D1011006

FORESTFALL

ALSO BY LYNDALL CLIPSTONE

Lakesedge

FORESTFALL

LYNDALL CLIPSTONE

HENRY HOLT AND COMPANY
New York

To B.,
I will find you in the dark of
the world Below.

Henry Holt and Company, *Publishers since 1866*
Henry Holt® is a registered trademark of Macmillan Publishing Group, LLC
120 Broadway, New York, NY 10271 • fiercereads.com

Our books may be purchased in bulk for promotional, educational,
or business use. Please contact your local bookseller or the Macmillan Corporate
and Premium Sales Department at (800) 221-7945 ext. 5442 or by email at
MacmillanSpecialMarkets@macmillan.com.

Library of Congress Cataloging-in-Publication Data

Names: Clipstone, Lyndall, author. | Clipstone, Lyndall. Lakesedge.
Title: Forestfall / Lyndall Clipstone.
Description: First edition. | New York : Henry Holt Books for Young
    Readers, 2022. | Series: World at the lake's edge duology; book 2 | Audience:
    Ages 14–18. | Audience: Grades 10–12. | Summary: As Leta struggles with the
    consequences of her deal in the World Below, Rowan realizes the tethering spell
    still connects them and he desperately tries to bring her back.
Identifiers: LCCN 2022017585 | ISBN 9781250753410 (hardcover)
Subjects: CYAC: Magic—Fiction. | Love—Fiction. | Fantasy. | LCGFT: Fantasy
    fiction. | Novels.
Classification: LCC PZ7.1.C5955 Fo 2022 | DDC [Fic]—dc23
LC record available at https://lccn.loc.gov/2022017585

First edition, 2022
Book design by Michelle Gengaro-Kokmen
Printed in the United States of America

ISBN 978-1-250-75341-0 (hardcover)
1   3   5   7   9   10   8   6   4   2

ISBN 978-1-250-88106-9 (special edition)
1   3   5   7   9   10   8   6   4   2

You, my love, the foremost, in a flowered gown,
All your unbearable tenderness, you with the
　　laughter
Startled upon your eyes now so wide with
　　hereafter,
You with loose hands of abandonment hanging
　　down.

　　　　　　　　—D. H. Lawrence,
　　　　　　　　　Letter from Town:
　　　　　　　　　The Almond Tree

Darkling I listen; and, for many a time
　　I have been half in love with easeful Death,
Call'd him soft names in many a mused rhyme,
　　To take into the air my quiet breath . . .

　　　　　　　　—John Keats,
　　　　　　　　　Ode to a Nightingale

Chapter One

ROWAN

I was the monster in the world.

I was the monster in the woods.

And though I was spared, all still feels ruined. Torn apart by claws and teeth.

It's midnight as I cross the hall. Pause at the landing and look down through the arched window. Cold glass, moonlight on the locked garden below.

Harvestfall has eclipsed Summersend. The trees are hung with leaves that are dying or dead. The ground is dewed with early frost. In the altar beneath the jacaranda tree, at the center of the lawn, a single candle has been lit. Illuminating the blackened streaks that still mar the wooden icon frame, turning the Lady to a shadowed shroud.

I feel the same. Dark as ink, dark as the Corruption that stained the shore, dark as the poison that filled my veins.

There are scars left from what we did. The locked garden. The ruined altar. Earth cut up, a fallen tree skeletal in the moonlight. Deep wounds torn across the ground that look like they were made by claws. All remnants of the destruction I caused when I became a monster. When I meant to drown the world.

The Corruption is gone now. Mended. *I'm* mended. And yet. And yet.

I watched the world tear open. I watched Violeta Graceling—the girl I love—vanish into the dark. Held her in my arms as the poison claimed her, as she spilled her blood beneath the dual altar and called to the Lord Under. In that last, terrible moment when the shadows closed in, I heard her voice as she demanded he take her, alive, to the world Below.

Then she was . . . gone.

I thought I knew grief. After my parents died, after I lost Elan. Thought I knew the way it softened in hurried moments and returned when the world was quiet. But this is new. This is a sudden violence. It catches me by the throat when I am at my most unguarded.

At night, after I drift into restless sleep, thoughts of Leta rise, always, though I don't want them. I wake alone in the dark. The spell she marked on my wrist aches and burns. Like she's still tied to the other end. And every time, I can't help reaching out. My hand on the bed, fingers clutched at a vacant space.

I hate myself for it. The way I expect to find her there. Grief isn't a tithe that can be paid with blood. There's no way to escape this hurt. This is a pain that I can't work free from.

Once I called her a ghost. And now, ghostlike, she haunts me. Awake. Asleep. All I see is Leta. How she looked when she crossed the shore, went into the water. How she looked when I carried her to the altar. How she kissed me that last time, her mouth tasting of blood and poison.

She said it was her choice. That she wasn't afraid. That her sacrifice would keep us safe.

With a sigh, I turn away from the window. Peel the gloves from my hands. I go quietly down the stairs. Though everyone is long asleep, I don't want to risk disturbing them. I need to be alone. Tonight is my first observance since it all happened. The first time I've come—uncorrupted—to the dual altar in the parlor.

The room is dark when I step inside. I close the door behind me. Draw back the curtains and let moonlight pool over the floor. The air is draped with the faded scent of smoke. Beneath that, a hint of old blood.

The dual icon hangs in shadow, but I don't move to light the candles that line the altar. Instead, I kneel down. Keep my eyes fixed on the floor. I touch the boards, feel them rough beneath my ungloved fingers. There's a faded crimson stain left behind from when Leta cut herself. Gave her blood to make that final promise.

And this is where—long before that—I cut myself and gave my blood and heard no answer.

I find a sparklight. Touch it to one of the candles. The flame wavers, and I feel the warmth against my face. Now I can see the mark on the floor more clearly. The blood, dried to a faded red, is the color of a pomegranate.

Everything blurs as unwelcome tears fill my eyes. I force them away. Force them back until my vision is spotted with darkness. With a ragged breath, I finally look up at the icon. The Lady is bronze and gold. Her hands outstretched. Light blooms at her palms like brilliant flowers.

Beneath her, the Lord Under is shadows and smoke and darkness.

I stare at him. The silhouette of his cloak. The sharp outline of his antlered crown. Here is the creature who saved me when I drowned. Caught hold of me as I fell beneath the water. Whispered to me as the lake stole my breath. Asked what I would offer in exchange for my life.

I've never known him the way that Leta does. To me, he was only ever a voice in the shadows, a presence I *felt* rather than saw. Like the lingering traces of a nightmare or a half-forgotten memory. And though I called to him so many times—after he killed my father, after I realized he meant to take my family to punish me—he never responded.

But Leta could see him. She could *summon* him. She spoke to him, she promised herself to him, and she walked into his darkness.

I press my hands against the stained floor. Her blood, my blood. So many unanswered pleas and ungiven promises. Sometimes I think of how different it would have been, if I'd

4

not broken my vow when I turned thirteen and he came back for me. If I had gone with him.

It's so easy to regret. To think how I could have chosen differently. But it doesn't matter now. I am here, with a life stolen from the sacrifice of others. My father, my mother, my brother. And now . . . Leta.

I light the rest of the candles at the altar. Dip my fingers into the salt, then scatter an offering beneath the icon. I start to chant. Hating my voice, the way the notes catch on my unsteady breath, my throat still rough with held-back tears.

The Harvestfall litany, when sung by others, calls up images of tilled fields and bonfire smoke. Of barren branches, and the slow transition toward long nights. But when I sing it, the litany sounds like a wound. It sounds like mourning.

My hands start to shake. I press them harder against the floor. Close my eyes. I reach for the light we're told is there. The light the Lady became when she made the world. The golden magic that's strung through everything. It's been so long since I felt it. When I was Corrupted and made observance, there was only cold. A sense of vacant darkness.

Now I wait, trying to feel beyond that familiar silence.

The candles burn. Smoke streaks the air. I swallow, and it tastes like ash.

For a long while, there's only stillness. Then heat pulses against my palms. I feel a pull. Startled, I look up at the altar. But this isn't magic. This isn't the Lady.

It's something closer. A wound, still tender.

I raise my hand; slow, uncertain. A thread is tied to my wrist. I stare as it gleams through the dark; a thin golden line that shifts and flickers, like a candle flame. My heartbeat rises as I watch the thread stretching into the shadows. I feel the pull, the strange pulse of heat, the wounded hurt.

Then, with a sudden rush, colors light over me. Peach and rose and gold. And a figure emerges. Pale freckles, pale skin, hair like summer embers. *Leta*.

She's there, just beyond the dark. Dressed in black lace with her hair unbound. I gasp, the noise cutting sharply across the silence. She looks up. Her silver-gray eyes are wide and blank. And I want, so wretchedly, for this to be real. Different from those haunting visions that drag me from sleep, every night.

Slowly, I get to my feet. Certain that in the next moment, the next heartbeat, everything will fracture, and I'll wake alone. My hands pressed to an empty altar.

I whisper her name, more desperate than any plea I've ever made beneath this shadowed icon. "Leta?"

The blankness in her eyes is replaced by recognition. She looks at me, all unbearable tenderness. I am filled with longing. Her lips part. Her mouth shapes a word—*my name?*—but I can hear no sound.

I reach toward her. My hand trembling in the space between us. The thread glows brighter. The other end is knotted at her wrist. Near the sigil left from the spell she cast to save me, when I was almost lost to the darkness.

I touch her there. On her wrist. At the feel of her skin— cold, impossibly cold—my breath comes loose in a shallow, jagged sob. I'm overcome by all I've wanted to say since she left. "Leta," I whisper. "I miss you, so terribly. I don't even know if this is real. But I . . ."

I trail off as the light begins to blur, and everything turns dreamlike. Leta takes hold of my hand. She doesn't try to speak again. Her lashes dip, a single tear spills down her cheek. And then, she starts to fade.

I clutch for the thread tied between us—tied from my wrist to hers—but all I feel is shadows. I try to pull her into my arms, but she is mist and embers. A pale wisp, replaced by the flicker of altar candles. Slowly, I kneel. Press my hands to the floor. She is gone.

I'm alone in the parlor. Overcome by a taunting blur of thoughts. All the hopes I once had for a life with Leta. The future I wanted to offer her. Books stacked on the library shelves. Her garden, bright with flowers. The two of us alone in my room, in the moonlight.

Then, a jolt of pain goes through me, so blisteringly fierce that my fingers curl sharply against the stained boards. Like I have claws. Shakily, I sit back onto my heels. Unlace my sleeves. Blood wells at my wrists. The scars where I cut myself countless times for the tithe have turned to open wounds. My blood, it isn't red. It's *black*. And around the sigil that Leta marked on me, the day I became a monster, there are shadows pooled beneath my skin.

Just like before, when the Corruption was overtaking me.

I touch a questioning finger to the sigil mark. The Corruption was cleansed in that last, terrible ritual where Leta went to the world Below. I watched the shore heal. Felt the darkness leave my body. And inside me, where a monster once slept, there was only silence left behind.

I am mended. I am supposed to be mended.

I'm still staring at my wrist, at the spell and the too-dark blood, when footsteps come down the hall. There's a flicker of candlelight. Then a soft knock on the door. Florence steps hesitantly into the room. She has a shawl wrapped around her shoulders, held in place by a carved, wooden clasp.

She looks at me, then at the altar, and her face turns solemn. "Are you all right?"

"I'm . . . not sure."

She takes another step toward me. Her brows rise when she notices my bloodied wrists. I start to pull down my sleeves to hide the cuts. But it's too late. She's already seen.

"Rowan, what have you done? Did you hurt yourself?"

The *again* hangs unspoken between us. I curl my hand over my wrist. "No." She watches me, waiting for me to say more. But I can hardly understand what just happened, let alone try to explain it. Silence draws out. Finally, I sigh. "There are still bandages in the drawers."

She puts her candle down beneath the altar. Tucks back a piece of hair that has come away from the braids she wears, twin rows at the sides of her head, the strands loosening to waves as they fall past her shoulders. She goes over to the table beside the chaise and opens the drawer. The box with bandages and a jar of Clover's honey salve is still inside. Left from when I would come here after the tithes.

I feel strange, hollow, as I watch her take the box out of the drawer. It's been months since the last time I went to the lake, cut myself, and bled into the ground. But the memory is so vivid.

The cold slither of darkness. The Corruption devouring me. The poisonous magic that ruled my life for so many years.

Florence lowers herself to the floor beside me. Balancing the box on her folded knees, she opens it and takes out the supplies. With a linen cloth, she starts to clean my wounds. I force myself to keep still. There's part of me that wants this so badly. To let her take care of me. To sit here and feel the gentleness in her touch as she wipes the blood from my wrists.

But the sweet smell of the salve makes me sick. All I can think of is the night Leta followed me when I gave my tithe. We came back here afterward, and I told her about my connection to the curse on the shore. It was the first time I'd ever shared that secret. I expected the worst . . . that she would be disgusted, that she would fear me. Instead, she held my hand and promised to follow me into the dark.

My chest goes tight, and a strangled sob comes from my mouth. I clench my teeth against the sound. Before Florence can react, I roughly take the cloth from her and gesture toward the door. "I don't need your help. You can go."

She hesitates a moment. I know she wants to reach for me. She twists her hands in her skirts, watches me as I finish cleaning the wounds, tie bandages around my wrists. Quietly, she asks, "Before I leave, will you tell me what happened?"

I run my fingers down the inside of my arm. The sigil has

gone silent now, but when I touch it, I imagine I can still feel that pull, that *pulse*. Still see the thread of light, stretching away into the shadows.

I spread my hands; palms upturned. "I saw Leta."

Florence gives me a guarded look. "What do you mean?"

My eyes go to the floor, the faded stain beneath the altar. "When I made observance, instead of light or magic, *she* was there. I looked into the shadows, and I saw her. I spoke to her. And afterward, this happened."

I gesture to my wrists, now bandaged. Florence watches me, her brow creased. Slowly, she moves forward. Puts her hands on my shoulders. She's careful, deliberating as she struggles to choose her words. "Rowan. She is dead."

"She was *there*."

My voice catches. I take a sharp, wretched breath as I try to fight against it, the slow creep of doubt. Leta can't be dead. She can't be *gone*. It was so real. The way she appeared before me, the pull of the spell, the thread tied between us. Her moods laid out in a wash of colors. The twist of my heart when she soundlessly shaped my name.

I've been haunted by memories of Leta since she left. But this wasn't another dream, a desperate wish cast across the night when I'm alone, in the dark. This was *real*.

Florence slides her hands gently down my arms. "I know how difficult this has been for you. I thought, perhaps, if we had a pyre—"

I pull away from her. "No."

Her fingers knot around the fringed ends of her shawl.

She looks at the altar. The movement of the candlelight makes the figures in the icon seem, for the barest moment, like they are . . . alive.

Sighing, Florence lets her hands fall to her lap. "Violeta gave herself up to keep you safe. She tore herself apart for all of us. To reach for her like this . . . It's a dangerous path to follow."

"What other choice could I possibly make, after she risked so much for me?"

"Rowan, my love. You need to let her go."

I close my eyes against more unwelcome tears. Trying instead to picture myself in the locked garden at midsummer twilight. A slender moon in the gloaming sky. Leta, with her skirts tucked back, showing me her scars as she confessed the truth of her connection to the Lord Under. How she gave her magic to him in exchange for Arien's life—a trade that left Arien with darkness in place of his alchemy. How she blamed herself for all he had suffered because of that darkness.

That evening in the garden was the first time I realized I loved her. That I wanted her to stay with me, wanted to give her a place where she wouldn't ever be hurt again. But safety was never something I could offer. All I did was make everything worse.

"Florence, I don't care what I become." My voice is a growl, reminiscent of how it sounded when I was changed by the Corruption. I swallow against the remembered taste of mud and poison. "If it means I can find her, then I don't care what happens to me."

She draws back. For just a moment, her expression turns raw. Cast heavily with depthless grief. Then she takes a breath. Her features settle into the familiar, resolute mask she's worn since my father died.

I know she wants to care for me, but I can't let anyone close. Not again. I have to face this—my ruin, my hurt, my destruction—alone.

Florence gets to her feet and picks up her candle. I swallow down my guilt. Try to forget the feel of her hand, gentle on my wounded arm. "It's not just yourself to consider," she says quietly. "Have you thought about Arien? What will happen if he loses you, as well?"

All I can do is shake my head. She pauses for a beat, then with a tired sigh, she goes out of the room. The silence left behind is tangled as thorns.

I put my hands back against the floor, press my palms over the faded marks on the boards. Before, my whole world was the Corruption. Poison in the earth. Poison in my veins. It wasn't *easy*, but I was able to face it single-mindedly: the hunger, the demands, the tithes I paid with my blood and my body.

I've never really *thought* how it would be on the other side of it all. I was a monster, and then I wasn't. I was alone, and then I wasn't. But Florence is right. I stole Arien away, brought him here to use his magic for my own gain. And now, because of me, Leta is gone. The only family he had left.

I take a deep breath. Blow out the candles. Tendrils of smoke wreathe the altar frame. For just a moment, the silhouetted icon looks exactly the same as the outline of Leta when she appeared before me.

I need to find out if what I saw was real. To put myself back into the shadows, where I can reach to her through the darkness. I need a way to poison myself, willingly.

I was a monster, and then I wasn't. And now, to find Violeta Graceling, I need to become that monster again.

Chapter Two

VIOLETA

There's no sky in the world Below, but I know that night has fallen.

From beneath the trees I've watched the light change from dappled shadow to faded gray to full dark. Now the heartwood forest is striped crimson against the shadows. The trees have bloodied bark and slender leaves. Their branches are strung with mothlights: tiny glass lanterns lit by luminous wingbeats.

In the distance, just beyond the haze of mist, is a thicket of brambles. Taller than me twice over, with thorns longer than my fingers, it goes all around this part of the forest in a neat, unbroken ellipse. The wall has only a single gate, an arched structure made from vines and serrated leaves.

The gate has never opened.

At least, not for me.

I reach for a mothlight, unhook it from the branches. With the jar clasped between my hands, I set off on the path that leads toward the bramble wall. My lace-hemmed skirts brush against the ground as I walk. I'm all in black, dark as the shadowed forest. A wide silk ribbon at my waist, sleeves of translucent moth wings, a mantle of cobwebbed lace.

It's cold here, always cold. Coldest at times like this, when the shadows cross the path and drape between the branches. I miss the sunlight. The heat and brightness, the languid weight of the air.

An icy wind stirs through the trees, raises prickles on my skin. I raise the jar between my hands, hold it close to my face, so I'm bathed in silver light. For a brief moment, I let myself imagine I am in the world Above, and it's Summersend. And when I breathe I can feel the sun go far down inside my body, to turn my heart and ribs all golden.

Then I push the memory away.

I've reached the thorns. I stand before them, looking over each curve of bramble, each folded leaf. Slowly, I reach out, press my hand to the gate. On my palm, the scar that cuts in a crescent across my heartline throbs softly in time with my pulse. From beyond the wall, I can hear the sound of footsteps. I feel a pull from the center of my chest. The kind of stirring that comes when like calls to like.

I hear the rustle of thorns, the stir of leaves. Beneath my pressing hand, there is only air. But then I blink, and with one brush of my lashes—*down, up*—I miss whatever tenuous magic allows the gate to open. When I look again, the brambles

15

are unchanged, still set tightly together. My hand still pressed against the woven vines.

The only difference is that now, the Lord Under is before me.

Outlined by hook-sharp thorns, he gleams in the dark, casting a glow that twins the mothlight I hold. Pale hair, pale hands, pale eyes. And though I'm here in this skyless forest, when I see him, I think of a moon. Full and sharp and white. I think of fields covered by midwinter frost.

There's a soul in his arms, the body wrapped in a silken shroud that turns it to a featureless shadow. He looks me over, silent a moment. "What," he says, "are you doing here?"

I hold up the mothlight that I brought. "I've come to help you."

His brows rise, and the bared edge of his teeth catch the pale gleam of my light. The moth dances inside the jar, its wings fluttering rhythmically. "I can see well enough in the dark, Violeta."

Then I uncurl my fingers and show him what I've held, clasped close to the center of my palm. "And I have this."

His gaze falls to my hand. The seed is large and round, amber dark. It was rough when I coaxed it loose from the cone I found, half buried in the debris of the forest floor. But I've worried at it with my fingers so much that the edges have become smooth.

The Lord Under brushes past me and makes his way to the path. "I thought I'd given you enough to occupy yourself, without you having to haunt me through the woods like a little ghost."

"Like a ghost?" There's challenge in my voice as I echo his words. I wait to see if he'll rise to meet it. When he doesn't respond, I go on. "Is that what you call it, what you've done to me?"

Irritation flashes in his eyes as he glances back over his sharp, mantled shoulder. "You really want to argue this again? It was your choice. If you have regrets—that isn't my concern."

It *was* my choice to make the bargain that led me here. I was desperate to protect Arien, to protect . . . everyone I loved. And in spite of the hurt, in spite of the danger, as the threat of the Corruption grew, I went willingly to the altar and summoned the Lord Under. I asked for his help. In exchange for his magic, I gave up the most precious thing I had—the memories of my family.

Everything I had of them is lost, swept from my mind. I know I must have loved them. That we had a life together, when I was a child, before they died. But it's all gone. There's only emptiness now. A terrible, unending *ache*.

I chose it all. The pain. The sacrifice. To risk myself, to come into the world Below and cast that final spell. I welcomed the darkness. I let the Corruption devour me. All I've given up, each step I've taken that's led me here, it has always been *my* choice.

That doesn't make it hurt any less.

I bite my teeth together until my jaw aches. Try very hard to keep my voice steady when I speak. "I don't *regret* this."

"Have you forgotten that you begged me to spare you from death?" His eyes narrow, lit coldly with a surge of anger.

"What I've given you is a gift. One I've not granted to anyone else, ever."

I curl my hand into a fist, trapping the seed in the darkness of my palm. "Maybe I'm not a soul inside a tree. But I'm not truly alive, either."

"*Enough.*" He raises a hand. Shadows stir up from the ground, striking jagged shapes into the air around us. "If you want to help me, then hurry up. Otherwise, you can go back home."

He turns away and continues to walk, not waiting to see if I'll follow. The word—*home*—is barbed as the thorns keeping me trapped in this part of the woods. My eyes fill with a sudden rise of tears. I blink them away fiercely. The thought of crying in front of the Lord Under right now feels worse than anything else I could do.

I breathe out a frustrated hiss between my clenched teeth and go after him, my skirts caught in one hand so I can walk fast enough to catch up. We fall into step, both of us tensed with our separate anger. The shrouded form in his arms must be heavy, but he bears the weight carelessly. His cloak brushes the ground behind him, a trail of swirling shadows. We move in silence, our footsteps over fallen leaves the only sound.

I follow him into the woods. It's a different path than the one I took from my cottage. That path is narrow, weaving through moss-covered stones that line the way like sentinels. Here the trees are taller, the mist wrapped silver-thick around their crimson trunks.

We pass beneath branches strung with mothlights. Step

over hollows of roots that are circled by pale, luminous mushrooms. Aside from my cottage, most of this walled-off, thornbound space is filled with heartwoods. But eventually, the forest becomes more sparse, and we reach a grove where a bare piece of earth is framed by two older, taller trees.

The Lord Under turns to me. The irritation from before is still in his eyes. With a clipped, tense motion, he indicates the shrouded soul in his arms. "Is your life here so truly wretched, Violeta? Would you prefer to have given it up completely?"

I try not to think of it, the moment I awoke and discovered the truth of our final bargain. He mended me, just as I had asked, but the only way I could remain alive was to stay in the world Below. And that, even that, was my *choice*. When I fell into a fury of hot, wretched tears, the Lord Under told me he could make the hurt stop. That I could let death claim me.

But when I sacrificed the memories of my family for the power to fight the Corruption, it was for eternity. I'll not remember them in *either* world. If I had accepted his offer, and given up my life, my soul would be alone. Without my parents, and without Arien—when his time comes to depart the world Above. And in that terrible moment at the heart of the bone tree, to be alone was more unthinkable than being here.

I shove past the Lord Under, go over to the bared space and kneel down. He shifts back a few paces to wait, the soul held carefully against his chest.

In the tree behind him there's a carved alcove with an altar set inside it. The icon is blotched with damp, a blur of mildew and moss, and the shelf beneath is draped by hardened rivulets of melted wax.

It makes me think of the altar at Lakesedge, how I knelt at observance with Arien and Clover and let them see my magic for the first time. Warmth teases my fingertips, and I feel the faint hum of power gathering across my palms.

Carefully, I unfold my hand and look down at the seed. I dig a small hollow in the earth, dirt embedding in dark crescents beneath my fingernails. I press the seed into the ground, and cover it. I reach into my pocket and take out my pen.

When I push back my sleeve, the cold air makes me shiver.

Alchemical sigils line my arm. A reminder of everything I did in my seventeenth summer. A reminder of everything I've given up. The spells I cast as I worked and fought and failed to drive back the Corruption that threatened to claim Lakesedge Estate—and its lord. All of it mapped out, sigil by sigil, forever on my skin.

I set the pen to my wrist. Sketch over the spell I once used in that other life, that other world, to awaken a forgotten garden. Memories rise of tender heat, of hands gentle against my scars. I close my eyes and force the thoughts away. I can't think of *him*, not now. I'll be undone.

I bite the inside of my cheek, concentrate on the pain until the memories subside. They fade slowly—too slowly—leaving behind a persistent ache at the center of my chest.

Once I've written the spell, I press my hands flat against the ground and close my eyes. My magic stirs awake, and the sigil sparks alight. I picture a thread spun from my hands, slowly woven around the seed, until it forms a glimmering net that draws tighter and tighter.

This is the first time I've used alchemy in the world Below since I mended the Corruption. The power I used that night, when I called down the darkness and welcomed it inside me, is gone. Now I only have the small remnants of magic from before. Faint as a single flame burning softly in the dark.

But still, when I draw on my power, it *hurts*. The same way it has ever since I sacrificed the memories of my family. All their warmth and light is gone now, replaced by the desolation of a moonless night.

As I cast the spell, an ache of absence fills me. The magic moves through my veins with unbearable coldness, as though my blood has turned to ice. Longing overwhelms me, for things I've lost, things that are impossible to retrieve. My breath starts to catch. My ribs feel tight, folded too close against my heart. My mouth tastes of blood.

I try to listen to the forest, the way the air whispers around me like a voice I can't quite hear. Slowly, painfully, I take hold of my power. It blooms reluctantly and I press it, hard, into the earth. The seed splits open; roots spiraling downward as branches begin to rise.

My hands tremble as I fight to keep hold of the spell. A gasp escapes my parted lips, and I bite down against it. Force out more power. Then, with a final *rush*, the tree breaks through the earth and pushes up—bark and leaves rasping against my palms.

I drag myself free of the spell and slump forward, my eyes

still tightly closed. The magic dissolves around me with a softened *hush*. I press my lips together, feel the sting from where I've bitten them. I lick away the wet smear of blood.

The Lord Under puts his hand on my shoulder. His thumb marks a path against my clavicle, almost tender. But I push him away. "Don't *touch* me."

He steps back, leaving space between us. I take a few more ragged breaths, steadying myself, then slowly get to my feet. The tree rises above me, a new heartwood spun into existence entirely with my magic. I let out a fractured sound—somewhere between a laugh and a sob—as I look up at the crimson branches, the needle-fine leaves. A heady, painful *pride* fills me. I want to give in to it, delight in it, but instead I squash the feeling down.

To be proud of myself for this . . . would be a betrayal.

The Lord Under examines the heartwood for a long moment before he turns toward me. There's a strange cast to the lines of his face, as though I've unsettled him. Slowly, he reaches out and tucks a loose strand of hair back from my cheek. He hesitates, his finger ribboned by one of my curls, before he draws away. "Thank you for your help, Violeta."

Begrudgingly, I reply, "You're welcome."

He moves closer to the tree. I pick up the mothlight, hold it out for him so the light glimmers against the crimson bark. He pauses for a moment, one hand pressed to the trunk, his splayed fingers pale and starlike. Then he rakes his claws down the length of the tree. It splits instantly beneath his touch, baring an inside that's glossed with sap.

My chest tightens, and an anxious, jagged shiver goes down my spine. Watching the tree peeled apart is like seeing my own skin torn away. My ribs folded open, my heart laid out. It makes me feel strange and sick and small. I think of the Lord Under with the soul in his arms. I think of myself devoured by poison as he carried me through the forest.

I close my eyes, turn my face away. But it's no good. I can still hear the tree as it takes the soul. The creaks, the groans, the shift and shudder as the wound starts to heal over. My hand that holds the mothlight trembles. As the glass tilts, light flickers across my closed lids, and the moth flutters a protest against the inside of the jar.

I swallow down my anger, my hurt, my fear. *I did make the right choice. I did.* Staying at the Lord Under's side, with all the pain of what I've sacrificed, is better than to be alone inside a heartwood. There, I'd have nothing except the same ache as when I use my magic. A barren loneliness, an empty darkness, a razed field.

Leaves rustle as the tree knits closed. After a few beats of stillness, I open my eyes. The tree is whole. Just smooth bark, as though it has always been this way. There's not even a scar. I swallow down the last traces of bitter nausea that linger in my mouth. Wipe my sweat-slick palms against my skirts.

The Lord Under looks between me and the heartwood. "If you're to make a habit of this, you'll have to develop steadier nerves."

I scowl at him. "I'll keep that in mind."

He regards me for a moment, then folds his sleeve over and

23

reaches out to wipe away a smear of blood from beside my mouth. His lashes dip, and he offers me his arm. "It's late. I will walk back with you."

I hesitate for a moment. Hold the mothlight to my chest, the wingbeats inside the jar matching the pulse of my heart. I'm still angry with him, but there's been a shift between us. He let me help him—I grew the tree; I held the light. The smallest tilt of balance, one tiny shred of power clutched tightly in my fist.

I run my tongue over my bitten lips. Go to his side. Tuck my hand into the crook of his elbow.

We make our way back out of the grove. He's so much taller than me, and the top of my head barely reaches his shoulder, but he evens his pace to match mine so we can walk beside each other.

When we reach the narrow path that leads to my cottage, I draw away from him, expecting him to leave. But he continues on, following me down the slope.

We always part here. Except for that first day, after I awoke in the bone tree. I still remember how I felt when he brought me to the cottage, seeing it rise up from the depths of the hollow. The sharp despair that caught me by my throat when he explained to me that this place—a house in the woods, encircled by a wall of thorns—was how he'd met the terms of our bargain. That he had made me a *home* in the world Below.

It feels strange to be here now, on that same path, to hear the echo of his footsteps behind me as I walk. I turn to him and lift my brows in question. "Do you think I'll get lost? Or don't you trust me to go where I'm told?"

His mouth tilts into a sharp smile that gives away nothing. "Perhaps I'm being polite and seeing you safely through the woods."

I shake my head at him, huff out a quiet laugh. I walk on, and he follows. Trailing me like a shadow.

As the path leads us into the hollow, the ghost mushrooms clustered beneath the trees light the air with a pale glow. Past their luminous shimmer, I see a wooden altar nailed to a branch—peeled paint and lichen, the icon weathered away. A row of stones that might have once been a wall. A curved iron shape that looks like a gate, opening into nothingness.

My cottage comes into view slowly, the gleam of the front window faintly visible through the mist. Set beneath two enormous heartwood trees, it's more forest than house. The walls are made of roughened wood that still bear scraps of crimson bark. Tangles of ivy hold together a roof of woven branches. There's a wreath on the door, leaves and bellflowers. Just like the one that decorated the front door at Lakesedge.

I could almost find it beautiful, if only I could forget what lies beyond the nearby trees. The brambles that make a wall around this part of the world Below, separating me from the rest of the forest.

I turn to the Lord Under. Look up at him. In this moment, with the shadow-striped trees behind him like the painted background of an icon, he seems as unbreachable as the thorn-snared gate. Light glints on his claws, the points of his antlered crown. He is a god, the forest wrapped around him like a cloak. I am a girl, trying to draw strength from scraps. A fallen seed, a spark of magic, my fierce, human heart.

"I want to help you again," I say, "next time you claim a soul."

His eyes narrow, and he gives me an assessing look. Slowly, he nods. "You can help me when I have a soul to be placed in these woods."

"Not just here." My heartbeat rises. I curl my hands to fists, feeling the rasp of earth still gritted on my skin as I press my nails to my palms. When he doesn't respond, I point to the distance, where the brambles are barely visible, a shade darker than the mist. "I want to go beyond the wall of thorns."

The Lord Under follows my gaze. "Your home is here."

I let out a frustrated sigh. "Who is out there that I should fear so terribly?"

"No one."

"Then why won't you let me leave?"

I stare up at him, my anger kindling alight again as I wait for him to answer me. It's late now, and the darkness presses around us, slipping in from between the trees. But I can still see myself reflected in his gaze. My white skin faded paler by the frosted-over color of his sclera. My red hair like a flame through lamp glass.

With reluctance, he says, "The rest of the woods are not safe for you."

"I was safe enough in your woods when you needed me for the Corruption."

"You were. But things are different now."

Unconsciously, I touch the scar that cuts my heartline, the blackened crescent left from where I gave my blood to summon him, the day I decided to ask for his help. I can still feel the rush of power that filled me that first time, when he showed me what I could have after our trade.

But that bright, fierce strength he granted me lasted only for a single, full-moon night. Now the only power I have is what remained after I gave up my magic to him in exchange for Arien's life, long ago in the Vair Woods. The scraps that were so much a part of me they couldn't be taken away.

"You could make me stronger again."

The Lord Under cups his hand against my cheek. He's not gentle, exactly, but he's . . . careful. It would almost be tender if not for the way he looks at me. His eyes are cold, filled with a warning not to press him further. "I have met the terms of our bargain, Violeta. You have a life beyond death and a home in my world."

My voice dwindles to a roughened whisper. "You know this isn't what I asked for."

His thumb strokes a brief arch against my cheek before he moves away. My skin feels strangely bare without his touch. He lets out a breath that turns to a plume of mist. "This was the only way I could mend you. The only way I could fulfill my promise."

I look down at my arm. Through the sheer lace of my sleeve, I can see the delicate edges of the sigil marked on my wrist. The spell in the shape of a sunburst. At the sight of it, my vision wavers and a single, treacherous tear spills loose, trailing slowly down my cheek. I scrub it away. Close my eyes tightly to capture the rest of the tears before they can fall.

At first, I cried so much whenever I thought of what I had lost. *Who* I had lost. Endless tears that overwhelmed me, my despair a thing I could drown beneath. The waves of a lake, swiftly rising. Now, I only let myself take tiny sips of grief. Like my sadness is a poison I can become immune to, dose by dose.

Swallowing down a rising sob, I open my eyes and turn to the Lord Under. "If you won't let me go past the wall, then please . . . just tell me the truth. What is hidden beyond the thorns?"

In answer, he extends his hand to me. And though my fingers tremble, I don't hesitate to reach out and take hold.

Chapter Three

VIOLETA

The Lord Under leads me past the cottage and into the forest beyond. Bordered by a half circle of sentinel heartwoods, the space is all moss and scattered leaves. A constellation of moths dances past us when we enter the clearing, stippling the air with silver light. I gather up my skirts, ready to walk farther, but the Lord Under draws me to a stop at the center of the grove.

I look around, confused. We're still far from the wall, the thorned gate completely hidden beyond the slope of the ground. "I thought—"

He pulls at my hand, the motion both gentle and insistent. "Kneel down."

I shake my head, my eyes still pinned to the distance. He strokes his thumb against my wrist. We look at each other, a shiver in the air. He inclines his head, voice softening. "Trust me, Violeta."

Slowly, I lower myself until I'm kneeling on the ground. It's cold, and the leaves are wet with melted frost. I shiver as dampness starts to seep through the knees of my stockings. "I asked you to take me beyond the thorns. Why are we here?"

Frowning, he stares past me into the trees. "All I want is to protect you. Surely you can understand how that feels, wanting to keep someone safe." He turns to me, levels me with his pale gaze. "Especially after what you gave up."

I scrunch my hands into my skirts. "I don't want to talk about that."

I haven't spoken of what happened at Lakesedge—not to the Lord Under, not even to the listening silence of the trees—since I awoke and discovered the true form his promise had taken. That I had become a liminal creature, bound to the world of the dead, so far from the *home* I wanted to go back to and everyone who was waiting there for me. Whose lives I had saved, at the cost of my own.

I glance at my wrist, where the sigil is veiled by the sheer fabric of my sleeve. It aches, how badly I want to touch it. But even that small gesture, my hand against the spell, is impossible. Too raw, too fragile. A sigh escapes me, and I lace my fingers together in my lap to keep myself from reaching.

The Lord Under kneels down in front of me. His cloak spills out across the ground in a wash of shadows. He touches a claw beneath my chin, tilting my face upward so he can look into my eyes. "I know it hurts. I know . . . you loved him."

I weave my fingers more tightly together, trying to keep very still. Fighting to hold back my grief, though it feels as unstoppable as a storm. "I said I don't want to talk about it."

"You've never let the hurt in, not since you awoke at my altar."

I bite down on the sob that wants to spill loose. I am strung tight, my tenuous control frayed to a single thread. "Fine," I snap, spitting out the words. "Yes, it hurts. Of course it does. But I made my choice willingly. What I *didn't* choose was to be kept here as your prisoner."

He traces down the line of my jaw. I put my hand over his, not sure if I want to shove him away or let him move closer. As I hesitate, his fingers slide to cup the back of my neck. "Close your eyes, Violeta."

I turn my face toward the trees. "No."

His voice lowers until he sounds almost tender. "I'm going to help you. You're in no danger with me."

The exhaustion that's a constant of my life here—born of watchfulness and fractured sleep and the fight against unwelcome memories—washes over me like a tide. In spite of everything, I let my eyes sink closed. Some of the tension loosens from my shoulders, and for a moment, I almost relax.

Then I feel the cold brush of the Lord Under's magic against my skin. My eyes snap open and I pull away, breaking the circle of shadows that have started to unfurl around us. "What are you doing?"

He still has his hand on the back of my neck. His claws press gently against my nape, drawing me closer. More shadows spiral out, darkening the grove until all I can see is the pale outline of his face, his hair, his antlered crown.

"I'm not going to hurt you." His words have the cadence of a spell woven through the trees, settling over me like mist. "I want to *take* your hurt, Violeta. You've kept it locked up for so long. Let me take it from you."

I close my eyes slowly, my teeth dug hard into my lip. It's still sore, bitten and bloodied from when I cast the spell.

I think of how it felt when I fought the Corruption. How I let the darkness in, how I let myself be devoured. I think of the seventeen summers I had in the world Above. All that I left behind. The life I might have had with Arien. The future I might have had with . . . the boy I loved. The razed-clear space, like a blackened field, that I see whenever I try to remember my family.

The pain is a snare of brambles in my chest, all hurt and sharpened thorns. I feel the last, frayed thread of my control finally break, and everything I've held back spills through me. I feel it all, the grief and the sorrow and the despair that I've tried so hard to inoculate myself against. The ache of all I have lost.

It's gone, all gone.

And I am dead.

And I am here.

I let out a ragged breath, and my head bows forward. I start to sob; loud hiccupping cries that tear from my throat with a primal, trapped-animal sound. It doesn't feel like my voice. I cry, wretched and ruined, and the Lord Under takes my hurt.

Takes it the way he took my memories, took my blood, took the promises I made to him at the altar.

The wind rises, shivering through the branches with an ominous whine. The crescent scar on my palm starts to burn, the ache unbearable. I open my eyes and stare down at it as the pain spreads farther, radiating along the inside of my arm.

The sigil on my wrist—it *glows*.

My sobs turn to sharp, stuttered gasps. I clasp my hand over the spell, trying to breathe through the hurt. Shadows shift and flicker around me like candlelight dancing against the dark. Slowly, the pain from my wrist starts to soften—the bright ache now a dull, persistent throb.

Then, a strand of light unfurls between my fingers. I watch, unsettled, as it stretches away from me, drifting out into the trees. It hovers for a moment then curls like a question mark, like it's beckoning me forward.

Everything has faded, blurred. I'm in the woods with the Lord Under right beside me. Dirt beneath my nails, the knees of my stockings dampened by melted frost. But at the same time . . . I'm somewhere else.

Slowly, I get to my feet. The spell-light spirals away from my wrist. The sigil beats and beats alongside my pulse. Prickles rise over my skin. My throat goes tight; my heart pounds hard against my ribs.

And then—the forest changes.

I'm on a path that winds through orchard trees heavy with fruit, their branches covered with lush, bright leaves. The glimmering thread still stretches forward. I take one tentative step, then another, following the thread until I reach a clear space filled with wildflowers. My bare feet sink among constellations of yellow dandelions. The light filters down through the branches, patterned with leaves.

This is my garden. The garden at Lakesedge that I grew with my magic.

As though from a distance, I see myself sitting on the ground beneath a tree. There's dirt on my palms. My skirts are folded back, my legs bared. The scars on my knees—crimson and cruel—cut starkly against my pale skin.

A voice comes, a voice I never thought to hear again. "Leta?"

"Rowan."

I've not spoken his name aloud since I came here. I've kept it pushed aside, locked up with all my grief. And now, when I finally allow myself to whisper it, his name tastes both sweet and bitter, like a sedative draft that's been stirred with honey.

Somewhere in the distant forest, the shadowed magic thickens as I kneel on moss-damp earth and feel the press of the Lord Under's claws against my skin. And here, in my garden, I watch Rowan through a veil of tears as he moves toward me.

He looks exactly the same as on that last, stolen night we spent together; his dark hair unbound, a flush across his fawn-gold cheeks, the scars on his throat visible through the unlaced collar of his shirt.

He comes closer and closer, until there's only a breath of space between us. We stare at each other. Carefully, I raise my hand. I'm so afraid I'll break whatever dream holds us here. My fingers tremble as they brush his cheek. His eyes widen at my touch. The warmth of his skin, the rasp of his scars, sends a thrill of heated longing right through me.

The thread at my wrist glows brighter and brighter. Magic flares, hot, across my palms, and I feel his moods—bleak despair, pale hope—everything as delicate as spider silk. The spell I cast to draw him back when the Corruption threatened to change him, devour him, the tether created by the sigils that mark us both . . . In this strange dream, this vision, our connection is still *there*.

"Rowan." I hold the shape of his name against my tongue, a desperate wish. "I'm—I'm *sorry*."

He presses his hand over mine, leans his face against my palm. "Please—" he says, voice rough with tears. "Please— stay. Don't vanish into the dark again."

Emotions wash over me, mine and his, despair and desire. I surrender to them, shift closer, my fingers sliding past his jaw to curl into his hair. Pain breaks loose from where I've forced it to sleep, nestled beneath my heart, caged behind my ribs. And everything I've held back, that I thought I'd never be able to tell him, spills out in a rush. "I had to protect you and Arien, and everyone. But I didn't know it would end this way. I didn't know I'd not be able to come back. I want—I want—"

My words choke to a sob, because all I want is impossible. His gaze darkens, full of tender ruin. He bends to me, his words casting over my lips. "Leta, I will find you. I will bring you home."

I want to eclipse the space between us. To turn the glimmering spell-thread into something unbreakable. I want magic and power and strength. More than anything, I want a way to make this *real*.

I tangle my fingers tighter in his hair. His breath catches, a sharpened sound.

I kiss him.

He groans against my mouth; all hope and desolation. Magic sparks at my fingertips, and the spell gives an aching *pull* at my wrist. The thread weaves around us, tighter and tighter, until we're shrouded in golden light. His fingers dig against my waist.

I kiss him like I did in the garden when he was overtaken by the Corruption. Caught up in the same thrill of longing and danger. And as we press closer together, poison and shadows seep in like a threat, but I'm not afraid. Rowan starts to change, the boy eclipsed by the monster. I cling to him, and our kisses turn feverish. His nails are like claws. His teeth are sharp. He tastes of darkness, of my own spilled blood. His touch is fire, a hurt that sparks and burns through my entire body, as fierce and bright as my magic.

I want, so desperately, for this to last forever. To find whatever alchemy could make this real. But all too soon, Rowan's hand draws back from my waist. His mouth rasps a final caress over mine. The thread unspools, the glimmer of the spell paling slowly, until the light vanishes entirely. The sigil at my wrist gives a final *pulse* . . . then it turns silent.

Rowan dissolves into mist-gray shadows.

My knees turn weak, and I crumple to the ground. The world Below comes back in scattered pieces of shade and mothlight. I'm bowed forward with my fingers dug into the earth. The ominous rise of wind has died to silence, and at the border of the clearing, the trees stand motionless.

I fight desperately to keep hold of the vision, the flare of magic that lit the spell-thread, the heat of Rowan's kisses. The feeling that—for just a moment—we were together again. But the warmth fades from my skin. My power quiets to a muted throb. I curl my fingers against the ground, feel cold mud embedded beneath my nails.

The Lord Under still has his hand at my nape. It seems that no more than a moment has passed here while I was lost in the vision. The shadowed ends of his magic are still in the air, trailed around us in gently shifting strands. I don't want to be touched by him, or his power, right now. I can't bear it. I push him away, sit back on my heels. Scrub my dirt-gritted palms across my cheeks and wipe away the lingering tears.

He gets back to his feet, half-turned. I see his face in profile, and though his gaze is studiedly downcast, I can tell that he is watching me.

"Tell me," he says, guarded and careful. "What do you think?"

Slowly, I look around. And I realize this space, which was once nothing more than leaves and moss, is now . . . a garden.

Ferns cluster beneath the heartwood trees, interspersed with strands of midnight-dark hellebores. Wild roses spill fragile petals across the ground and pothos vines drip their stripe-leafed strands from the branches above.

I stand up, feeling unsteady. Take a tentative step forward.

I'm on a path, lined with pale mushrooms that light the air with a silvery glow. It's like the garden at Lakesedge the first time I saw it beneath the moonlight, all secret and shadow. Now, seeing it here, replicated, sends a flicker of magic across my hands and makes warmth dance at my fingertips.

Understanding weights my chest with the gravity of what the Lord Under has done. "You used my hurt to make this."

He nods slowly. "Yes, I did."

"But why?"

His brows knit together for a moment before his features smooth. He makes a sound that is not quite a laugh. "You're welcome," he says, as though I have thanked him. He gives me a look, mouth tilted, and then goes on. "You are not my prisoner, Violeta. This world is your home."

I rub the back of my neck, still feeling the prickle of his claws, my other hand restlessly tangling in the folds of my skirts. I look around the garden, teeth worrying at my lip until I taste blood. "It's beautiful. But this isn't an answer."

His smile fades, and his expression turns cold. A flare of something dangerous marks his gaze. The ends of his cloak turn back to shadows again, trailing out across the ground toward me. Tendrils of darkness lap at my feet like ink-dark waves. I curl my toes inside my boots and bite the inside of my cheek, forcing myself to be still as he moves closer.

"I cannot give you what you ask, Violeta."

I curl my hand around my wrist, press down against the sigil. Blurrily, I realize that in my vision, when the thread unfurled into the trees, it went in the direction of the wall. To the arched gateway, the locked door that will never open for me. I press harder against the spell, a frustrated sigh caught in my throat.

I stare up at the Lord Under and meet his gaze evenly. "What are you hiding from me out there beyond the thorns?"

"Nothing." His teeth are bared. And though he bites out the words, there is unmistakable honesty in the way he looks at me. "I am hiding nothing from you."

The silence extends, becomes leaden. My hands tense to fists, sparks of magic hot against my palms. Abruptly, I turn away from the Lord Under and put my back to him. "I want to be alone."

He hesitates a moment. I hear the shift of his boots, the rustle of his cloak, as he paces back and forth. Then, he stills. Quietly, he says, "Good night."

I don't respond. He moves past me as he makes his way out of the garden. I watch as he slips between the trees, and the shadows of the forest close around him. He is gone as swiftly as if he'd vanished, leaving me with only the gentle rustle of fern leaves and the faint creak of branches overhead.

The tiredness I've fought against finally overwhelms me. I breathe out another ragged sigh and start to walk slowly back to my cottage, keeping my arms folded around my waist. As though I can hold together all the emotions threatening to riot through me.

My cottage is a single room with a bare space of earth for

a floor. The walls are the same rough-hewn panels as outside, the wood marked with patterns like whorled eyes and scraps of crimson bark. The branches that form the ceiling are covered with leaves, and a tangle of ivy makes a canopy above my bed.

The fire has burned down to only a scatter of coals, and my room is almost dark. But I'm familiar enough with the space that I don't bother to light the single lantern. It was a gift from the Lord Under to use with the candles he gave me, wondering aloud if I might like to make observance at one of the many altars in the forest. I haven't, yet, instead saving the candles to burn when I am alone. I like to watch the light dance while I try to make my mind go still, then exhale to turn the flame into a trail of smoke.

I take off my muddy boots and untie the sash of my dress, slipping free of the silken fabric, replacing it with a pale night-gown that's hemmed in cobwebs. I go over to the fireplace, add new wood to the coals. Sit by the hearth with my hands outstretched. The flames burn higher. The air grows warm.

I'm filled with impossible longing for all I've given up. For *Rowan.* I want to see him again, to hear the tender way his voice shaped my name. I curl my fingers around my wrist. Feel the beat of my heart, the beat of my magic. I close my eyes and see the spell-thread, stretched out through the forest, toward the wall.

I need to go out beyond the thorns. But no matter how much I ask or argue, the Lord Under will only lock me tighter in what he insists is not a cage. He wants me here, only here, inside this replica of the world I left behind. A cottage built from the woods, a garden grown from tears, a chest full of dresses sewn from spider silk.

I know him well enough to understand that the truth of his words—there is nothing hidden from me beyond the wall—are deceptive as a lie. My whole existence here is proof of how he bends words to his will, as though honesty is a heartwood to be reshaped beneath his claws.

Something is there, out in the world Below. Something he doesn't want me to see. Maybe something to do with my magic . . . the tether that might still tie me to Rowan. The Lord Under's determination to keep me *here* only lends more weight to it.

But I have no way to breach the thorns. I've paced their borders countless times, searching for a way through. My only chance is the gate that never opens, except when the Lord Under comes to this part of the forest.

I lean my chin against my knees and stare into the fire. As I watch the flames lick over the wood, a plan begins to form. Slowly, I get to my feet, ignoring the protest of fatigue that weights my limbs. I pick up my cloak and put it on over my nightdress. I step into my boots, knot the laces tightly.

The lantern is in an alcove above my bed, a new candle set inside. I take it down carefully. Slip my sparklight into my pocket. Then I go back out into the garden, and walk over to where the Lord Under disappeared between the trees. From the path, it's the barest sliver of space, impossibly narrow. As I draw closer, though, the space widens. I turn sideways, fit myself through the gap.

For a moment I'm caught, leaves in my hair and branches snagging at my skirts. Then I'm on the other side, in the shadowed woods. When I look behind me, my cottage—woven walls and a smoke-streaked chimney—is barely visible.

I tuck my hair under the hood of my cloak and tie the ribbon tight at my collar. Beneath a bower that's tangled with ivy, two arched branches frame a narrow path that leads into the shadows.

I light my lantern, and I walk into the forest.

Chapter Four

ROWAN

The next morning is muted weather. A gray sky that matches my mood. Wind full of leaves. Air that smells of stove ash. I find Arien and Clover in the stillroom, side by side at the table beneath the window. The light from outside is dim, screened by clouds that promise rain. They have a candle on the table, brought in from the kitchen altar. The small flame stirs, caught by a draft when I walk into the room.

Clover looks up at me. She smiles, tired, and takes off her glasses to rub her eyes. Arien stifles a yawn. None of us have been sleeping well lately. We move through the house somnambulantly. Drowsing away the afternoons, then awake at midnight.

Sometimes I'll see Arien when I pace the halls in the dark. We'll pause together beneath the landing window and look up at the sky. As though the patterns of stars might hold some answer to all of this.

43

Or I'll find Clover in the library, where the portrait of my family watches over empty shelves. Her arms folded on the table. A pile of notebooks beside her. A pen tucked loosely in her hand.

I know their dreams must be as haunted as mine. Filled with thoughts of the final ritual and all that came after. The way the ground tore open. How Leta told us she had to mend the Corruption in the world Below. The moment when she walked into the lake. The way our tentative hopes were shattered after she returned, and the poison claimed her.

When she fell into my arms, begged me to take her to the parlor, and we all watched as she called to the Lord Under. As she vanished into the shadows.

The stillroom is a narrow, low-ceilinged space. I have to duck beneath the flowers strung up to dry between the rafters. Dead leaves and dried petals rustle against my hair. I brush them away. Clear my throat. Move closer to the worktable.

Arien makes room for me on the bench. I sit beside him. "I have a favor to ask you both."

He looks at me curiously, chin propped on his hand. "What do you need?"

I touch my bandaged wrist, feel the ache of scar and spell. Try to find the right words. As I hesitate, my eyes fall to the table. There's a piece of paper torn from a notebook, with a sketch inked on it. I look closer. It reminds me of an image from an icon. A figure with a crown of flowers, petals shaped into a halo. An eye, a cheek, a soft-edged smile. The features are familiar, though I can't place why.

Then I realize. "Oh. It's—it's Elan."

Arien puts his hand quickly over the page, smudging the ink. He starts to blush. "I was just using his face as a reference." He indicates toward the stairs that lead up to the library. "From the portrait."

"Right," I manage. "The portrait."

I think back to the day in the library when Leta uncovered the portrait of my family. That way she looked at me. Her sharp, silver eyes full of accusation. From the first moment we met, she knew me. Truly knew me for what I was. And even then, when I hated her so much, I was drawn to her. Because of that knowing.

She knew I was a monster, but she didn't turn away.

Arien ducks his head, embarrassed. He cut his hair after the ritual, and now the jagged ends fall unevenly around his face. I put my hand on his shoulder. I feel shaken by this reminder of Elan. This is the nearest we've come to mentioning my loss—or his—ever. Arien has kept his hurt over Leta closely held. A weight pressed to his heart.

"It's a good likeness, Arien."

He folds the paper. Hides it beneath a stack of notebooks. "Thank you."

Clover pokes at him with her elbow. Her mouth twitches into a playful smile. "Will you draw me next?"

Arien glares at her. He adds another notebook to the pile that hides the portrait. "Rowan, you said you wanted a favor?"

Slowly, I take off my gloves. I first started to wear them after the Corruption began, along with tightly laced shirts and a heavy cloak—even at the height of summer. I wanted to keep as much of myself hidden as possible. And though the Corruption has been mended, the habit remains.

Now I feel bared, vulnerable, as I untie the laces at my cuffs and fold back my sleeves. I unwind the bandage from my wrist. Stretch out my arms. "I need your help with this."

Arien and Clover both fall silent when they see the marks on my skin. The wounds look worse than ever. Blackened cuts, streaks of darkness stretching along my forearms. Bruises that pool like shadows beneath the sigil on my wrist.

Arien touches the mark of the burned-out spell. Tentatively, he presses down.

"Ash!" I jolt back, wrench myself away from his touch as pain cuts sharply through me. I clench my hand over the sigil as darkness clouds my vision. My breath turns rough, echoing loudly in the small space of the stillroom.

Clover leans toward me, horrified. "Rowan, what's happened to you?"

My teeth bite down against the inside of my cheek. I taste blood and earth and bitter herbs. A rush of emotions tears through me. Hurt, loss. The silver-sharp cold of endless night. It's the same way I felt at every tithe. When I went to the lake, let the darkness inside me.

Finally, I unclench my jaw enough to speak. "I've seen Leta."

"What do you mean," Arien says, a guarded hurt in his eyes, "that you've *seen* her?"

Carefully, I touch the lines of the sigil. "The spell she marked on me . . . I felt it change when I made observance."

I tell them everything. How I looked into the shadows at the altar and saw Leta there. How I felt the Corruption wake up inside me when I reached for her. How my scars bled, and lines of poison streaked my skin.

Clover pulls at the end of her braid. She leans closer, gaze narrowed at the spell on my wrist. "That sigil shouldn't be active any longer. Once a spell is cast, all the alchemy is gone. It's only the mark that's left behind." She chews her lip. "At least, that's how it works when *we* use magic. But since this spell came from the Lord Under . . ."

She holds out a hand, then hesitates. Though we worked together for almost a year of hopeless, bloodstained rituals, I've rarely let her touch me. When my blood was needed for her magic, I'd set the knife to my own wrist. Bind my own wounds afterward.

Now, I push my sleeve farther back, offer my arm. As she examines the lines of the sigil, I'm overcome with the same mix of longing and refusal as when Florence tried to comfort me. I clench my fists. Struggle against the urge to shove Clover away.

Her mouth moves, shaping soundless words. Light sparks from her fingertips, and her eyes shimmer, golden. Her magic is warm against my skin. Gentler than the fierce, sharp heat of the spell Leta cast. The feel of it, this difference in their alchemy, sends a new flood of grief through me. With effort, I force myself to keep still.

Arien leans in close, watching as the sigil reacts to Clover's touch. Beneath my skin, the pooled darkness uncurls. It trails, like spilled ink, toward the crook of my elbow. Down across my palm.

Arien makes a low sound beneath his breath.

"It still has magic," I say, sure enough that it's not a question.

"It still has magic," Clover agrees, her expression grim. "There shouldn't be *power* in a burned spell. But it's still . . . awake."

"Leta told me that when the Lord Under works magic on someone, it leaves a mark." Arien holds out his hands, showing us the pale, fernlike pattern of his scars. He was wounded when the Lord Under saved him at Leta's request, after the second ritual failed and the Corruption tried to claim him. He stares at the marks solemnly. Then, with a heavy sigh, he goes on. "Maybe it's been the same for you, Rowan. Her power and that spell were from him. So it's *stayed* in you."

Clover nods slowly, her eyes filled with a mix of fear and sadness. "And this reaction . . . it's like the Corruption. Like there are still traces left. It was inside you for so long. Each time you fed it your blood, you made it more a part of you. We mended it from the lake and the shore, and I thought—but maybe we didn't—maybe it hasn't been mended from you." She tips back her head. Sighs wretchedly. "We have to find a way to stop this before it spreads even farther."

"No," I tell her. "That isn't the favor I came to ask."

She lets out an incredulous laugh. "It's not?"

"I don't want it mended. I want to find a way to make it worse. I want to reach Leta, using the spell."

"But Violeta is . . ." Clover darts a glance toward Arien. Trails into silence.

None of us have spoken of it, what it meant when she turned to shadows in my arms that day at the altar. She left no body to burn. We had no pyre.

"She isn't dead." My teeth bite down against the word. I spit it out, fierce. "You *know* she isn't dead."

Clover looks at me unhappily. "Please, don't ask us to do this."

"You used my blood in the rituals. How is this any worse?"

"In the rituals I had no other choice! But this—" Her voice chokes. She takes off her glasses, presses a hand to her face. She swallows, hard, as she blinks back her tears. "What happens if the Corruption overtakes you again? What if you're lost completely? Without Violeta's magic we've no way to call you back."

Call me back. The taste of poison fills my mouth at the memory of Leta, the vision at observance. How I bled, how I felt the shadows rise within me when I saw her across the vacant dark. "I'm willing to risk that."

"If you lose control, we won't be able to stop you."

It hangs unsaid between us. A truth that turns the silence to a sickness.

If I push this too far, if I fail, the poison will destroy me.

For so many years I fed my blood to the lake. Went in secret to give my tithe. Let the Corruption devour me slowly. Even at my worst moments I hadn't truly wanted to die. I didn't want that to be my legacy.

But right now, I'm not afraid of death.

"I'm only here because of the sacrifices of everyone around me. My parents. Elan. And now Leta. What right do I have to my life when that was the cost? It's never been *mine* since the day I drowned and the Lord Under saved me. If I have to risk myself to get Leta back, then so be it." I clench my hand around my wrist. Lines of darkness radiate from the sigil. Gleam blackly in the candlelight. "You will make it worse. You *will*."

Clover scowls at me, tears still bright at the corners of her eyes. "Stop being so awful, Rowan. We're not going to do this. We won't be complicit in your destruction."

"You're already complicit. We *all* are. Leta wanted to burn herself down. She lied and cheated and threw herself into danger. But in the end, none of us held her back."

"Don't you think I know that? Violeta made a reckless, foolish choice, but she never should have paid so dearly for it. She was my *friend*, Rowan." She pauses to take a breath. Gathers herself before she can go on, in a halting whisper. "I miss her, too. But this isn't the answer."

Arien slaps his hands down, hard, against the worktable. His palms thud against the wood, the sound cutting sharply through the tense air of the stillroom. We look at him, startled. He glares back at us. Two splotches of bright color mark his pale cheeks.

"Can you both just—stop!" He rakes at his hair, sighs

raggedly. His voice lowers, wounded. "She's my *sister*. Don't you think I should get a say in what happens?"

"Arien . . ." I put my hand on his arm. "I'm sorry."

Before he can respond, a rhythmic *knock knock knock* echoes through the house. We turn in unison toward the sound. The knock comes again. Clover wipes the tears from her eyes, puts her glasses back on. "Someone's at the door."

She smooths a hand over her skirts as she gets to her feet. Arien and I follow her out of the stillroom and into the entrance hall. Arien studiedly avoids my gaze as I walk beside him. His face is sharp with sorrow. It reminds me of how Elan looked, in those last, grief-filled years before he drowned. His narrowed features, his fatigue-shadowed eyes.

And just like with Elan, I own a share in this, in Arien's hurt.

The door opens to reveal a girl waiting outside. She has oak-brown skin and dark, curly hair that she wears tied back with a wide, silken ribbon. I stare at her, confused. Then a recollection comes of her face—more entranced, less fearful—at the Summersend bonfire. Calathea Harkness, the keeper's daughter.

"Thea?" Clover says, confused. "What are you doing here?"

Thea doesn't answer. Her attention is fixed on my bared arms, on the sigil with the raised lines of poison around it. She falters back, an involuntary step. Gravel from the front path scatters under her boots. I quickly pull down my sleeves and retie the laces on my shirt cuffs.

Nervously, Thea looks between me and Clover. "I brought

51

the case you ordered for Arien. The alchemical case. You do . . . remember, don't you?"

I notice, now, that she's carrying a paper-wrapped parcel, tied with twine. My head starts to ache. I press my fingers to my temples, breathe out slowly. All the days since the ritual have blurred together. But I have a vague recollection of a conversation we had about ordering an alchemical case to be made. Arien sketching a design for Clover to take to the village.

Clover pushes the door open wider. She gives me a warning look. "Of course we remember! Please, come inside."

Thea steps warily into the house, the parcel held tight in her arms. She ducks her head at me, an awkward nod, then follows Clover into the hall. Arien and I trail after them, both of us still lapsed into a tense silence. When we reach the kitchen, he pauses. Takes a breath, as though to steady himself. Then he walks into the room where Thea has put the parcel down on the table.

I linger back, one shoulder leaned against the doorframe, and watch Arien open the parcel. He cuts the twine with scissors from the stillroom. Folds the paper back carefully.

The new case is made of carved wood, polished to the color of amber. Inside there is a larger space to hold notebooks and pens, then tiny compartments for storing other materials. Arien looks at it, his eyes welling with tears. He touches the case gently. Traces his fingers over the wood. "It's beautiful, Thea."

The sides of the case are carved with a pattern of moons, the phases marked out from full to crescent. When Clover notices it, she smiles. A soft blush rises over her freckled cheeks. "It's perfect, Thea. You're—you're so clever."

Thea twists a curl around one finger, shoulders squared with pride. "I like intricate work. Those tiny compartments were a wonderful challenge." She quiets, her brow creasing. She looks searchingly around the room. Noticing the absence of one person for the first time. "But doesn't Violeta want one, since she's an alchemist as well?"

Arien and Clover exchange a look, then Arien clears his throat hesitantly. "Leta is—"

I cut in, before he can finish. "She's still deciding."

He bites his lip, then nods slowly. "Yes. That's right. She hasn't decided yet."

Clover stares at me helplessly. She knots the end of her braid around her hand, her restless fingers tangling in the strands of hair. Her voice turns low, imploring. *"Rowan."*

I stand very still. My pulse beats sharply at my throat, my wrists. The taste of blood and poison is in my mouth. I know what I should do. What is right. Tell Thea, tell everyone, that Leta is dead. Burn a pyre for her in the fields outside the village. Chant the mourning litany.

And I know—equally—those things are *impossible*.

Without speaking, I turn and leave the room. As I walk up the stairs, I hear Thea give an awkward, nervous cough. "Did I upset him?"

"He's always like that," Clover replies, voice strained. "Don't worry. It's not your fault that he has no manners."

I don't look back. When I cross the landing, I keep my eyes determinedly ahead as I pass the window. I don't want to see outside; the view of the ruined garden, the sun-sparked lake.

I go into my room and draw the curtains, let silence snare around me. Cold and deep.

Stretched out on my bed, I roll back my sleeve, press my fingers against the sigil. Pain flares bright, sharp enough to steal my breath. My pulse beats wildly against my fingertips. As the hurt washes over me, my vision starts to blacken. This time, I let the darkness come rather than forcing it away.

It swallows me whole.

My fingers clench against my palms, my nails sharp as claws. Blood fills my mouth as my teeth sink into my lip. The world turns blurred. In a single blink, the outline of my room—dresser, bed, unlit fire—is gone. Replaced by a shadowed dreamscape.

I see slender, pale trees. I'm in the forest behind the estate. The sun has set, leaving a streak of crimson at the very edge of the sky. The light drips like blood between the branches. It's cold, colder than any Harvestfall night. My breath plumes in the air. Beneath my feet, frost covers the ground.

As I walk through the forest, I hear the hush and sigh of water in the distance. The sound grows louder as the trees part. I step out onto the windswept shore, and the lake stretches before me, its inky surface cut by reflected shards of vanishing sunlight. A form lies at the edge of the water, half-wrapped in a shroud. I can only make out the barest details. A curved cheek. A pale hand, fingers tangled with lake grass.

Myself, as a child, the night I drowned.

Slowly, the air starts to darken. Clouds gather across the sky, and the light turns heavy, shadowed. When a cold drift of wind sweeps them aside, the shrouded form—my five year old self—has gone. And Leta is there, standing on the shore.

I'm overcome with hurt and hope. This isn't the vision from the altar. Blurred, surreal. She is here, right before me. Her dress is dark as midnight. Her hair is tied back, and her shoulders are bare, a pale curve from neck to clavicle. The ends of her skirts trail over the ground like shadows.

I take a faltering step toward her. Afraid all this will shatter. That she will vanish. But she falls into my arms, sighs my name with a tattered breath. *"Rowan."*

I bury my face against her shoulder. Press my lips to the bared edge of her collarbone. She's so cold. My breath forms beads of condensation on her skin. I kiss her neck. Clutch tightly at her waist. "I saw you," I tell her, a sob caught in my throat. "I saw you in the dark."

Leta makes a soft, desperate sound. She presses fiercely against me. Whispering, her voice ragged. "I made you a promise, when I was last on this shore. Do you remember? I promised to come back to you."

Her fingers circle my wrist, find the spell. Her thumb marks the center of the sigil, and a rush of power floods over me. I gasp, caught by the sudden force of it. The air turns bright. A thread—the same thread of golden light I saw last time—ignites between us. Strung from her wrist to mine. I feel the strength of it. This strange spell that weaves us together.

On the ground, beneath us, our shadows make a darkened

line. An echo of the path that opened at the final ritual. The path that Leta followed into the world Below.

Gently, I take her face between my hands. Determination sets a fire in me as I stare down at her. Lit by the spell, she gleams, brilliant as starlight. The tenderness I feel for her, it *hurts*. All I wanted was to be with her, in a way that I hardly allowed myself to believe possible. For the two of us to have a life without fear or danger or death. And when she vanished at the altar, I thought I had lost everything.

The tether burns brightly between us. The sigil aches against my wrist. I bend to kiss her. I feel her sigh against my mouth, feel the barest brush of her lips on mine.

As she starts to fade, I breathe against the curve of her ear, "I am going to find you, Violeta. That is *my* promise."

Chapter Five

VIOLETA

I keep to the woods rather than following the path. Leaves tangle my hair, and twigs scrape against my skin as I move through the trees. Every few steps I pause to gather scraps from the forest floor. I fill the pockets of my cloak with leaves that are brittle and brown, handfuls of sticks that clatter like bones, a cone like the one I gleaned the seed from to grow the heartwood with my magic.

The gate appears in the distance, framed by two ivy-laced trees. On the path, my footprints from before are still visible in the soft mud. A newer row of prints is marked in the opposite direction, left by the Lord Under. I follow them now, setting my feet into the hollows shaped by his boots.

My pockets are heavy with the newly added weight of collected debris. My cloak drags as I kneel beside the wall, where the thorned palings of the gate are embedded in the ground.

When I set the lantern down behind me, the flickering light throws my blurred shadow against the brambles until it looks like a spined, faerie-tale beast.

I roll back my sleeves and start to clear away the earth at the base of the thorns, digging out handfuls of wet leaves and clotted mud. Then I hurriedly empty out the pockets of my cloak, piling the kindling that I've gathered at the base of the thorns.

I take the lantern, my fingers leaving muddied smears on the glass, and carefully lift the candle from inside. Gently, I tilt it, the flame elongating as wax puddles and drips. The fire wavers for a moment, then it catches, moving greedily across the leaves and fern fronds and broken branches.

I watch it all burn. Smoke coils up through the brambles, spiraling around the thorns as the flames rush swiftly over the wood. I watch the fire rise and spread, welcoming the heat on my face and the new brightness that cuts through the gloom.

Then, above the crackle of the flames, comes another sound. A jagged noise that could almost be . . . *a laugh*. I shove myself back to my feet and look anxiously at the top of the wall. Magic sparks at my fingertips, and the sigil on my wrist gives a *pull*. My eyes sting from the smoke as I stare intently at the space above the brambles.

But all I can see is a stretch of shadowed sky, veiled by mist. No one else is here. It's only me, my nervous heartbeat, and the empty, smoke-washed air.

I curl my fingers against my palms and let out a shallow breath. As though in answer, the sound—that almost laugh— comes again through the trees. A cold rush of wind sweeps over me, making the flames in the brambles stutter. From behind the smoke, a shadow appears, outlined by the forest canopy. It darkens, coalesces into a solid shape.

A girl is standing at the top of the wall.

Small and delicate, she has tanned skin and unruly dark gold hair that drapes around her narrow shoulders. She's balanced carefully, her bare feet just visible beneath the hem of her skirts. The top of her face is hidden by a bone-pale mask that's carved like the face of a deer. The two jutting antlers at the top are woven with strands of ivy.

Aside from the mask, she looks . . . human.

I take a halting step back, my mouth open, a soundless gasp of shock caught in my throat. In the haze of smoke and the gloom of the forest, the girl doesn't seem real. It's impossible that there could be someone else here in the world of the dead, let alone someone like *me*. An ordinary girl with mud on her dress and tangles in her hair.

I swallow, press my bitten lips together. "Who are you?"

She twines a strand of hair carelessly around one finger. "Who are *you*?"

Another rush of wind stirs through the forest, sending a cloud of ashen smoke against my face. I start to cough, and my name comes out rasped. "Violeta."

"Violeta." The girl gathers up her skirts delicately and takes a step closer to the edge of the wall, leaning forward to peer down at me through the rising flames. A smile pulls at the corners of her mouth. "I've heard whispers of you, the Lord Under's pet. But I hardly let myself believe it."

59

"I'm not his pet."

"A little hard to protest while you're standing in a cage."

I gesture to the fire. "I won't be for long."

She starts to laugh, a louder version of the same sound I heard before. Letting go of her skirts, she raises her hands. There are marks scored on her wrists, more haphazard than any of the alchemical sigils I've seen Arien or Clover use. But the pale light of magic starts to gleam from her hands, and behind the mask her eyes turn golden—the same way that Clover's do when she casts a spell.

The wind grows fierce, tearing at my skirts and whipping strands of hair across my face. The branches of the heartwoods groan in protest as the air hisses sharply through their leaves. The fire rises higher through the brambles, the thorns now amber and orange amid the brilliant flames.

Then the strange girl claps her hands together, and everything goes completely still. When I try to take a breath, nothing is there. My lips part helplessly, and my lungs *ache*. I stumble back from the gate, my hand clutched to my throat. My mouth shapes a desperate protest, and my nails scrape my skin. Darkness clouds my vision, and I hear, as though from far away, the urgent, choking sound of myself trying to breathe. My knees buckle, and I falter to the ground.

And in this airless void the fire dies instantly, the flames gone out as suddenly as an extinguished candle.

Some of the burned brambles fall away from the wall, a tangle of charred wood and blackened leaves. The girl watches them drift down with mild curiosity. Her gaze shifts in my direction. Slowly, she lowers her hands, and with a burst of pressure, the air floods back in. I bury my fingers in the ground and hunch forward, coughing, then drag in an enormous breath that tears the insides of my lungs.

I glare up at the girl, my mouth twisted into a snarl. "Why did you do that?"

"To stop the fire, obviously." She smooths a hand down her skirts and shakes her hair back behind her shoulders. "Did you think I was going to *help* you?"

Incredulity drags a laugh from my aching throat. The sound tangles, becomes a sob that I can't bite back. "No, why would you help? Why would anything in this ash-damned world be on my side? I only gave my entire *life* to save it."

My anger rises swiftly, and I'm all instinctive motion, an animal in a snare with their teeth at a captured limb. I wrench myself forward—pen in my fingers, ink at my wrist. Draw over the lines of the sigil, then cast the pen aside and thrust my hands into the ruin of charcoal and scattered kindling at the base of the brambles.

My fingers pass over a shattered branch, a handful of soil, and then the cone digs into my palm as though it has been pressed there. I clutch it tight, close my eyes, and call on every thread of my too-small, too-faint power, sending it into the smoke-blackened earth.

The hurt of before tears through me brutally, an ache of grief and desolation. I let out a cry as I clasp the seed, force my magic down against it. It's a hundred times more painful than when I grew the heartwood tree for the Lord Under. Like my whole body has been driven beneath the soil, my limbs outstretched in the clotted dark, my mouth full of leaves, roots breaking past my bones.

The seed splits open, and the heartwood rises up between my hands, so fast that the roughened bark scrapes the skin from my palms. I scream with the effort of it, and the brambles are forced apart with a sound that matches my own howl. The thorns bend back, and a slash of light appears, twin to the space I slipped through in the forest above my garden. Beyond are the woods—trees and mist and shadows.

Without thought, without hesitation, I shove myself forward. The thorns fight against me, ripping through my cloak. One cuts my cheek; another tears loose strands of my hair.

I feel as though I'm beneath the Corruption again, at the very end of the spell when I called down the poison and let it devour me.

I kick against the earth, digging my boots into the mud, crying out as thorns cut my palms. I'm lost in the dark, caught by pain and the erratic sound of my panicked breath. Then, in a rush, I tumble through and land on the other side.

I lie on the ground, gasping. The branches above are a dizzying blur. The girl leans over me, her antlered outline splitting into four, then two, before my vision settles. Behind the mask, her expression is one of open shock—lips parted, brows raised.

She looks from me to the ruined brambles and lets out a low whistle. "The Lord Under is going to be *furious* with you.

I can't believe you did—" She shakes her head as she gestures to the gate, the new heartwood cleaving the archway into splintered halves. "*That*."

I spit out a mouthful of dirt. "Did you think you're the only one here with magic?"

"Apparently not." She examines me a moment longer, eyes darting to my thorn-scraped arms, the freshly inked sigil. Then she holds out a hand, offering to help me up. I don't move, and she laughs softly. "Come on, I won't bite. Promise."

I let her pull me to my feet. Everything tilts unsteadily when I stand, and I close my eyes against a rush of nausea. The girl slips her arm around my waist, easily bearing my weight as I sink against her. My forehead presses into the curve of her neck. Her skin is shockingly, unexpectedly cold.

At the feel of it, I jolt back and move away from her. Nervousness prickles down my spine. I stretch out my hand, making sure she keeps her distance from me. Blood from my grazed palm drips slowly onto the forest floor. The girl glances down at it, then touches her fingers to the edge of her mask.

I fold my arms across my chest, trying to hold back a shiver. "Will you tell me your name now? Or do I have to fling myself through another bramble wall first?"

Begrudgingly, she smiles at me. "My name is Fawn."

Then she pauses, eyes narrowed to the distance. We both fall silent as the unmistakable sound of footsteps echoes through the woods. She clutches my arm and drags me back into the shelter of the nearby trees. I start to speak, but she claps a hand over my mouth. Wide-eyed, she shakes her head.

Strands of mist weave across the ground, tangling at our feet. The footsteps draw closer, and my heart goes still as I hear a sharply familiar sigh. The shadowed shape of the Lord Under casts against the trees. He stalks back and forth in front of the archway, slowly taking in the damage. He touches his claws to the heartwood I grew and swears beneath his breath.

I grit my teeth, trying to be as still and silent as the forest, but leaves crackle around my boots. The Lord Under turns quickly toward the sound. "Violeta."

His voice is low, my name bitten out like a curse. Unbidden, a gasp escapes me beneath the press of Fawn's hand. His attention snaps in our direction. It's like all the trees fall away and I am standing right before him with nothing to hide me, pinned beneath his furious glare.

Fawn leans close and breathes a single, urgent command against my ear. "*Run.*"

We run into the woods, moving so quickly that the forest becomes nothing more than a blur of light and shadow. The crimson of heartwood trunks, the green of branches, the haze of swiftly rising fog. I trip against a snarled root, but Fawn drags me back up before I can fall.

My hand slips into hers, solidarity replacing the wariness I had of her before. We are two girls in danger. And there is no time to look back, look forward, to do anything except clutch her hand and trust her to lead me through the forest.

I can't hear anything except the sound of our feet and my labored breath as it tears from my burning lungs, but I am certain the Lord Under is right behind me. All I can think is how foolish I've been. These are his woods, his world. There's nowhere I can go to escape him.

Fawn and I stumble out into a clearing. Our path ends at an impenetrable row of heartwoods. I pull away from her and go back and forth along the trees, searching for a way through, but they grow so close together that it's impossible.

It starts to rain, a sudden shower of heavy drops that fall down through the branches. The water is black, like ink, like poison. Fawn stands with her hands on her hips, her skirts trailing across the sodden ground.

She sighs in disgust as she waves a hand that sums up the mess I've caused—the ruined wall, the Lord Under's fury, the cage of trees that has trapped us in the clearing. "No wonder he kept you locked up. You're an utter *disaster*."

"You can insult me all you like after we find a way out of here."

My boots cut a desperate path through the mud as I reach the far end of the grove. I drag my hand across the trees, searching. Then, my fingers catch between two trunks. I skid to a stop, pressing closer to peer into the narrow space.

Fawn sloshes over to me through puddles that have begun to form on the ground. She considers the space with a scowl. "We won't both fit. I ought to give you up to him and take my chances."

Behind us, my name comes ringing through the rain-drenched woods. *"Violeta!"*

I grab Fawn by her wrist and pull her close against me. With a burst of strength and impulsive panic, I shove us both inside the hollow. Now, hidden by the trees, we're tangled up in a knot of limbs and muddied skirts, my breath clouding the air between us as I try to stay quiet.

The inky rain pours steadily down, filling the bottom of the hollow beneath us. I curl my toes inside my boots as water seeps through my stockings and wish with every piece of myself that I was safe.

Fawn raises her brows at me. "What's your next clever idea?"

I clench my fists. My magic starts to stir, but there's no spell I can cast that will solve this. "I don't know."

"I should have left you behind. Oh, it's no good. If he catches us now, I'll be in just as much trouble." She sighs with irritation. "I think I can fix this. But I'll need something from you."

I look at her, confused. "Like what?"

"A *trade*," she hisses. "Have you truly come to the world Below without any understanding of how magic works here?"

"When I cast magic, I use a sigil."

"Forgive me for not being an *alchemist*." She draws out the word like it's a curse, her mouth twisted. "Now, quickly, tell me what you'll give up to keep us hidden."

I spread my hands, look down at my empty palms as I try to think. All I have is myself: rain-chilled skin, my fingers cut by thorns. My heart beats rapidly inside my chest. The ache of it, the lingering burn of my lungs, makes me think of when Fawn used her magic to put out my fire. How all the air went out of the forest, and I sank, choking, to the ground.

"Breath?" My voice quavers with uncertainty. I swallow and try again, managing to sound more certain. "I will trade you one breath."

She nods grimly, then moves closer, reweaving the knot of our limbs as she leans toward me. She takes hold of my wrist, her thumb circling over my pulse. "Ready?"

I swallow down a shiver as the Lord Under's voice snarls just outside the trees. "I know you're here, Violeta."

I look at Fawn. Her eyes, shadowed by the mask, have already begun to turn gold. Quietly, I shape a single word. *Yes*.

Fawn catches my face between her hands and crushes her mouth to mine. She's rough and fierce, her fingers tightening against my jaw until I gasp in shock and my lips part. Her knee pushes between my thighs and a shard of heat carves through me. I've never kissed anyone except Rowan, and as her tongue sweeps mine, I'm filled with fear and desire, the two so entwined that I don't know where one ends and the other begins.

Outside the tree, wind howls through the branches as the rain pours down in a torrent. There's a bone-deep sound, an endless groan, and the heartwoods begin to shift. The hollow reshapes, and the trees seal closed around us, locking us in like two souls placed in a heartwood.

Fawn pulls back, leaving me with my mouth open and my lips bruised. She smiles at me as she exhales, and I watch my single, surrendered breath come loose.

My heart goes still. My lungs go still. This is so much worse than whatever I felt before when she used her magic on the flames. Now I am trapped, held, desperate. I feel my body scream—it cries out for me to fight, to stop this, but there's nothing I can do. Nothing at all.

I can't even make a sound as I crumple to the depths of the hollow, my eyes closed, lost in the darkness.

Chapter Six

ROWAN

The vision releases me, unhooking its claws from my throat. It was more vivid, more painful, than what I saw at the altar. But still, it wasn't enough. As the shadows clear, I feel restless, desperate. It's the same way I'd feel when I was called to the tithe. My chest tight. My heartbeat rapid. My mouth laced with bitterness.

I'm left motionless on the chaise beneath my open window. My fingers are still clasped around my wrist. The sigil aches, circled by new bruises. Lines of darkness etch across my arm. When I press down against the spell, the lines start to spread. But the strange magic that drew me into the vision stays quiet.

I sit up. Turn to the row of candles on my windowsill. I light them, one by one. Watch the flames stutter as they start to burn.

A knock at my door startles me. I get to my feet. Then

pause, look down at myself. My crumpled shirt, my ruined arms. With a sigh, I cross the room, dragging a hand through my hair. My fingers catch on the tangles. I twist the strands back into a knot, tie them with a scrap of cord.

When I open the door, Florence is out in the hall. She's carrying a tray that's set with a covered bowl and an enamelware cup of tea. She adjusts the balance of the tray. Holds it out. "I brought the dinner you missed."

"I'm not hungry."

She looks me over. Her eyes are flinty, unreadable. Her gaze lingers at my wrist, the streaks of darkness around the sigil. "Don't you mean to say, *Thank you*?"

I try, hopelessly, to smooth the creases from my shirt as I step aside to let Florence into my room. "Thank you."

She sets the tray down on a low table beside the chaise, then notices the row of candles on the sill. "You shouldn't let them burn so close to the curtains."

Pointedly, I pull the curtains open farther. Cast her a glance, my brows raised. "Better?"

Her mouth twitches into a smile, though her eyes are still troubled. "Your food is getting cold."

I sit down on the chaise. Take a sip from the tea while I look at the food. There are mushrooms, cooked into a rich sauce, parsley scattered over the top. Black bread. A dish of salted butter. I have no appetite, but I pick up the spoon and stir it around the bowl. If I don't at least *attempt* to eat, Florence will never leave me alone.

"Is Thea still here?" I ask her.

"She left after dinner. Clover is walking her back to the village." Florence hesitates, then goes on softly. "Arien told me that Thea was asking about Violeta."

My jaw clenches. I nod, tightly. "We made an excuse for her."

She looks at me for a moment, fingers curled over the silver keys she wears on a chain around her neck. She fidgets, dragging the keys back and forth, then lets her hands drop to her sides. She's uncharacteristically restless. "Next month will be the Autumndark bonfire. Maybe that would be the right time to . . . tell everyone that she is gone."

I put down my spoon. It hits the edge of the bowl with a clunk. "I don't want to talk about this."

"You're the lord, Rowan. You have a duty—"

"I'm not going to the bonfire to stand before the villagers and *chant* and act like everything is fine. And I'm not going to tell them—or anyone—that Leta is dead."

"You can't lie about it forever."

There's no condemnation in her eyes. She's only . . . sad. I stare down at the floor. Avoiding her gaze. "It isn't a lie, Florence. You were there. You saw what happened after the ritual."

"I know you don't want to face it. I know it hurts. But I think it might help, if you let yourself mourn her."

Her words are meant with kindness. But coming so close to the vision I just had of Leta, they twist at my heart like a blade. I think of the lake and the pale trees. The frost on the ground. Our shadows making a path toward the water. My final, desperate promise as she faded. *I will find you.*

71

I stand up and go over to the door. I left it open, and now I look pointedly out toward the hall. "Thank you for dinner. I'd like to be alone."

Florence hesitates; then she trails slowly out of my room. As she passes me, she touches my shoulder. Her hand is gentle. "Arien deserves the chance to grieve his sister properly."

"I *said* I don't want to talk about this."

Her hand falls back. She turns away. I listen to the sound of her footsteps on the stairs, growing quieter. Guilt lodges heavily in my chest. I can't deny the truth of her parting words. I'm ashamed of it, the way Clover and I argued about Leta in front of Arien. Neither of us even thinking to ask how he felt.

On my windowsill, the candles flare and flicker. I extinguish them with a rough, sharp breath. Smoke trails around me as I pick up my gloves from the dresser.

I walk out of the room. Close the door behind me.

I make my way to the other side of the house. The hallway is dark, and my boots echo across the bare floorboards. When I pass the library, I glance through the door at the portrait of my family. It hangs solemnly between two empty shelves. Moonlight outlines the faces of my mother and father in silver. But Elan is pooled by shadow. His eyes turned onyx.

At the landing, I pause beneath the arched window. Put on my gloves. Tie the laces of my shirt cuffs tightly at my wrists. I can't escape the familiarity in this. The way it feels like I am going to give another tithe. With a deep breath, I climb the stairs to where Leta and Arien have their rooms.

I clench my fists as I pass Leta's closed door. I've not been here since before the ritual. Now, I try not to think what I'd see, if I went inside. Her unmade bed. A cast-off dress left crumpled on the floor in a tangle of lace. The book of poetry I gave her, the page still creased where I marked it.

I turn instead to Arien's room. His door is open, but he isn't in there. With a sigh, I go back down the hall. I can still feel the pull from Leta's room. It's like a cold echo against my spine. Not fading until I'm past the landing. Until I've gone down the stairs, put an entire floor of the house between me and that memory-haunted space.

In the kitchen the fire is banked, the windows shuttered. But a gleam of light comes from the stillroom. Through the partly opened door I see Arien. He's at the worktable, bent over a notebook. His alchemical case is open. He's filled some of the compartments with ingredients. Jars of salt. Charcoal. Dried flowers.

He looks up when he hears my footsteps. We stare at each other. I'm the first to break the silence. "I owe you an apology."

His mouth tilts into a grim smile. "You owe me about a million apologies, honestly."

I go into the stillroom, sit down beside him. "Arien, I'm sorry. I should have asked you about Leta. About what you wanted."

"I don't know what I want." He stares distractedly at the worktable. The notebooks and pens and half-finished sketches. His voice is quiet, hardly more than a whisper. "I'm so *angry* with her, Rowan."

73

The guilt in his voice fills me with a rush of sympathy. Gently, I say, "You're allowed to be angry."

"I thought if I went with her to the ritual, she would be safe. I should have known what would happen." He bites his lip, trying not to cry. "I let her go. At the ritual when the ground opened up, I *told* her to go."

"It wasn't your fault. She made a terrible choice when she bargained with the Lord Under, and that was because of me. If I hadn't been overcome by the Corruption, if she hadn't needed to stop me, then . . ."

"So, it's not my fault, but you're going to blame yourself?" Arien gives me a half-hearted smile. "What did she trade to the Lord Under for the power to stop you, and to mend the Corruption? She never would tell me."

I pause for a long, pained moment. I don't want to tell him, either, but he deserves the truth. No matter how terrible. "She . . . gave up her memories of your family. In this life, and the next."

Speaking it aloud, I'm overcome by the same despair as when I first heard Leta's tearful confession about the trade. Arien's smile dims instantly. He pales, horrified. "You mean—"

"She will be alone, even in death."

His gaze shutters. Tears fill his eyes, but he presses a hand to his face and stops them. "I don't know what is worse," he says miserably. "That the Lord Under could be so cruel, or that Leta could be so wretchedly *foolish*. She gave so much for us, and I know it was her choice . . . but it *hurts*. Everything hurts."

I put my hand on his shoulder. Wanting to comfort him.

Feeling helpless. "Florence thinks we should let her go. Build a pyre in the mourning fields, tell everyone she is dead. If you want that . . ." I trail off, hardly able to say it. But I owe him this. I owe him a choice.

Arien tugs at his hair and frowns at me, his expression conflicted. "Have you *really* seen her?"

I hesitate, then nod. "Yes. Twice now. At the altar, and just before, when I was in my room."

"Show me the sigil again."

He reaches to me, and I push back my sleeve. Lay my arm on the table. "It's still *there*," I tell Arien. "Our connection, that she made with this spell."

His fingers hover above the mark on my wrist. "And you think if we make it stronger, then we can use the connection to find her?" A flicker of hope lights his eyes. But then he shakes his head, troubled. "What if we fail? If you burn yourself down, just like Leta did?"

"It feels like a fair risk, my life for hers."

He lets out a harsh, sad laugh. "*Ash*, if you give your life to save Leta, she'll never forgive either of us."

I can't help but laugh, too, though my throat feels tight. I blink, hard, as tears blur the corners of my eyes. "I truly hope it doesn't come to that."

Hesitantly, Arien touches the sigil. He presses down, and a flash of pain spills through me. I swallow back a hiss, try to bear through the hurt. For the briefest moment, as lines of darkness shimmer across my skin, I imagine that I can feel— *magic*. The ghost of Leta's power.

Arien frowns. He starts to murmur to himself, tracing the lines of the spell. "Blood. Salt. Iron. Silt. Mud." He shakes his head again. "It shouldn't even *work*. It's not a proper spell. But . . ."

He turns to the worktable and snatches up a notebook. Flips quickly to a blank page. Starts to draw a sigil, matching the one on my wrist. He pauses, brow creased, then adds more lines. A second mark, beside it. The shape of the new spell is . . . familiar, somehow. I squint, trying to place it. Then I see it transposed. Not on a scrap of paper but inked on the inside of Leta's arm.

"That's from the spell Leta used to help you in the ritual."

"It's an amplifying spell," Arien explains. "Generally, it's used to amplify magic. But if my calculations are right, it should amplify whatever *this* is," he says, indicating my arm. "I'm going to try and replicate what happened at the altar, when you first saw her."

"Arien, I—"

"Don't you dare thank me for this." He tears the page from the notebook. Blows on the ink to make it dry, then shoves the paper, folded, into his pocket. "Come on. Let's do this now, before anyone sees us."

I go out into the dimly lit kitchen. Arien doesn't follow right away. In the stillroom, I hear him rifling around in his alchemical case. There's a clink of jars, the scrape of a drawer being shoved closed.

"Where do you think we should cast the spell?" I glance around the room. My attention lingers on the door that leads to the parlor. But that doesn't feel right. Then I move to the window, open the shutters to reveal a dark space of moonlit garden. "When I saw Leta in the last vision . . . I was at the lake."

Arien comes out of the stillroom. He chews his lip thoughtfully as he takes his cloak from the hook behind the door. "Then maybe we should go there. If the visions are connected to where she's used her magic, being at the lake might make it stronger."

I take two candles from the altar and set them into jars. After lighting them both, I pass one to Arien. A sound echoes from farther inside the house, and we exchange a wary glance. With his finger at his lips in a shushing motion, Arien opens the back door slowly. We tiptoe outside, trying to be as silent as possible.

Decaying leaves crunch underneath our feet as we go across the garden. We keep our heads down. The candles shielded close to our chests. When we step over the scar that marks the ground, I glance at the ruined altar. The darkened icon is more like the shadowed silhouette of the Lord Under than the golden features of the Lady.

That dark image stays with me as we follow the path into the woods that border the lake. Outlined against the pale trees. Framed by the iron gateway ahead. Picked out by stars in the sky above the shore.

We step from the forest, where trees give way to bare earth. It feels strange to be here again. I haven't come to the lake since the last ritual. The ground is mended, but outside the faint circle of our candlelight, everything looks blackened. Like the Corruption is still here.

I pace along the line of the shore, then lower myself to the ground beneath the tallest of the pale trees. Arien kneels beside me. I watch as he takes a collection of things from his pockets. The folded paper with the sigil he drew. A pen and some ink. A small glass vial.

He spreads the paper on the ground, weights it with stones to hold it flat so he can copy the spell. He motions to my arm. "Push back your sleeve."

I look at him, confused. "What are you doing?"

"I'm using Leta's spell, then amplifying it. Which means I have to draw it on you, like she did when she cast it the first time." He shakes his head, mutters to himself. "I'm certainly not going to draw it on *my* arm, and end up bound to you forever."

I take off my gloves, set them aside. Fold back my sleeve. Stretch out my arm. Arien draws over the sigil already on my wrist, then adds the new lines of the amplification spell. He waits a moment until the ink has dried. He caps his pen, puts away the paper. "Now, hold still."

He leans over me. His eyes darken with a blink—turned from gray to pure black, the transformation unnervingly swift. Shadows start to unfurl from his hands. I take a breath, taste ash and smoke. Carefully, Arien touches my arm. His fingers trace the sigil.

He hesitates, eyes narrowed, teeth dug into his lower lip. Then he presses down on the center of the spell.

The pain is white hot. A sudden, inescapable *hurt* that steals my breath and turns my vision blank. Darkness spirals through me in a swift, cold *rush*. I bite the inside of my cheek until my mouth fills with blood. Force myself not to move. Beneath the sigil, lines of darkness spread rapidly all the way across my arm, down over my fingertips.

Arien grimaces as he watches the poison move beneath my skin. He draws back, flexes his hand; then he grabs my wrist and presses down again. A cry catches, ragged, in my throat. The pain is teeth, is knives, is ruin.

Finally, he lets me go. I clutch my wrist as my vision blurs. I am shadows. I am claws. I am a hungry, endless darkness. I feel the *pull* of magic unwinding through my veins. My breath turns slow. My pulse sluggish. I slump against the tree. Tilt my head back, stare unseeing at the branches above.

Arien wipes his hands against his trousers and settles back onto his heels. He watches me with weary resignation. I shift, discomforted. "You don't have to stay."

"Actually, I do. Someone needs to be here in case things go badly."

I press a hand against my face. Magic coils around me in heavy strands. Turning my bones to lead. But when I try to fall beneath it, let it overtake me, all I can think about is Arien. His anxious silence. The apprehensive way he watches me. "I can't relax with you *looming* there."

"That's why I've brought this." He holds up the glass vial. I look at it more closely. It's like the sedatives that Clover gave me, so I could sleep through the worst of my nightmares. But the liquid in this vial is a different color. Dark red, instead of brilliant green.

"You're going to drug me?"

Arien raises a brow at my incredulous tone. "That's really where you draw the line? Yes, I'm going to drug you. It's doubly concentrated, so it probably tastes twice as awful as the one Clover makes. Enjoy."

He shoves the vial toward me. Inside the glass, the sedative looks like blood. My hands have started to shake, and when I open the stopper, some of the liquid spills out. Arien sighs, irritated. He puts his hand around mine. Helps me raise the vial to my mouth.

The sedative is strangely thick. It burns all the way down my throat, leaves behind an aftertaste of rust. I swallow hard against the nausea that follows.

I lie down, curl up on my side with my face pillowed on my folded arm. Night air drifts, cold, against my skin. I listen to the hush and sigh of the lake. My fingers dig into the earth. I close my eyes.

Sleep rises over me, swift as floodwater.

It's like drowning.

It's like coming home.

I'm sunk so deep that I can't move. I can't think. From far off, I hear a stilted whisper. I can't make sense of the words it says. But I feel, with terrible certainty, that if I could listen closer, could just *hear*—

I open my eyes. The whole world has flooded with dark green light. The lake has gone, and the pale trees have been replaced by pines that are cloaked in mist. They're endlessly tall, branches covering the sky. Bark the color of blood.

I *know* where I am. I've been here before. When I fell beneath the water. When the lake almost claimed my life.

I'm in a world where no one living should walk.

The darkness opens to me. It welcomes me. I see black water. Black blood. A silver moonscape. Trees and trees, and a path at the center.

And on the path—*her*.

Chapter Seven

VIOLETA

The trees release us. Fawn and I tumble heavily to the moss-damp ground, caught up in the trailing fabric of my cloak. I catch a glimpse of the forest where we've landed—pale trees with scraps of lace tied to their branches—then Fawn grabs my arm, her fingers digging painfully against the cuts, and drags me to my feet. She shoves me away from the hollow where we hid, and we keep running, into the other side of the woods.

It's my first proper sight of the world Below outside the wall. I haven't been here since I mended the Corruption. It's different from how I remember. The air is full of secrets and hidden things, and the shadows play tricks as we pass. Whorls of bark become narrowed eyes or sharp-toothed smiles. Shapes appear from the dark, and they're like *creatures* . . . with feathers and horns and scales. I turn, try to see them more clearly. But they slip away, melt back to leaves and mist.

Finally, we emerge in an alcove made of granite stones. Three of the walls are still standing, but the other one has collapsed into a tumble of lichen-smooth edges. There's an altar at one end, the shelf lined with mothlights that glimmer through the dark. The icon—of the Lord Under—is weatherworn. All that's visible are his pale eyes and the sharp points of his antlered crown.

Fawn sinks down onto a piece of the broken wall with a sigh. "We'll be safe here for now."

She takes off her mask and scrubs at her face. Beneath, she is girlish and pretty, with round cheeks and long-lashed eyes. But then the light around her jawline blurs, and it's as though her features change—her mouth too wide, her teeth crowded close, a second set of liquid, amber eyes blinking at me from beneath her brow bone.

I smother a gasp, and she looks at me sharply. The strangeness that I thought I saw vanishes. She's just a girl with leaves caught in her hair and a flush across her cheeks from our hurried flight through the woods.

Fawn puts the mask back on quickly, mouth curved into an embarrassed smile. I turn away, feeling awkward, like I've seen her unclothed rather than unmasked.

"Sorry," I stammer. "I didn't mean—"

She waves a hand. "It's fine."

I move away from her, sit on the opposite side of the wall

with my face toward the trees. My chest aches, my lungs are raw, and I can't catch my breath after running so far. I feel like the night I drank a whole handful of stolen sedative vials—half caught in a dream, unable to focus clearly.

For the barest moment, the shadows in the forest transform again. This time into another, more familiar shape. A long cloak. Dark hair and gold-flecked eyes. A scarred hand outstretched toward me.

"Rowan?"

His name slips free before I can help myself. I take a step forward, expecting the shadows to blur and fade, close over him. Instead, the sigil on my wrist begins to beat, faint but steady. A soft glow of magic lights my fingers.

His head snaps up. Our eyes meet. He is more monster than boy—limned with darkness, poison shifting beneath his skin like drips of ink, his fingers curled to claws.

I see his mouth part, light catching on too-sharp teeth as he whispers my name. An ache spills through me, all hurt and loss and want. And then, beneath the pain, is a small, fleeting *hope*.

I press my fingers to my wrist. Touch the spell—gentle at first, then more insistent. I wait, breath held, for the thread to unfurl between us like it did before. I feel a muted pull, and a pale glimmer lights the air. But then it stutters and fades, and I am alone at the border of the trees.

I blink hard, press my knuckles to my closed eyelids, and look again. There is only the drip of leftover rain, the subtle murmur of souls inside the trees. A sharp, disappointed sob escapes me. I clench my teeth, try to swallow it down.

Fawn gently touches my arm. "What's the matter? What did you see?"

"It was—nothing. Just the shadows, playing tricks."

"I heard you call out a name. Was that someone from your life in the world Above?"

"Rowan." My hand goes to my wrist. Slowly, I trace the shape of the spell as I try to find the words to explain. "He was . . . the boy I loved. I bargained with the Lord Under to protect him, to save him. I wanted to go back. I promised to go back, but I . . ." My voice catches. Tears well in my eyes, spill slowly down my cheeks as I go on. "I know that I'm dead, and it's impossible for us to be together. But I've *seen* him—in a vision—and it felt so real."

Fawn rubs her thumb against my arm, makes a comforting noise low in her throat. She guides me over to the wall, and we sit down together. "He must have been very special, for you to make such a bargain."

"Yes, he is. He—he was." I stare across the alcove, my gaze fixed on the altar as I fight back more tears. I take a few, ragged breaths, trying to hold myself together.

The adrenaline that carried me here has faded, and I hurt all over. My cloak has caught the worst of the thorns, but my palms are deeply grazed. I push back my sleeves, revealing scratches on my hands and wrists, still beaded with blood.

Sighing, I press a fold of my cloak against one of the cuts. Fawn reaches into her pocket and draws out a scrap of lace, like the ones fluttering in the trees above. I take it from her, tie it awkwardly around my wounded arm.

She watches me for a moment, expression thoughtful. "If

you died, how did you come to be *here*, rather than inside a tree like the other souls?"

I show her the scar across my heartline. "I bargained with the Lord Under when I was a child. Later, he came back to me. He told me I was . . ." I trail off because it feels foolish to say it. *Special*. "He needed my help, and in return he granted me a place in his world."

Fawn looks at me closely. Behind the mask, her eyes have widened. "You're the girl who mended the Corruption. So *that* is what you meant when you said you saved the world. I didn't realize you were being so literal." A smile plays at the corners of her mouth. She shakes her head, laughing dryly. "The Lord Under told me you were dead."

I start to laugh, too, at the ridiculousness of it all. "And he didn't even tell me you existed. He built me a cottage and a garden, gave me a place to live inside that wall of thorns. When I asked what was outside, he said nothing was there. That he wasn't hiding anything from me."

Fawn rolls her eyes. "For someone who can't lie, he is very good at avoiding the truth."

"Yes. I've noticed." I lean back against the wall, my laughter dwindling to a sigh. "So how did *you* come to be here?"

She frowns, shaking her head. "I have no memories of a life in the world Above. Until I met you, I didn't think it was possible. Your connection to Rowan"—she pauses on his name, smiling wistfully—"sounds very rare. A bond that could outlast death. It doesn't sound like tricks or shadows. It sounds . . . real."

I cast her a wary look. "What do you mean?"

Fawn shifts closer to me until our knees are touching, and puts her hand over mine. Behind the mask, her gaze is veiled. "If there was a way to use your bond to Rowan, to see him again . . . would you do it?"

My pulse quickens, and all the longing I've worked so hard to push down, the grief I've tried to avoid feeling, rises up again, sharp and sudden. "Yes. Of course I would."

Fawn clasps her hand more tightly around my own. "Would you let me . . . help you?"

I stare at her wordlessly, parsing out what she means. "Your magic," I say, my pulse gone wild as desperation aches through me. I stare down at the sigil on my wrist. "You can use it to reawaken the spell?"

She nods slowly. "I might know a way."

With a quaver of doubt, I think of our exchange inside the hollow. "But it would involve a trade."

Her mouth tilts into an apologetic smile. "Yes, it would." She strokes her thumb across my knuckles, as if to reassure me. "You needn't decide now. I'll give you time to think it over."

Behind the mask, her eyes are soft. *She wants to help.* I know how reckless, how foolish this is, to offer more pieces of myself to a world that has already taken so much. But I came through the thorns because I wanted truth. And if there is a way to reforge my connection to Rowan, then I have to take it. "Yes. I'll trade with you."

She smiles wider, revealing prominent eyeteeth. And just like before, when I imagined that her features shifted, for just a moment her teeth look *sharp.*

I look at her more closely. She tilts her head, smile dimming with confusion. The otherworldliness I thought I saw fades. She's just a girl, and her expression mirrors my own. A tentative, fragile hope.

"So," I ask her, "how do we start?"

Fawn gets to her feet and goes over to the archway that leads back into the woods. "I'll need to gather some things for the spell, first."

I pick up one of the mothlights from the altar and follow her out of the alcove. The archway opens to a narrow path that winds through a copse of slender trees. They have pale bark and ribbon-strung branches, and the trunks are spotted with marks that look almost like . . . eyes.

The landscape here is different from the thorn-hemmed part of the woods that surrounds my cottage. The ground isn't moss but hard-packed earth, and tangles of star jasmine spill alongside the path in curlicues of leaves and pale flowers.

Between the vines, the ground is studded with gleaming bones.

Among the bones and leaves, there are other things. Jars filled with crimson liquid. Burned-down candles. Small, silken moth cocoons. There's an altar nailed to one of the trees. The icon has faded, but I can make out the curve of a mouth, soft. The sharp jut of twin antlers. A spill of pale hair.

The crowned silhouette must be the Lord Under, but it doesn't quite seem like the other icons of him. I pause, trying to look more closely, but Fawn pulls at my hand and urges me to keep walking.

A hush moves through the air, and pale flurries fall over me, soft as feathers. They land on my hair and skirts, cover the grim decorations beside the path. I catch one of the flakes on my palm. It's like a tiny flower, made of ice.

Wonderingly, I fold my fingers closed, open them again to see the snowflake melted to nothingness. When Fawn looks at me, I explain, shyly, "It's the first time I've seen snow."

"You'll be sick of it soon." She tucks a strand of hair back behind her ear and laughs. "Come on, it's not much farther."

The snow starts to fall more heavily, covering the ground. As we pass between the trees, they change again, becoming taller and thinner, their trunks clustered with more of the charcoal orbs. I shiver, feeling the tree-eyes watching me.

I turn to Fawn, who is still empty-handed. "What did you need to gather?"

She lifts a shoulder, demurring. Her attention shifts to the branches above us, and she pauses a moment. Head tilted, as though she is listening. I listen, too, but I can hear only the sounds of the forest. Leaves and mist and soul-whispers.

Then a noise in the trees makes me startle. I falter back, pulling away from Fawn. She smiles at me, but there is no softness in the way she looks now. Only bare, fanged teeth. "It's not a *something* I need for the spell. It's someone."

In the trees surrounding us, the leaves stir with movement that isn't the wind. A shadow moves overhead. The branches groan, as if pushed down by a heavy weight.

There's a creature, above.

The mothlight slips from my hand, falls, and shatters.

There's a tiny brush of wings. The moth dissolves. I tense, magic sparking through my veins and across my palms, as the creature comes down through the trees and lands before me.

She could almost be another human girl if I didn't look too closely. She's small and curved, with flawless, russet skin. Her hair is long, glossy curls; the same pallid ivory as the Lord Under's hair.

But then she steps into the light, her wings folding together to form a feathered cloak. Her feet are clawed, three toes— birdlike. She blinks at me. Her large, dark-pupiled eyes are surrounded by a cluster of smaller, keener orbs. A gaze so depthless I could drown in it.

My stomach tightens. I take another step back, widening the distance between us.

"Well," the creature says. Her voice is deep, like the crumble of coals in a long-burned fire. Her gaze slips past me, landing on Fawn. "What *have* you found?"

I look between them, realization settling over me in leaden horror. *They know each other.* Fawn pushes back her mask so it rests on top of her head, the sharp curve of the antlers following the line of her hair. A cluster of eyes blooms at her temple, lashes fluttering discordantly before her features settle.

"You're not—" The word dies on my tongue as I look from Fawn to this new, feathered creature. *Not human.*

"No," she agrees. "We're not."

Once I feared the monsters in the woods; made of stories and nightmares, they were an easier threat to face than the truth of Arien's darkened magic. But these creatures are not a story that I've told, or a dream that's slithered through the dark.

They're real.

Fawn catches hold of my arm. Her grip is like ice, even through the sleeve of my cloak. Betrayal stings me, followed swiftly by anger at my own foolishness. I think, desperately, of the power I once had, strong enough to bring down the Corruption. Now, by comparison, my magic is gossamer soft, ineffectual as spider silk.

I don't have the strength to fight these creatures. But I can't let them see how helpless I am.

My hands curl to fists. I reach for the delicate threads of my magic. Take hold of them and *pull*. Light flares between my clenched fingers. Flickers, dims. The creatures exchange a glance. A note of wariness passes between them. Fawn's grip on my arm loosens slightly.

I pull at the threads of my magic again.

It comes awake with a rush, a fierce blooming heat. As my power rises, pain lances my chest, and my vision blurs. I hiss out a ragged breath. My magic is a wound, will always be a wound, aching with the sorrow and loss of my carved-out memories. My parents, our life together, our connection in the world Below.

I swallow down the terrible hurt, the taste of my despair. Let the pain burn through me, burn me down until I am only power. My magic flares, immeasurably bright, a silver glow that casts over Fawn and this new creature. Illuminates their wide, wary eyes, the fear painted starkly on their inhuman features.

I clench my teeth. Spit out a furious command. "Let me *go*."

Fawn's hold on me falters. I shove her back, drag myself free. She stretches out her hands in a gesture of surrender.

"I'm sorry I deceived you, Violeta." Even her voice is different now, less girlish. A hollowness to it like the sound of the wind before a storm. "But I did speak the truth. I know a spell that will help you see Rowan. Or at least . . . Owl does."

The feathered creature—*Owl*—looks at my magic-bright hands, then raises a brow at Fawn. "She's an alchemist."

Fawn nods, her mouth drawn into a grim line. "She is."

Owl makes a low noise beneath her breath. "*Ash*. What has he done? He'll be the ruin of us all."

"Right now," I interrupt, "you should be more concerned about *me*." I'm nervous, my legs unsteady, but I keep my hands raised, my shoulders squared. I draw on more threads of power, force my magic to burn brighter, ignoring the splinter-sharp ache in my chest and the taste of blood in my mouth. "Is this the truth? Can I see Rowan again?"

Owl holds up her hand—delicate, five fingers, her nails sharp and shiny black. She doesn't touch me, but her claws trace the air beside my cheek. She looks at me for a moment, contemplative. "Yes. I can help you."

"And you will need a trade."

"I will." A flash of hunger crosses her face, and I am undone.

I feel the same as when I cut my hand and pressed it beneath the altar to summon the Lord Under. This is an inevitable wound, a hurt made by my own choice. But it's better than bound-up helplessness.

Rowan and I are still connected. I promised to go back to him. And maybe . . . maybe the strand of magic tied between us might somehow lead me *home*.

I step closer to Owl, the light of my magic dancing over us. "I tore my way through thorns to escape the Lord Under. I destroyed the wall he kept me caged behind. You can see what I'm capable of doing." I let the light flare brighter, struggling to keep my power steady, trying not to show how much effort it needs. "I will trade with you, once. That is *all*."

Her eyes flicker in a discordant blink. Then quietly, she asks, "What will you offer?"

I unclench my hands, release the tangled threads of magic. They fade, and the grove turns dim.

This all tastes of danger. But Rowan is *there*, beyond the dark. I'll do whatever it takes to find him. I let out a sigh, remembering the breath I sacrificed to Fawn. My fingers flex open and closed as I try to think of another token.

I meet Owl's eldritch gaze, trying for a steadiness that I don't feel. Roughly, I push back my sleeve. At my wrist, the scrap of lace I used as a makeshift bandage is now soaked through, crimson as a heartwood tree. "Blood. I offer my blood."

She moves toward me soundlessly, until the hem of her feathered cloak brushes my boots. She touches a clawed fingertip to the soft place beneath my chin. Mist slips and slithers around me, and ice begins to crystallize in the ends of my hair.

Her hand drops back, and she smiles. "Untie the bandage."

My fingers are already at my wrist, unwrapping the sodden lace to bare the deep cut left by one of the thorns. She takes hold of my hand and presses it between her palms. Pauses for a moment, her eyes lingering on my sigils. Then she twitches her wings and brings my wrist to her mouth. Her teeth sink into my skin.

I start to scream. It rings through the forest, tangled through the trees until it's no longer my voice, no longer human. Owl's cold tongue licks over my wrist, lapping up the blood.

The forest melts away, and the pale trees with their ribbon-strung branches vanish into the coiling mist. There's a blur of textured shadows, like I'm in a room after a candle has been blown out and my eyes haven't adjusted to the darkness.

Then a house grows up in place of the trees. Shuttered windows with ivy woven between them. A bellflower wreath pinned to the door. I push it open, my fingers leaving a bloodied print against the handle. My wrist is a smear of crimson, cut with a jagged tear that I refuse to look at. To let myself regret what I've done.

I gave myself willingly—my breath, my blood. And, as the familiar shape of Lakesedge Estate rises out of the dark, I know the risk was worth it.

I am here. I am home.

With my arm cradled to my chest, I make my way inside. The entrance hall is still the same, all faded loveliness. The carved banisters that frame the stairs, the arched window on the landing above, the ceiling light with its trail of cobwebs.

I go down a corridor that opens in front of me, walk to a

room where the furniture is draped like shrouds. The window is wide open, baring a stretch of midnight sky. *The parlor.* The dual altar is lit by only one candle, and though the Lady shows clearly, wreathed in gold, the small flame is not enough to reveal the Lord Under.

My breath catches as someone steps out from the shadows. Rowan is there, standing before the open window. Light and shadow ripple over him, like he is beneath the surface of the lake. His sharp, beautiful features are still more monster than boy. His throat is circled with strands of sedge grass that are woven tight as a snare. His eyes are crimson, blood clotted at the corners like unshed tears, his pupils wide and dark.

He holds out his arm. Gaze fixed to mine; he touches the spell. I reach to my own wrist in an echo of his gesture. Beneath the blood and the thorn cuts, the sigil marked on my skin has begun to glow.

Rowan presses down. I press down. My veins burn with wild magic. The spell-thread lights between us, the strands pulling tighter and tighter as I'm drawn toward him. A rush of memories fills my mind in rapid, brutal flashes. A knife drawn over a scarred wrist. My own voice calling out a name. The shore of the lake when it was still Corrupted, my hands shoved deep into the blackened ground.

I move closer to Rowan, until I'm encircled by his shadows. He takes my hand. His fingers lace through mine, and blood is slick between our palms.

"Rowan," I breathe, a prayer and a plea all at once.

"Leta," he replies, his voice sounding like the waves.

He raises a hand, fingers stained with ink, tipped with claws. But even like this, when he is no longer a boy of honey and tender words but instead a creature made of darkness, it feels so *right* to be near him again.

I fall into his arms, clutching at him as my fingers smear blood against his skin and knot tangles in his hair. Beneath our feet the floor begins to shudder. There's a sharp *wrench* where the spell joins my wrist, the thread pulled wire-taut, lit so brightly it hurts my eyes.

Rowan puts his hand to my cheek. He is shadows and poison, but he touches me with such carefulness, such devotion. As though I am not a girl but a painted icon; all gold and candlelight, encircled by flowers.

"Stay with me, Leta." His voice is the lake. I want to let it drown me. *"Stay."*

"I will," I promise. "I will."

Magic sparks fire over my grazed palms, and the air turns hot as the Summersend bonfire. I drag him closer, until I can feel the rapid echo of his heartbeat against my own chest. My face upturned; I feel the rasp of his desperate breath over my mouth. Then I crush my lips to his, kissing him deeply.

Rowan tastes of blood, the bitterness of a sedative. Burned sugar, black tea. He growls low in his throat as he kisses me back, his teeth in my lip, his tongue dragging rough against mine. All around us, the light starts to shatter piece by piece. The forest closes back in, and the two of us are at the center of a ring of stones, the granite charred like it's been burned. The trees beyond are skeletal, all the leaves torn from their branches.

This is the ruined grove, the place where I died. Where I was devoured by the Corruption.

I look up. Darkness boils across the sky. The Corruption starts to spill down over me, closing out everything else until I'm lost beneath it, overcome by the feel of endless teeth and endless claws.

At my wrist, the tether burns. Rowan is still there, somewhere beyond the darkness. I reach for him—the boy I love, scarred and poisoned and beautiful.

I reach for him, but he is gone.

Chapter Eight

ROWAN

I'm on the shore. In the moonlight, the lake is black. The scars on my wrists have opened again. Darkened blood spills through my fingers. The thread of Leta's magic is still tied to me. Lit up with a pale glow, it stretches away, pulled taut into the darkness. The light stutters, and the magic gives a single, terrible *wrench*.

But everything I saw in the vision made from Arien's sigil has vanished. The shadow-blurred parlor. Leta, sorrow and wonder in her voice when she spoke my name. The heat of her kisses as the spell wove between us.

All that's left behind are my final words, like an echo in the air.

Stay with me.

Beneath my feet, there is a path marked across the ground. It leads into the water. I start to follow.

Distantly, I hear Arien call out to me. "Rowan, stop! You can't—"

On my wrist, lines spiral out from the sigil. Covering the inside of my arm, the crook of my elbow. Darkness beats alongside my pulse. I can feel how it wants to spread farther. Become an inextricable part of me.

I take another step forward. Stars fill the sky above the lake. Beneath, the water shimmers with their reflected light. A wave crests against my feet.

Arien grabs hold of my arm. He starts to drag me back. My bloodied hand clenches the empty air. I open my mouth to speak, but all that comes out is a snarl.

I struggle, trying to pull free. Arien forces me back, away from the water, as I fight against him. My teeth are bared. My fingers clawed. Poison is in my veins, speared through my heart. His hand locks tighter around my wrist, and he drags me to the edge of the forest. My knees give out, and I sink to the ground.

I try to get back up, but Arien pushes me down. I growl at him. "Let me *go*. I have to get back to her, Arien. I have to—"

More darkness spirals loose from the sigil. It crosses my palms, bands my fingers. My vision starts to blacken. The ache in my chest is a twisted knife. A familiar *pull*. The same demanding hunger of the Corruption. I am ink and mud and poison.

I'm lost, I'm lost, I'm lost.

Arien shoves his hands against me. Magic rushes out, smoke-like, from his palms. A sharp, cold burst of power tears through my chest. I'm stilled for a moment; then I gather myself. Twist loose from his grasp. I reach for his throat; he clamps his hand around my arm. Anger sets his features. He glares at me with magic-darkened eyes.

His voice turns fierce. "Rowan. *Don't*."

Hurried footsteps sound from the trees, followed by a frantic shout. "Arien!"

A flare of light sparks over us, a sudden flash. Clover rushes across the shore, her eyes lit gold, her expression furious. She grabs my wrist. Her power burns through me. I bite my tongue. Taste fresh blood.

"Enough!" She digs her nails into my arm. "Rowan, *stop*!"

I stagger back, consumed by heat and brightness. I let out a hiss as Arien pushes me to the ground. Mud seeps through the back of my shirt. Cold against my fevered skin. Arien and Clover lean over me. Their hands are on my chest. Their magic weaves around me, a snare of light and shadow. I arch upward, eyes pinned to the moonlit sky. Blackened water spills from the opened cuts on my arms.

All I can think of is Leta, tied to me still. Leta, in the world Below. The sigil at my wrist gives a final pulse. The last, pale light of the spell-thread fades. But I don't want it gone. Not the spell or the pain or the poison. Once it goes quiet, Leta will be lost, faded into that shadowed dark. I'll never be able to reach her again.

"*No—*" I struggle, trying to get free. "You can't—"

My voice is raw. I can feel the lake in my lungs. Clover grabs hold of my shirt. Twists the collar tight in her hand. She drags me toward her. She shoves a vial to my mouth, and bitter liquid pours over my tongue. I choke on the draft, trying to spit it out, but her fingers press against my jaw, forcing me to swallow. The familiar blur of the sedative floods through me.

It works quickly. My limbs go loose, my heartbeat sluggish.

Arien and Clover hold me, trapped, for a moment longer. The feel of their magic against my skin is unbearable. I choke, struggling to breathe. I want to be anywhere else but *here*.

Finally, they release me. I curl forward, gasping. I'm shaking all over, uncontrollable shudders that I can't hold back. Clover puts her hand on my shoulder. Strokes a gentling circle against me. Then she catches hold of my chin. "Look at me. Are you still *you*?"

I try to focus on her as another shudder tears through me. My skin is sweat streaked, though I am unbearably cold. I glare at Clover and Arien. "I'm not going to change into a woods wolf and devour everyone."

Arien raises a brow. "Aren't you?"

"Not yet."

Clover shakes her head at us both. She lets me go, then takes a ribbon from her pocket and starts to tie her unbound hair back into a braid. Her cheeks are bright with anger. But when she speaks, she is on the verge of tears.

"This was so completely *reckless*. You could have been hurt, worse than this. You could have—" She cuts off, lips pressed together. Shakes her head when the words don't come.

Arien knots his fingers in the cuff of his shirt. "I had to try, Clover. I had to know."

She stares out at the lake. Blinks rapidly, fighting back tears. "I just . . . don't want to lose you—either of you—as well as Violeta."

Arien looks at her solemnly. "But if there's a chance that Leta might still be alive, how can we *not* try to find her?"

With a sigh, Clover gets back to her feet. Holds out her hand to me. I hesitate, turning to look across the shoreline. The path I saw, that led to the water, is gone.

I close my eyes. Picture a thread stretched out across the darkness. But no matter how hard I try, how far I *reach*, there is only silence.

I take Clover's hand. Let her help me up. Slowly, we make our way back to the house. Arien and Clover stay on either side of me. Their steps slowed to match my unsteady pace. I clutch the remaining candle jar. Everything outside the circle of its light is blurred to shadows. The trees, the garden, the scar on the ground.

Back inside the kitchen, I pull a chair close to the hearth and sit down. Clover sits on the floor beside me. Carefully, she takes hold of my wrist. Pushes back my sleeve. She places a questing finger against the sigil. I wince. My skin is a ruin of bruises and blood. My veins are still dark with poison.

But when she touches me, the darkness doesn't spread or spiral farther.

She traces over the new marks that Arien inscribed on the spell. "You tried to amplify it?" She raises a brow at Arien, who nods in confirmation. Her mouth curls into a sad, distant smile. "That was a good idea. And how . . . did it work?"

She looks between me and Arien. She's still angry, but beneath that anger is a small flicker of hope.

"It worked," I tell her. "But it wasn't enough."

The kitchen door opens, and Florence comes into the room. She stares at us all for a drawn-out moment. Her gaze settles on me. My bloodied wrists. The incriminating new sigil marked on my skin. She shakes her head. Sighs. Then picks up a cloth and comes over to me.

I fold my sleeve farther back. Let her take my arm. Sit, unresisting, as she wipes away the blood. She's silent, troubled. Finally, she asks, "Rowan, please . . . tell me what, exactly, have you done?"

I start to explain the visions I've had of Leta, how the one at the shore with Arien's spell was both the strangest and the most *real*. "We're still bound by the spell she marked on me. And when we're together, in the visions, the connection between us feels stronger. But—it never lasts. I try to keep hold of her, but each time, she vanishes."

Florence sets aside her cloth. Starts to unroll a clean linen bandage. "And the magic hurts you, when you try to find her."

"That doesn't matter."

She cuts me an irritated look as she finishes tying the bandage around my arm. "It *does* matter."

Arien takes the paper from his pocket and shows Florence the spell he used. "We need a way to make the connection last for longer, without the risk of Rowan being overtaken. I thought if we went to the shore, it would help. It was where we mended the Corruption, and where Leta used the magic from the Lord Under. But something is still missing."

Clover takes the page from Arien. "Let me see."

Her brow furrows as she reads over the sigil. Arien shifts closer beside her. They fall into a silence that reminds me of the days they spent in the library, heads bowed over notebooks as they prepared for the rituals. And in spite of everything, there's a strange comfort in this.

The magic, the poison, the risk . . . it's all better than being helpless.

I close my eyes and picture the lake. The path that led into the water. I can't shake the sense that if I'd tried harder, gone farther into the shadows, I'd have been able to draw Leta back from the darkness.

"We need to make the power stronger," I tell Clover and Arien.

Clover narrows her eyes. Musingly, she traces patterns in the ashes at the hearth. They look like half-formed sigils. She bites her lip, thoughtful. Then smears the patterns away with a rough *swipe*. "The altar and the lake are both places where Leta communicated with the Lord Under. But it wasn't the first place she made her bargain."

Arien gets to his feet. He stares at the fire. Light shifting over his features. His expression is troubled. "We need to go back to where I died."

I look at him. His fingers stained by magic, his eyes still dark. The signs of his alchemy, transformed by the Lord Under.

Arien and I—we share this common thread. Both of us gone close to the border of death. Returned, marked forever.

"You mean the Vair Woods," I say. "The woods near your village."

He nods solemnly. "The woods where Leta made the bargain that saved me."

Florence steps between us. She takes my hand, looks searchingly into my eyes. "Rowan, I miss Violeta so terribly. But if this goes wrong . . ."

"Leta saved me," I tell her. "She saved all of us. I'm not going to lie and burn a pyre for her. Tell everyone she's dead. I can't let her go like that. But I'll not ask anyone else to risk themselves. I can do this alone."

Arien snorts. "Yes, because that turned out so well for you the last time." He indicates the scars on my throat. The marks left from my final, desperate attempt to save Elan from the Lord Under.

Clover makes a sound of agreement. "The only way this will work is if we're together." She takes off her glasses. Clutches them inside one mud-stained fist. Tiredness marks her eyes. Turns them shadowed. "If Violeta is really there, if there's a chance we can find her, then we all have to do this."

I bow my head to her, to Arien. "Together, then."

Florence presses her lips into a thin, trembling line. "I know I should tell you all not to go. But . . ." She trails off, tears spilling down her cheeks. Then she pulls me into an embrace.

Slowly, I put my arms around her. It's been so long since

I let her hold me like this. It feels so strange. I've wanted her comfort, but now I'm here, I don't know how to let myself soften.

We stay, unmoving, for a long while. Then she draws back. Gives us all a stern look. "I'll be waiting for you. Come home safe."

"We will," I tell her.

Arien manages a faint smile. "Don't worry, Florence. What's a little more danger after everything we've done, so far?"

"Oh yes, that's very reassuring." She brushes her hands over her skirts. "You should leave at first light. I'll pack some things for you."

"I can help," Clover offers. Together, they go out of the room. Arien and I remain alone beside the hearth.

Outside, the wind starts to grow stronger. It rattles the shutters. Comes beneath the door with a low-pitched whisper. A shiver casts between my shoulder blades. I move closer to the fire. Thinking of the Vair Woods. Moonlight woven through the trees. All of us at the center of the forest. Circled around a place where a child once lay dying.

"Arien, do you—" I hesitate, uncertain of the right words. "Do you remember it? When the Lord Under came to you?"

His cheeks start to flush. He pulls at the edge of his sleeve. "I was just a baby when we went into the woods. Leta was the one who remembered most." He goes quiet. The weight of our shared knowledge turns the air leaden. Leta's memories of their life before, with their family, are now gone, forever. "I

106

remember the night when our village burned. And that I was frightened. When the Lord Under appeared in the woods, he was just shadows and a voice. But I knew he was *real*."

I nod slowly, thinking of the times when the Lord Under spoke to me. The first time, when he saved me. The second, when he came back to claim my life. He was only ever a voice in the darkness. Yet his allure, his cruelty, his *power*—it had a weight.

I felt it then. I feel it still, when I kneel in observance at the dual altar. A heaviness across the candlelit silence. As though he is watching me. And now I'll go to the place where Leta first bargained with him. Attempt to bring her home from his world.

Quietly, with my eyes downcast, I tell Arien, "We will have to travel close to Greymere to reach the woods."

"I know." He lets out a weary sigh. I can tell his thoughts are turned to the past. To the village that feared him. The cruelty of the woman who raised him. "When I left—when I let you take me away—I didn't care what you wanted from me. I only cared that I wouldn't have to hide who I was. I knew a monster wouldn't be afraid of my magic."

"For what it's worth, I'm sorry that I frightened you."

He waves away my apology. "I wasn't frightened."

My mouth tilts into a rueful smile. "Oh?"

"I knew what Leta would do if you hurt me. You're a monster, but she's *much* more frightening than you could ever be."

I manage a laugh. "Agreed."

Arien laughs, too. Then his face settles into seriousness. He squares his shoulders, resolute. "I'm not afraid to go back, Rowan. Not if that's what it takes to find her."

As we sit together, fallen into silence, I try to imagine how things will look when we return from the Vair Woods. It's impossible. All I have is the taste of poison in my mouth. The ache of magic at my wrist.

I slide my fingers under my sleeve. Press against the sigil. Hold fast to the memory of a thread tied from me, to Leta. Binding us together.

I hope that I've made the right choice. That our strange, liminal connection will echo stronger at the heart of the woods.

Chapter Nine

VIOLETA

When the darkness clears, I'm still in the ruined grove. Everything from my vision—Rowan, the thread of magic, my whispered promise—has faded. There is no sign of Fawn or Owl. No bloodied ribbons or loosened feathers. No voices beneath the wind. Even the thickening snowdrifts are unblemished by their footprints.

Desperately, I grasp hold of my wrist. Press against the sigil as hard as I can. With my eyes closed, I can *almost* feel the spell that connects me to Rowan. It's barely decipherable, but the magic is there, still there, beating through my veins like a second pulse. And he is somewhere beyond.

And I am alone, in the grove where I mended the Corruption.

Footsteps crunch over the snow, and I look up, startled. Power throbs in the air, a magic that tastes of salt and ash, familiar enough to make my heartbeat stutter. I let go of the sigil and climb quickly from the stones. Make my way hurriedly to the far edge of the grove and slip between the trees.

From behind a row of scarred, blackened heartwoods, I watch the Lord Under step out of the shadows. He walks slowly, the hood of his cloak pulled down low, obscuring his face. As he moves closer, mist spilling out in a trail behind him, anger rises through me.

I think of the last time we stood here, when we made our final bargain. When he knelt at my feet and I gave him my promise, I thought I had measured out my words so carefully. *Make me safe from the Corruption. I'll never forget you.* He told me he would mend me, and let me go home. Instead, he gave me a life beyond the borders of death. He sent me home by making part of this world mine.

It's cold—so cold that the blood from the thorn cuts has frozen on my arms. But despite the frost-laced air, I am feverish with fury. So angry that waves of heat are radiating from my skin. I storm forward, out of the trees, and shove my arm toward him. The sleeve of my cloak falls back, baring the sigil.

"When the poison claimed me, you said I could never return to the world Above. That I was dead. So *why* am I still bound to Rowan with this spell?" He remains silent. I take a sharp breath, move another step closer. "I want you to tell me the truth."

"Well," says a lilting voice, "there is truth, and there is *truth*, isn't there?"

I come to a sudden stop, my boots kicking loose a scatter of

110

snow. A gloved hand comes free of the cloak and pushes back the hood. And it isn't the Lord Under at all, but a strange, pale creature.

Unlike Owl or Fawn, the creature that stands before me could never be mistaken for a girl. Her skin is bloodlessly pale. Her hair the blue of melted frost. Her eyes are enormous, solid black beneath arched brows.

She holds herself as regally as a faerie queen, her chin tipped upward, a smile on her full lips. She's clad in black, and the wide skirts of her dress are embroidered with a marbled pattern, splotches of charcoal and silver, a trim of intricate lace. She wears a spun-steel crown that's shaped into feathery, ghostlike antlers.

She's not a girl, but *monster* isn't quite the word for her, either. My voice, so determined before when I thought I spoke to the Lord Under, now lowers guardedly. "Who are you?"

"You may call me . . . Lady Moth."

A cold drift of wind shivers through the trees, scented by smoke, as though someone has just blown out a candle. Shivering, I wrap my cloak tighter around myself. "*What* are you?"

Her eyes run over me, taking in the muddied hem of my nightdress, my ragged cloak, my wounded arm. An unsettling sharpness gleams in her expression, and her smile stretches wider. "Surely you know by now. After all, you've met my sisters. And I *know* you've met my brother."

"You're all—" The word catches in my throat, comes out as a whisper. "*Gods?*"

Lady Moth picks up her skirts and steps delicately toward

me. "Did you think the Lord Under was the only one?" She smirks, then makes a small, derisive noise. "He'd like you to believe that, I'm sure. But no."

Silently, I turn over her words. Trying to understand what it all means. "But how . . . ?"

Her smile widens, as though she's delighted by my confusion. "The world Below is divided into bordered lands, much like the world Above. There, each place is tended by a noble family. Our world is no different. Each region has its own caretaker who watches over the souls within that domain."

I think of the world Above, how Rowan is lord of all the lands that stretch from the Vair Woods to Lakesedge Estate. It's strange to imagine the world Below as similar. Divided into borders and bound by their own version of our village rituals. Bonfires beneath an invisible moon, the trees delivering ribbon-tied branches in a yearly tithe.

And then there's my place in all this. How, when I was poisoned, and the Lord Under carried me through the forest, those strange silhouettes had appeared alongside the path. How he built my cottage, cut off from the rest of the woods by the wall of thorns.

The truth is a bramble vine, slowly wound over me with a crushing pressure, until I can hardly breathe. "He wasn't hiding anything from me. I was the one he was hiding . . . from all of you."

Lady Moth looks at me accusingly, and I feel so *watched*, the same way I did when the tree eyes were on me as I walked through the woods. "He told us you were dead. Just another soul, claimed like any other. He's gone to such lengths to keep you secret, hasn't he? His little human girl. His *pet*."

I fold my arms across my chest. "I am not his *anything*."

"He's broken so many rules for you, Violeta. You must be very special to him." She edges closer, a conspiratorial tilt to her smile. "Tell me: Is he special to *you*?"

"No. He's not." But even as I protest, I can't stop thinking of how I let him touch me when we were in the garden. The way it felt when he cast the spell and took my hurt, the silence of his chest as he held me, the stroke of his claws through my hair.

And in spite of everything—my confusion, my anger, my flight through the woods as he pursued me—an unbidden blush spreads across my cheeks. Lady Moth captures my face between her hands. She presses her thumbs against my skin and laughs when she feels the warmth.

"Oh, I made you embarrassed. Truly, I've no idea why one of our kind would want a *romance* with a creature like you. But he's always had peculiar taste. He'd be gentle with you, I think—or try to be, at least. You'll not be any use to him if you're broken."

"I've no wish for your romantic advice."

She shakes her head, laughing quietly to herself. Then her gaze fixes on my bloodied wrist. Instinctively, my fingers curl around the sigil. "You do have wishes, though, Violeta. What are you chasing out here in the woods?"

As I stand before her—this monster, this *god*—I feel as though I'm balanced on a knife-edge. I take a slow breath, trying to anchor myself. The faint heat of my power begins to spread across my hands.

I step closer to Lady Moth and meet her gaze evenly. "I wanted to find the truth."

"You wanted to find *Rowan*." At the sound of his name from her sharp, sly mouth, I start to pull away. But then her voice lowers, and she goes on, "If there was a way to go back . . . would you take it?"

A stillness comes over me, sudden as a spell. Each word feels like a danger. The pause before I speak is a glass-shard thing. It will draw blood if I grasp it too tightly. "It depends on what I would have to do." My mind is a blur, filled with calculations more complicated than any of Clover's alchemical formulas. "I could—really go back, and be with Rowan again?"

Lady Moth strokes her thumb against my cheek, humming to herself. Time seems to slow. Everything feels like honeyed wax melting a path down the edge of an altar candle. Then her expression darkens, and her smile splits to a jagged, hungry *grin*.

Her grip begins to tighten against my jaw, her gloved fingers pressing, hard. "I didn't mean you'd go back to the world Above, and that boy you gave your heart to. I meant *back* where you belong."

"No—I don't—" I try to push her away, but her hand slides down my arm, catches hold of my wrist.

"My sisters are foolish children to have helped you. Almost as foolish as my brother. He nearly ruined everything with the

114

Corruption before you mended it for him. It should have finished there, with you destroyed by the poison and the balance of our world restored."

Her fingers press sharply into my arm, against the wound where Lady Owl took her payment of blood. I let out a cry and jolt back, trying to pull away. Power hums through my body, sparked in response to the hurt. The crescent mark throbs wildly at the center of my palm. Blood drips over the ground, leaving crimson stains on the snow.

I raise my other hand, grasping for the threads of my magic. Light burns over my fingertips as I glare at Lady Moth. "I *earned* my place here."

She bares her teeth. Tightens her grip, drags me toward her. We're so close that I can see the slender veins of darkness under her pale skin. "You play at being brave," she snaps, "but you're a girl in a world of gods. My brother thinks to keep you at his side, but the dead should stay dead. There is only one thing you can possibly *give* now, Violeta."

Her hand slashes out and grabs my throat. I twist against her, my feet sliding over the snow. Her eyes are glazed with a cold hunger. The harder I struggle, the more pleased she looks.

I think with longing of the strength I once had—the power to end a curse, to call a god out of the dark. A single, desperate word echoes in my mind. *More.*

Now my power is the barest warmth over the grazed palms of my hands. A single candle flame in the shadowed dark. But I reach for those small traces as I fight against Lady Moth. The air sparks as I clutch for her wrist, trying to drive my nails into her skin. I picture threads of light snared around her fragile-feeling bones.

Her fingers tighten brutally against my throat. Darkness eclipses my vision. I start to sink, my limbs turned boneless. Everything narrows, until all I can hear is the snarl of the wind as it tears through the branches overhead.

Then a tide of black water washes over the ground, freezing in jagged ribbons across the snow. The Lord Under strides out from between the trees, his teeth bared in a bladed snarl, his face is a mask of incandescent rage. He raises his hand, claws sharp, and magic spills through the air.

He shakes his head, disgust in his voice as he growls at me, "You ungrateful little *beast*."

Then he turns to Lady Moth and snaps out a word I can't comprehend. It rings from his mouth and echoes through the ruined grove. Everything *stops*. Even the snow stills, the flakes of ice turned to motionless static.

Lady Moth's eyes widen. She stares at the Lord Under in helpless fury. His shadow-wreathed claws hook sharply against the air, and he wrenches downward, tearing Lady Moth away from me. I fall to my knees, coughing raggedly as I struggle for breath.

More shadows rise from the ground. They snare around Lady Moth, capturing her with tightening strands. The Lord Under snarls that strange, formless word again. "Sister. Give me one reason why I shouldn't carve you to pieces right now."

Lady Moth sneers at him, a trail of blackened blood oozing

from her lips. "Are you really going to waste your time with me, while your little pet lies wounded in the snow?"

His eyes narrow at the word *pet*. "Violeta can take care of herself."

"She's certainly taken *care* so far. Running away from you. Trading with Fawn and Owl. Trying to find her way back to the world Above."

The Lord Under glances at me. He's distracted, and his grip loosens. Lady Moth works her hand free from the snare of magic. Her eyes glimmer with a golden sheen, the same way that Fawn's did when she cast a spell.

A cloud of moths spirals down from the trees, and the magic that's trapped her comes apart. She dissolves into a whirl of wings. The grove is lit up—briefly, luminously, silver—before she vanishes into the dark.

The Lord Under glares after her, uttering a wordless curse beneath his breath. Then he paces over to where I'm crumpled in the snow. "I warned you. I warned you of the dangers in the woods. If I hadn't gotten here in time, Moth would have torn your throat out."

I dig my fingers into the cold earth and meet his gaze, unrepentant. "I am still bound to Rowan. The spell I cast, the spell you gave me to stop the Corruption devouring him, it connects us. All this time, there's been a chance for me to see him again. To go *back*. And you hid it from me. You kept me locked away in that cage you built."

Furious bursts of shadows lash around him. With his teeth

clenched, he lowers his voice to a snarl. "Whatever tenuous connection you *think* exists between you and Rowan Sylvanan—it changes nothing. The life I've given you here is all you have left. There is no way to go back."

He thrusts his hand toward me, offering to help me up. I ignore it, shoving myself unsteadily back to my feet. I let out a cry, my throat still raw. "What you gave me can never match what you have stolen. You took me from my family and my home. You took all the memories I had of my mother and father. You took *everything*."

He glowers at me, face marked by sharp exasperation. "I have given you everything. A home, a life beyond death. Don't act so blameless, Violeta. I have stolen nothing. You offered yourself to me, along with the memories of your parents. You were so eager to sacrifice yourself to protect everyone you loved, whether they wanted it or not."

I storm toward him. Magic sparks in the air as I strike his chest. He takes a step back, hands raised, shadows spilling from his palms. Mist rises from between the ruined trees, and the snow turns to rain, a scatter of ice-cold raindrops the color of ink, spilling over the path.

I lift my own hand, echoing his gesture. The small, pale flame of my magic lights the air between us. "You used me."

"Yes," he says, fierce and unrepentant. "I did. I needed a willing vessel to contain the Corruption because that was the only way it could be mended. And I meant to let it destroy you."

The blunt honesty in his words sends me reeling. I knew it, all along I knew that he planned to discard me. But hearing it laid out so plainly turns my anger to blistering heat. A forest fire at the center of my body.

My mouth twists into a snarl. "That's all I've ever been to you. A means to an end."

"Yes. You were."

I strike him again. He doesn't move, doesn't fight back, doesn't relent. I hit him and hit him. He stands, still and silent, until I'm breathless, slumped forward with my fists knotted in his cloak. I press my forehead against his chest and start to cry large, ugly tears that fall hotly down my cheeks.

The Lord Under lifts his hand, strokes his claws through my hair. I can feel the leashed-back anger in his touch, in the way his fingers tremble, and the stilted motion when he draws in a breath. "You were a means to an end. You gave me what I needed: the power to end the Corruption and a way to contain it. I meant to let you die, to claim the power from your hurt and despair, to place you inside one of my trees. That was how it should have ended between us."

"I hate you," I sob. "I hate you, I hate you."

I have never felt such despair. I want to shove him away, tear him to pieces, see him turn to dust. I want to pull him closer.

Tenderly, he wipes his thumb against my cheek. When I chance a look at him, his expression has softened incrementally. "I meant to let you die," he says again. "But then you called me back. When you demanded my help, you were so brave, even in the face of your ruin. And I realized . . . I didn't want you gone."

119

"How can I believe anything you say?"

He stares at me a moment. Hesitates, as though measuring out his words. Finally, he says, quiet as a vow, "Because I care for you, Violeta."

I shake my head, incredulous. "You *care* for me?"

Unflinchingly, he meets my gaze. "I care for you so much that I've broken the rules of my world. Risked the anger of my sisters. All so I could keep the promise I made to you on my knees at the center of this very grove."

Slowly, slowly, his arms go around me. I tighten my grip on his cloak and start to cry harder, my sobs echoing loudly beneath the branches of the heartwood trees. He pulls me close, and I feel as though I've been swept up by some fearsome nighttime creature. All claws and endless wings.

The shadows start to dissolve. The inky rain softens, melting to a dewdrop-fine mist. I bury my face against his chest and let out a fractured, wounded breath. "I want to go home."

He trails his claws through my hair again. But although he touches me gently, when he speaks, his voice is as cold as a frost-laced field. "You *are* home."

I taste rust and copper, and realize my nose has begun to bleed. My eyes sink closed. The ground tilts, my knees turn weak. I crumple. The Lord Under catches me, the motion practiced.

He lifts me into his arms, and he carries me away into the forest.

Chapter Ten

VIOLETA

The Lord Under carries me to my cottage. He opens the door, goes inside with me still in his arms. I start to struggle against him, and he puts me down, roughly, at the end of my bed. I sit on the unmade quilts with my knees drawn up and my wounded arm cradled against my chest, glaring at him through my leaf-tangled hair.

He reaches to me, claws beside my blood-soaked sleeve. With a sharp, angry breath, he tells me, "You're lucky this is all my sisters did to you. You're lucky that I'm the worst thing in these woods, the only one who doesn't wish you harm."

"Yes. *Lucky* is exactly how I feel right now."

His eyes turn cold, and he motions to the ribboned bow at my collar. "Take off your cloak and let me see the cut."

One-handed, I start to unknot the ribbons that fasten my cloak. My fingers are numb and awkward; all I do is make the knot tighter. Frustrated, I let my hand fall heavily to my lap. "I need your help."

He sighs again, then kneels before me. My stomach tightens at the sight of him like this, in a simulacrum of when we bargained in the ruined grove. I close my eyes as I feel the snag of the ribbon against his claws. Keep them closed as he pulls the knot loose. My cloak falls away. I shiver, newly cold without the weight of the fabric.

The Lord Under starts to untie the laces at my wrist so he can fold back my sleeve. A strange prickle of heat replaces the cold on my skin, when he touches me. I open my eyes, push his hands away. "I can do the rest."

I clench my teeth, peel away the bloodstained fabric. My breath hitches, becomes a gasp. The cut is a garish, bloodied *slice*. I shudder, feeling sick. Held in captive horror by the crescent print of Lady Owl's teeth gouged into my arm.

The Lord Under stares at the wound. He is motionless, stilled by muted fury. The few, pale flames left alight in the fire are enough to line his face in gold, the way he might appear if he were painted in an icon. Shadows move across the floor behind him, curved to brutal angles.

Slowly, he raises his eyes to meet mine. "What did you trade to my sisters?"

I square my shoulders. Look down at him, still kneeling at my feet. I refuse to apologize for what I did. Even now, marked by how badly it ended. "Breath, to Fawn. Blood, to Owl."

"And to Moth?"

I gesture to my throat, which still aches from her choking grasp. "She didn't want to trade."

His claws flex, then curve against his palms. A slow spill of shadows starts to trail loose from his clenched hands, dimming the pallid firelight as they spiral over the floor. His gaze slips past me, narrowed toward the darkened corner.

When he speaks, his voice is shaded by a quieter anger, like a sheathed blade. "Violeta, what more do you want from me?"

I think again of the moment in the ruined grove after the vision of Rowan faded. When the light came back, and the spell-thread turned silent. How, despite everything I tried, he was still unreachable. "You've made it very clear that everything I want from you is impossible."

I get to my feet and push roughly past the Lord Under, crossing the room to the chest where I keep my clothes. My boots leave a trail of mud printed across the floor.

He calls after me. "You want to go *home*? I've given you my whole world as your home."

I snatch a ribbon from the chest and wrap it, awkwardly, over the cut as a makeshift bandage. "You weren't even able to give me the truth. Were you just going to keep me hidden away forever, rather than tell me about your sisters? Was it so *important* that I thought you to be the only god?"

He gets to his feet, and the shadows rise around him like a storm cloud. He glares at me across the darkening room. "Your safety is what's important. My sisters and I are bound by rules set out by the Lady. Rules that stop us from destroying one another. But you have no such protection. Given the chance, my sisters will take *everything* from you."

I pull my bloodstained nightgown over my head. Let it drop, crumpled, on the floor. Rummaging through the chest, I start to search for a new dress. "If my safety is so important, you could have given me enough magic to defend myself. I don't even have the power to mend *this*."

I turn to him, thrust out my bandaged arm. Magic sparks across my hand. It quickly dims, as though to prove my point.

"You can't—" he begins, then falters. His eyes go from me to my discarded nightgown. We both fall silent. An unnamable, heated feeling rises through me when I realize how *bared* I am, standing here in only my camisole and my underwear.

A fierce blush rises swiftly over my face. I reach unseeing into the trunk and grab the topmost dress—a loose, silken shift with moth wings sewn into the sleeves and hem. Pull it on quickly.

I bend down to unlace my muddy boots, step out of them. Then I cross the room barefoot, my skirts trailing behind me like shadows. I pause before I reach the Lord Under. The space between us feels like a spell that needs to be warded against.

Slowly, I push back my sleeve. Hold out my wounded arm. "If you care so much about my protection, the ability to heal myself would be a wonderful place to start."

"A wound like that can't be mended with alchemy."

"Then maybe *you* should mend it for me."

He hesitates, contemplative, then crosses the space between

124

us in a single stride. He takes my hand, turns it palm-up. Drags his claws over the scar on my palm.

A scatter of sparks comes from my fingers, unbidden. I flinch, caught by a conflict of feeling. The way it reminds me of when Rowan touched me like this, when my magic was still a hidden secret, and he pressed his fingers to my heartline. Drew my power from me.

The Lord Under looks down at my bandaged wrist, his gaze obscured by the pale line of his lashes. "You know if I mend you, it will require a trade."

"Of course," I snap, irritated. "*Of course* it requires a trade."

I pull my hand from his grasp and go to sit back down on my bed. I've given so much to him, to his sisters, to this whole *world*. The thought of relinquishing even more sets my teeth together in a snarl.

He watches me for a moment, then walks over to the fireplace and starts to add more wood to the stove. "Believe me, Violeta, I'm not exactly delighted by the thought of trading with you again. Each of our bargains has caused unending trouble. But my magic requires a price."

"Yes. I'm aware how magic works in this world. And as for *unending trouble*—that feeling is entirely mutual."

He shakes his head with a sigh of disavowal. "I'll need to clean the cut, first. You have until I'm finished to decide what to offer."

I try to school my features into unconcern. "Fine."

He fills the kettle and sets it on the stove to heat, then he takes down an enamelware bowl and a jar of salt, laying them

125

out on my kitchen table. It's strange to watch him doing such ordinary, human things. When the kettle begins to hum, he even picks it up with a cloth folded around his hand, the same way I do.

He pours hot water into the bowl. Stirs in a heaped spoonful of salt. Then he brings it back to the bed and sits down carefully beside me. "Give me your hand."

I let him take my hand. With unexpected gentleness, he reaches for the knot on the makeshift bandage. He's so close to me, our shoulders touching, his knee pressed to mine. Trying to distract myself from his nearness, I push back my hair from my face, loosening a scatter of leaves. The ends of my curls are damp where the snowflakes have melted.

I twist a scrap of leaf between my fingers. "What was it that you said to Lady Moth to make her let me go? That word—" I try to repeat it, but my mouth can't shape the sound. "Was it a spell?"

"No . . ." He trails off, silent for long enough that I'm certain he won't tell me. Then, with resignation, he says, "It was her name."

"Her name?"

"Her true name. I used it to compel her."

"You mean . . . To make her obey you?"

"Yes." For the briefest moment, he seems almost embarrassed. "It's not a power I use often, but it was the fastest way to make her stop."

I think again of the word he spoke, the arcane sound of it that didn't fit to my ears. It's unexpected to think that names—such a tender, human thing—can hold such power over the creatures of the world Below. "Do *you* have a true name?"

He huffs out a soft laugh. "Were you hoping to compel me, Violeta?"

At my wrist, the knot slips undone. He draws the ribbon loose, moving with oppressive slowness. It slides over my skin before, finally, falling away.

I turn away from him and stare fixedly out of the window. "If I could compel you, it would certainly make things easier."

He laughs again, louder this time. "Unfortunately for you, it's not quite that simple. When the Lady made this world, I was created as her equal half, the dark to balance the light. My sisters came later, once my forest grew so large that I was unable to tend the souls alone. Their names were given to me to maintain the balance."

"So the compulsion wouldn't work on me, either."

His mouth tilts into a wry smile. "No."

"Unfortunately for *you*."

"Oh, I don't know. Perhaps I'd miss your arguments eventually." He folds up the bloodied ribbon and sets it aside. I draw my arm back closer against myself, trying not to look at the wound. He dips a cloth into the bowl of water, wrings it out. Nodding to my arm, he warns, "This is going to hurt."

I clench my teeth, braced for his touch, but when he presses the cloth down, I can't help jolting back. Pain sparks through my body, sharp and sudden. I knot my other hand in my skirts and force myself to be still.

Stubborn tears bead at the corners of my eyes as he rasps the salt-soaked cloth over every inch of the cut, washing away the blood. Time passes in a blur, marked only by my jagged breath, the sting of my held-back tears. Finally, he lets me go.

I cradle my arm to my chest. Let out a fractured exhale. The dull ache of the wound is a welcome relief, now.

The Lord Under puts the cloth and the bowl down onto the table beside my bed. With careful deliberation, he turns to look at me. "Have you decided what you will offer?"

The word—*offer*—fills the small space of my room. I'm in the Vair Woods, five years old with Arien in my arms, desperate to escape the night. I'm beneath the altar, fingers sticky with blood and pomegranate juice as I whisper to the shadows. I'm at the lake, the path opened before me, calling me into the darkness.

My hands curl to fists, the heat of magic burning uselessly beneath my skin. I hate that I've come so far only to feel like the same girl who pressed her bloodied palms to the parlor floor and laid down promises like a petaled offering.

I want to tilt the balance between myself and the Lord Under. To fight him the same way I fought through the thorns, with fire and determination, with power that's come from my own, human self.

Unbidden, my gaze falls to his mouth. My thoughts fill with treacherous images, persistent, even though I try to push them away. My lips against his, my breath casting over his skin as he is overcome by my touch. How it would feel to be the one in power, instead of the opposite.

A nervous tremor catches in my throat, but I swallow it

down. Try to sound careless as I tell him, "I might kiss you, in exchange."

He arches a brow. "What makes you think I want to be kissed by you?"

I spread out my hands, feigning nonchalance. "You don't have to accept. But that's what I'm offering as my trade."

He stays very still, but his expression flickers. I've caught him by surprise. A wary light colors his eyes, and then he starts to fracture. His features split apart, the way they often did when I first was able to see him, before I could hold a fixed image of him in my mind. A cluster of eyes rises on the arch of his cheek. His mouth carves into *two* mouths, all fanged, both drawn into a scowl. A row of slashes flutters at his throat in time with his stilted breath.

It pleases me that I've unsettled him, even for this fleeting moment. I put my hand on his knee, lean forward, driven by an irascible urge to *push*, to plunge myself back into the thorns. "If you'd prefer another trade, then perhaps you should make the offer. I promise to give it my full consideration."

His teeth snap together, loud enough that I can hear the click. His features resettle back to the cold, sharp planes of his face. The uncertainty in him vanishes, and his hand covers mine, claws pressing down. "A kiss. That's your trade?"

The sound of it from him stills me. A heartbeat passes, then I manage to steady myself, respond without stammering. "Yes."

His voice turns slow and languorous as honey. "You're certain?"

I nod, all words gone.

His eyes gleam with unreadable emotion. It isn't desire—not quite. If anything, it reminds me of the way he looked when he dipped his claws into the cut pomegranate I'd left for him at the altar. I *thought* I'd turned this precarious balance in my favor, but now it slides back in the opposite direction as his claws trace over my cheek.

A throbbing heat blooms at the pit of my stomach. He tucks back one of my curls that's fallen loose, then trails lower, past the side of my throat to the wingbeat of my pulse. He moves so slowly that it aches. His hand goes down my arm, and he encircles my wounded wrist.

I sink back onto the bed, stretched out beneath him. His hair spills down as he leans over me. He's so close that I can feel the movement of his chest as it rises and falls, each slow breath. Then he pauses. For a long moment we stay like that, the space preserved between us.

He's waiting for me to kiss him. That was how I worded the exchange.

I'm too overcome for pretense. I reach to him, a glimmer of magic lighting my fingers, and shakily trace the line of his mouth, the curve of his lips. He smiles, baring the fanged edge of his teeth. Then I draw him toward me. Press my mouth to his.

It's the barest touch. Gossamer light. But still, it sends a wave of heat right through me. Turns my bones to syrup. Faltering, I shift back. He pulls away instantly.

I start to sit up, but then he takes my hand. My fingers clench closed, the motion instinctive. He unfolds them gently, touches the place where the crescent scar curves blackly across my heartline. His head bows, face hidden by the fall of his silken hair.

Slowly, slowly, he kisses my palm.

A tattered sound escapes me before I can stop it. "Oh—"

I let out a shallow breath. Clench my thighs against the wretched *want* that's unspooled through my entire body. His breath is cold. I feel frost unlacing all over me. My eyes shutter closed. I think of secrets, of power, of names. A name for *him*, beyond the title known to everyone.

It's there, like a golden flicker behind my eyelids. I can't shape the word, but I can taste it in my mouth. Sugar melting on my tongue.

He laughs softly, and I feel the hum of it against my hand. Then he sits back. I open my eyes and stare up at him, trying hard to ignore the sink of disappointment as he moves away.

My blood is on his fingers. Keeping his eyes locked on mine, he raises his hand to his mouth. He licks my blood away. He takes his time.

"You're horrible." I feel drugged, my eyelids heavy, my body turned numb. "You're *truly* horrible."

My hand is still trapped by his grasp. He turns my arm over and gives the wound an assessing look. "Mending this won't be pleasant."

"Nothing about you is pleasant."

He smiles. There's a faint smear of my blood on the edge of his mouth. "What a mercurial creature you are."

"Just get on with it already."

He wraps his fingers more firmly around my wrist. With a sudden rush, shadows coil over my wounded arm, binding me with darkness. The cut begins to burn and ache. I choke back a cry. The pain is countless needles driven into my skin, over and over. A thousand times worse than the bite itself, or how it felt when the Lord Under cleaned my wound.

I twist against his grasp. He tightens his hold, unrepentant. "I'm the lord of the dead. Did you think I could mend you without it hurting?" His voice lowers, halfway between a caress and a threat. "You have felt power like this before."

I have. And that's what makes it so terrible. The echoed memory of what he did to save me comes rushing back. How he took me into the heart of the forest, laid me down on an altar, and tore the poison from my body with his power. The thought of it—being mended, the despair when I learned the cost of my promise—sends a new hurt through me, overlaying the tremors of pain.

I try to breathe steadily. To picture myself in a stream, the sensation like waves. An ink-dark tide, rising higher, until I am lost beneath the surface. Sweat beads my temples and the back of my neck. It takes all my effort to hold myself still. *It will pass, it will pass.*

Finally, the Lord Under releases my hand. "There. It is done."

I sink back onto the bed, curl up on my side. Still lost beneath the surface of the waves, the hurt. Everything is muffled, dark, until I slowly let the light back in.

Guardedly, I look at the wound. It's healed into a blackened scar, curved like a sickled moon. It crosses the spell on my wrist, the moon eclipsing the sunburst shape of the sigil. I trace my fingers across the new mark, then down to the matching scar on my palm.

"That's twice now," I say to the Lord Under, "that I've been marked by you."

He hums, inscrutable. "Let's try not to make it a habit." Looking down at his claws, stained with my blood, he sighs roughly. A sound that's edged with the last traces of his burned-out anger. "Why do you fight it so much, what I've given you?"

"Because fighting is all I have left." I start to turn away, folding myself into a spiral beneath the quilts, but he catches my shoulder and pushes me onto my back. There's a moment of shock. I'm held, too stunned to move. Then I slip out from beneath him, catching him off guard, and I push him down against the bed. Lean over him, my hands braced on either side of his shoulders.

He stares up at me, the ethereal cast of his features marked in shadow as I bend closer. My hair drapes around us like a veil, dead leaves still caught in my curls. "You asked before what I wanted from you. Do you *really* want to know?"

The look he gives me is all challenge. "Please. Enlighten me."

"I want *more*." It comes out like a warning, or a prayer, or both. "More power, more strength. Magic I can use to protect myself. I'll not hide behind thorns any longer. I want to be strong enough that I'll always be safe in this world full of monsters. I want . . . to be like you."

Hunger flashes briefly in his eyes—it's faint, like a flame

133

that's just begun to lick at scraps of kindling. "You want to match me. To be my equal."

I swallow, struck by the sudden impulse to close the distance between us. I wonder if I would taste my blood on his mouth if I kissed him right now. With effort, I force myself to keep still. "Yes. That's what I want."

Quiet closes over the room. Slowly, the sounds of the forest seep in from outside, the rustle of leaves, the shift of branches, the whisper of souls. The Lord Under doesn't move. He lies captured beneath my pressing hands, looking at me as though I am a knot to be unpicked, as though the answer to countless secrets is written over my skin.

Finally, he nods, the movement so small it's almost imperceptible. "I promise you: The next time Moth crosses your path, you'll be the one to put your claws to her throat." With a slight smile, he glances at my hands, still pressed to his shoulders. "Figuratively, at least."

Slowly, I ask, "How will it work?"

"We will need to go back to the place where I mended you. To the bone tree."

At the sound of that name, spoken smoothly in his voice, I see a shape emerge from the darkened woods, eerie and pale. The bone tree, the enormous heartwood that grows at the center of the forest. A bleach-white monument that is both sepulcher and altar, the place of my death and rebirth.

My ears start to ring, filled by an ominous hum. With difficulty, I manage, "When?"

"I will come for you tomorrow, at dusk."

I shift back, let him out from beneath me. He moves slowly, careful to keep space between us. We sit, side by side, on the edge of my bed. Not touching. I stare down at the new crescent mark on my wrist.

Outside, the heartwoods stir quietly as mist trails through their branches. I picture the wall beyond the trees, the torn-open gate sealed shut again with a touch of the Lord Under's claws. "Until tomorrow—don't close the thorns."

He shakes his head. "I've no wish to be dragged across the forest to rescue you if anything makes its way inside the wall."

I can't bear the thought of it. To be caged, even if only for another night. "If you're that worried, then stay here with me tonight."

He makes a sound, too sharp to be a laugh. "I don't sleep."

We look at each other. I've never seen him so unsure, so unsettled. I wish I could feel more pleased. But heat has begun to prickle across my skin again, and I can feel a flush rising on my cheeks. The distance between us suddenly feels at once too close and endlessly wide.

Before he can move, I put my hand on his arm. It takes me as much by surprise as it does him. We both stare down at my fingers, knotted into his sleeve.

I straighten my spine. Try to keep my voice steady. "You don't have to sleep. But I want you to stay."

He doesn't respond. I let go of his arm, lie down on my side, with my face turned toward the wall. He doesn't move for a long while. I stay very still, waiting for him to leave. But then I feel the weight of him settle next to me. He stays fully dressed,

135

not even taking off his cloak or his boots, as though he can't surrender completely.

I lean back against him, uncertain. Slowly, he puts his arm around me. He smooths my hair aside, so it won't fall into his face, and rests his forehead against my shoulder.

I close my eyes and listen to the sound of him breathing. I hadn't known that I missed it so much, someone else beside me as I went to sleep. I let myself soften against him. Edges into hollows. He's so sharp and cold. It makes me very aware of the rhythm of my heartbeat. How I am flesh and blood. How he is none of those things.

And yet, in his arms I could almost feel safe.

But as the fire burns down and stillness settles over the room, I reach toward the sigil on my arm. Trace my fingers over the spell, newly bisected by the crescent scar. Holding my breath, I hesitate, then tentatively press down. There's a small flicker of heat on my skin, a quaver beneath my fingertips that might be nothing more than my own pulse.

The visions I've seen of Rowan—shadowed and dreamlike— feel like an offering to be laid at an altar. A fragile, flower-strewn, candlelit thing. And now, in the quiet space before sleep, I let myself admit my secretive hope.

That I might follow the thread tied between us and go back to the world Above. That with enough power, I can find my way back to him again.

Chapter Eleven

ROWAN

We leave in the dark, riding silently away from the estate. At the arched iron gateway, we draw our horses to a stop. I look back to the house, to where Florence stands by the door, holding a lantern. The single light flickers like a pale star as she raises her hand in farewell.

Behind her, vines cover the walls of the house in trailing, inky lines. A pattern twinned by the marks on my arms, where my veins are mapped darkly by poison. Where a garland of indigo bruises frames the sigil on my wrist.

The way to the village takes us through orchards. The road is dim beneath a lowering sky, and the clouds are so heavy they scrape the trees. The first strands of daylight reveal a world turned to a miserable gray. Rain starts to fall, and we pull up the hoods of our cloaks.

Arien doesn't know how to ride, so he sits behind Clover. It reminds me of Leta. When we rode together, after I took her and Arien from their cottage. The curve of her back against my chest. The strange protectiveness I felt, despite how dangerous I knew it was to *care*.

Now I feel the same—just as fierce and reckless. I want her safe. I want her *home*. Want it so badly that I'll risk everything.

It's just past dawn when we reach the village. I've not been here since the Summersend fire. I try to avoid it as much as possible. Even like this—in the quiet of early morning—the village unsettles me.

A few people are outside already. They cast wary glances in our direction, and as we pass, I can hear the nervous murmur of their voices. I pull the hood of my cloak down farther, bow my head as I try to ignore them.

Arien looks back at me. He wears a borrowed pair of my gloves, and a cloak that once belonged to Elan. He tugs at the collar, tucks it more tightly against his throat. Clover glances between us and shakes her head. "Can you both try not to look so *suspicious*?"

I force myself to straighten my shoulders, and let the hood fall back from my hair. I look ahead, just in time to catch the attention of Keeper Harkness. He's in front of his cottage, saddling a small gray pony.

I want to ignore him, but Clover cuts me a warning look. With a sigh, I pull to a halt and nod in greeting. "Keeper Harkness."

"Lord Sylvanan." With an edge of uncertainty, he says, "I didn't expect to see you until the Autumndark bonfire."

He glances from me to Clover to Arien—who pulls at his sleeves, fidgeting with the laces on his cuffs. I arrange my face into what I *hope* is a neutral expression. "We're just passing through. We have errands in the next village."

Arien clears his throat. "Yes, errands," he agrees.

Keeper Harkness frowns at us all. "I thought—"

Before he can finish, the door of his cottage opens. Thea steps out into the rain. She's dressed for travel, in sturdy boots and a heavy cloak. Her hair tied up in a braided crown.

She holds a rolled-up piece of parchment, wrapped in a waterproof cover. A satchel filled with wooden palings—the kind that would repair an altar frame—is slung across her shoulder. She looks at us, and manages a small smile.

"Hello. You're all out very early." She takes the reins of the pony from her father. Steps into his offered hand as he helps her into the saddle. "Thank you," she says to him. Then, brows knit, she asks us, "Where's Violeta?"

Twin splotches of red mark Clover's cheeks. "I—She—"

"She stayed behind," Arien cuts in, too quickly. "At the estate."

Thea's frown deepens. Her eyes track over me warily as I motion to Clover. "We should go. We have a long ride ahead."

Wordlessly, she nods. We start to ride forward, keeping our eyes fixed straight ahead as we pass the rest of the way through the village. Once we're out on the road, I quickly turn down a narrow path, guiding my horse into the fields. I look back, once, to check that Clover and Arien have followed me. Then I spur my horse to a gallop, until the village is far behind us.

The fields we ride through are fallow, the earth left bare from the final harvest. On the night of the Autumndark bonfire, I'm supposed to come here. Chant the litany, light a candle, make an offering.

Memories rise, like ghosts, of when my father was lord. The villagers would line the field as he knelt to pour salt and handfuls of petals over the ground, to consecrate the earth.

He wore the mantle of lord like a cloak, perfectly cut. Bearing the weight of duty so naturally. If *I've* borne the weight at all, it's only been so that I wouldn't be crushed by it.

Eventually we leave the open ground. Following a path that winds through a grove of olive trees. At my wrist, the sigil gives a sharp *throb*. I glance down. On the bared stretch of skin before the edge of my gloves, I see the lines of poison. Darker now, heavier. They shift, flicker, as they move beneath my skin.

There's a familiar hunger in this hurt, this ache. But I'm not afraid. I welcome it. The spread of shadows. The rising taste of silt on my tongue. The way my lungs feel snared by thorns. How the scars at my throat feel sharp.

This isn't the Corruption, with demands of bloodied tithes. I'm bound by no curse. Only Leta. A connection made from my promise. From her magic. From the spell-thread tied between us. The fierce *love* wound through me, following the darkness in my veins.

It will take almost two full days to reach the Vair Woods. We ride without stopping, except to briefly rest the horses at an empty wayside. Then we go on again. Avoiding the road, I choose a path that's hidden by the trees. The orchards are gone now. We're in the wilder forest. The air turns cold as the sunlight is eclipsed by woven branches.

Night comes early at Harvestfall. Soon, dusk has begun to pleat shadows through the woods. The clouded sky, barely visible through the trees, is the color of ash. The wind turns quiet.

My skin starts to prickle, and I can't escape the feeling that I'm being watched.

I glance back over my shoulder and realize I'm alone. Arien and Clover must have fallen behind. Sighing wearily, I pull my horse to a stop. Get down from the saddle. I knot the reins in my hand, walk over to the side of the road to wait for them.

At the edge of the clearing is a fallen tree, with spindled roots stretching overhead. An enormous moth flutters out from beneath them. I flinch, startled, as it circles me, close enough that I feel wingbeats on my face. I catch a clear impression of it before it vanishes into the darkening sky.

The ache at my wrist gives a sharp, insistent pull. I fold back my sleeve. The bandage covering the sigil is stained with too-dark blood. I take off my gloves. Slide my fingers beneath the bandage and press the spell.

I search for the tether that binds me to Leta. At first there's only quiet darkness. Then it changes into bright, hot pain. Darkness crowds across the edges of my vision. I let go of my wrist. Lean back against the tree. Close my eyes, trying to catch my breath.

The sound of hoofbeats comes from the distance. I straighten, turn toward the road. But instead of Arien and Clover, it's—Thea.

I stare at her, a knot of apprehension in my stomach. The path we're on is far from the main road, and I chose this way knowing we'd not meet another rider. At the sight of me, alone, she draws her pony to a sharp halt.

She looks around anxiously, her hands tightening on the reins. Beneath her hood, dark brown curls frame her face, escaped from the braided crown. "Where are Arien and Clover?"

I drag a breath through my clenched teeth. It's effort, to speak while magic riots through me. "They fell behind. I'm waiting for them," I tell Thea. Her eyes shift from me to the darkened woods. Her expression is lined with fear. "Is something the matter?"

Another gust of wind stirs the trees around us. Thea shivers, rubs her arms. Glancing doubtfully at the road, she gets down from her pony and faces me. "There are rumors about you in the village."

"Yes. I'm aware."

"Rumors about you . . . and Violeta."

At my wrist, the sigil gives another *pull*, then dampens to

142

silence. Thea's gaze drops to my hands, and she bites her lip. Lines of black band each of my fingers now, like rings made of shadow. I clench my fists, wishing I'd put my gloves back on. "What rumors about Violeta?"

Thea casts another nervous glance toward the road. "That you sacrificed her."

The taste of poison creeps across my tongue. Mud and ink, silt and smoke. I try to remain still, to hold back the hungering tremor of magic. *She can't know.* But the rumors about me have never been far from the truth.

Carefully, I ask, "And what do *you* think?"

"I don't know." She wavers, then, steeling herself, she takes a step closer. "But I'm not going to let you hurt anyone else."

"Anyone else?" I look at her, confused. Then realize what she means. Why she's so afraid and determined at the same time. I can't help but laugh. "I have no plans to sacrifice Arien and Clover. Or anyone, for that matter. Now, you need to leave. You'll have a long ride back to wherever you're supposed to be."

"No."

I scowl at her. "It wasn't a request, Thea."

She folds her arms across her chest. "I'm not leaving."

Silence draws out. We stare at each other. Her eyes are bright with the promise of tears. I cast around helplessly, knowing whatever I say will only make things worse. Then, from far off, I hear the sound of another horse. The lilt of Clover's voice as she calls out through the trees. "There you are!"

Thea lets out a sigh of relief as Arien and Clover come into sight. "Sorry," Arien says with a rueful smile. "We took a wrong turn in the trees and got lost."

My tenuous hold on the magic loosens, and the poison spirals further through me, marking blackened lines across my skin. My throat feels tight, snared by sedge grass. It's hard to speak. When I do, my voice sounds strange. A lake-washed tone. "You see," I tell Thea pointedly, "they are very much *un*sacrificed."

Clover dismounts, then helps Arien down from their horse. "What's going on? Thea, why are you here?"

Thea rushes forward, pulling Clover into an embrace. She buries her face against Clover's shoulder and starts to cry. "I couldn't let him hurt you!"

"Oh!" Clover gasps, startled. She puts her arms around Thea. "We're safe. I promise you, we're safe."

Arien smothers a cough. "I wouldn't exactly say that."

Clover glares at him. She takes a folded handkerchief from her pocket, gives it to Thea. Gently, she says, "Really, Thea, we're all right."

Thea sniffles as she wipes her face. "She is gone, though. Isn't she? That part is true. Violeta is gone."

Arien and Clover exchange a stricken look. Clover takes Thea's hand. "Thea, we—"

"I appreciate your concern," I interrupt. "But you really need to leave."

Arien turns sharply at the tone of my voice, still lake washed and shadow dark. His eyes dip to my forearm, where the bloodied bandage shows beneath the edge of my sleeve.

I swallow down the taste of ash, of blood. With a ragged sigh, I manage to gather control. Some of the darkness clears from my vision. The snare at my throat loosens.

Thea stares at me in horror. She wavers, as though about to flee. Then she squares her shoulders. "I'm not leaving. But if you won't tell me the truth, I'll go back to the village and tell them all that you *did* sacrifice Violeta."

Arien gives me a *look*. He sighs roughly, shaking his head. "There's been so many lies, Rowan. I'm tired of it. Maybe if we'd had a single, honest conversation with Leta before the ritual, we wouldn't *be* in this mess right now."

Clover puts her arms more tightly around Thea. "We can tell her. We can trust her."

I want to refuse. It feels impossible, to tell the truth. All I've done—all I've *ever* done—is keep everything hidden. Held my secrets close. It was always easier to lie. To hope it would spare everyone else from pain.

But Arien is right. Leta and I both caused so much hurt with our reluctance to be honest. Maybe if we'd been more open, we'd have found choices other than tithes, than dangerous bargains.

Now, faced by the chance to be honest with Thea, I feel a strange, dizzy *relief*.

Carefully, I push back my sleeves. Untie the bandage. Show her my arms. The scars, the sigil—with Arien's addition marked in newer, sharper lines. The wreath of bruises around the spell. "Violeta Graceling has given herself to the Lord

145

Under. She's in the world Below, and we are trying to bring her back with an alchemical ritual."

Thea draws her fingers across her chest in a protective gesture. She looks at me, as though seeing me clearly for the first time. "You're death touched." Her hand flexes, like she's trying to grasp hold of an explanation. "That's why you're . . . this way."

"Yes," I tell her plainly. "I drowned as a child, and the Lord Under saved my life. Leta made a similar bargain in her childhood. And because of that, and many other things, she is still alive in the world Below."

I see her waver as she takes this in. Then she turns to Clover. "All of us are raised with whispers of the Lord Under. What might happen if you go to close to the border of death. I never thought—"

She trails off. Shakes her head. Clover puts her hand on Thea's arm. "I know it's a lot to comprehend. But you've seen me work magic before."

Thea squares her shoulders. "Yes, I have."

"This is the same magic, more or less. You don't have to be afraid. There's a connection between Violeta and Rowan, made with her alchemy. We're going to use it, to reach her."

Thea glances at me. She's still wary, but it's the nervousness of someone who has seen a myth made real. "I always knew alchemy was more than what a village healer might do," she says with an incredulous laugh. "But this . . . Clover, do you really think you can all bring her back with magic?"

146

Clover and Arien look at each other, and they both nod. "We're going to do everything we can to try."

Thea bows her head to me. She clears her throat, embarrassed. "I'm glad it's not the truth; that you're a monster, or that you hurt her."

A sharp ache spreads through my chest. *I am a monster*. But despite the honesty of this moment, I'm not ready to share that part of my story with Thea. Instead, I turn away, gather up my reins, and prepare to get back onto my horse. "So now you have the truth of it," I tell her over my shoulder. "No one will be sacrificed. No one is in danger, except for me. And that's a risk I'm more than willing to take."

Gently, Clover says, "It's almost nighttime, Thea. Do you want me to ride with you back to the village?"

"No," Thea says again. "I'm not going back. If you're trying to find Violeta, then I want to go with you. I want to help."

Clover tugs at the end of her braid as she looks toward me. She raises her brow, a silent question. I let out a rough sigh. "Fine. If you're coming with us, then hurry up. I want to reach the wayside before it's completely dark."

Thea scrambles to get back on her pony, while Clover holds out a hand to help Arien remount. We make our way back to the road, ducking beneath the roots of the fallen tree. Another moth flutters out from inside it as we pass. It vanishes into the branches above. Leaves a trail of silver motes in the air.

Shadows lengthen as we ride out of the woods. Once we

reach the road, the sky is dull. A line of pale crimson, like a streak of blood, marks the horizon.

None of us speak. I stare blurrily ahead as we pass fallow fields. Foreboding sinks over me, a heavy weight.

Finally, beneath a clouded sky, the wayside cottage comes into sight. It's not the same place where I stopped with Arien and Leta last summer. This cottage is smaller, a single room. As we dismount and tend to our horses, my memories drift back to that other wayside, that other night.

The story Leta told Arien about a brave maiden. A monster. A labyrinth. How she cut to silence when she noticed I was listening. It's a story she will never be able to tell again. She gave it up to the Lord Under, along with all the other memories of her family.

Inside the cottage, I light the fire while Clover fills a kettle at the sink in the corner and puts it onto the stove to heat.

We divide up slices of plain travel bread. Thea offers a parcel of spiced tea. There's a teapot on a nearby shelf, along with a stack of enamelware cups. Clover takes them to the sink in the corner to wash. Then she makes the tea, pours it into the cups.

We all sit together, crowded close by the hearth. Thea looks around the room, sips a mouthful of her tea. There's a quiet laugh in her voice as she says, "This might be fun to do again someday. When things are less dire."

Arien glances at her over the rim of his cup. "I appreciate your belief that this won't be a complete disaster."

"Really, Arien," Clover raises a brow. "After all my excellent lessons, you should be a little more confident." She looks around the room with a wistful sigh. "Maybe one day everything will be . . . uneventful again."

"Have our lives *ever* been uneventful?" Arien makes a face at her, and she shoves him. "Hey!" he cries, clutching his cup against his chest so it won't spill.

Clover rolls her eyes. "Okay then, if you want to be so picky. Everything after this can be uneventful for the first time."

"I look forward to it," Arien says.

Thea laughs. Clover puts down her cup and takes a notebook from her satchel. While she leafs through the book, Arien moves closer, a pen in his hand.

He draws a line of sigils on the page. The markings are familiar, though I can't place where I've seen them. Clover looks at the symbols, frowning. She scratches one out, writes in another.

Thea watches Clover, wistful and curious. Their eyes meet and they exchange a shy smile. But neither of them moves.

I remember the awe I felt when I first saw Leta use her magic. Even though I was familiar with alchemy, there was a new wonder in seeing it worked by her hands.

I shift closer to Clover. Nodding toward Thea, I murmur quietly, "You could show her how the magic works."

She gives me a startled look. Her cheeks flush with shyness. Lowering her voice to a whisper, she asks, "Are you actually giving me *romantic* advice?"

"Um. Yes." I tug a hand through my hair. Feeling an answering flush on my own face. "And this is just as awkward for me, if you wondered."

Clover spreads the notebook out in her lap. Hesitantly, she beckons to Thea. "Would you like to see?"

"Yes!" Thea says quickly. Arien snorts back a laugh at her eagerness. Clover glares at him. Thea clears her throat. "I mean, yes please."

She takes her teacup and goes to sit beside Clover. Their shoulders touch as she bends to look at the page. Clover traces her finger across the sigils.

"We need a way to strengthen the magic, without it causing more . . . damage." They both glance toward me. "If we redraw the spell in the same place, all the power is concentrated together. So I've deconstructed the sigils. Written like this, it should protect Rowan from being harmed."

Arien looks at her askance. "It *should*? You just told me to be more confident."

Clover presses a hand to her chest, pretending to be wounded. "My own words, used against me!"

Thea shakes her head at them both, and they all start to laugh. I want so badly to join in with their good-natured playfulness. But I am too jittery and restless. I flex my hand, watch as more bruiselike blotches encircle my wrist. There's a rasp whenever I breathe. When I swallow, I taste dirt. It's as though I'm already in the woods. Trapped by thorns, by longing, by poisoned magic.

I get to my feet, make my way outside. Clover, her expression turned serious, moves to follow me; I wave her away. "I'm fine. I just need some air."

The space between the cottage and the road is covered by fallen leaves. I crunch through them, walk over to a nearby altar. The wooden shelf is scattered with leftover offerings.

One candle remains among the rivulets of melted wax. I still have a sparklight in my pocket. I set the light to the wick. The candle flares, the icon illuminated by its small flame. The paint on the image has faded. The top half is veiled by cobwebs.

It makes me think of the dual icon in the parlor at Lakesedge. The way that Leta looked when she appeared, wreathed by darkness.

I unlace my sleeves. Fold them back. The sigil stirs at my wrist, a muted heartbeat. Darkness shifts beneath my skin, mine and not mine.

Slowly, I lower my hands to the earth. The clouds draw back, and moonlight spills over me, cut by the branches of the tree above. I close my eyes. I don't chant. I don't even think the words of a litany. I don't reach for the magic strung through the world.

Instead, I think of other trees, the color of blood, their trunks shrouded by mist. Think of my voice calling Leta's name into a silence that swallows all sound.

The door of the wayside cottage creaks open. Arien steps outside. He has Elan's cloak huddled around himself against the cold. He looks at me for a moment. Then comes and sits down next to me at the altar. I draw my hands back from the earth. Wipe the dirt against my knees.

Arien frowns at the lines on my arms. The bloodstained scars, the bruised sigil. "You're *fine*, huh?"

"I'll be fine enough."

"Yes, obviously. How could I think otherwise?" He reaches for my wrist. His fingers move carefully over the lines of the spell. More of the darkness spirals loose when he touches me. He frowns. "This is getting worse."

"I've noticed. I've been trying to hold it back, but . . ." I trail off, biting against a hiss of pain. Arien lets me go. I curl forward, wrist clutched against my chest. I want to tell him it doesn't matter. But I can't form any words.

Arien sketches a spell on his arm, then reaches to me again. Shadows wrap around me. His magic is cold, but even though it hurts, the touch of his power is a welcome ache. It moves through my veins, a slow creep of frost, as it silences the poison.

I think of Leta, dressed in cobwebs and moth wings. I've already drifted so close to the edge of ruin. But I'm resolved to it, this risk. I won't turn back. Even if I'm destroyed, it doesn't matter. I will pay whatever price it takes to save her.

Slowly, Arien lets me go. He glances at me, one brow raised. "So . . . was Elan as completely reckless as you?"

In spite of everything, I start to laugh. "Oh, he was much worse. His entire life was spent plotting the most ridiculous schemes and dragging me along."

"Sounds familiar." Arien pushes at my knee with his own,

then offers a faint smile. "Hopefully he would approve of *this* ridiculous scheme."

"Oh, I'm certain he would."

I think of what lies ahead tomorrow. How we'll go to the woods. How I'll let the darkness in. I wish I was more certain of what will come after I step into the shadows.

All I know for sure is that in the Vair Woods, this will end. One way or another.

Chapter Twelve

VIOLETA

At dusk, the Lord Under is waiting for me beside the ruined gate. It rained steadily all through the night, and now the forest is cloaked by mist. The heartwood leaves are jeweled with water, and sparkling necklaces of cobwebs are strung between their branches.

I'm dressed in a gown made of fragile lace that leaves my arms bare. When I walk out of the trees, my skirts stir the mist into eddying swirls.

The Lord Under turns at the sound of my footsteps. Our eyes meet, and the silence between us shimmers. He was gone before I awoke, but I have hazy memories of him beside me while I slept. His arm around my waist, the touch of his claws against my hair.

Now, as I move toward him, foreboding winds through me, a clambering vine with thorns that catch my chest. My hand circles my wrist, finds the place where the new scar meets the sigil. I press down, feeling only my pulse. The vines tighten further.

I look at the wall. The tree I grew, which cleaved apart the thorns, has become even taller overnight. The bower of its branches casts a heavy shadow on the ground, and as I step into this shadow, the air is cold enough to raise goose bumps on my bare arms.

The Lord Under holds out a large, folded garment, tied up with a ribbon. "Here. I mended your cloak."

My mouth lifts into a puzzled smile. He unties the ribbon, revealing my cloak, each torn place sewn closed with tiny stitches. The inside has been newly lined with cobalt silk—the color of the woods at dusk.

I put my back to him and lift aside my hair. Carefully, he drapes the cloak over my shoulders. Then he turns me gently around so we face each other. Slowly, he ties the ribboned fastenings at my throat. Heat prickles over my skin, and my palms feel warm with magic.

"I—" My voice comes out unsteady. I pause, take a breath. "Thank you."

"Try not to throw yourself into any more thorns while you're wearing it."

I trail my fingers over the cloak. The new stitches make a delicate, asymmetrical pattern, like the curve of a fern frond. Laughing, I say, "I'll do my best."

The Lord Under puts his hand against what remains of the gate. As he traces his claws over the brambles, they part farther, leaving a wider space for us to walk through. I take a mothlight from a nearby tree and gather up my cloak.

Before we leave, I turn back to look at the damage I caused. The torn-apart gate. The tree at the center of the thorns. When I last came here, I was driven by a singular *want*—to unlock the secrets on the other side of the wall.

Now I know what lies beyond, but I'm still so uncertain of what I'll find at the other end of the path. Even my hope for what this power will bring—strength, protection—feels so easily shaken. All I'm sure of is that I want this. The *more* I craved in my struggle against the sister gods.

I want to reforge the connection between myself and Rowan. Press my fingers to the sigil and summon him at will. Follow the thread into the dark and find my way . . . home. Where I'll be with him—not just for a brief moment of stolen kisses and desperate promises, like in the visions. But *forever*.

Side by side, the Lord Under and I walk into the woods. The ground is damp from snowmelt, remnants of the storm stirred up by Lady Moth. As we follow the path deeper into the trees, the forest changes around us. The trees shift closer together, their branches a woven archway. Though the sun has set, a strange light turns the sky to a lilac haze. And everything is washed by a peculiar scent, a heady perfume like incense and crushed flowers.

The path starts to slope upward. The trees creep back, revealing shapes buried in the shadows between them. The remnants of stone walls, open doorways that lead to nowhere, icon frames filled only with lichen and decaying leaves.

And then, at the end of the path . . . is the bone tree.

Encircled by mist, its bleached-white trunk and leafless branches fill the sky in a skeletal canopy. I falter, stilled by the sight of it. This is the heart of the world Below. This is the place where I was brought to be mended, where I awoke and learned the price of my survival.

As we walk toward the tree, a strange feeling starts up in my chest. The threads of my magic shift, uncurl. Like there's something asleep within me that has begun to wake up. I wrap my cloak around myself, tighten the ribbons at my throat. The Lord Under gently touches the small of my back. I take his hand. A spark of power lights between us—the pale gold of my alchemy, the clouded dark of his shadows.

In a clear space at the end of the path is a wooden altar, encircled by candles that have already been lit. The icon frame is weathered, laced by cobwebs and moss. And it's empty. In place of a portrait, the frame shows only the bone tree—pale and endless, carved all over with a delicate pattern.

I kneel slowly, moving with habit rather than thought. My fingers slip into the earth at the base of the altar, just like when I made observance in the world Above. My eyes dip closed, and I reach into the quiet darkness.

I think of the light threaded through the world. The Lady who made the earth, who *became* the earth. The Lady who made the Lord Under. Creation, destruction, the ability to speak a name and make it full of magic and power.

From the shelf beneath the icon, the Lord Under picks up a woven circlet of branches, curved like a halo. "Bow your head."

But I don't bow. Instead, I take the branches from his hands.

An amused smile plays across his features as he watches me set the crown on my hair.

Then a sound comes from the path below. I get to my feet, turning back to look at the forest as new snowflakes start to drift through the air. Three figures emerge from the mist between the heartwoods. Lady Moth. Lady Owl. Lady Fawn.

They come forward in a line. The snow falls heavier, the whispers in the trees dampen to a hushed, desperate stillness. The Lord Under draws himself up taller. A low, defensive growl echoes in his chest. Shadows lash around us, darkening the air.

He is pale fire, cold and fierce as he gazes down at them. "I thought it was clear when last we spoke that you are to keep to your own corners of the woods."

Lady Moth looks from the Lord Under to me, frowning at the sight of the wreath on my hair. "Brother. A human girl has no place in our world."

"I am ruler of the Below. What I do is my own concern."

Lady Owl glares at him, her eyes glittering with anger. "What you do has been our concern since the Corruption escaped your control and almost destroyed our world. She's a girl—a dead soul—and you have no right to keep her here."

"Violeta is mine," the Lord Under snarls. A shiver goes through me at his words. *Mine.* "She has a right to whatever I give her."

Lady Fawn bares her teeth, sharp behind the bone mask. "We will not allow you to do this."

I take a step toward them, slow and deliberate. The wind

158

catches my cloak, it drifts back in a billow of bright silk. My hands are at my sides, fingers pressed to my palms. Power wakes beneath my skin. The air sparks around me.

I stand before the gods. I refuse to be afraid. "I traded my blood and breath and safety to be here. I gave up my life. This is my choice, and you will not stop me."

Lady Moth tilts her head, and her mouth curves into a scathing smile. "Little mouse. What power do you have against us?"

I reach to the Lord Under and take his hand. Our eyes meet with veiled understanding. Magic hums between our clasped fingers with an eager heat. I think of my hands in the earth, seeds splitting between my cupped palms. Think of the way it felt when his power wove through mine as I mended the Corruption.

Now, I brace myself as his magic washes over me, through me. As I draw on my own power. The air fills with shadows that are sparked with gold. Our power encloses everything. The forest darkens. The air turns cold. I gasp out a breath laced with frost. A sharp, heavy pressure crushes down on me. Everything tastes of salt and smoke and mist.

Then there's a crackle, and the light comes in.

The sister gods have gone. Only a slight movement in the heartwoods beyond the path shows they were ever here at all.

The Lord Under stares at the place where they vanished. Gradually, his shadows dim. He looks down at our hands, our fingers still laced together. There's a strange expression on his face. A quiet, confused awe.

His mouth tilts into a rueful smile. "I've never shared my power like this. None of us have. Until I met you, I didn't think it was possible."

A surge of adrenaline rushes through me. My heartbeat spikes, echoing the pulse of my magic a few moments earlier. "I will *not* let them hurt me."

"No," he agrees. "My sisters . . . they want you asleep in a tree, not alive in our world. But you are right, my Violet. You have earned your place here."

I slip my hand from his and walk toward the tree. There's a blank space at the center of the carved trunk. Roughly the shape of an arched doorway. I press my palm flat against it. The tree is *warm*, burning with a heat that feels alive, as though there's blood flowing, hot, beneath the surface.

The Lord Under touches his claws to the trunk, and the scrollwork pattern begins to move. I draw back my hand, caught between horror and fascination as the archway opens. When last I came here, it was in his arms. Carried into the dark as the poison claimed me.

The girl I was *died* in this place.

Now, we walk together into the hollowed darkness. Inside, the ground is soft beneath my feet, and the air smells of rain. Beyond the glow from my mothlight, the cavernous space is larger, even, than it appeared from outside.

After a long while, the corridor opens to a circular room. It's empty except for a raised dais at the center, made of the same filigree-patterned bone as the outside of the tree. I move forward, my light held high. When my fingers trace the edge of the dais, a splinter of bone pierces my skin. Blood wells up. I stare down at the cut, my heartbeat echoing loudly in my ears. Slowly, slowly, I reach out and smear a streak of blood across the bones.

Light flickers. I see an image, overlaid. The memory of when I was last here, like a dream that's spilled from sleep. I'm still in the cavern, at the dais. But now there's a figure atop it, lying deathly still. A girl, with white skin and tangled red hair. Her chest rises and falls faintly, as though she's not dead but soundly, unbreakably asleep.

Her whole body is filled with shadows.

I take a breath and close my eyes. When I look again, the girl is gone.

The Lord Under comes to stand beside me. He takes the mothlight from my hands and sets it in a niche on the wall. Neither of us has spoken of the price, of what I will trade for this new power. I press my lips together. Swallow past the tightening of my throat. "You haven't asked what I will offer you."

He goes silent, a careful pause. Apprehension tracks down my spine, shiver by shiver. His features fracture for the barest blink. His reply is measured, each word held close before he speaks it. "I don't want to trade with you. Not this time."

"What do you mean?"

His face resettles. The eyes, the mouths, the slashes at his throat, all fade back to silvery marks that are barely visible on his pale skin. With effort, his expression settles, too. It's like watching someone put on a well-worn mask that has, for the briefest second, slipped.

"This isn't the same as casting a spell. I am giving you a share of my power. I am giving you half of all I am."

I shiver again, a tremor that goes right down to the center of my body. *Half of all I am.* Half of his strength and shadows and inhuman magic.

The power in my veins sings with a new resonance. My chest feels tight, my skin feverishly hot. I'm trembling when he holds out a hand to me and helps me climb onto the dais.

He stays close as I sit down on the edge of the platform. And in the petrichor-scented gloom of the alcove, I'm overwhelmingly aware of how human I am in comparison to him. His skin is so cold, and his claws are so sharp.

"What will I be?" I ask him. "When this is done?"

He strokes his thumb against the scar on my palm. "You will have power. So much power."

His words and his touch send a rush of emotions through me. Despair and longing. Deep within my chest I feel the shape of a name—his name—that's almost, but not quite, formed into a word I can speak.

I touch his chest, feel the silence where a heartbeat would be. The space between us narrows. He bends until our foreheads touch. A sigh tangles between our mouths. He strokes back a wayward strand of hair from my cheek and whispers my name. *"Violeta."*

And I want his name in return, want to chant it in reply like an echoed litany. But I am speechless, all words lost to the cold of him.

I want to press my lips to the hollow of his throat. Mark

kisses like a claim against his skin. Instead, I draw back. I put my hands flat against the dais on either side of me. Feel the worn-smooth bone of its surface. "I am ready."

A mothlight burns behind the Lord Under, turns him to a silhouette. Slowly, he places his hands on my shoulders. The air fills with shadows and the familiar taste of his magic. Ash and salt, black tea, moonless nights.

I let my eyes close as my pulse speeds up. Power hums through me, a different feeling from my own magic. I scrunch my hands closed, feel the *throb throb throb* of the crescent scar on my palm. I'm about to cross a line that should not be crossed. But I don't want to turn back.

My power sparks awake. It matches the cold slither of his shadows. I let it in, let it spill through me. As this new dark magic slides though my body, everything fades away. The Lord Under vanishes into the shadows. I am alone.

It feels right, for this moment to be mine, entire. I was the one who asked for this power, who chose to claim it for myself.

Carefully, I step down from the altar. The ground beneath my feet is no longer softened earth but stones, interlaid with a delicate pattern. Softened light shines from the distance. I start to walk toward it. At first there are only the path and the walls, air that smells faintly of the perfume I noted before in the forest. Incense and crushed flowers.

Then the light grows brighter. In the distance I see a door carved from crimson wood. There's a wreath on the center, bramble vines woven into a circlet, sharp with thorns that are as long as my fingers.

The door opens as I approach. I step into a high-ceilinged chamber, aglow with candlelight. The air is honey and amber, languorous with a haze of smoke. An arched window fills the wall at the opposite end of the room. Beyond the glass is a stretch of mist-draped sky. And beneath the window is a figure, outlined against the pale light.

As I move closer, I can pick out details, features. Bronzed skin, golden eyes, hands that gleam with immeasurable, wondrous magic.

I hear a sound that is not a sound. A voice that is not a voice. I stand before the Lady as her words trace over me like a caress.

You hold the fire of the world in your hands.

I'm on a path between rows of trees. The grayed shadows of the world Below shift and flicker around me as I move forward. The sunlight fades, and the sky is moonglow silver. The air turns the color of stars. The sigil on my wrist starts to beat with a frantic pulse, like a moth caught inside a jar. There's a hiss, a rush, and all the breath is gone from my lungs.

Then the vision fades, and I am awake, back inside the bone tree.

The Lord Under watches me carefully as I sit up. "How do you feel?"

"I—" I stare down at my hands, feel the hum and burn of new magic. "I feel very . . . different."

He helps me down from the altar. We walk together back out into the forest. My skin is so terribly cold, like all my warmth, all the softest, most sunlit pieces of myself, have been razed clear. The power flows through my veins with a fierceness I can barely contain; I feel as though I will come unstitched, spiral apart until I am tree and leaf and flower. Just another part of this beautiful, terrible world.

Outside the bone tree, we pause, a measured distance between us. I look restlessly at the path that leads back into the woods. My fingers curl with the impulse to slide beneath my sleeve and touch the spell. I need a place to be alone, where I can test my new power, see how far I can reach into the dark.

Beside me, the Lord Under is suddenly still. He turns with a sharp motion, and I flinch back, startled. He can't know what I intend—can he?

But his focus moves past me, eyes narrowing at the forest. I look, too, expecting one of his sisters to appear from the trees. Instead, I hear a strange sound carried on the wind. It's like the whispers of the souls. Except, while the voices that murmur in the heartwoods are calm and restful, this sound is pained and frightened.

I take a step forward, trying to hear the sound more clearly. The Lord Under puts out his hand, stopping me from going any farther. His gaze is lit with an eagerness that frightens me. It has the same peculiar hunger that I saw when I summoned him, when he stepped out from the altar and stood before me that first time.

"What is it?" I ask, my voice hushed.

With effort, he drags his attention from the sound. "There have been many lives taken in the world Above. I need to claim their souls."

Chapter Thirteen

VIOLETA

At the Lord Under's words—*claim their souls*—my mind starts to turn, my thoughts so swift I can barely grasp them. To claim a soul, the Lord Under must cross the border between worlds. That's how I first met him in the Vair Woods, when Arien was close to death.

And if *I* could cross that border, with my new power, and the spell-thread that ties me to Rowan, our connection would be so much stronger.

I turn to the Lord Under. Trying—and failing—to hold back my eagerness. "I want to come with you."

He doesn't even consider it for more than a second. Already on the path, he turns back to say, "Absolutely not."

I gather my skirts. Walk faster, to catch up with him. "Are you saying I *can't* come to claim a soul, or that you won't *let* me?"

With a sharp breath, he draws to a stop and takes hold of my shoulders. "My answer is no. The *why* is immaterial." His hands slide down my arms. His fingers lace through mine, and he looks toward the path. "I'll walk you back home before I leave."

I bite down against the inside of my cheek. I want to argue. But if I press him, he'll only be suspicious. I can't let him know why I want to follow him so badly. I swallow back my protests and nod. He stares at me for a beat, a flicker of wariness in his eyes. I try to keep my face neutral.

Then he tightens his grip on my hand, guides me to walk forward. I follow him away from the bone tree. When we reach the bottom of the slope, Lady Moth is waiting. She pushes back her hood, and a drift of snowflakes scatters through the air around her as she steps out onto the path.

She watches us, one feathery brow raised above her depthless gaze. "I thought you'd be on your way to the mourning fields, Brother." Though her voice remains innocent, there's a sharp edge to her smile. "I hear there have been many dead near the Vair Woods."

The Lord Under takes a slow step forward, his fingers flexing against mine. "What would you know of that?"

Idly, Lady Moth examines her claws. "You've been so distracted. Perhaps some of our magic slipped through into the world Above. But of course, that's only a guess. Who could say what truly happened?"

"Those lands are under my protection. If you have

transgressed, Moth—" He bares his teeth, a serrated line of anger. Leaves the threat unspoken.

The Lord Under and Lady Moth stare at each other. The air grows more tense with each beat that passes. Moth glowers at him, all challenge. "And what of *your* transgressions?"

Her attention flicks toward me. I fold my arms. "You don't need to talk about me as though I can't hear you."

She flicks back a strand of pale blue hair. Straightens her antlered crown. An enormous gray moth flutters down from the trees and lands on her shoulder. "I'm surprised, Violeta. Doesn't it anger you, what my brother has done? He destroyed Lord Sylvanan's life—and yours as well—with the Corruption. He tricked you into sacrificing yourself in order to mend it."

"I didn't mend it for his sake."

Sighing, she turns back to the Lord Under. "A life for a life, that should have been the punishment when Lord Sylvanan refused to pay his debt. But *you* wanted the power that came from all his fear and pain. And now you have someone who will give you more power than a curse ever could."

Give him power.

The Lord Under studiedly avoids my gaze. Nervous sweat prickles at the nape of my neck, then starts to track slowly down my spine. I clench my teeth, try to force the feeling away. He gave me power because I demanded it. I am the one who gained strength from this, not him.

I step closer to Lady Moth, let my magic rise, a cold kiss over my skin. I picture myself with claws at her throat, matching

168

her own ruthlessness. Our eyes meet, and her features start to shift and fracture. Her mouth divides into a blur of sharp teeth, her cheeks dapple with bruise-like splotches that writhe and dance.

I stare at her levelly. "Whatever he's gained from me I've claimed for myself in equal measure."

Her face gives another blurred shiver; then reshapes into the flawless mask of before. "You'll never be truly his match. You may wear a crown and walk at my brother's side, but that doesn't change what you are and where you belong. A soul has only one rightful place in our world."

I close my eyes and think of a word—a name—the command I heard the Lord Under use against this creature when she tried to harm me. "*Chmah*. You will leave us."

Lady Moth's eyes widen. She looks from the Lord Under to me, her face twisted in fury. "This cannot go unanswered."

But even as she speaks, she's started to fade. More of the gray moths surround her, a cloud made from silver dust and delicate wings. She vanishes, leaving behind a drift of snow-flakes across the path.

I swallow, feel a sharpness burn all the way to my stomach. The word that was once not a word at all to me, that wouldn't make sense in my mouth, now lingers on my tongue with a taste like nectar. An overripe, sickly sweet thing. I resist the urge to scrub my sleeve against my lips.

The Lord Under lets out a startled laugh. He looks so *shocked*, the expression so rare and strange on his sharp, ethereal features. "You spoke her name."

I'm shaken, too. But I try not to let it show. "What did you *think* would happen when you gave this power to me?"

He doesn't answer. Instead, he looks down at the ground, eyes narrowing. Around my feet, pale flowers have grown from the earth. Delicate leaves and petals curl up over the toes of my boots and brush against my ankles. Startled, I take a step back. More flowers grow from the place where I've walked.

I stretch out a hand. Golden threads of light spill loose from my fingers, spiraling upward to the mist-drenched sky. The forest *glows*. The heartwoods are luminous crimson, their leaves silver sharp. The voices of the souls, which were only whispers before, now sing through the air.

This is my power. I am woven through the forest. I have the strength of the world Below.

The Lord Under clasps my hand. Leads me back to the path, back toward my cottage. As we walk, more flowers and vines rise from my footsteps, lining the path with petals and pale green leaves. Power hums through my bones, the intensity overwhelming.

I feel so *changed*. With a crown of branches on my hair and ruinous magic in my veins, I am the girl who was poisoned on the altar. I am the girl who took the hand of death.

When we reach the wall of thorns, another sound starts up, a sharper, more urgent call than the voices of the souls in the trees. I can hear them—the newly dead in the Vair Woods.

My hands crumple in the fabric of my skirts as I look in the direction of their voices. This is where I'll have to go, to reach the border between the worlds.

Beside the archway that leads into my part of the woods, I pause. Step away from the Lord Under. "I can find my way from here."

He gives me a warning look. "Remember what I said. Don't wander until I return to you."

I glance at the path that goes back into the forest. The place where it curves between the trees. The ground marked in shadows. "What did Moth mean, before, about her magic and the Vair Woods? Have your sisters done something to the people there?"

"My sisters can't understand how I let you help me, how I made another bargain with you after you were poisoned. They can't forgive the imbalance I caused with the Corruption." He sighs, chagrined. "I admit, I *was* ruthless. I loved Rowan Sylvanan for his pain and his fear. It gave me such strength to hurt him. But it went too far."

It's a shock, to hear him admit his fault. To hear Rowan's name spoken in his ethereal voice. For a moment, I can't make a sound. "*Too far* is perhaps the biggest understatement you've ever made. You wanted power. All you gained was destruction."

He exhales sharply, clouding the darkness with frost. "I won't apologize for my nature, Violeta. But I want to make amends. I've given you half of all I am. You have so much power, and it changes everything."

I shiver, and the feel of magic in my veins burns with a new resonance. "Has this . . . put you in danger, also?"

"I can't predict how my sisters will respond when they

realize what this means," he glances meaningfully toward the gate in the wall. "Which is why you need to go home and stay there until I return."

I curl my fingers against my palm, press down against the crescent scar. "I'll do my best to keep out of trouble."

He sighs at my teasing. "That is, I suppose, the most I can expect from you."

I go through the archway, walk a few paces along the path. Then I sidestep into the shadows between two heartwoods. Wait for a moment. Once I hear the Lord Under's footsteps, retreating, I tiptoe back to the wall and tuck myself beside the newly grown tree.

I draw up the hood of my cloak. Imagine the mist has gathered around me, until I am covered by the darkened pieces of the forest. Hidden from view, I peer through a gap in the broken thorns and watch the Lord Under walk away. His cloak spills out behind him, a trail of shadows.

When I'm certain he is far enough away not to notice me, I slip back out through the gate and follow him.

I avoid the open path, let a thicket of heartwoods hide me. This is the opposite direction from where I ran with Fawn when I first escaped. It's gloomier here, in this part of the world Below. The light ripples as it filters through the trees, and ghost mushrooms glimmer in circles between clusters of ferns. Silver moths dance past, close enough that I feel the brush of their wings.

After a long while, the trees start to thin. Beyond, I see a walled space that's like the ruins where Fawn and I took shelter.

Except that here, at one end, is a flight of stairs that leads upward to a hollowed doorway, framed by two stone pillars. The space beyond is only darkness.

The Lord Under climbs the stairs swiftly, taking them two at a time. At the top, he pauses and glances back at the forest. I duck behind a tree. Hold my breath, listening for the sound of his footsteps. But there is only silence. I wait a moment longer, then carefully peer out from where I've hidden.

He is gone. There are only the stairs, the archway, and the darkness.

I crumple my hands tightly into my skirts. Before I can lose my nerve, I go up the stairs. More vines unfurl as I walk, weaving around the banister and the pillars that flank the archway. Pale, star-shaped flowers bloom between the dark green leaves. They fill the air with a scent so sweet I can almost taste it— syrup and overripe berries and burned sugar.

A tendril of the vine uncurls as I move close, stretches through the air toward me.

The archway looms at the top of the stairs. I put out my hand, reach into the darkness. It feels cold, but I can't tell what lies beyond. I take a deep breath, step forward, and cross into the lightless space on the other side of the door.

The world turns instantly to shadows. They enclose me, an impenetrable darkness. My eyes are open but I can't see anything. Everything narrows to the rasp of my breath, the echo of my heartbeat, the pulse of magic at the center of my palms.

I bite my lip, tasting blood. Tension coils through me. Then, with a sudden flare, the light floods in. A golden hue that I haven't seen, ever, in the world Below.

I stumble forward.

I'm in a field full of flames. A row of pyres burns beneath a clear night sky. There are dozens of them, arranged in a crescent that echoes the moon above. I glance around cautiously, but I don't see the Lord Under, or any of the people who should have come to the field to mourn the dead. Everything past where I stand is blurred, like the opaque surface of water. I can't even feel the heat from the pyres. I'm both here and not here.

Slowly, I step closer to the flames. The bodies are laid out on beds of branches. Their bloodless skin is streaked with veins of darkness. It's the same—the same poison that I saw so often on Rowan. The darkness that veiled him, spilled through him as he became a monster.

This was what Moth meant, when she said their magic had come to the Vair Woods. These people have been poisoned by magic from the world Below.

I shake my head, not wanting to believe this terrible truth. Moth said I'd distracted the Lord Under. That's why they could send magic here, to poison these people. I'm stilled by the cruelty of it; countless lives destroyed in a struggle for power between the gods.

I push back my sleeve, look at the scar left from my trade with Lady Owl. The gods have hurt me and everyone I loved. But I was willing when I came to the altar and called on the Lord Under. I was willing when I offered my breath and my blood and my kisses.

The dead laid out before me never chose this.

I'm so distracted that I almost don't see the Lord Under as he walks between the pyres. Just in time, I slip away, moving into an empty field on the other side of the firelight.

From the dark, I watch him as he comes toward the flames, steps *into* them, sparks rising beneath his feet as his boots crush the coals. His face is all desperate tenderness.

Light glints against the sharp points of his claws. I'm struck by awe and horror as he bends close to the shrouded form on the pyre. Shadows wreathe his fingers as his hands pass gently over the body. It crumbles beneath his touch. Ash drifts into the air. I blink, my eyes stinging, as the flakes settle against my skin and my eyelashes.

The Lord Under gathers something into his arms. A charred bundle of fabric and bone and darkness. A soul.

With the flames at his feet and the night sky at his back, he gleams like a pale moon. Remote and powerful, all stark beauty. The power in my veins gives a muted *pull*, and the golden threads that connected me to the forest Below start to light through the air, extending toward him.

I suck in a breath, command the magic to quiet itself. It starts to dissolve. But the Lord Under pauses. He stares into the darkness, his frosted-over eyes narrowed exactly in my direction. For one endless, helpless moment I'm held captive. Certain he has seen me. I take a slow, faltering step backward, deeper into the field and farther away from the flames.

The spell on my wrist starts to ache. And even though I don't touch the sigil, light starts to rise from my skin. The magic unfurls again, threads trailing loose from my fingers—not toward the pyres and the Lord Under, but away into the distance. To the other side of the field.

The Lord Under hesitates for another moment. Eyes still pinned to the dark. Then he cradles the soul to his chest and turns around, walks away. The light from the flames is a wall between us. I am hidden again. I let out a quiet, relieved sigh.

Out beyond the field, I can see striated shadow: dark on dark, the shapes of endless trees. My heartbeat rises.

The Vair Woods.

The place where I ran as a child with Arien as our village burned, so desperate to keep him safe. Where the Lord Under came to us, two children lost in the woods, and I offered him my very first bargain. It was the moment everything changed. When I gave up my magic in exchange for Arien's life. When I forged the bond that reawakened when I came to Lakesedge.

That night in the woods I took the first step on the path that would lead me . . . here.

I walk away from the flames. Move closer and closer to the forest. The pyres dim behind me, eclipsed by rising darkness. I don't look back. My path to the trees is like instinct—breath through my lungs, the beat of my heart.

Memory snares me when I reach the woods. I was so much younger when I last came here. But the trees still seem enormous as they cut tall and silver against the night. Silent branches, silent sky. It's like stepping back into the world Below. Even though the trees are pale gray, not crimson, and the ground is covered with drifts of golden leaves.

The Vair Woods have that same, hushed stillness. The same feel of secrets and monsters hidden just beyond the shadows.

My fingers curl against my wrist, press down over the sigil. I think of promises made beneath a midwinter moon, promises made on the shore of the lake. I walk into the woods, my skirts a shimmer of spider silk, a crown of branches on my hair.

The trees part, and I'm in a clearing beneath a canopy of branches and starlight. A small fire burns at the center of the grove.

And there, beyond the flames, is Rowan.

Chapter Fourteen

ROWAN

We wait at the border of the Vair Woods. Watch the sun as it sets. The trees here are tall, with branches that swallow the darkening sky. Their crimson-lit outlines reach toward us. Like sharp, clawed hands. Inside the woods, where the light is already gone, the wind stirs with a low, ominous murmur. The whispered words of a secret, a spell.

Thea adjusts the strap of her satchel. With a small, nervous laugh, she says, "I've never gone this far from home before. I guess the farthest I've been was your village, Arien. I could see these woods from the square in Greymere on tithe day."

Arien moves slowly toward the trees. He traces his fingers across a lowered branch. Picks loose a strand of ivy that's woven there. "It's all so familiar." He twists the ivy strand into a knot. "I've dreamed of the Vair Woods so many times. It's strange to actually be here again."

Clover gently touches his shoulder. "Are you all right?"

He nods, gaze fixed on the ivy clasped in his magic-darkened fingers. "I . . . think so."

I take out a sparklight. Touch it to the wick of the lantern I've brought. Hold it up, let the pale glow mark the path ahead. "Come on."

We walk in silence, the four of us. Follow the path as it weaves narrowly through the woods. Arien stays ahead. The light from my lantern casts his shadow against the trees. Behind us, Clover and Thea collect sticks and fallen leaves from the ground. Place them inside Thea's open satchel.

Soon, the path is less defined. Cut by stones and tangled grass. It slants down, uneven. The ground is eroded, carved with deep trenches. We move carefully, eyes on our feet. The air smells like smoke. It's faint. As though there's a bonfire lit, far off beyond the woods.

I picture Leta here. A child, with Arien in her arms. I knew already how fierce she was. The depths of her protectiveness. But now, standing in the place where she faced death and bargained with the Lord Under, I realize how much her life changed when she brought Arien into these woods.

What happened that night has left a mark. On her, and on this place. I can feel it, an echo in the air. A scar on the earth. It's the same way I felt whenever I was near the lake. The darkness left from my own bargain. The memory of where I crossed into the world Below. Alive, dead, alive again.

Arien leads us to the center of a clearing. The ground is bare. The sky above filled with stars. He kneels, his eyes already dark with magic. He's quiet, his shoulders hunched. All of him tensed as he watches the woods. As he *listens* to the forest.

He puts his hands against the earth. "I think this is the place."

I go over and kneel beside him. Take off my gloves, touch the ground. Beneath my palms, the hints of power I felt before are now a steady *pulse*. "Yes," I murmur. "This is right."

I roll back my sleeves, unwind the bandage from my wrist. Arien grimaces when he looks at the sigil. The raw lines of my scars. The inky bruises on my wrists. I can feel the poison. Rising, hungry. Called by the magic in the ground. It spills eagerly beneath my skin, tracking in jagged veins down my arms, across my fingers.

Sighing, Arien pushes his hair back from his face. Then he takes out his pen and the piece of paper with the deconstructed sigils written on it. "I'll try and space them out as far as I can."

He inscribes the spell in careful pieces. A symbol at the center of my palm. A symbol in the crook of my elbow. A row of smaller, arcane marks to connect them. He repeats the pattern on the other side. Then he motions for me to unlace my shirt. I draw the knots loose, tilt back my head. Stare at the branches above as he writes the sigils over my throat and across my collarbones.

Something sharp and shadowed unhooks from me. Presses between my ribs. Slithers with inquisitive languor through my veins. It's both strange and familiar—Arien's magic, Leta's spell, and the left-behind traces of power in the woods.

While Arien works, Clover and Thea make a circle of stones. They pile up the collected leaves and branches. Set them alight. Smoke winds upward in slow tendrils. Turns the air gray. The wood they've gathered is damp. As it burns, the fire smells like dust and death.

Arien takes out a vial of sedative and presses it into my hand. Together, we raise the vial to my mouth. I drink, shuddering at the bitter taste. As soon as I swallow, my body turns heavy. My vision blurs. I take a deep breath. It catches, like there are thorns inside my chest. The darkness of the woods moves toward me. Shadows blotch the edges of the grove.

Clover puts another handful of leaves on the fire. Then she comes to stand beside me. She scrapes aside my hair. Touches the nape of my neck. Her palm is warm with magic. A flicker of heat against my skin.

Magic clouds the air—a mesh of light and shadow. Arien takes hold of my wrist. The sigils he inscribed on me ignite, one by one. It *burns*. A ruthless ache through my whole body. Flakes of ash melt on my tongue. The world turns crimson. The color of sunset, of blood.

Clover's voice is soft beside my ear. "Be careful."

Her words are half plea, half warning.

"I will," I manage.

Then I can't speak anymore.

Pain sparks across my skin. My veins run with fire. I lie down at the center of the clearing. Think of the rumors that have followed my whole, stolen life. *Death touched. Monster.* But it's because I am death touched, because I am monstrous, that I can be here. That I can reach into the dark. Find Leta on the other side.

I stare at the fire. Watch the light fading behind the flames. Arien and Clover and Thea start to blur, then vanish. I slip beneath the spell. My heart clenches. The world stills. I'm alone in the Vair Woods, overtaken by poison and magic.

And then, out in the velvet night, I see a shape.

A shadow, a figure, a girl.

Leta.

She's all dark. Dark lace, dark cloak, dark eyes. Her ember-bright hair is upswept. Caught back by a wreath of branches that she wears like a crown. A drift of wind stirs through the trees. Catches her cloak. It billows behind her, a flash of cobalt lining.

I get to my feet. Take a step forward. Dry leaves crumple beneath my boots. "Leta." Her name spills from me in a ragged whisper. *"Leta."*

She's ethereal in the pale firelight. A creature from one of her stories. A brave maiden. A faerie queen. But the expression on her face is unchanged. The way her eyes widen with fear, with hope. Her bitten lips. The flush rising over her cheeks.

"Are you real?" she asks, all despair and tenderness. "Are you *real*?"

I take another step toward her. Slow, hesitant. Afraid that everything will fracture. "Yes, Leta. I'm real."

She moves forward, and I move forward. Slowly, slowly, I

reach to her. She reaches to me. My hand trembles beside the pale outline of her fingers. Only inches remain between us. But it seems like forever, that moment before we finally touch.

I catch hold of her. The air lights with a sharp rush of power. Leta sighs out a desperate, startled breath—"Oh!"—as I pull her against me. The tether throbs with colors—silver; charcoal; deep, dark green. All of our moods tumbled together. Fear. Despair. Desperation. Hope.

The sigils burn like embers across my skin. The air *glows* with rioting magic. The spell takes hold of me, of Leta. There's a sharp *pull* as the thread unfurls between us, tied from her wrist to mine. It surrounds us with a fierce brightness, pulses in time with our hearts.

I bend to her. Press my lips to the corner of her mouth. Whisper against her skin, words punctuated by kisses. "I've searched for you all this time. Ever since I took you to the altar. Ever since I watched you go into the dark."

She looks up at me. Tears glimmer in her lashes. "And here I am."

I kiss her again. Trace a path down the line of her jaw, the curve of her throat. My fingers circle her wrist. I press against the sigil. She gasps. The spell winds between us, tighter and tighter. But the power—Leta's power—it's *different*. Sharper, colder. A darkness reminiscent of moonless nights, bitter tea. The blackened water of the lake.

It's familiar, and not familiar. I've felt this magic before, but not from her.

Shakily, I draw back. Put my hand against her cheek. She's cold, colder than she's ever felt to me. As I touch her, she shivers.

And then her features *change*.

Her face is covered by a mask, made from bones. Shadows wreath her hands. The branched halo on her hair turns to thorns. Her silvered gaze is a new moon. Impenetrable, blank, depthless.

I stare at her wordlessly. Try to piece together what it means, this strangeness. Her frostbitten skin, her changed power. The way the shadows cling to her—draped over her shoulders, pooled at her feet. "Leta, what have you done?"

Her voice catches, she tries to hold back a sob. "Something very foolish."

"What—What do you mean?"

With a wretched sigh, she drags me close. She kisses me, her mouth painfully cold against mine. She tastes of salt, of tears. The spell-thread tangles around us, and her power rushes over me. It steals my breath, my words, my everything. Poison writhes beneath my skin.

"Leta." I say her name like a vow, a promise made at an altar. "Come home with me."

Her kisses turn fierce—her teeth at my lip, drawing blood. Her fingers drag over my throat, down the open collar of my shirt. Mapping the path of the sigils. I burn everywhere she touches me.

I kiss her back, desperate and feverish. Surrendering to the force of her magic. On my wrists and throat the cuts reopen. The collar of my shirt and the ends of my sleeves are wet and black.

Blood spills from my throat, from my arms, drips between my fingers.

I am death touched. Full of shadows and darkness, a monstrousness that's never left me because I couldn't let it.

I couldn't let her go.

"Stay with me," I whisper again. "Please."

Hands clutched in my bloodied shirt, she gazes up at me. I watch as she shifts from girl to *other*—bones and thorns and shadows—then back again. She goes terribly, wretchedly still. A rush of emotions floods the tether—from Leta, to me. Deeper than fear, fiercer than hurt. A darkness so immense that it feels like drowning.

"No," she says. "No, no, no."

A sound cuts through the air. A sound I can't make sense of. It's a voice but not a voice. Words that are not words. A low, deep, snarl. Filled with bitter, endless *fury*.

I'm caught by horror, like a knife at my throat. It starts to rain, blackened water pouring down through the trees. The darkness beyond the grove turns liquid. It washes toward us, becomes a shape. A sharp-edged silhouette. A pale gaze. Opalescent claws. An antlered crown.

The Lord Under.

So many nights I called his name. I willed him to appear. And now, I see him. Truly see him. A chaos of impossible features. Fanged teeth, cold eyes, a face that won't settle into coherence. Fear scrapes down my spine.

I pull Leta against my chest. Wrap my arms around her protectively. The Lord Under looks at us both. His mouth tilts into a cruel, fanged smile. Recognition lights his face as he nods to me. "Rowan." Then his attention cuts to Leta. "I'm sorry. Have I interrupted you?"

His anger spirals through the grove with brutal cold. The rain freezes to shards of ice, held motionless in the air. Frost crackles over the ground. He raises a hand, shadows pooled at his palm. They ooze down. His hooked claws are an unspoken threat.

But Leta steps toward him, unflinching. She glares, furious, and raises her own hand. Sparks light the air as she gestures toward me and the shadows in the woods. "This is why you didn't want me to come with you. Because you *knew*—"

The Lord Under snarls. His claws cut through the air. The frozen rain scatters around us, daggering at the ground. His shadows rush up. Catch hold of Leta, circle her wrists. His eyes narrow, a fierce, feral gaze. "Chase the ghosts of your past all you want, but there is no escape from death, Violeta."

She cries out as his shadows bind her. The spell-thread draws taut between us. Our emotions snare together until I'm lost in a haze of crimson anger, blackened grief. The magic inside me is wild now. It's all I am, this poison, this darkness. I surge forward, pulled entirely by instinct. My voice is the depths of the lake. The sound of thorns. I bite out each word as I command the Lord Under, "Let. Her. Go."

He turns sharply toward me. There's a wrongness in it— to face death while I am alive. To speak to him. To be *looked at* by him. To hear the sound of his voice as he answers me. "She cannot go back." He lifts his hand, and more strands of shadowed magic spill out from his palm. Snare tighter around Leta. "Show him, Violeta. Show him what you are."

Furiously, she shoves at him. At our feet, the earth splits. Branches spear up from the ground and make a wall of blade-sharp thorns between Leta and the Lord Under. Shadows curl like vines between them. She wrenches herself from his grasp. Turns to me, tears spilling from her eyes.

"I'm sorry," she says wretchedly. "I'm *sorry*."

Leta stares at me with eyes gone black. And I see, for the first time, the full force of her transformed power. It's sun and smoke. A brilliant, terrible confusion of *dark* and *light*. She's no longer a girl but a creature of ink and midnight, lined in gold. As remote and beautiful as the stars. And not human. Not anymore.

She went to the Lord Under. She stepped into the abyss. And the darkness crept back. I'm pinned in place by realization. The true horror of what she's done. All I can do is look at her, the girl I love, gone into the dark and come back changed.

I can't let this be the end. I can't let her be lost.

"Leta," I say. "I love you."

I reach to my wrist. Press down hard against the sigil she marked on me. Pain and power tear through my body, white hot. The deconstructed spell is now a single, conflagrant *blaze*. Leta clutches at my hand. She's pale frost, moss, moth wings.

The light flares brightly, then stutters, then fades. As shadows encircle us, she whispers to me, "And I love you, Rowan."

I take a step forward, unable to see anything except the tether. Tied between us. Like a line from the poem I gave her that took the place of my own words. So I could explain how I felt. How terribly I loved her.

A seal on your heart, a seal on your arm.

Then another strand weaves through the tether. Delicate as spider silk, unbreakable as fibered steel. The Lord Under's magic threads between us.

We stand in the Vair Woods, the three of us. The Lord Under with his shadows clouding the air. Leta with her cold, new magic—the power of the world Below. Me with my blood turned to poison. I am bound to Leta by the spell she cast to save me. She's bound to the Lord Under by her unbreakable promise.

And I am bound to both of them.

The shadows close in; the forest darkens. Piece by piece, Violeta Graceling dissolves into mist. I reach for her, but she's a ghost. She is smoke and ash and flames. She is gone.

The trees rise up. The heat of the fire shimmers in the air. I drag in a desperate breath as the world shifts. Arien kneels beside me, his hand at my wrist, fingers pressed against my pulse.

I shove him away and get to my feet, then stagger forward. Trying to catch those last traces of shadows. To keep hold of the dissolving strands of the tether. But my bloodied fingers clench over empty air. Out beyond the fire there's only the Vair Woods. Lit by flames and moonlight.

"She's gone." My voice sounds wrong, the words choked with bramble vines. "She's gone. *She's gone.*"

Clover takes hold of my shoulders. Stares up at me, her expression fearful. "Rowan. You're—"

In the fire, branches collapse into a crumble of coals. Sparks cascade into the sky. Heat blisters over my face. The world goes white.

I start to cough, feeling the wash of water inside my lungs, my throat, my mouth. My vision shutters. I feel thorns wrapped tightly around me. The magic, the poison, spills through each cut and scar and wound on my skin.

I know that I've changed. I made myself a monster to find Leta. But she is *gone*, and now I can't turn back. There was a line, and I've long since crossed it. I'm so far past that it's invisible.

I'm lost, I'm lost, I'm lost.

Chapter Fifteen

VIOLETA

I find Rowan. I find Rowan in the woods. He is here—really *here*—not a magic-laced vision, not a memory that haunts me like a ghost. This is every dangerous, wretched wish I've allowed myself to have, come true at the center of the Vair Woods. I hardly dared to let it in, this desperate longing, but we are *here*, we are together.

I move to him, reach for him. My magic weaves shadows through the trees, turns the air cold. The tether bright with my new power; it feels *alive*. With the spell-thread tied between us, I fall into his arms.

Rowan slides his fingers over my wrist, presses against the sigil. His moods spill over me in a cascade of colors and emotions. Fierce desire, stark despair, and a hope that is fragile as shattered glass. We are connected—now and forever. A bond that spans life and death and two entire worlds.

He whispers against my skin, words that are all prayer and promise. "Come home with me. Stay with me."

I clutch at him, press close to him. Feel the warmth of his chest, the frantic rhythm of his heartbeat. He is human and here and *mine*.

But then—another thread of magic draws tight around me. Draws me back. I am caught, bound by a power that is not my own. The Lord Under appears. His fury turns the air to ice and his shadows snare around me. I am torn from the woods, from Rowan, from the world where I thought I could never return.

"Let go of me!" I try to pull free, lash out with my own magic. Shards of light cut through the dark as I fight against him. "I want to go back. I want—"

His claws tighten, dig into my arm. He snarls at me, the sound like a whetted blade. *"No."*

We are back at the pyres. A barren field beneath a bone-white moon. All I want is to run back into the woods. To find Rowan again. I start to cry. Hating myself for it, unable to stop. Through a haze of hot, furious tears, I glare at the Lord Under. "All this time, when I wanted to go home, you said it was impossible. But I am *here*. This is *real*. I want to go back. I want to *stay*. Let me go."

In answer, his claws sink deep into my wrist. I cry out, striking him. Sparks of magic flash and burn as my fist pounds his chest. He drags me against him, his pale gaze fixed to mine with unassailable *rage*.

Shadows surge up around us, and everything blurs. The

world beyond the pyre flames—the field, the woods, and Rowan—is lost to the darkness. We travel back across the border in a rapid, nauseating *rush* that steals my breath. I stagger out of the archway, into the world Below, disoriented.

Pain cuts sharply at my wrist, and the spell-thread that tied me to Rowan, so strong only moments before, is silenced. I turn, horrified, and see the doorway to the world Above is sealed over. A blank space of impenetrable stone.

The Lord Under catches hold of me again, pulls me toward the stairs. I stumble after him, fighting with each step. My wrist pinned by his claws, my power lashing through the air around us. When we reach the bottom, he lets me go.

Desperately, I clutch at my aching wrist, the severed spell-thread trailing around me. I reach for Rowan, trying to reforge our shattered connection. The sigil *burns*, and magic spills uncontrollably from my hands. Veins of indigo lace my arms. My new power is a torrent of ice beneath my skin.

"Violeta," the Lord Under says, unflinching. "The past is lost to you. If you can't let it go, you'll be destroyed."

I'm overwhelmed, lost beneath a flood of hurt. The ache of all I've sacrificed—my love, my life, my *family*—is an untended wound. My eyes shutter closed, and I see a barren world where there is only me, alone, forever. Loss and loss and loss.

All I can do is fight to keep hold of the thread, the magic, the last connection I have to Rowan and the world Above.

Shadows rise, torn loose from my hands, and I think of Arien in our cottage room. His terror and the lack of control, his rioting magic. Bruises spread across my skin. Blood pours from my nose. I curl forward, my arms wrapped around my waist.

I hear the Lord Under's voice, sharp as a blade as it cuts through the darkness. "Call your power back."

I bite down, hard, against my tongue. Spit out a mouthful of blood. "I can't."

I won't.

"Call it *back*, before it tears you apart."

My heart pounds with an erratic, frantic rhythm inside my ever-tightening chest. I let out a ragged gasp, struggling to breathe. My power is only hurt and chaos. I'm being destroyed in a fight between magic and memory.

Sobbing, helpless, I close my eyes and picture my power, clasped like a seed between my hands. I think of trees and mist and a quiet forest. A cottage beneath two heartwood trees.

It feels like ruin to push everything else away—all my thoughts of Rowan, of Arien and the lost memories of my family, of the world Above. But I do it. I force them into darkness and think only of *here*.

I start to crumple, catch myself against a nearby heartwood before I can fall. My fingers clench at the roughened bark. I let my head slump forward, lean against the tree. Slowly, slowly, the hurt subsides. The shadows clear. My power resettles, sunk beneath my skin, curled inside my veins. All that is left is a hollowed ache at the center of my chest. A fierce, desperate *grief*.

I open my eyes and look across to the Lord Under. He stands at the base of the stone staircase. Watching me in a way that's scoured clear of all emotion—like a mask he's placed on, deliberately.

I scrub my sleeve across my mouth. Swallow down blood that wells from my bitten tongue. "What else? What else have you *lied* to me about?"

There's a shift, a flicker. His eyes turn cold. He has a soul in his arms, brought from the pyres. Now he turns his attention to it, refolding the shroud over ash and bones. "You have no right to accuse me of lying, Violeta. Not after what you've done. You made me a promise. Then you *used* me, and my magic. With all I've given you—"

"All you've given?" A harsh laugh catches in my throat. "You're the one who used *me*."

He turns away, brushes past me as he goes to the path. I follow him as he carries the soul into the trees. Vines spear up beneath my feet as I walk, a trail of brutally sharp thorns left through the woods behind us.

The Lord Under doesn't answer me. There's no sound except the angry hitch of his breath, the crush of his boots on the undergrowth. He moves swiftly, and I struggle to keep up, pushing my way through the trees. More vines uncoil from my footsteps, the thorns interspersed with crimson roses.

By the time we reach a grove of heartwoods, the air is thickly laced with perfume, so sweet that my throat burns and my head aches. The Lord Under pauses beside a tree that's smaller and newer than the others in the grove. He regards me for a drawn-out moment.

"What you want is impossible." He sighs harshly and turns toward the heartwood. Ready to carve it open for the soul.

I shove past him, put my own hand flat against the trunk. The scar on my heartline throbs and throbs. Fernlike patterns of frost appear on my skin. I swallow, tasting blood. With my eyes locked to his, all challenge, I scrape my blunt nailed, unclawed fingers down the tree.

The bark splits open, baring pale insides. My stomach twists nauseously at the sight of it—the gloss of sap, the naked depths of the heartwood. But I refuse to turn away.

The Lord Under watches me a moment. Then, he steps closer. He offers the soul to me. I feel the balance tilting between us—he's waiting for me to falter, to back down. But I don't. Without hesitation, I take the soul and place it inside the hollow space.

The shards of wood snap together like hungry teeth, piercing through the shroud. The bones and ash within dissolve, wisping the air with colorless smoke. I think of a candle burned out, a trail of soot in the empty air.

As the wound closes over to smooth, crimson bark, there's a small, treacherous part of me that revels in this. The icy rush of magic through my veins, the feeling of strength, of the *more* that I craved when I was just a girl lost in the woods.

But beneath the pride, I am simmering with heated fury.

I turn to the Lord Under so quickly that he's caught by surprise. I push him roughly against the tree. "If what I want is so *impossible*, then why was I able to see Rowan, and speak to him, and *be* with him in the world Above?" I shove at his chest, striking him. "Why did you hide it from me, that our connection stayed beyond death?"

He catches my hands before I can hit him again. "I couldn't predict it would last in this way."

"I want to go back. I want to go *home*."

The Lord Under's magic clouds the air, the darkness of it twinned by the shadows spilling coldly from my own hands. We glare at each other. Matched, power for power, anger for anger. It starts to rain, fast and swift. Pouring down through the trees, making a pool at our feet. The thorn-studded earth turns to blackened mud.

He stares at me, defiant. Jaw sharp, teeth set in a snarl. "Everything I've told you was the truth. You *can't* go back. This is your home. This is your *world*."

He's still against the tree, where I pushed him. I catch hold of his cloak, wind the fabric tight in my fist. I tug at it— insistent—until he bends, until his face is level with mine. The space between us narrows and narrows until it has completely vanished.

His breath hitches, the way the air stirs up before a storm.

And then . . . he kisses me.

At first, I am still. Shocked by the feel of his mouth on mine, impossibly soft. He is so *cold*. Then I knot my fingers tighter in his cloak, and I kiss him back. His lips part, and the softness is gone, replaced by the sharp edge of his teeth.

There's hunger in it now, the way he kisses me. As though

he's starved and I'm something to be devoured. There is no tenderness here, from either of us. It's all bared fangs and bruising touches. His claws on my skin, my hands still gripping his cloak. Shadows surge around us, and I taste the ashen bitterness of my new, dark power.

My hand slides to his waist, my fingers dig in, and I move closer, pushing him harder into the trunk of the heartwood. My lips are at the hollow of his throat. The place where there should be a pulse is quiet and still. He shudders when I kiss him there, and I feel the tremor against my mouth. Then—with a low, rough snarl—he spins me around, so I am the one pressed against the tree.

I can feel the shallow *throb* of the soul inside the heartwood, flickering against my spine. The Lord Under gazes down at me, a conflict of emotion in his eyes. Heat and hunger. Unsettled confusion. Our breath echoes loudly across the incremental space between us.

"Violeta—" he begins.

I think of the promise I made in the ruined grove. To love him, to worship him. Think of all the power he's gained from my hurt and despair. A power that is now *mine*. I rock forward, crush my mouth against his. I catch hold of him with my kisses and my shadows both, let him feel what I've become.

I poisoned myself in the dark for him, and now I *am* poison; I *am* darkness.

He kisses me back, his hands fisted into my skirts, crumpling the lace. His claws press against my bare thigh, and a gasp spills from me. He smothers the sound with his mouth. I wrap my leg around him, and his hand slides down. He touches my knee, traces the curves of the deepest scars that mark my skin.

My back arches, and I let out a tattered breath. The sigil on my wrist starts to beat with a frantic pulse, like a moth caught inside a jar. I put my hand over it, feel the spell grow hot against my palm.

Then I press down.

All of a sudden, the world turns to lilac and dusk. Instead of the Lord Under's claws I feel Rowan's hands. Rough, soft, gentle. The way he touched me when I showed him my scars in the garden, the night I worked my magic for the first time. When I told him the truth of my past—how I'd bargained for Arien's life, how it left his magic darkened, how I blamed myself for all the hurt he had suffered because of that darkness.

And when I cried, and Rowan held me, I realized how much I cared for him, knew how far I'd go to keep him safe.

The Lord Under raises his head and looks at me. He sees my stricken expression and my fingers pressed hard against the sigil. He takes my hand and moves it away from my wrist. The tether turns quiet.

We stare at each other for a moment; then he pushes himself away from me. His breath is rough, his hair tangled. He turns and gazes fixedly at the shadows just beyond where we are standing. "You would have been much less trouble if I'd put your soul into a tree."

"Oh, really?" I wrench my skirts back down. I'm feverish

with a hateful mix of anger and desire. "Maybe remember that next time you want a *vessel* for the Corruption."

My words are sharp, but they come a beat too late to cut him the way I intended. I move to the other side of the grove, where a low, stone wall is set between two heartwoods. I slump against it and try very hard to ignore the kiss-bruised feel of my mouth.

Gradually my heartbeat settles. The rain, still falling, starts to cool the fever from my skin. I wrap my cloak around myself and pull the hood over my hair. Countless impossible wishes rise through me. So hopeless that I can't give them voice. I want to go back to the world Above. I want to be with Rowan.

Shakily, I touch the sigil on my wrist and see the blur of colors behind my closed eyelids. "Answer me honestly. Can I ever return?"

Slowly, the Lord Under walks over and leans against the wall beside me. His expression is troubled. He looks almost . . . *sorry*. "You are not human, Violeta. Not anymore."

My eyes start to fill with more tears, but I fight them back. The truth of it aches. That Rowan and I are bound together by magic that reaches across the worlds, but I'll never be able to find him. I wish I were home with him in the garden and the sunshine, with flowers all around us.

Instead I'm here with a creature of death, and my only home is in the shadows.

"What about the tether, then? The sigils I inscribed on Rowan—the sigils *you* taught me—there's power there, still. I know you felt it when we were in the woods."

He edges a step closer, eyes on my wrist, where the sigil is visible beneath my sleeve. "You and Rowan and I . . . we are all connected. There is power in it, the spell woven between us all. My magic. His despair. Your love. It won't let you go home. But . . . you can use it, to help me. To help this world."

I glare at him, an incredulous laugh caught in my throat. "Why would I *ever* help you again?"

"You saw, tonight, what my sisters did."

A heartbeat passes. I remember a world turned quiet except for the roar of flames. A soul in each pyre, each life stolen by Lady Moth's cruelty. "So, punish them," I snap. "Lock them up, steal their magic, twist their words into an unbreakable bargain. Do all those things you're so good at."

He cuts me an irritated look. "It's not that simple. I am bound by rules. I cannot stand against them in a way that *lasts*. But with your power alongside my own, I can make them answer for this. I need your help."

"No," I correct. "You need *me*."

Slowly, the Lord Under raises his hand to my cheek. His fingers trace the curve of my jaw. "Yes, I need you. I can't do this alone, Violeta." His touch is lulling, careful. He lowers his voice, the words turned to a spell. "This world is yours now, too. Help me keep it safe."

My eyes sink closed, and I lean against his palm. It troubles me, the feel of the balance tilting between us once more. I wanted power to find my way back to Rowan, not to help the Lord Under exact revenge on his sisters.

But I can't escape it, the brutality of what they did. The

200

villagers laid out in the mourning field; their bodies snared by poison. The sister gods, their fight should have been with *me*— not the people in the Vair Woods.

I open my eyes, look up at the Lord Under. "If I agree to this . . . it doesn't mean ~~you~~'re forgiven."

"No," he agrees softly. "I'd not expect your forgiveness to be won so easily."

His hand lingers against my cheek for another moment. Then he steps away from me. "I've more dead to claim from the pyres. I'll walk you home; then I'll go back."

"I don't need to be watched. I can find my own way."

"It isn't you who I'm concerned about." He looks pointedly at my arm, at the scar left by Lady Owl's bite. Visible through the sheer fabric of my sleeve. "I don't want you to encounter my sisters, especially not right now—with what we have planned."

"And what *do* we have planned, exactly?"

"I think, at this moment, the fewer details you have, the better. In case you run into them before we are prepared."

The beginnings of a headache start to bloom across my temples. Sighing heavily, I press my fingers against my forehead. Then I turn my back on the Lord Under and continue walking, doing my best to pretend that he isn't behind me.

The rain falls heavily as we walk through the woods. By the time we pass beneath the thorned archway, the air is so thick with clouds and mist that I can hardly see more than the ground beneath my feet. My cottage is hidden beneath a veil of gray, the trees above dripping with inky water.

We reach my door. The Lord Under pauses for a moment and looks again at the scar on my arm. "Stay inside until I return."

I glower at him. "You can trust me not to get lost in the woods."

"It's not that I don't trust you. The real question, my Violet, is if you trust *me*."

My stomach knots at the sound of the endearment he once used so often. I press my lips together, trying—and failing—to erase the feel of how he kissed me.

He leaves without waiting for my answer. I watch him walk back to the path. The shadowed ends of his cloak bleed into the mist. The trees close around him, and he slips between two heartwoods, disappears into the forest.

I open the door of my cottage and go inside. The fire is still alight, bathing the room in a faint, golden warmth. I sit down on the edge of my bed to unlace my boots. As my fingers work at the laces, I notice how the veins on my wrists have turned starkly blue. One of the many ways I'm marked by this new power.

I have a home. I have magic that can match the gods. I have the strength to keep myself safe. But all I can think of is the tether, the spell, the way it felt to be with Rowan in the Vair Woods.

Safety, like everything else from the Lord Under, comes at a price. And much as I want this, I can't turn away from my past.

Not yet.

Chapter Sixteen

VIOLETA

I take off my boots and my cloak and my dress. Let them fall to a crumpled pile of rain-wet, mud-stained fabric. Barefoot, I cross my room and stand beside the fireplace. I pull the wreath from my hair and hold it out above the flames, picturing the woven branches burned away to ash and smoke. Just like the pyres in the mourning field.

But I can't do it. I can't let go.

With shaking hands, I set the wreath down carefully at the end of my bed. My heart still beats erratically, loud inside my ears. I press my fingers to my wrist, search out my pulse. The rising throb beneath my skin feels like it should belong to someone else. Not to me.

I am dead. And that is all I'll be, forever.

I let my hand slide down my arm. Touch the sigil, still aching with a faded heat. I trace the lines of the spell and close my eyes. Reaching again for the magic that was strung between me and Rowan in the Vair Woods.

But no matter how hard I try, how desperately I *reach*, there's only a soft, distant flicker—like a faded echo.

He's too far away. This is not enough. For all the strength of my new power, I can do nothing to cross the distance between us.

It would be so easy to give up, give in. Except for one, undeniable fact.

That, when I asked the Lord Under about returning to the world Above, he didn't answer me *no*.

He told me I'm no longer human. That he's given me half of all his power. Hidden beneath those words is a veiled truth—about my magic, about our connection. And maybe, if I can find a way to uncover it . . . If I can speak with someone who knows the ways of this brutal world . . .

I think of the lake, how I washed to the shore numbed and windswept after I mended the Corruption. A bone, a branch, a piece of driftwood. How I lay in Rowan's arms as the poison started to devour me. What sacrifice is too much for a chance to go back, to be with him again? Not blurred by dreams or death, not tied by a breakable thread of magic. But *with* him, forever.

I put my hands over my face, let out a ragged sigh. Feel the burn in my lungs as I remember the horrible emptiness, when Lady Fawn stole my breath.

Anything—that's what Rowan traded for his life, and the same word rises easily to my own lips now. I whisper it—a sound that tastes of shadows and pyres and sacrifice.

Slowly, I get to my feet. I go to the chest in the corner and take out a new dress, a dark silver gown with an embroidered sash. I leave my feet bare, let my hair fall loose around my shoulders. At the door, I hesitate, then turn back to pick up the wreath. I place it on my head.

I step out into the woods, closing the door firmly behind me.

Out in my garden, the ferns lie curled against the earth, and the petaled hellebores are folded closed. Everything is asleep beneath the mist-wreathed night.

As I move toward the heartwoods, a trail of vines marks my path from the cottage, leaves and thorns sprung up in each of my footsteps. When I reach the trees, they part for me, trunks reshaping into a scrolled arch that opens to the forest beyond. I step through, slowly, and hear the trees breathe a quiet *sigh*.

The path ahead lights up with clouds of moths. Their wing-beats turn the air silver.

The forest encloses me. Branches bend to stroke my hair, flowers bloom at my feet. When I reach the wall of thorns and pass beneath the tree I grew, the shadows of its branches settle over me like a shawl made from midnight.

Beyond the gate, the forest is quiet. Heavy with a watchful stillness. But as I walk, there is magic—strands of heat and light—that glimmers between me and the woods. An endless, golden web connecting me to the world Below.

I duck under hanging mothlights, move past altars covered by scattered offerings. Slip through shadowed groves filled with whispers. And then the path narrows, and the trees give way to an alcove made of lichen-covered stone. The glassless window reveals a darkened stretch of forest. The icon at the far end shows a pale-haired, antlered creature, too small and delicate to be the Lord Under.

It's the place I came with Lady Fawn. When I thought her just a girl like me, in search of a way through the woods.

I turn toward the listening dark, stretch out my hands. I call to her. "Please. Fawn. I want to talk to you."

There's a hush, a rustle, and the branches above start to stir. Fog drifts through the stones in pale strands, gathering into a shape that swirls like smoke before a figure emerges.

Lady Fawn wears a gown of silver lace with the skirt split to her thigh, and though her feet and shoulders are bare, she doesn't even shiver at the cold. Her eyes, behind the hollows of the mask, travel over me, from the wreath on my hair to the flower-strewn ground.

"Well, well. Look at you. So changed." Her mouth tilts into a sharp-cornered smile. "Tell me: How was your visit to the mourning fields?"

I clench my hands, digging my fingernails against my palms. The crescent scar throbs at the center of my closed fist. "I saw what you and your sisters did. The lives you destroyed. No matter your fight with the Lord Under—or with me—those you killed were blameless."

Unperturbed, she goes to the altar at the far end of the alcove and picks idly through the offerings there. Examining a wilted flower, she asks, "Was that why you've come here, to *scold* me?"

I let my hands fall to my sides, unclench my fists.

Begrudgingly, I shake my head. "No. That wasn't why." I start to pace in a half circle, vines curled beneath my restless footsteps. "I want . . . a truce."

Fawn drops the flower back onto the altar. She turns to face me, eyes narrowing. "Why would I ever agree to that?"

We regard each other, the silence between us turned precarious, filled with danger. I take a step back, press my palms to the wall behind me, trying to ground myself. Ivy unfurls against my hands, trails down to drip greenery over the tumbled stones. "Because," I tell her. "We have a mutual interest."

She folds her arms, leans back against the opposite wall. "Please. Continue."

"You, and your sisters, want me gone from this world. I—I want to leave."

My confession hangs in the air, woven into the mist. Fawn makes a sound beneath her breath, almost a laugh—but too low, too cold.

She moves closer to me, her steps measured, deliberate. "You want to go back to him, that monstrous boy you loved. I know you saw him when you went to the pyres—my border crosses beside the Vair Woods." Her voice lilts, she waves a careless hand. "Truly, you should thank us for what we did to the villagers. It was a good trick, following the Lord Under to gather a soul so you could have that tender reunion."

"It was no *trick*."

She shakes back her hair, her glossy curls rippling in the silver forest light. "Did Rowan even recognize you, when you stepped out from the pyres with your cloak and your crown?"

I dig my fingers into the ivy-covered stones. Trying not to think of Rowan, the awe in his eyes when he saw me in the Vair Woods. The way he kissed me and whispered promises against my skin. All of it feels so close held. A secret I refuse to share.

I turn my face toward the trees. "I'm not discussing him with you."

"What did he see, I wonder, when you came from the pyres? A vision, a shadow, a ghost. A girl who walks at the heels of a god." She waves a hand in the direction of the icon. "That's all you'll ever be to him now. Someone far beyond his world."

"You could never understand what lies between us."

Fawn ignores me. Musingly, she goes on. "Monstrous, beautiful, tortured Lord Sylvanan . . . I expect he loved you even more when he saw you like this—though he might have hated himself for it."

"Enough." I cross the space between us in a heavy stride. We're of the same height, with the jutting antlers of her mask matched by the woven branches on my hair. "You want the balance restored to your world. The rules unbroken. All of that will happen when I am gone."

Her eyes light with sharp, feral hunger. "Or I could just destroy you. My brother isn't here to save you now."

She advances toward me, her teeth bared. But I don't falter back. At my feet, sharp-thorned roses bloom from the earth, spilling crimson petals across the ground. Frost starts to fill the air, making our breath crackle. I feel my power rise, flood through my veins.

I look at Lady Fawn evenly. Shadows wreathe my hands, alongside sparks of light. "I don't need him to save me."

Darkness—my darkness—clouds the air. She pales, taking in what I have become. The power I have claimed that allows me to walk these woods without fear.

Then she starts to laugh. "Oh, Violeta. What have you *done*?"

Apprehension prickles down my spine. I curl my fingers sharply against my palms as my power surges. More shadows slither up from the ground, tangling at Lady Fawn's feet. Her features start to flicker. The bone mask overtakes her face, her antlers sharpen. Her eyes gleam crimson.

I step toward her. Meet her eldritch gaze. "Tell me plainly—is there a way for me to return? Not to the pyres, but forever?"

A smile dances across her fractured mouth. "Not while you are bound to my brother. While you have his power—and his promise—you will never be free."

"So *tell* me," I say, leaning closer, more shadows rising around us. "How do I get free?"

She stares at me, silent. Her face shifts further, fangs curved from her parted lips, a constellation of tiny stars pinpricked across her crimson eyes. "There is only one way to unbind yourself from him. With sacrifice."

The laden meaning in her words sends a shiver through me. The Lord Under and I are connected; we always have been. Ever since the Vair Woods, when I bargained with him to save Arien's life. He is inextricably woven through my entire existence. Even the strength I have now is drawn from him.

I shake my head as though I can escape the horror of it. "To free myself, I should *destroy* him?"

Fawn sighs heavily, gives me a scathing look. "Why are you so loyal? You're nothing to him but another fearful *girl* kneeling at his altar. He'll ruin you, Violeta, the same way he'll ruin our world."

"If he knows you've asked me this, you'll be the one he ruins."

"Hm," she smiles, unbothered. "You'll not tell him. This is the only hope you have to find your way home."

A flare of anger heats my skin, tightens my chest. She's playing with my life as heedlessly as she did with the lives of the villagers near the Vair Woods. With a snarl, I clench my fingers, and my magic winds tighter around her. She makes a choked sound.

I drag her toward me until we're a breath apart. "And I suppose once I've destroyed him, then you will take his place?"

"No," comes a voice from outside the alcove. "*I* will."

The mist stirs, transforming to a cloud of moths. They pour in through the window, filling the air with shimmering wings. Lady Moth strides out of the forest, her dress the color of a waning moon, her frost-blue hair bound with a gossamer veil. She raises a hand, and the moths swoop down to land on her skirts, her veil, her bare arms. Then, with a shiver, they melt away.

My hold on Lady Fawn falters. She pulls loose from my magic and steps lightly back, leaving delicate footprints on the ground. She frowns at me as she brushes a hand over her dress, smoothing the places where my shadows clung.

I look between the two sister gods, an incredulous sound caught in my throat. "You claim the Lord Under has transgressed . . . but you harmed innocent people to prove a point. You want to kill your own brother."

Lady Moth lifts a shoulder in an impassive shrug. "Sometimes the only way to match power is with power. He wouldn't listen to us, so drastic measures were required to get his attention."

"After all you've done, why would I ever entrust this world to you?"

"I *care* for this world. This is the only way to restore the balance." Her eyes narrow. She takes a slow, single step toward me. "This is the only way you can ever be free. Unmake your bond to him, return to your world, and leave me here to rule."

Her countless eyes shift and flicker, the blurred reflection of my own face looking back from the depthless dark of her gaze. I can feel my resolve begin to waver, and I'm filled with undeniable longing. I want to agree. The shape of it—a desperate, wretched *yes*—forms in my mouth.

With effort, I swallow it back. Push down my desperation until it becomes a snare in my chest, a tangled knot. "Leave me alone."

Moth extends a placating hand. The light catches against her claws, and her smile is cold. "We won't wait forever, Violeta."

"I *said*, leave me alone."

I feel the weight of her secret name against my tongue. The world goes still, everything strung tense. But before I can speak, Moth lets her hand drop back. She and Fawn exchange a glance, then they turn slowly and go toward the archway. I watch as they slip out of the alcove and into the forest. They walk away without looking back. Shadows lengthen as they reach the trees. The darkness swallows them whole.

I am left alone, with only the heartwoods and the souls and the rising unsteadiness of my breath. The last flare of my magic fades to shadows at my fingertips, like the smoke from a burned-out candle. I let my head drop forward, closing my eyes against the burn of tears.

The trees bend gently to me through the open ceiling of the alcove, touch my shoulders with their branches. More tears spill free from my eyes. I scrub them away, then give in, too worn down to fight any longer.

I'm so tired. Of cryptic words, of trades, of the cruelty of gods.

With a ragged sigh, I leave the alcove, walk out into the forest. More of the trees bend toward me as I follow the path back through the woods. After a long while, the thorn wall rises in the distance, blurred by my tears.

As I draw close, the heavy shadows beneath the tree at the center of the gate peel loose, gather up into a solid form. The Lord Under watches me approach. There are flakes of ash in his hair. In the half-light of the forest, he's pale and remote, beautiful and terrible.

He frowns at me as I reach him. "I told you to stay in the cottage."

I wipe my face on my sleeve, then push past, walking back through the gate. From over my shoulder, I snap, "If this whole world is my home, then I have the right to go where I wish."

"You are not a prisoner."

He starts to follow me along the path. I spin to face him. "What am I, then, to you?"

The muscles in his jaw tighten. He takes my hand, laces his fingers through mine. Slowly, he leads me over to one of the trees. There's a scar on the bark from where it's been sealed closed—this must be where he's just placed a soul from the mourning field.

He guides my palm flat against the trunk. Beneath my touch, the soul beats softly. It feels calm. Safe.

So far removed from the storm in my own heart.

The Lord Under looks down at our hands, pressed to the heartwood. "You know exactly what you are to me."

"No. I don't."

He stares at the tree a moment longer—then his lashes dip; his voice turns solemn. "I draw strength from remembrance. From the lord who rules the lands Above and makes observance to me at his altar. From all those who fear the shadows. From those who are death touched, marked by me and left alive. Whenever I'm worshipped or feared, it gives me power."

I pull my hand from his, step away from the heartwood. "I'll not *fear* you."

His arm goes around my waist, and he presses close, so the curve of his chest echoes the arch of my spine. He bends down, his mouth against my pulse. His sigh shivers, cold, across my skin. "I want all of you, Violeta. Your hate, your fear, your devotion. I want you to stay with me, and share my power, and rule my world."

He kisses the side of my throat. I feel the press of his teeth, sharp, beneath the softness of the caress. My breath hitches, and I think of myself with claws and shadows. A girl of frost and moonlight and *power*. I would never die. Would never be alone, bereft of the memories of my family while I sleep inside a heartwood tree.

I'd be so far away from Lakesedge. From Arien, from Rowan, from everything in my past that I gave up.

Shaking my head, I step away from the Lord Under. I draw my cloak around me, pointedly tightening the ribbons at my throat. "I am going home now. You don't need to follow me."

"Tomorrow," he says, voice even. "We'll stand against my sisters. We'll right the balance of this world."

I watch him walk away. The sweep of his cloak, the fall of his hair over one shoulder, the way his boots crush heavy prints into the moss-covered path. There are so many ways the Lord Under has wronged me. He's deceived me for his own gain. He gave me death when I asked for life.

And yet, faced with the chance to betray him, to go *home*, all I feel is uncertainty.

Chapter Seventeen

ROWAN

I dream of teeth and claws and darkness. I'm being kissed. Kisses that are in turn soft and sharp. There's a sigh. Leta's sigh. Then another sound. Lower. Colder. Like the wind, deep in midwinter, when it whispers icily across the lake. I should be afraid. Instead, as the claws scrape over my skin, I'm lost in feverish heat. I'm wretched with desire.

My eyes snap open. I'm sprawled out on my back, tangled in bedclothes. My heart is pounding. Sweat beads over my skin. Each time I blink, there are more images from the dream. Teeth. Claws. Kisses. Sighs in the dark.

I stare up at the ceiling, trying to parse out what I saw. What it meant. Soon my longing turns to a knot in my stomach. I feel anxious, trapped. I shove back the bedclothes and sit up.

I'm in a strange room, small and bare. Whitewashed walls, the window covered by a pale curtain. I'm almost certain I've never been here before, but something about this place feels . . . familiar.

The door creaks open. Clover peers inside. Behind her, I catch sight of a narrow hall. The gleam from a stove fire in the room beyond. The scent of woodsmoke drifts in, caught up on her skirts, as she steps into the room. She closes the door behind her. Moves tentatively toward the bed.

"Oh." She presses a hand to her face. "Oh, you're awake."

She starts to check me over. Her fingers mark my pulse, touch the sigils on my arms. I try to speak. My throat feels rough, and the words come out slow, rasped. "How long have I been asleep?"

Clover sits down on the edge of the bed with a sigh. Her hair is tangled, her braid undone. Behind the round frames of her glasses, exhaustion shadows her eyes. "You've been *unconscious* for two days."

"Where are we?"

Brow raised, she glances around the room. "Don't you recognize it?"

I look again, but nothing reveals any clues. There's just the bed I've slept on, another empty frame, and the curtained window. "*Should* I recognize it?"

"We're in Greymere. This is where Arien and Violeta lived before you . . ." Clover trails off, searching for the right phrasing.

"Before I came and ruined their lives? It's okay, you can say it. It's the truth."

She gives me a *look*. "Where they lived when you first met them."

I examine the room again, searching for traces of Leta and Arien. Of the years they spent in this house. At Lakesedge, Leta would leave discarded ribbons, books, and dried flowers, like a faerie trail all through the house. And everywhere that Arien pauses for more than a moment ends up covered by stacks of notebooks, pens, and paintbrushes.

But this cottage—the place they grew up, spent most of their lives—is plain and bare. Only dust and cobwebs.

"Why are we here now?" I ask Clover. "What about Arien—and their mother?"

"Arien was the one who brought us here. We needed somewhere to keep you safe while you recovered."

I start to get up, already tensed with protective ire. "*Ash*," I hiss beneath my breath. Furious with myself. "After all Leta did to keep her brother safe, I've brought him back to the person who hurt him most."

Clover holds out a hand. "Stay there. You need to rest. It's all right, she's gone. The house was empty when we arrived. No one lives here now. Which was lucky, truly. You were a *mess* when we dragged you in."

She gestures to the open collar of my shirt. Alongside the deconstructed spell that lines my chest are newer sigils, marked in Clover's neat hand. They're copies of the original spell Leta cast to hold back the Corruption. Darkness pools beneath the marks, stirring and writhing, in constant motion.

Queasily, I touch one of the inscriptions. A hot, bright flare of pain spikes through me. My chest goes tight. I drag in a labored, thorn-edged breath. Wait for the hurt to settle.

217

It subsides into a dull ache, but the taste of dirt lingers in the back of my throat. With effort, I say, "This doesn't feel the same as Leta's magic."

Clover gives me a pointed look. "Not all of us make trades with the Lord Under for our power. This isn't the same as what Leta did for you. It's a stopgap at best; and it won't last long if you aren't careful."

Warily, I fold back my sleeves. Look at my arms. Stark, black lines radiate out from the sigils. Stretched from my elbows all the way down to my fingertips. I flex my hands. The darkness shifts, uncoils. Spreads beneath my skin with a slow, inquisitive motion.

A wet rasp shudders all the way through my lungs. I start to cough. Clover stares at me, stricken. "It's all right," I manage. "I'm still *me*."

Clover sighs. "Forgive me if I'm not reassured."

She watches me intently until my breath turns vaguely steady. Then she gets to her feet and goes over to the door. "I'll bring you some tea."

Alone, I sink back against the wall. My fingers creep toward the sigil on my wrist. I touch it, slowly. Remembering Clover's warning to *be careful*.

All that happened in the Vair Woods feels like a nightmarish vision. I held Leta in my arms. We were together. I found her, just as I'd promised. But it wasn't enough.

Searchingly, I press the center of the sigil. The space just above my pulse. A spark of power lights through me. For the barest moment, the tether comes awake. Then sharp, sudden pain sears through my chest. Each sigil in the new, fragile web of alchemy on my skin feels like a deep-carved wound.

I let go of my wrist with a stifled cry. My head bows forward. My eyes wince closed. I picture myself with Leta, in the darkness. How she was *changed*. Her dark eyes, her shadowed magic. And how, just before she vanished, another strand of power joined the tether between us.

The Lord Under.

I think of desperate words, spoken into the shadows. Promises made at altars. How the Lord Under has been in my life since he saved me. His presence its own kind of scar, its own kind of poison.

I'm bound to him. Bound to Leta. Bound to them both.

Was that why I dreamed it—kisses and claws, softened heat, caresses that felt like frost? Warmth flushes my cheeks. This connection feels impossibly intimate. Too secret a thing to ever put into words. And even as I fear it . . . I'm drawn by it, too.

With a sigh, I clench my hands into fists. Darkness pools at the center of my palms. A persistent throb that echoes my heartbeat. It aches, thinking of Leta. How the spell-thread wove so tightly between us. How close she was to being *here*.

How, in spite of everything, she is farther away than ever.

The door opens again. Clover comes in, trailed by Thea. She gives me a careful look from behind Clover's shoulder. "Are you feeling better?"

"A little."

I shift to the edge of the bed. Clover passes me the tea she's made. Dryly, she says, "The baseline for *better* is fairly low at the moment."

"Well." Thea laughs softly. "I'm glad you're not dead."

I laugh, too. Drink a tentative mouthful of tea. It's spiced and sweet, made from the leaves that Thea brought. But there's an unmistakable hint of bitterness after I swallow. I can tell it has been dosed with one of Clover's medicines.

I hold the cup between my hands. Trying to hide my reaction to the taste. "So, Thea, has this satisfied your desire for adventure?"

"A little." She smiles, realizing she's echoed my earlier response. "I suppose."

Clover sits down on the bed next to me. Quietly, she asks, "Will you tell us what happened in the woods?"

I take another sip of tea. Put the cup aside. "I saw Leta. And it wasn't a vision. She was *real*. But when I tried to draw her back, it all went—wrong. The Lord Under appeared. He wouldn't let her go."

"Oh," Clover says, helpless. "Rowan, I—"

"It wasn't just him. I don't think she *could*—" I falter, suddenly unable to hear anything except the words he spoke to Leta. *Show him what you are.* Her tearful apology when she revealed her new power to me. I grasp for the words to explain. "Leta is . . . changed."

Clover tugs at the end of her hair, fingers trembling. "Changed how, exactly?"

I shake my head, search for a way to describe how Leta appeared in the woods. A creature of smoke and shadows,

220

cloaked in darkness. "She looked like she should be painted at an altar."

"You mean . . ." Thea swallows nervously. Her hand creeps up, draws a protective line across her chest. "You mean, she looked like a *god*?"

"She is bound to the Lord Under. She has his power; she wore his crown. Her magic felt like death." I watch the horror on their faces as they take this in. "I was close to her—so impossibly close—but it made no difference. She *couldn't* come back."

My vision starts to blacken at the edges. I feel the darkness push against the sigils. Clover watches me, biting her lip. Her eyes shimmer with unshed tears. "Rowan, we can't go on, not like this. You're going to destroy yourself."

"I'm bound to her, Clover. I can't let her go."

She puts her hand on my knee. "Violeta isn't dead. What she is might be . . . *worse*. If we aren't careful, we'll lose you both."

Clover starts to cry. Thea sits beside her, takes her hand. Suddenly the room feels too small. The walls are pressing in. I get to my feet. Pull my sleeves back down to cover my arms. Tie the laces tightly at my cuffs.

I go out into the hall, closing the door behind me.

The rest of the cottage is just as bare as Leta and Arien's old room. In the kitchen, all the furniture is gone. The window lets in a square of faded sunlight. Outside, the leafless branches of an apple tree cast an elongated shadow across the floor. The whole house has been swept clear.

221

At the far end of the cottage is a small, built-on room. With walls of wood instead of plastered stone, and a low, sloped ceiling. It's empty, like the other rooms. But it still carries the scent of varnish and linseed oil.

Arien is inside. He stands by the window. Leaning forward with his elbows against the sill. He looks up when I come in. His eyes are bloodshot, tearstains on his cheeks. With a weary smile, he says, "Mother never allowed us in here. This was her workshop, where she painted the icons."

"I'm sorry," I tell him. "I'm sorry that you had to come back here."

He lifts his shoulder, a tired shrug. "We needed somewhere you could rest. This was the closest place I could think of." Glancing around the room, he moves a hand across his face. "It was late when we came through Greymere, but Clover spoke with the keeper briefly. We—we wanted to know what to expect when we arrived." Arien pauses. He shakes his head, laughing dryly to himself. "Apparently, the week after you took us away, Mother traveled to Anglria. She went to paint icons in the capital."

I go to stand beside him. The window overlooks the fields behind the cottage. A forgotten garden, bordered by a row of leafless cherry trees. I feel so wretched. Unable to think of any way to make this better. "Arien, it was—brave of you, to do all that. Thank you."

He looks at me, then his gaze traces the line of my throat. The new marks holding back the poison. "You don't have to apologize. After what you did, trying to find Leta, I think we're even." Sighing, he turns back to the window. "All the time I lived here, I wanted to run away. But Leta wouldn't leave. At least, not until you showed up. She always said there were worse dangers out in the world. I never thought that Mother felt the same as I did. I guess . . . that once we were gone, she was free."

He says it carelessly, but I can feel the hurt beneath his words. How he blames himself. I'm caught by guilt and anger, remembering the day I first came here. The bruises on Leta's arms. The burns on Arien's hands, and how their mother's delicate features had twisted in fear when she revealed the truth of his power to me. *I've tried to mend him. But there's so much darkness.*

I put my hand on Arien's shoulder. "*Nothing* that happened here was your fault. None of it."

He makes a choked sound, snorting back a laugh. "Are you really *comforting* me, after you showed up and threatened me, so you could use my power?"

I start to laugh, too. "Listen, I'm trying my best."

We stand together for a moment. Then he looks at me, his smile fading. "I heard what you said about Leta. If what you saw is true . . . does that mean she belongs to the Lord Under now?"

"I don't know, Arien."

We exchange a solemn glance. He takes a shuddering breath, then bows forward. Leans against me. With his face buried in my chest, he starts to cry. Sharp, pent-up tears that wrench through him.

I falter, uncertain, then put my arms around his drawn-up

223

shoulders. All I can think about is Elan. He was so angry after our parents died. He knew I'd kept secrets from him. We argued, all the time. Once, we fought so fiercely that he struck me. I let him hit me. Let him hurt me.

Then he cried, and I held him. And I felt exactly as helpless as I do right now.

Clover steps into the room. Her face crumples at the sight of Arien, crying. She comes over to us, quietly. Puts her hand on his shoulder.

We stand together as his tears soften into ragged sobs. Then he draws back, wipes his face on his sleeve. Clover looks at him, eyes dark with sorrow. She lowers her head. Gently, sadly, she says, "I know it hurts to consider this, Arien. But we can't try the spell, not again. It's too dangerous. We have to let her go."

Arien's tearstained cheeks flush bright with anger. "No!" He glares at Clover, then shoves her hand away from him. "I won't burn a pyre and tell everyone Leta is dead. It's not true. She isn't gone, not like that."

"Arien, my love—" Clover begins, but he pushes past her. Storms out of the room. His footsteps echo sharply down the hall.

Clover spreads her hands helplessly as she watches him go. She presses her lips together, fighting not to cry. I've never seen her look so lost. Not even during the worst of our time fighting against the Corruption.

With a rough sigh, I go back into the hall. I reach the kitchen just as Arien rushes outside. The door slams closed behind him.

Thea is by the stove, banking up the fire. Our travel satchels are near the hearth. Already packed for the return journey. She closes the drafts, then looks mournfully at the door that Arien just slammed. "When we go back to the village, I can tell my father that Leta died from an illness," she offers. "That you had a pyre at the estate. Would that be better?"

I can't answer her. We stand in silence. She scrunches her hands in her skirts, her face stricken. "I know you mean well," I manage, finally. "But—" I shake my head, unable to finish.

Arien's cloak—the cloak that once belonged to Elan—is folded beside the satchels. I pick it up, bundle it in my arms. A fleeting memory is dragged to the surface of my mind. Elan, wrapped in the same cloak, the last time we walked to the village with our father. I sigh, push the image away. Turning toward the kitchen door, I go outside.

Away from the closed-in cottage, the Harvestfall air feels cold and sharp. I breathe in deeply. Trying to clear away the scent of dust and linseed oil. The ghosts of those vacant rooms.

The space behind the cottage is almost as tangled and unkept as the garden at Lakesedge. The plants—mostly herbs and vegetables—have either died or gone to seed. Beyond the garden is a line of orchard trees. Bare branches that twist against the clouded sky.

When I step onto the dew-wet grass, I realize I'm still barefoot. I stop to roll up the cuffs of my trousers. Then follow the path left by Arien's boots through the overgrown weeds.

I find him at the edge of the orchard. Where the ground is covered in decaying leaves. I shake out Elan's cloak, drape it across Arien's shoulders. He huddles into it with a sigh. Silent

225

tears drip over his cheeks as he stares past me. Eyes fixed on the distance. "If we let her go, will it stop hurting?"

I want to tell him the grief will soften. That we can find our way out of it. But the words die in my mouth. Instead, with a raw ache, I admit, "No."

I start to pace along the row of trees. Walk to the edge of the orchard. Faint sunlight cuts through the heavy clouds. The field past where we stand is lined with beehives, now dormant in the cold weather. Beyond that, in the distance, I can make out the shadowed line of the Vair Woods.

I touch my wrist, press down. Feel the faint hum of the tether. It isn't gone. I'm still tied to Leta, even with her darkened magic. Her connection to the Lord Under. How *changed* she was when we met in the woods.

And even now, with her lost beneath the shadows, I don't think I can let her go. There's a thread tied from her soul to mine. If I burned a pyre, told everyone she was dead, there would still be a bond between us, deeper than magic.

My fingers trace the lines she marked on my skin. I can hear her voice, the way it changed and softened when she first tried to explain her bond with the Lord Under. Why she asked him for help, despite how patently foolish it was. *He needs me. We are connected.*

Connected.

My hand drops away. I look back at Arien. Poison shivers through me, pushing up against the rows of makeshift spells. Yet for the first time since I can remember, a small spark of *hope* lights inside me. "I know how to find Leta. I know how to bring her back. But I'll need your help."

He looks at me, troubled. "What are you going to do? I don't—I don't want you to keep poisoning yourself. I don't want to give up, but Clover is right. We can't use the spell again."

"No. This isn't about poison. I know another way."

He tugs at his sleeve, hesitating. A flicker of tentative curiosity lights his eyes. "What do you mean?"

"Leta and the Lord Under have been bound together since she met him as a child. That was why she could see him, and speak with him, and walk alive into his world. She summoned him at the altar to make her bargain. They were connected." I push back my sleeve and show him the sigil on my wrist. "Leta and I are connected, too."

Arien bites his lip, his expression darkening. "When you saw her at the pyres, you said she looked like a—" He pauses, unable to put it into words. "She looked like *him*."

"Yes," I confirm, holding back a shiver at the memory of her changed features, lit ethereal by the moonlight. The cold burn of her power in the air. "If we had an altar, then maybe I could reach her. All the other times—at the lake, in the woods—I was trying to find my way to her. But if we do this, she would be drawn to me. I could *summon* her."

It feels so strange to speak the words out loud. But once I do, a surreal calm settles over me. A hush falls between the barren trees. Everything turns still and quiet. In the distance, the shadows from the Vair Woods pool deep against the horizon.

Arien stares down at our feet, which are sunk in the piles of decaying leaves. He nods, slowly. He's resolute. The same way he looked when I told him how I'd help him use his magic, how I wanted him to fight the Corruption. "So," he says, "what do you need me to do?"

"I need you to paint an icon."

Chapter Eighteen

VIOLETA

I walk through the woods, alone in the layered, velvet night. As I pass between the mist-filled trees, I think of the world Above. How the sky would be starless dark, and beneath it, how the lake would be washed black. Like the water was Corrupted again.

My dress is the same color as that kind of night, made of spider silk and tied with a trailing sash. I carry the wreath of branches loosely in my hand.

The Lord Under meets me inside a grove of heartwoods, where a stone arch frames the path to the bone tree. I've spent all night turning over the impossible bargain offered by his sisters. Torn between longing and despair.

I want to go back to the world Above, back to Rowan. But more than anything, I want everyone I love to be *safe*. I've paid so dearly for their protection. I made my bargains, and let the

Corruption devour me, to stop the risk, and the hurt, the cruelty. To bring an end to *exactly* the type of ruin that I saw in the Vair Woods.

If I destroy the Lord Under, let Lady Moth claim all his power, everything I've sacrificed will be undone. Right now, all I can do is help him restore balance in this world. Use my power to keep his sisters from hurting anyone else.

After that . . . perhaps my own path through all of this will be clearer.

Briars rise around my feet as I cross the path to meet him, leaving behind a trail of thorns. The trees bend to me, their branches stroking my hair. The Lord Under watches the forest as it changes, comes alive to my presence. Quietly, he says, "The woods answer to you, now."

I look down. Roses bloom between the vines, their petals as red as blood. I can't tell if he is pleased or disturbed by this evidence of my new power. "Yes. I suppose they do."

He takes a slow step toward me. "You know, you never answered my question." There's a deliberate idleness in his voice, but his hands are clenched, tense, at his sides. "Do you trust me, Violeta?"

I look down at the wreath, still held between my hands. Then, carefully, I place it onto my hair. A slow curl of magic whispers beneath my skin with a coldness that makes me shiver. Beneath the translucent sleeves of my dress, my forearms are traced with darkened veins. Like a leaf, held up against the sky.

I sigh out a cloud of pale frost. "I trust you. If I can't—then what is even left?"

He reaches for me, and his claws mark the curve of my cheek. "Sometimes, you're all I can think of." He laughs, mirthlessly. Then his voice turns low, the words reluctant, as though he doesn't want to admit this but can't stop himself. "For all my power, it feels, sometimes, that I'm the one to be held, spellbound, by you."

Lined in shadows, he gleams pale against the dark, reminding me of the way he looked when I summoned him at the altar, when I knelt and pressed my bloodied hands against the parlor floor.

Cold shadows of magic bloom across my fingertips, and unnamable emotions rise in my chest, sharp and bittersweet. "Maybe that's all I am now. Magic and poison. You mended the girl and left the Corruption."

His claws cast another touch against my cheek. A brief flame of hunger licks through his eyes, then he draws away from me and turns toward the path. "It's time to go."

The air hums with the murmur of souls. More flowers rise from my footsteps as we walk together through the forest. I can see the magic threaded between me and the heartwoods that surround us. Endless threads that burn bright as captured stars.

Once I was awed by the endlessness of this world. Now, I feel so far from the girl who walked into the lake, driven by hope and foolish bravery. Believing that she could visit this world of monsters and leave, unscathed.

The ground slopes upward, and the trees alongside the path shift closer. The crimson trunks and the shadowed places between them take on the look of paneled walls. Like I am in an endless corridor, where I'll walk and walk but never find a door, or a window, or any way out. Then, a gleam of white splits through the gloom. The bone tree emerges, tall and pale, towering above the rest of the forest.

We climb the slope toward it, heartwoods lining either side of our path. Their branches bowed like supplicants. The arched entranceway to the bone tree is closed again, the carved bark sealed over. The altar at its base is lined with unlit candles.

I kneel down and place my hands to the earth. The ground shivers beneath my palms, and black-petaled hellebores bloom around my fingertips. One by one, the candles on the altar spark alight, heat from their flames caressing my face.

The Lord Under stares past me, his gaze fixed on the empty icon frame. "This world was once mine, entire, until my sisters were created. And now, it will be mine again."

His words are such a grim echo of last night, that it's like I'm back in the alcove with Lady Moth again. Her ruthless offer, it's undeniable allure. Slowly, I get back to my feet. Wipe the dirt from my hands onto my skirts. I look, searchingly, at the Lord Under. "You want to *destroy* them."

The silence stretches out, a slow heartbeat between us. Cold apprehension prickles over my skin in a sharp, endless shiver.

Finally, he nods. "I have no choice."

"When I offered to help you, this isn't what I meant. How does their destruction restore balance?"

"Because, after we go to the heart of the tree and speak

232

their names, they will be stripped of their power. They will be turned back to ash, to dust, to the light threaded through the world."

"So this is, what, a redistribution of matter?" An incredulous laugh catches in my throat. I refused to help Lady Moth, yet here I am about to seal her fate in the exact same way.

"If it helps you to think of it as such."

I stare at him, shaking my head. "You've always had their names. You could have stopped them at any time."

The Lord Under presses his hand to the bone tree. The scrollwork pattern begins to shift, and the arched doorway opens at the center of the trunk. He touches my arm, gently, and guides me forward.

As we move past the altar, our bodies cut the candlelight, striping the corridor ahead with pale gold and muted shadows. Then the light fades away, and the corridor turns dim.

"I've never been able to stop my sisters. Not in a way that lasted." He casts an unrepentant look back at me, over his shoulder. Then he pauses, expression softening. "None of this was ever possible without you, Violeta. I told you before that my sisters and I are bound by the rules of our world. To ensure the balance, our power is enough to hurt one another, but not to destroy."

"So, you need my magic, because it isn't bound by the same rules as your own?"

He hesitates, veiled by the paling light. "No. That isn't the only reason."

This feels like a test. A proof of the trust I promised him, outside in the woods. A shiver goes through me, but I swallow it down. "And what," I ask, "was the other reason?"

He turns away, continues to walk forward. I follow him. The corridor opens to a room, a narrow sepulcher made of woven branches. Different from the room we came to last time, where he gave me his power. Countless tiny lights glimmer from high above, like stars shimmering down through branches of the tree.

The quiet between us stretches out, filling the hollow dark as the Lord Under moves toward me. "It isn't your magic I need, Violeta. I need *you*." He takes my hand, presses his thumb to the scar on my palm. Watches, as sparks of light drift up from my fingertips, my magic stirred awake by his touch. "I never thought it possible—to share my power in this way— until now. You are my equal half, my cleaved moon. Together, we have the strength to hold the balance of this entire world."

He looks at me with more tenderness than he's ever shown. Beneath the pale fire of his gaze, I am undone. An ache of loss springs suddenly from the center of my chest. I think of his voice in the parlor, when I first summoned him. *We are connected.* I think of promises made and promises broken. All my choices lined up, a macabre alchemical calculation.

Destruction. Strength. Resurrection.

My magic shifts. Strands of power rise, shadows threaded gold, darkening the air as they curl toward the Lord Under. I draw him close. He raises a hand, traces his claws against my cheek. He's slow, careful. Painstakingly gentle. I'm not sure if he's afraid I'll break, or that *I'll* be the one to break him.

More shadows spill around us as I wind my fingers through the pale silk of his hair. He makes a sound that I feel, midwinter cold, across my skin. I press my toes into the earth, stretch taller, eclipse the final space between us.

I kiss him.

He hesitates a moment, held captive by the press of my mouth against his. Then his hand goes to my hip, his touch alight with held-back longing and tremulous desire. He sighs; a formless sound full of hunger. I drag him against me, feeling the sharp edge of his fanged teeth as his lips part.

Gold shimmers behind my closed eyes, the brightest light I've seen in this shadowed, juniper-dark world. I shiver and shiver and shiver. His claws dig against my waist, pulling me closer to him. The pauses between our kisses turn ragged, filled with things too wretched to put into words.

On my wrist the sigil burns. I slip my fingers under my sleeve and press down. Magic lights my palms, and the world tilts into overlaid images—sunlight and shadow, mist and brilliance. Claws tracing the curve of my ribs, my waist, my hips. And then, a touch that's rasped and rough but still softened, still hopelessly human.

There are monsters, and there are *monsters*: There's a boy who was cursed and a creature who rules the dead. There are razored teeth at my throat and honey-sweet whispers in my ear. Poison and poetry and I am here; I am Below; I am kissing the Lord Under inside the bone tree. I am *there*, at Lakesedge, with Rowan. Curled together beneath an open window, light spilling over us, the room filled by the feverish cadence of our breath.

I don't know if it's the lingering magic from the tether or my own relentless desire, but I feel him, too, I feel him here, I feel them *both*. Rowan—the tender way he touched me, burned onto my skin alongside these new, sharp fingers. The desperate way we kissed as we lay entwined on his narrow bed—like we knew it would only be that once, that last time—lingers over my fresh, bruised mouth.

I release the pressure on the spell, severing the connection. The heat and warmth and memory fade. I'm back in the cold and in the dark. The Lord Under stares down at me. Unnamable emotion clouds in his pale eyes. He sighs, a fragmented breath that casts across my lips.

"I love you, Violeta." He leans close, his mouth against the shell of my ear. "You are going to give me so much power."

I'm halfway lost to his tender confession, to the frostbitten burn of his kisses on my skin. But his words echo over and over in my mind, until they are all I can hear. *Give me, give me, give me.*

I know what I have to do. My only choice.

I shove him back against the wall of the sepulcher. The space is so narrow that it only takes a single, faltering step. He lets out an audible gasp as his back meets the woven branches, and the air clouds with frost. I put my hand flat against his chest. My heart is beating very fast, his not at all.

I whisper a single word. It tastes of ash and mist and the salt of my tears. *"Rvth."*

His eyes widen. He goes instantly, horribly still. "How—"

I press my hand harder against his chest, power uncoiling

236

from my fingers. The tree shudders; the curved pattern on the bark beginning to move. Pale, rootlike tendrils unfold and snake around his wrists, his throat. And then, spears of whitened bones wrench out from the tree, tearing through him.

He doesn't fight. He can't.

"How?" I echo. My mouth tips into a bitter smile. "How do you name a creature who has no name? You give them a name. You speak it deep in your heart, make it real. I've known you. I've loved you. And now, I've named you."

Power rises through me in an eager rush. I crook my fingers, and more of the roots and the bones close around him. But there's no joy in it, this fierce magic. This is the darkest power. This is every memory of my family erased, the blackened scar left where he cut them from my heart. This is Arien's hands, burned by candle flames while I am powerless to help him. This is Rowan, devoured by a darkness that stole everything, consumed his entire life.

The Lord Under tries to reach for me, but his wrist is caught, pierced by a curve of bone. The edges of him start to blur. His features split into an imperceptible confusion. Mouths drawn into fractured snarls, slashes at his throat turned jagged as he gasps, countless eyes that fix me with a cold, relentless glare.

"I offered you power. I offered you a whole world." He fights out stilted breaths. His lips are bitten, bloodied. "What more would you have of me?"

"No more lies."

"I've *never* lied to you, Violeta."

My fingers dig into him, hard against the cold plane of his silent chest. "I want the *truth*."

He bares his teeth. The shadows of my magic are strung between us, tangled around my fingers, pooling at my palms. And even like this—captured and ruined—he looks at me with fierce, unshakable defiance. "If you want the truth, then ask the right questions."

I let the words out slowly, lingering over each one before I speak. "Am I truly dead?"

His mouth tilts into a hard smile. "No. At least . . . not in the way you think."

My heartbeat spikes to a frantic rhythm. I think of my despair when I awoke in the bone tree, learned that my life was forfeit and I was bound to this world. "What have you *done* to me?"

"I saved you. I mended you. And when you awoke and believed yourself to be dead, I realized that if I met the terms of our bargain—the Corruption gone, a home built from the forest—then I could keep you. I wanted you here, and *mine*, so I could draw more strength from you. From your fear, and your heart, and your magic. I couldn't let you go. I knew how much *more* I could be, if you stayed at my side."

"You had no right!" I'm trembling with fury, all my senses lost to solid, depthless *rage*. "All you have ever done is *use* me."

"I needed your power." His lashes dip, gaze faltering as another pale spear of bone cuts through him. "I didn't intend for my feelings toward you to . . . deepen, like this. But the way I healed you meant you were so bound up with my power, and my world, that even after I realized I cared, it was impossible to release you."

"Then tell me," I hiss, my teeth clenched together. "Tell me how to *unbind* myself."

"There is no way. Whatever chance there might have been to undo our connection before, once you claimed a share of my magic . . . it was too late."

The sigils on my arms flare alight. Sparks cascade through the air as I clench my hand to a fist, feel the crescent scar throb painfully at the center of my palm. I dig my feet hard into the ground and pull at the shadows strung between us.

The Lord Under snarls, a terrible sound. Blood paints his teeth as more shards of bone pierce his chest, jutting sharply on either side of my pressing hand.

"I love you, too," I whisper. My confession is an ache, a wound. "But you tricked me. You trapped me. You stole away my *choice*."

We stare at each other in tense, hopeless silence. Then I tighten my hold on the magic again and more of the tree closes over him. A shard knifes through his throat, and he spits out a mouthful of blackened blood.

Shadows fill the sepulcher, blocking out the starlike glimmer of the lights above. The walls start to blur and fade. The whole of the bone tree is lost beneath a shroud of darkness. I am alone, at the center of a night-black void.

And then, far in the distance, a voice begins to speak. It sounds like sunlight and pollen, leaves and honey.

No one god can rule the world Below.

I'm in a corridor. There's a floor with delicately patterned tiles beneath my feet. The walls are paneled with crimson wood. An enormous, open doorway frames a room that is hazed in smoke. The sickly sweet perfume of decaying flowers lies heavily in the air.

The Lady stands beneath the same arched window where I first saw her. She turns toward me, limned in brightness. She feels closer, *realer*, than when I last was here. The weight of her presence turns me silent. This is the awe I felt when I touched the earth and a bright rush of magic spun from my hands, the awe I felt when I first stepped into the world Below.

Violeta. You should not be here.

"I know." All I can do is kneel. I bow my head, put my hands against the tiled floor. A shimmer of warmth passes beneath it, a feeling like breath, like a pulse.

Yet you have the power of death beside your beating, human heart.

There's no condemnation in her golden voice, but a sting of shame burns through me. I look up at her, lift my hands from the floor to show her my upturned palms. "This power is mine. I gave my life for this. The Lord Under brought me into his world, and I took what I had to, so I could survive."

She regards me for a long, drawn-out moment, then she steps down from the dais and moves toward me. The folds of her cloak are like sunset as they float, diaphanous, behind her. Light flickers over the floor as she walks, and flowers bloom under her feet, their stems pushing up between the wooden boards.

The same way the forest changed for me, as I walked through the heartwoods.

The Lady touches beneath my chin with her gold-tipped fingers. Tilts my face upward until our eyes meet. Her gaze is brilliant—stars and firelight—as her smooth, bronze-skinned features shift. A row of eyes, fringed with heavy lashes, blink open down the line of her forehead. Curved, delicate fangs appear when she smiles.

I made your Rvth. I made his sisters. They are—and always have been—creatures unchanging, who thrive on rules and power, with ways that may seem ruthless to a human girl. And yet . . . it's because you were human that you are here. He thought to use you, to bend you to his will, but your humanity has changed him in return.

Her hand cups my cheek as tears spill from my eyes. "Even if he loves me, I have to destroy him. It rights the balance. His life for mine. And then—I can go home."

It is one way to right the balance, yes. A god destroyed, another in his place. But is that truly what you want? Do you think you could return to your human life, with his blood on your hands?

"I—I don't know. What should I do?"

You're the only one who can make that choice, Violeta. What do you see when you look at yourself? You, a girl who loved a god enough to name him?

I stare down at my outspread hands. Then I push back my sleeves and bare my arms. Reveal all the marks left on me, left by what I've done and gained and sacrificed because of the Lord Under.

My wrists, veined with ruinous magic. The scar on my palm, from when I first summoned him to the altar. The sigil he taught me that I used to save Rowan. The scar where he healed Lady Owl's bite. "What will even be left of me, if I don't carve him out?"

There's only one way to find that out for certain.

Her hand draws back, fingers tracing a line of heat across my jaw. The light darkens, piece by piece. Strands of power spill from my opened palms. They're stretched out into the distance where the bone tree stands, towering above the rest of the forest. Where the Lord Under is held captive, imprisoned by my words and my power.

He watches me, his features a portrait of suffering, a blur of eyes and teeth and ink-dark blood smeared across his mouth. He whispers my name. I feel his magic shiver through me. A frost-laced field, a midnight moon, the Vair Woods in the depths of winter.

I picture a thread, thorned and black, wrapped around my hand.

I close it tight in my fist, and I pull.

Chapter Nineteen

ROWAN

At the wayside cottage, halfway between the Vair Woods and Lakesedge Estate, we begin to make the icon frame. It's late. Night laid out under a starless sky. The pale moon swathed by clouds. Rain drums steadily over the thatched roof. Inside, the fire burns low in the hearth.

None of us have slept. We're all wide awake, restless in anticipation of what lies ahead. What will happen once we're back at the estate. When the icon is finished, the altar built.

We left Greymere early, at first light. The cottage, with its door closed and shutters drawn, felt abandoned as soon as we stepped outside. Arien lingered behind as we readied the horses. I watched him from the place where I'd stood last Summerbloom, waiting for him and Leta to come with me.

Head lowered; he pressed one hand to the front wall. Traced his fingers slowly across the line of roughened stone.

He was silent a long while. Then he turned away, to where Clover stood with the reins of their horse in her hand.

"Come on," he said, voice quiet. "Let's go. There's no reason to stay here any longer."

Once we left, he didn't look back. Not even when we reached the woods. Where, behind us, the slope of fields hadn't quite cut across the last view of the cottage. The clouds gathered. Light turning dim as it started to rain. We rode through the trees in silence. Shadows washed the forest as the sun set, and evening lined the path behind us.

Now, at the wayside, we sit in the single room. Crowded close to the hearth. Thea's carpentry tools are spread out on floor, alongside the pieces of wood from her satchel. She frowns, bent over a notebook. Marking out a design for the icon frame.

I hold a cup of tea, dosed with a vial of sedative. The same type Arien used when we first tried the spell beside the lake. The crimson liquid has stained the tea, made it the color of blood. I clasp the cup between my hands. Feel heat across my palms. Drink deeply, swallow down the burn and bitterness. I wait for it to numb me.

I'm overly aware of my heartbeat. The rise and fall of my chest. The movement of the fire. The flickering candle Thea lit, to better see her work.

In the corners of the room, shadows pool like spilled ink. There's a strangeness in the air. Everything feels *sharpened*.

I glance around, look at the others. But they're all fixed on the icon work. Arien, a notebook in his lap, his pen held loosely in one magic-stained hand. Clover, watching Thea as she pieces out a rough shape from scraps of wood.

"Really," Thea says, mouth tilted into a smile. "You're doing me a favor. I should at least *pretend* I wasn't out here with you all. And I can't go home with all my supplies, or my father will be suspicious."

Clover leans toward her. She raises a brow teasingly. "Don't worry, Thea. Your secret is safe with us."

They laugh. Arien rolls his eyes at them.

No one else can feel it. That out beyond the darkness, something is *there*.

Beneath my skin, the poison writhes. Blackened tendrils dip in and out. A shard at my wrist, a band across my thumb. It presses against the wards. Searching, testing. Coiled against the magic that holds it—barely—in check. Trying to find a way through.

I swallow more of the bitter tea. Turn my face to the flames. Feverish sweat beads at my temples, the nape of my neck. I watch Thea as she sharpens her blade. Ready to make notches in the corners of the frame.

In the depths of the fire, a shadow stirs beneath the coals. A shape emerges. Gone by the time I've blinked. I drag a hand through my hair. Move away from the hearth and sit, leaning against the wall.

Arien glances up from his notebook, where he's been leafing through the pages. Examining the sketches he's drawn in between calculations. He frowns at me. Raises a brow in question. I shake my head, stilted. "I'm fine."

He watches me for a moment longer, still frowning. Then, with a sigh, he turns back to his work. He sets aside the notebook. Riffling through his satchel, he takes out a square of blank parchment paper. He spreads it across the hearth. In the light of Thea's candle, bowed forward, he starts to sketch. All of him tensed with focus.

For a long while, the room is quiet except for the scratch of his pen on the page. The scrape of Thea's tools as she starts to carve the wood.

My eyes feel heavy. I put down my cup. Let my head drop back against the wall. Outside the space of firelight, the shadows lengthen. The darkness in the corners of the room has weight behind it. As though whatever magic I touched at the heart of the Vair Woods has clung to me. *Followed* me. And now it waits, watches.

I see more blurred shapes, like the one that arose from the coals. Antlers, woven with vines. Pale, drifting feathers. A moth, with silver wings. And Leta, magic strung around her hands. Her fists clenched, white-knuckled, as she draws the strands of power tighter and tighter.

I close my eyes in a slow blink. Look again to the corner. The ghostlike images are gone. Now there's only the bare floor. A few crumpled leaves, drifted in from outside. A cobweb draped between the walls.

At the hearth, the others are still immersed in work. The icon frame half-carved, a sketch taking shape on Arien's page. I think of the space between *now* and *after*. How we're out in the dark, in this cottage surrounded by barren fields. How I have to hold myself together for another night.

I picture the estate. See it as though staring across a distance. The house, with vines tangled over the walls. The garden, cut by a blackened scar. The lake beyond, water reflecting the clouded moon. And me, bowed at the newly made altar.

There's a rustle of paper. Arien gets to his feet and comes over to sit beside me. Shyly, he holds out the parchment. "What do you think?"

I look down at the page. He's taken the fractured story I told: Leta in the woods, a wreath on her hair, the shadows at her hands. He's captured it perfectly. I'm stilled by it, hardly able to speak. "Arien—" I begin, then falter.

The shifting lantern light turns the smudged, feathery sketch to a figure caught in motion. The curve of Leta's cheek, the tangled fall of her hair. The fierce way she stood against the darkness.

Arien pulls at his sleeve. "It isn't finished. And maybe—" he pauses, bites his lip, then lets out a nervous sigh. "I'm not even a real painter. Maybe the icon won't be right."

I put my hand on his shoulder. Trying to ignore how my fingers tremble. Poison covers each of my knuckles, a heavy band of solid black. Like rings, made of shadow. "I can't think of anyone better for this," I tell Arien. "This is *exactly* right."

He takes the parchment back. Gives me a small, grateful smile. I sit beside him, silent, watch as he adds more details to the image. In the corners of the room, the shadows start to shift again. More of the strange, blurred shapes flicker across my vision.

But I keep my eyes fixed to the page as Arien works. Think only of the altar. My knees on the ground. My head bowed low before this new icon. Leta, reaching out to me. A forest of crimson, mist-covered trees at her back.

Outside, the rain starts to quiet. When I look to the window, the sky is now a stretch of pallid gray. Early dawnlight turns the room to the color of ash. Of smoke.

Thea holds up the finished frame. It's small and square. Carved with a simple linework pattern. The wood unvarnished. On any other altar, it would look too plain. Incomplete. But here, it has the feel of a relic we've found in the forest. Buried under leaves and fallen branches.

"It's perfect," I tell her. "Thank you."

Smiling shyly, Thea wraps the frame in a length of cloth. She places it into my hands. It's like a ritual. The way she holds it out, eyes lowered, expression solemn. "Be safe," she says. "When you summon her."

"I will."

In preoccupied silence, we prepare to leave the wayside. All of us lost in our own thoughts as we move around the room. Arien rolls the parchment carefully. Ties it with a strand of twine leftover from Thea's supplies. We repack the satchels. While Clover goes outside to prepare the horses, I bank the fire. Close the shutters over the single window.

The sun casts pallid streaks over the horizon as we ride along the road. Passing silent fields, the bare earth silver with frost.

Once we reach the forest, we retrace the path we took on the way here. Going in single file on the trail that winds through the woods.

The clouds gather low, the wind bites cold. The air is heavy with the promise of rain. And I can still feel it. That *pull* of darkness. The watchfulness of the shadows. They stretch toward me as we pass beneath the trees. The taste of dirt creeps over my tongue.

We come to the fallen tree. Shadows gather around it, pooled in the hollowed roots. There's a blur, a shiver. A figure appears, outlined in dark against leafless branches. A silhouette, sharp edged.

The Lord Under.

I knot the reins in my hands, grip the edge of my saddle. My heartbeat rises, a rapid pulse loud inside my ears.

He stands as though pinned to the jagged trunk. His head bowed; face hidden by his pale hair. Then, he looks up. Regards me with his fractured gaze. Light cuts through him. He's just an image formed of shadows. A trick of my own, poison-laced mind.

Yet still, we stare at each other. As though this is real. Eyes bloom across his temples. The razored edge of his fanged mouth opens, shapes soundless words.

I clench my jaw, bite my teeth together until I taste blood. I still have the icon frame held in my arms. Now, I pull it close against me, feel the corner of it pressed hard into my ribs.

The image flickers, shivers. Then it fades. The Lord Under— the sinister vision of him—is gone. All that's left behind is the tree. Angular branches, upturned roots. Wood washed over with faded light.

We ride farther through the woods. The path curves, and the fallen tree is lost behind us. But the shape of what I saw lingers. My skin turns cold, and I think of how it felt when the snare of his magic lit up. Wove into the spell that binds me to Leta. How his voice sounded when he spoke to me in the Vair Woods.

A shudder passes over me. Down the line of my chest, the sigils *burn*. An ache that spikes from spell to spell. There's hunger in it now, the way the poison feels. It calls to me, the same way the Corruption once did, when it demanded a tithe. Familiar, though I don't want it to be.

I push it away. Push it aside. Imagine the darkness curled up within me. Asleep, waiting.

After a long while, the forest thins. The wilder woods give way to orchard rows. Overhead, clouds gather. Fading the sunlight until everything is like a dreamscape. One where all color has been leached away.

Everything smells of woodsmoke and earth. The scent reminds me of the Autumndark bonfire. It's drawing closer to the shortest day of the season, when we'll hold the festival. Flames bright at the center of the village square. The moonless sky beyond. It's such a distant, impossible thought. That I'll circle the bonfire stones. That Leta will be there to walk beside me.

When the village comes into sight, we draw away from the path. Shelter beneath a grove of olive trees. Hidden by a screen of branches, we all dismount from our horses. The close-grown leaves shroud everything but a small, half circle of sky.

Arien holds the reins to Thea's pony while she adjusts her satchel, smooths down her cloak. A wayward curl has spiraled loose from her pinned braids.

"Here, let me," Clover reaches to her and tucks it back. "Remember, if anyone asks, you spent a very uneventful few days near Ashengold, mending hive boxes."

Thea lifts her face against where Clover's hand lingers on her cheek. Laughing softly, she says, "And I didn't even get stung once."

Clover smiles shyly as she casts a guarded look toward Thea. "Will you come to the Autumndark bonfire with me? I promise there will be less danger than what happened in the woods."

Thea laughs again, louder this time. "You absolutely can't promise that. But," she quiets, expression turned serious, "I would love to go to the bonfire with you."

They stand together for a moment. Traced by sunlight that has broken fleetingly through the clouds. Thea puts her hand on Clover's waist, draws her close, and kisses her.

Everything stills. For a breath, the darkness loosens its hold on me. I close my eyes, and see pale gold.

Clover and Thea step apart, move back into the shadows. Clover, blushing, adjusts her glasses as she bites her lip against a pleased smile. Thea runs a hand over her hair, rechecking the pins that hold her braids in place.

She tightens her cloak, then collects her reins from Arien. Starts to lead her pony toward the village. When she reaches the main path, she looks back over her shoulder and waves to us. "Good luck!"

We wait, all of us quiet, until she is gone. "We should take the longer way around," Clover says. "So that nobody sees us."

Arien grins at her, one brow arched. "Yes, we wouldn't want to be too close to Thea."

Clover swats at him. "Don't even start."

He spreads his hands, feigning innocence. "I'm not starting anything!"

She flicks her braid over her shoulder. "I thought you might have prepared something poetic about finding love at the heart of danger."

"Sorry. Maybe next time."

We ride the rest of the way through the olive trees, our heads bowed low. Avoiding the branches that overhang the path. Leaves press against me—my shoulders, my cloak, my hair. Once we're past the village, back on the road that will take us the rest of the way through the woods, the promised rain finally starts to fall. Dripping steadily through the trees.

My head starts to ache. A dark, blurred aura slowly closes out my vision, blotch by blotch. Until everything is bordered in shadows. I try to ignore it, but even the hard edge of the frame pressed close to my ribs is not enough to ground me. By the time we reach the estate, I feel so wound tight that I'm about to snap.

I swallow back the taste of blood, of dirt. Take a breath that catches, a vine-tangled sound. I should be afraid of how close to the edge I've come. Instead, I welcome it. I am here, ready to walk into the darkness. One final time.

Lakesedge is silent and still as we come down the drive. A curl of smoke rises from the chimney. There's a lantern burning in the front window. It casts a small glow of light out through the glass, onto the ivy leaves that border the window frame.

The sound of our approach draws Florence from the house. She comes swiftly toward us, eyes widening when she takes in my appearance. "What happened? You look terrible!"

I start to dismount, the frame still held awkwardly against me. She catches my arm, tries to help me. When she feels how feverish I am, she draws back. Her face goes pale, shocked. Her eyes narrow at my throat. Where the line of new sigils is visible above my laced shirt collar.

"I'm all right, Florence."

She shakes her head, aghast. Takes off her cloak and drops it unceremoniously around my shoulders. One hand on my arm, she steers me in the direction of the house.

"This isn't as bad as it looks," Clover calls from the drive, where she stands with the horses. "We have a plan."

"Oh, what a relief," Florence mutters. "I can't wait to hear it."

Arien follows us inside. He closes the door, takes off Elan's cloak. The fabric is now drenched with rainwater. Florence lets me go, takes a step back to examine me again. She frowns,

253

lets out a weary sigh. Then, passing a hand over her hair, she walks ahead, into the kitchen.

Arien lingers behind, the cloak still folded over his arm. He digs through the pockets. Takes out another vial of sedative. In the dim light of where we stand, in the entrance hall, the bloodlike liquid inside the vial is almost black.

He takes the wrapped frame from my arms. Presses the vial into my hand. "Here. Drink this, then go and lie down before you collapse. I'll tell Florence everything."

Chapter Twenty

ROWAN

In my room the hours pass in a blur, filled with nightmarish visions. Fangs and shadows and claws. Thorned darkness. The fragmented outline of the icon Arien drew. Leta, veiled by shadows. A voice that calls to me from a place I cannot reach. *Be in the cold, be in the dark, let yourself be lost.*

When I wake up, I'm burning hot. Drenched in a feverish sweat. I sit up, peel off my filthy shirt, and drop it on the floor. My hair is knotted, strands stuck to my face. I drag my fingers through it, loosening the worst of the tangles. Tie it back with a length of cord.

There's a knock on my door, startling me. I get to my feet. Cross the room, moving unsteadily. Arien is outside. He has a rolled canvas held carefully in one hand. He looks at me and pales. On my bare chest, the poison has clouded into inky pools beneath the sigils. On my hands, another band of solid black marks each finger. This time above my knuckles.

"You look terrible," he says.

"Florence already told me that." I start to laugh, then it becomes a ragged cough. I reach for the finished icon. My fingers are stained with blood. Confused, I touch my throat. Realize the scars there have reopened.

Arien takes hold of my arm. Expression grim, he steers me across the room, over to the washstand. He sets aside the canvas, then pours fresh water into the sink. He dampens a cloth, presses it to my throat with a frustrated exhalation. *"Ash,"* he sighs. "You're a mess."

"Truly, you have no idea." I take the cloth from his hand, lean over the dresser. Elbows against the wood, my forehead to the mirror. We stand together in silence as I hold the cloth against my scars until the bleeding stops. I let out a heavy breath that fogs the mirror glass.

"It's a bit smudged," Arien says, apologetic. It takes me a moment to understand he's talking about the icon. "You're meant to work on it over months. Layer the paint after it dries. But . . . well, you'll see."

I drop the bloodied cloth back into the bowl of water, then start to search through my dresser. I pull out a clean shirt. Fight my way into it, the cloth stuck on my still-wet skin. I tug the laces closed at my collar as I move back across the room. "I'm sure it will be fine. We're not trying to make a shrine to the Lady. This is just . . . *Leta*."

Arien goes quiet as he carefully picks up the rolled canvas from the dresser. The gravity of what we're doing settles on me. The both of us. It's strange how this, after everything—the poison, the visions, that last desperate moment in the Vair Woods—has made it real. The realization that Violeta Graceling, with her scarred knees and uncombed hair, her complete aptitude for disaster, is akin to a—*god*.

Arien looks down at the canvas. He shifts it between his hands. "Where do you think we should put the altar? Not—in the parlor?"

I shake my head at the thought of the closed-up room. The bloodstains on the floor. Picturing the newer icon set in front of the dual altar makes my stomach churn. "No. Not there."

"What about . . ." His eyes drift to the window. The slope above the house, covered with barren trees. My window faces away from the garden, the lake. But I know what he is thinking.

"Yes." I pause. There's a tightness in my chest, and it's hard to speak. "That's a much better place."

Arien waits while I lace my boots. My cloak is still wet from the rain when I put it on. I tighten the buckles close at my throat. Draw the hood up over my hair. We go down the stairs in silence.

Florence and Clover wait in the kitchen. Clover holds the wooden frame Thea made, unwrapped now, in her arms. When we enter the room, Florence comes over to me.

She straightens the collar of my shirt. Tucks a loose strand of hair behind my ear. With her hands on my shoulders, she looks me over. Gaze turned serious. "You're certain you want to do this?"

"Yes, Florence," I say. "I'm certain."

She holds me for a moment longer, then lets me go. I walk out into the garden, followed by the others. The air is laden with heavy fog. Florence has a lantern, but her light does little to cut through the gloom. As we move forward, everything is lost beneath a shroud of white.

It's nearly the end of Harvestfall. Soon it will be half a year since Leta came to Lakesedge. Almost two years since Elan drowned. Longer since the Lord Under called to my mother, in the night. Since I woke and found my father dead on the lakeshore.

And even longer since my own death. When I fell beneath the water. When I made a promise that changed everything.

We cross the path. The mist thins as we reach the garden, slowly unveiling the gate. I locked it, on the day Leta left. But I've kept the key in my pocket. Tied, still, with the ribbon she wore it on, around her neck.

My hands are shaking. It takes me a moment to steady myself. To set the key inside the lock. Then I open the gate and go inside.

Autumn has shaded the rest of the grounds at the estate. But Leta's garden is a world turned gray. Broken branches, leafless stems, snares of bramble. A blackened scar cuts across the barren lawn. And at the very center is a fallen tree. Cleaved almost in half, the trunk stained by the Corruption.

This place is the heart of all I've lost. Where I sat with Leta and watched her work magic for the first time. Where I held her as she cried, and I saw her scars. Where I let myself hope that all I touched would not be ruined.

Where I became a monster who wanted to destroy everything I loved.

Arien brings the canvas forward. Clover helps him place it inside the frame. They set the icon down against the scarred trunk of the fallen tree. Florence puts her lantern beside it. The light from the flame outlines the makeshift altar, the outspread branches above.

"Oh, Arien," Clover gasps, softly awed. "It's so beautiful."

I bite the inside of my cheek. Overcome. Beautiful isn't the word for this strange, dark portrait. The sketch that Arien drew, transformed into a smudged, abstract, *perfect* image.

It's Leta. Outlined in scallops of darkness that might be shadows or might be lace. Like the dress she last wore to our final ritual. Her features are marked pale at the center of the image. The angle of her chin. The curve of her cheek. A wash of darker paint to indicate her downturned gaze. Her hair is a bright flame.

She's a faerie-tale creature. Little more than a dream. But her, still her.

Finally, I manage to speak. "It's perfect, Arien."

He nods, lips pressed together, tears in his eyes. Hesitantly, he touches my arm. "Do you want us to stay?"

"No," I say quickly. "I need to do this alone. Wait out there and I'll—I'll call you in, after."

None of us have spoken it aloud. As though it's a spell that will break if we say the words. *After I've brought her back.*

Florence looks at me, her expression solemn. She places a candle and a sparklight in my hands. Then she puts her arm around Arien's shoulders. I watch them walk back out through the garden. Picking their way carefully over the fractured path.

Clover stays behind for a moment. She glances at the altar. Then turns to me. Stares, levelly, up into my eyes. "I miss her, Rowan. Promise you'll be safe."

"I will."

With a nod, she goes toward the gate. Arms folded around herself against the cold. She gives me a small, encouraging smile. Steps out through the gate. Pulls it closed.

I'm left alone. Everything turns suddenly quiet. I take a breath. Feel the shift and slither of darkness against the sigils.

I place the candle Florence gave me at the altar. Light it carefully. My hand cupped around the wick to shield the flame. Then I get to my feet. Go over to the pomegranate bower.

This is the only part of the garden left untouched by the Corruption. The ground is covered by fallen leaves. But a few golden scraps still cling to the branches. Encircle the last ripe fruit. It's split, bearing crimson seeds. I twist it free from the stem.

Back at the altar, I kneel down. Everything feels so practiced, familiar. But my hands are shaking. I can barely unfold the knife. First I cut the fruit. Then my palm. It isn't a clean wound. The first cut doesn't bleed enough. The second *hurts*.

I should be used to this. I've done it so many times. But no ritual or observance has ever felt so *vital* as this. A spell, a girl, a love drawn out of the dark.

I grit my teeth. Press the blade into my skin. A hiss escapes me. I bite down, bite back the sound. Tears of pain fill my eyes as I drag the knife back and forth across my palm. I cut and cut. Until there's a deep ruin at the center of my hand.

Blackened blood oozes between my fingers.

I take the halved fruit and press it down into the earth. I close my eyes. I know I should say something. A chant, a litany. But no words fit. All I can do is murmur her name. "Violeta. Violeta. *Violeta*."

I say it over and over, until the words are colored. Like they've been painted. Rose, lavender, gold. I feel the hum of the tether between us. It beats in my wrist like a second pulse. I picture myself in the Vair Woods. My hand outstretched toward the trees.

The wind picks up. The altar candle flickers. I hear the sound of the lake, how it washes against the shore. The mist grows heavier. Everything feels soft. Enclosed. Distant.

I put my hand on the altar. Smear my blood across the frame. "Leta, *please*."

At first there's nothing. Only the wind through the empty trees. Frost starts to creep over the ground. The air grows colder and colder. It burns when I breathe. Like ice has formed in the depths of my lungs.

I hear a rustle, like branches parting. A shiver. A sigh.

And then—

My heart catches. The poison surges through me in a sudden rush, spirals free of the sigils that have held it back. I let out a helpless sound. My blood is lake water. The scars on my wrists are open wounds.

I let it come over me. Let it change me.

Maybe I won't find my way back this time. None of that matters. Not in this moment.

All that matters is Leta.

She's here, at the altar. Wreathed in shadows. Staring at me with disbelieving eyes. Her voice, caught on a sob, as she whispers my name. *"Rowan."*

I reach to her with my cut hand. Blood spills between my fingers. I think of all the times I've tried to keep hold of her, but couldn't. I'm darkness. I'm poisoned. I can hardly dare to hope.

Then my hand finds her cheek; I smear blood across her face.

I can touch her. She's *here*.

She turns against my palm. Her lips press my skin. She licks the cut, swallowing down my blood. I shudder, sickened. Filled at the same time by aching, ruinous desire. My whole world narrows to this moment. The rasp of her tongue. The frost of her breath. The sound she makes low in her throat. Yearning, desperate.

I pull her to me. We fall back against the altar. The candle gutters out, and smoke twines through the air in an upward curve. We're caught in a tangle of cloak and hair and hands. Kissing so fiercely that our mouths hardly meet. It's like a fight, full of sharpness and fire. I can feel the frantic beat of her pulse. The frantic beat of her magic.

I capture her face between my hands. Hold her still to kiss her more deeply. Her mouth tastes of my blood, coppery sharp. The tether lights between us. A flare of colors. I see her hope.

Her despair.

Her fear.

She starts to cry, hard. Her sobs stutter between our kisses. I draw back, look at her properly for the first time since she appeared. She's bloodied all over. More than the stain I left on her cheek. Slick with it, her arms crimson to the elbow.

"You're hurt." I run my hands over her. Search for the wound. Dimly, I notice that on my cut palm, the place where she kissed me has healed to a blackened scar. The same as the crescent marked on her own hand, since she summoned the Lord Under.

"It's not—" Her words are lost beneath tears. She takes a ragged breath. "Rowan, it's not my blood."

My confusion shifts to horror. Her depthless sorrow resonates across the tether. Her dress is soaked with blood. The lace on the front clotted. As though she held someone against her while they bled out.

"If it's not yours, then whose is it?" But I don't have to ask.

I know; I know. I saw it in the watchful shadows. In the darkness between hollowed roots and a fallen tree. The silhouette that appeared, blurred and pinned, in the woods. Arms outspread. Head bowed.

The Lord Under.

Leta puts her hands over her face and starts to *wail*. The sound is barely human. A bone-deep, heart-torn cry. It's the sound my mother made the morning they pulled my father from the lake. The sound of ruin.

I stare at her, wordless. I can't even comprehend what this means. What she's done. "Leta, how did you—how did you *kill* a god?"

She shakes her head, crying harder. I put my arms around her. Draw her close. Murmur useless comfort into her tangled hair. "You're safe; you're safe now."

"No," she sobs. "I'm not."

I can feel how frightened she is. Her heart is wild. Magic sparks between us, alight with her terror. I tighten my hold on her. Unsure of everything except that she is here. I've brought her back. And no matter what she's done, I won't *ever* let her go.

"Home," I manage. "Let's go home."

I get to my feet; then help her to stand. Try to lead her through the garden. She walks slowly, her gaze unfocused. I'm almost dragging her as we make our way along the path. When we reach the gate, it creaks open a sliver. Arien steps hesitantly inside.

He pauses a moment. Looks at the both of us. Then he

rushes to Leta and throws his arms around her. "Leta!" He starts to cry. "I thought we'd never see you again."

She doesn't speak. She rests her bloodied face against his shoulder. Stares blankly at the ruined garden with her tear-filled eyes.

Arien takes her hand. Pulls her toward the gate. "Come on. Florence and Clover are waiting for you. We'll go back to the house."

She falters. "Arien, wait."

But he's already gone. Leta grabs for my arm. Her fingers clasp tightly around my wrist. As we step through the gate, out of the garden, the ground heaves, a terrible shudder. Pain spikes at my temples. The sigils marked on my skin burn, fracture. Darkness pours over me. Through me. I start to choke against a tangle of thorns.

I feel Leta's hands on my chest. Then a strange, cold slither across my skin. She scrapes her fingers down the line of my throat, presses hard against the sigils. I cry out. Her touch is so sharp, it feels like she has claws. Blood and bitterness fill my mouth.

Then she pulls me against her. She catches hold of my wrist. Her thumb marks my pulse. The pain softens. The darkness starts to clear. The riot of magic and poison inside my body goes finally *still*.

I open my eyes and look around, confused. The house, the garden . . . everything has gone. Behind us there's no ruined tree or makeshift altar. There's only forest. Endless trees, so tall their branches cover the sky. Bark the color of blood.

"I'm sorry," Leta says, her voice distant. "I can't—I couldn't—"

Arien is a few steps ahead. On a narrow path that winds away into the darkness. "Leta." His voice is low, angrier than I've ever heard him sound. "Leta, what have you *done*?"

Chapter Twenty-One

VIOLETA

I am in the world Above, at the altar where Rowan has summoned me. I see my garden—still marked by the Corruption, but so beautiful that my heart *aches*. The air is all woodsmoke and fallen leaves and steady rain. Clouds veil the sun, but it's bright—so much brighter than the misted sky in the world Below. I am home. I want to stay here, so terribly.

But I can't.

The Lord Under's blood is on my hands, his stolen power in my veins. I've left behind a world unguarded, at the mercy of ruthless gods.

Arien starts to lead me toward the estate. I try to stop him, magic spilling through me in a desperate surge. Before I even realize what I've done, I draw him back with me—Arien and Rowan both—into the world of the dead.

The bone tree is beside us, a pale blur. And I'm overcome

with fear and ruin, remembering the sepulcher that's all thorns and sharded bone. I can't bear it; I can't be here, not now.

I bite the inside of my cheek until it bleeds, dig my nails sharply into my palms. *Not here, not here, not here.* Darkness billows around us, turning the world to striated shadow and pulses of crimson. I'm lost beneath the brutal ache of my new magic.

Then, with a rush, the darkness settles. The bone tree is gone, and we're deeper in the woods, at the center of a heart-wood grove where tangles of new ferns veil the ground. Arien and Rowan stand a slight distance from me, both of them looking around in shocked silence. At the trees, the mist, the covered sky.

Arien drags his gaze from the latticed branches overhead and turns back to me. He's silent a long while, staring in horror at the blood on my dress and on my arms. Then, very slowly, he asks, "Leta is this—the *Below*?"

I nod, all words gone.

Rowan reaches out to me, hand trembling in the air between us, fingers banded dark from the poison. "Why have you brought us here?"

"I didn't mean for this to happen."

He and Arien exchange a wary glance. Arien tugs a hand through his hair. I notice for the first time that it's shorter. He's cut it, and the jagged, uneven curls make him look so much older. "What *did* you mean, then?" he asks, eyes narrowed. Realization settles over him, and his voice wavers, raw with betrayal. "You never wanted to come back."

"Arien, no, it's not—" I falter, stare down helplessly at my bloodied hands. "I can't leave. I—I *can't*."

I turn away from them, fresh tears spilling over my cheeks. With a ragged sigh, Rowan comes toward me. He touches my arm, his thumb casting over the sigil marked on my wrist. "Leta," he says, "what have you done?"

I start to shiver, the rush of power I used to pull him and Arien back now dwindled. Pain spears through me, sharp as needles. I scrunch my hands closed, feel the drying blood on my skin. I'm crying so hard that I can't speak. I'm still in the dark heart of the bone tree with stolen power flooding through my veins. All I can hear are screams.

"I have to stay," I manage, "because no one will be safe if I don't. Not here, and not in the world Above."

Rowan takes my face in his hands and leans close, until our foreheads touch. He's trembling with anger, but when he speaks, his voice is gentle. "Tell me. Tell me everything that's happened."

I don't have words for it. What I've given up, what I've become. But the tether hums between us, so much stronger now. I feel the shift of Rowan's moods as the colors circle from peach to rose to ashen gray. All the conflict he's fought with himself since I walked into the dark.

I close my eyes and let my own emotions be caught by the magic. Let him see everything. All the mistakes I've made, all the pieces of myself I've given up as I've fought my way through the forest. The bargains, the tricks. The favors I owe.

And the end of it—the brutal end—inside the bone tree. "I took everything from the Lord Under. Everything."

"But he is death," Rowan says quietly. "How do you *destroy* death?"

And, with my mouth to his ear, I whisper the terrible truth. "I grew close to him. Close enough to name him and take his power."

Rowan steps away from me. Both he and Arien have turned pale. They already knew what I've become. They built an altar for me, summoned me from the dark. But there's knowing, and there's *knowing*.

Rowan turns his face toward the trees. "It's true, then. You belong to his world now."

His hands are clenched, his eyes closed. I can feel the bright throb of his hurt. And a stranger, newer emotion—envy, green and virulent as the sedative vials in Clover's stillroom. He's trying to push it down, that feeling, so I can't see. But it gleams, unavoidable, even as the darker layers of his shame and guilt wash over it.

"I don't belong here," I tell him, my voice low and sorry. A knot of wretchedness tightens in my chest. "But I've caused an imbalance with what I've done. And I can't leave until I've set things right." I take a deep breath, look between Rowan and Arien. Then haltingly, I try to explain. "There are gods. Other gods, like the Lord Under. I've been trying to find my way home, and I—I bargained with them, so they'd help me."

I push back my sleeve, revealing the hooked scar left by Lady Owl's teeth. Arien leans closer to examine the mark. He shakes his head, struggling to parse out what I've told him. "More gods?"

"They're his—the Lord Under's—sisters. Made to help him tend the souls, when the world Below grew too large for him to care for alone. It's like the world Above. How there's borderlands, each with a lord. The world Below is divided up the same way, with a death god for each place."

His forehead crumples as he takes this in. "More gods," he says again. "*Ash*, Leta. I thought what you did at the ritual was bad enough. But *this* . . . Rowan told me what you gave up, to save us. Our family—your memories of them, and your chance to be with them after you died. Your chance to be with—" His voice chokes. He presses his fist against his mouth. "To be with *me*. Leta, you've sacrificed so much to this world already. It deserves no more from you."

Tears blur my eyes at the fierceness of his words. "I have to fix everything. If I don't mend this imbalance—no one will be safe."

Arien takes a shuddering breath. He glares hotly at me, eyes dark with anger. "Well, we are *not* leaving without you. So tell us how we can help."

I put my hand gently on his shoulder. "You can't be here, Arien. It's too dangerous. Let me take you both home, and then—"

"No!" He folds his arms, defiant. "We will go back together, or not at all."

I pull him into an embrace. He doesn't push me away, but he stands very still, his arms still folded, all of him tensed. I close my eyes, sigh out a slow breath that turns to frost in the air. With an ache in my chest, I force myself to go on. "It isn't just the sister gods, Arien. There's something else—"

Before I can finish, a sharp rush of wind cuts through the air, sudden enough that it shocks me into silence. The light starts to change, turning dark as a bruise. Prickles rise over my arms as the temperature shifts toward freezing. Pale snow begins to fall from the clouded sky, and ice creeps over the ground beneath our feet.

I stare into the space beyond the grove, my heartbeat rising. Rowan moves forward, stands protectively beside me.

"What is it?" he asks. "What can you see?"

The snowflakes start to shimmer, flicker. They become wings, a fluttering cloud of moths that spills out from between the trees.

I raise my hand, and a flare of power ribbons my fingers. I step in front of Arien and Rowan. "Stay back."

More sounds cut through the air, above the noise of wing-beats. The snap of a branch, broken underfoot. A sharp, high laugh. Then Lady Moth walks out of the forest.

Half-hidden in shadows, she's a creature of luminous feathers and pale blue curls, her eyes as depthless as the lake at midnight. She looks us over, her attention pausing on Rowan and Arien in a way that makes my heart beat even faster.

There's danger in the way she moves toward us, unhurried, her mouth hooked into a cruel grin. In her arms, she carries a soul, wrapped in a long, silken shroud.

When she steps into the light, Rowan presses close against

my side. His hand tightens on my waist. "Is she one of the . . . sisters you mentioned?"

Lady Moth smiles at him, fanged and feral. "Lord Sylvanan." She tilts her head in mocking deference. "Allow me to introduce myself. I am Lady Moth, rightful ruler of the world Below."

Her gaze slides slowly toward me. The crescent scar on my palm throbs. The blood on my hands has dried now, making my skin feel armored. I think of the bone tree, of screams, of kisses tasting like death. Magic and darkness. A name that I wrote on my heart. "This is *not* your world to rule," I tell Lady Moth slowly. "There is no place here for you to claim."

She clasps the soul tighter to her chest. Her form shifts, jagged limbs and too-long fingers. The glint of too many teeth in too many mouths. "We had a bargain, Violeta."

"No," I say. "We didn't. I've made you no promise."

"I hoped you would be reasonable." Her expression turns sharp. There's challenge in every line of her body. "Perhaps this will change your mind."

She takes hold of the shroud covering the soul in her arms and pulls it slowly. The silken fabric falls away, revealing what lies beneath. I stumble back, my mouth opening in wordless shock.

There's a boy—*a boy*—caught in her arms. He's pale and still, but unmistakably . . . alive. Flesh and blood and breath, his closed eyes flickering, his chest rising in rapid, shallow movements.

Rowan lets out a ruined, ragged sound. He says a name. A

273

name I first heard cried at night in the dark of a ruined house. "Elan?"

Elan opens his eyes. He looks at Rowan, and his expression changes—numbness giving way to fear. "Rowan?"

His voice is the whisper of the trees, the air through needle-fine branches, the hum of shadows beneath my skin. Rowan takes a step forward. I catch his wrist, holding him still. The tether sears bright between us, a chaos of colors.

Arien clenches his hands, shadows gathered around his fists. He looks to me, waiting for my reaction.

"Let him go." I glare at Lady Moth, the shape of her true name already rising against my tongue. But before I can speak, she sets her claws to Elan's throat.

"I will destroy him, Violeta. If you dare speak my name, I will destroy him."

I force myself not to waver. Take a slow step forward. "Your fight is with me, not him."

Lady Moth strokes Elan's long, dark hair back from his face. He flinches as her claws catch against his cheek. She laughs carelessly. "My fight is with you? Well, if you lay claim to this part of the forest, then he is yours. And I choose to take my fight here."

"You can't harm him," I tell her, swallowing down my rising panic. "You're bound to protect the dead."

"As you can see, he is very much alive." She strokes her hand through Elan's hair again, her magic spilling over him in pale, cobwebbed strands. He makes a frightened noise, struggling against her as the strands start to tighten. "Now, give me what I'm owed."

The magic I claimed from the Lord Under spills through my veins, a rising tide of inky water. I curl my fingers against the cold bloom of power, let it gather at my palms. "I owe you *nothing*. Now let him go."

I raise my hand, but as soon as I move, Lady Moth tightens her hold on Elan. She bares her teeth at me in a vicious snarl. "Do you truly think you can rule in my brother's place? You are a girl, not a god, and this world does not belong to you."

Elan whimpers. He starts to shudder and blur, like he's dissolving into the dark. His eyes roll back. Blood drips from his nose. Streaks of silver twine through his hair, the color being leached away beneath Lady Moth's touch.

Everything moves in a blur. Arien shoves his sleeve to his elbow and quickly scrawls a sigil onto his arm. Shadows unfurl around us. Power burns cold across my skin. Lady Moth growls. Her name is on my tongue, but before I can speak it, her claws tighten against Elan's throat. I slash against her with my magic, sparks filling the air. She falters—teeth bared in a furious hiss—and I pull Elan from her arms.

Her magic uncoils from him in a brutal shudder, leaving behind a welt against his cheek that beads with blood. He falls heavily into my arms. He's cold—so cold. His throat is bruised, his left eye swollen closed. His hair is now almost entirely silver. He twists against me, crying out, "No, no, no!"

"Elan—" I try to hold him still. "Elan, I'm here to help, I—"

We stumble back together, a tangle of limbs. Rowan reaches to Elan, as his brother struggles in my arms. "It's all right, Elan," Rowan says. "It's *me*."

Lady Moth surges forward. I catch her magic against my raised arm before she can hurt Elan again. It snares me tightly, my wrists, my ankles. Her features shift—mouths and eyes and fangs. "You can't protect them, Violeta. A human girl will never rule this world."

I wrench my hand free from her magic, shove my palm against the ground. Leaves and thorns and petals spear up from the earth, cutting through the mud. At the outside of the grove, the heartwoods start to bow toward us, their branches groaning.

"Rowan. Arien." I look toward the trees. "Go, quickly. Take Elan and keep him safe."

They give me a final, desperate glance. Then Rowan gathers Elan up and carries him into the depths of the woods, with Arien behind them, shadows still clouded at his hands.

I take a deep breath. Indigo veins lace up my forearms as I call on more power, call to the forest, asking for protection.

Branches groan and shift. Slender roots pierce through the earth. The heartwoods weave together until they make a barrier between the path and the rest of the woods.

From behind the trees, I can hear Elan, his voice raised and frightened, and the lower tone of Rowan, trying to calm him.

Swiftly, I turn back to Lady Moth. I start to speak her name, but her hand lashes out and grabs my throat. My voice is choked to silence by the snare of her power and the cut of her claws. I struggle furiously as tightening coils wrap around my neck.

My mouth tastes of blood. I start to crumple, my face against the cold, snow-chilled ground. Everything blurs—Elan's frightened voice; the dissolving strands of Arien's shadows; Rowan, calling my name from beyond the trees.

I can't let them be harmed.

I can't fight Lady Moth.

I can't—

So I stop. I let her power wash over me. I feel it. I feel *her*. I feel her willingness to leave a path littered with pain and death if it means saving her world. I feel her cruelty, her ruthlessness, like it's mine.

It *is* mine. I want to pretend what I've done is not as cruel, not as ruthless. But we have both gone to terrible lengths to protect the ones we love.

I let it in, let it fill me. A cloud of moths swarms over me, wings beating against my face. I let her power come, all of it, the full force of her magic, until we're so bound up together, I can hardly tell where I end and she begins.

She bares her teeth. Light gleams over her claws as she raises her hand.

I twist against the magic, spit out a mouthful of blackened blood. Finally, finally, I breathe her name in a snarled whisper. "*Chmah*. Stop."

Moth snarls as the compulsion stills her. Her hold on me loosens, and she falls back as I drag myself up from the ground.

I'm over her, my knees on her shoulders, my hands at her throat, my magic wrapped around her in thick, dark strands.

I want to destroy her. And there's part of me that knows if I do this—steal her power, her breath, her existence—it will be as though I've destroyed myself. But right now, I don't care.

She twists beneath me, fighting against the magic that binds her. Then, in a desperate motion, she tears herself free, leaving a gruesome wound on her arm. She slams her fist into my chest, unleashing a burst of power.

I fall back, my heartbeat gone wild, fighting to breathe, to see, to hold myself together.

Wings fill the air. A cloud of moths encircles us, and then she is gone.

Darkness blotches my vision, and I close my eyes. I think of the heartwoods filled with urgent voices. The field of pyres and the Vair Woods beyond. And the last, desperate sound the Lord Under made as I stole his power, inside the bone tree.

Chapter Twenty-Two

ROWAN

The trees that cage us fall back. I rush forward, out of the grove. Elan held tight against me. Arien runs ahead to where Leta is on the path. She lies curled on her side. Pale and still. Her lips are stained with blood. Arien kneels beside her. Gently, haltingly, touches her arm. She gives a rasping cough. Her lashes flutter, and she sits up with a groan.

Arien helps her to stand. She scrubs her bloodied mouth against her sleeve. "*Ash*," she swears. "*Ash* damn it. Damn the gods. Damn everything."

She steadies herself, one hand at her chest. Her fingers clench in the bloodied fabric of her dress. She's breathing heavily. Her eyes are narrowed at the shadows between the trees. She's tensed; a wary, listening stillness. I listen, too, but the woods have gone silent.

Still, it's inescapable. There are *things* in that darkness. The same things that trailed me from the shadowed corners of the wayside cottage. Watching us. Waiting.

Quietly, I say, "Leta, we need to get out of the woods."

Elan curls against me, whimpering softly. I put my arms tighter around him. His hair has turned completely silver. As though that creature stole all the color with a touch of her claws. When he presses his face to my shoulder, I feel blood, hot. It starts to soak into the cloth of my shirt. I touch my fingers to his cheek, and they come away crimson.

Leta starts to pull at the hem of her dress. Trying, impatiently, to tear off a strip. She makes a frustrated sound when it doesn't tear. Holds out a hand, fingers crooked into a beckoning gesture. "Rowan, do you still have your knife?"

I glare at her, aghast. "You're not using your dress to bandage him. It's filthy."

She sighs heavily. Folds up her skirts and reveals a linen slip beneath. It's still relatively clean. She gives me a pointed look. "Does this meet your approval?"

I take the knife from my pocket, pass it to her. She cuts into her slip. Tears loose a long piece of fabric. It flutters palely as she reaches to Elan. Tries to press the cloth to his cheek. His whole body goes rigid with terror, "Don't *touch* me."

Arien watches the exchange, mouth set in a sympathetic frown. Gently, he takes the cloth from Leta's hand. Holds it out to Elan. "She won't hurt you," he tells my brother.

Elan snatches the cloth with a scowl. Presses it to his face. The pale fabric turns brightly crimson. Arien, brow creased with concern, turns back to Leta. "I know some healing sigils, but my alchemy can't mend something like that. We have to go home. He needs Clover to help him."

Leta folds the knife, passes it back to me. She sighs, her head bowed in resignation. "I have to set things right, first. I can't leave this world to the mercy of creatures like Moth." Her eyes scrunch closed. "Oh, I have ruined *everything*."

The tether darkens. Her fatigue, her despair spills between us in a wash of umber shadows. I put my hand on her cheek. Stroke a questioning arc against her jaw. "Is there somewhere safe we can go?"

Arien lets out an incredulous laugh. "We're in the world of the dead. An actual god just tried to kill us. Where could possibly be safe?"

I expect Leta to answer him teasingly. The way she always does. But instead, she gives us all a serious, dark-eyed look. When she speaks, her voice sounds like frost. "You will always be safe with me. I promise."

She tightens the ribbon on her cloak. Then, squaring her shoulders, she turns to the path that leads into the trees. Gestures for us to follow. We walk behind her, into the woods. The light dims as we move forward. A gloom pinpricked by the flicker of tiny lights. They're silver moths. Captured in jars and strung from the branches.

The trees shift and creak around us. Leaves whisper above our heads. It sounds like voices. Like hidden secrets. Leta stays ahead, her eyes narrowed warily on the shadows between the trees. Her boots leave shallow prints in the soft earth.

And in each place that she steps . . . flowers grow; thin

stemmed and dark petaled. Rising from wherever her feet touch the ground.

I watch as a branch bends to caress her hair. As more of the new flowers brush the train of her skirts. Feeling my gaze on her, she looks over her shoulder at me. In the pale light, her features shimmer. Her cloak spills behind her like silken wings. The crown on her hair is like jagged thorns.

A flood of her emotions comes darkly through the tether. A raw ache. A desperate sorrow. Her lashes dip, and she turns back to the trees. "This way. It isn't much farther."

We go down into a shadowed hollow. The forest presses in, crowding us close together on the path. Icy wind cuts through the shadow spaces between the blood-colored trees. The darkness beyond feels *sharp*. I tighten my hold on Elan, try to suppress a shiver.

This is where I came when I drowned. When I died. This is where I first spoke to the Lord Under. Where I promised him *anything* in exchange for my life.

It's haunting. Terrible. And conflictingly, undeniably beautiful.

Our path ends at a wall of brambles. It reaches, unbroken, through the woods on either side of us. The only way past is a jagged arch where the thorns are bent back. A tree grows at the center. The ground beneath it looks charred.

Leta gathers up her skirts and steps carefully through the archway. We follow her. Once we're through, she drops to one knee. Presses her palm against the ground. The vines on the wall start to move. Weave tightly across the opening, until the wall is completely solid. The space now blocked with fresh, thorn-edged tendrils.

Arien touches one of the vines. He sounds both impressed and nervous when he asks, "Did you make all of this, Leta?"

"Um." She hedges. "Not all of it." She turns toward the path. "I'll explain later."

On the other side of the wall, the air is dark. Heavy with fog. A path curves through the trees. Slopes downward into a darkened hollow. We follow it past candles and moths. Past glowing mushrooms and hollowed roots. Then, we step out into . . . a garden.

It's like the garden—Leta's garden—at Lakesedge. But a mirror image, set in reverse. Dark instead of light. Silver leaves, groves of ferns. Flowers the colors of a bruise. A vine weaves through it, prickled by thorns that are serrated as knives.

And beyond the thorns is a cottage. Shaped from the forest, with crimson walls and a branch-thatched roof. Seeing it fills me with a painful emotion that I can't name.

"This is my—" Leta hesitates over the word. Arien and I exchange a glance. "Where I live."

She opens the door. We all go quickly inside. Leta draws the latch, closes the shutters. The single room is lit by a fire. It burns dimly, low in the hearth. There's an unmade bed. A line of polished stones on the windowsill. An open chest piled untidily with dresses.

It's so much like Leta's room back at our house. And after the strange, replicated garden outside, the sight of this space—so familiar, so clearly *lived* in—sends a fresh wave of unwelcome envy through me. Irritated with myself, I try to hide how I feel. But it sings along the tether. Leta looks at me. Her cheeks are flushed. Our eyes meet, but I turn away quickly.

I help Elan over to the bed. He sinks down. Keeps the torn strip of cloth pressed to his face. Leta watches us for a moment, biting her lip. She wipes her bloodied hands against her skirts. Motions to another door on the opposite side of the room. It leads into a small alcove. "Let me . . . clean up. Then I'll see what I can do about that cut."

She collects a new dress from the chest. Goes across the room, shedding the outer layers of her clothes as she walks. Her cloak, her boots, her socks. She goes into the alcove. Closes the door behind her.

I pick up her boots, pair them neatly. Drape her cloak over a chair near the hearth. On the shelf above the fireplace there are rows of jars filled with dried flowers. I stare at them for a long time. "It's like the tea from our stillroom."

Arien raises a brow at me. "You're angry with her."

I pick up Leta's discarded socks. Hang them beside the cloak. "Aren't you?"

"I have plenty of reasons to be angry with her. But this isn't one of them. Would you prefer her to be out in the forest, in the cold?"

"Of course not."

He folds his arms. "It doesn't sound that way."

"I'm not sorry she's been safe, Arien. Safe or . . . whatever this is."

With a frustrated exhalation, he pulls out one of the chairs and sits down. He slumps forward, arms folded against the table. "I want her to come home. How is she even going to *set things right* with that . . . Moth creature?"

I drag a hand over my hair. Sigh heavily. The fight, Leta and that creature whom she called *Lady Moth*, is a blur of impossible horror. Elan, snared by magic, claws at his throat. The sister god, with her rows of fanged teeth. Her immense, liquid eyes. The frostbitten shiver of her voice.

"I don't know. But after what we just saw, I think—" I shake my head, hating to admit it. All I want is to be *gone* from here. "This doesn't feel like a situation we can leave behind."

I sit on the bed next to Elan. He's been quiet since we came inside. But now he offers me a wary smile. I put out a tentative hand. Touch his arm. Curl my fingers tightly in the fabric of his sleeve.

Almost two years have passed since he drowned. His jaw is sharper. His hair is longer. He's only the faintest, dry-leaf echo of the memories that filled my nightmares.

But it's him. It's truly him. Solid and *real*, beside me.

He looks me over with equal disbelief. As he takes in my changed appearance—the sigil marks, my new scars, the lines beneath my skin—his expression falters. He presses a questing fingertip to the inside of my arm. The poison starts to stir and shift. His eyes widen, but he doesn't pull away.

Then he starts to cry. He bows his head, the cloth still clutched to his face. His unwounded eye closes against the tears. He whispers, so quiet I can hardly hear him, "I'm sorry, Rowan."

"No, Elan. You—" I falter, overcome by a rush of grief and guilt. All the pain I've held inside me since I watched him drown. "You haven't done anything to be sorry for."

He gives me a beseeching look. "That night I followed you to the lake, I wanted to help. I knew something was wrong. I knew you were hurting. I thought maybe I could . . ." He trails off, more tears spilling over his cheeks. "Instead, I made it all worse."

I think again of that terrible night. The knife at my wrist. The ground, all starveling magic. The fatal moment when Elan stepped onto the shore. How the Corruption held me, *changed* me, so that when he sank beneath the waves, I was *pleased*.

I start to cry, too. Sharp, painful sobs, impossible to hold back. "None of it was your fault," I tell him fiercely. "*I'm* sorry, Elan. I couldn't save our parents. I couldn't save you. I couldn't even stop you being hurt again, before. Please . . . don't ever, *ever*, think I would blame you for what happened."

He throws himself against me. Buries his head into my shoulder. "I want to come back," he says, a rasped whisper. "I want to stay with you."

"Whatever happens, you will be safe." I hold the word in my mouth like a prayer. *Safe*. "I'll not let anything harm you again. None of us will."

He nods, lips pressed together. I close my eyes. Rest my face against his hair. We sit together until our tears soften into an unsteady silence.

So many nights I woke to a sound or movement in the shadows. Certain it was him. I'd call out, desperate for him to stay.

But the sounds always faded. The light changed. He was lost. Dead and drowned.

And yet I have him alive, in my arms.

The door on the other side of the room opens, and Leta comes back out. She's scrubbed the blood from her hands and face. Her hair is loose, the strange halo of branches gone. She crosses the room toward us, buttoning her clean dress. Through the loose, gauzy sleeves, I can see the new mark on her arm. The strange black scar that joins the sigil.

She crouches down beside Elan, kneels at his feet. They regard each other for a long moment. Then, nervously, he asks, "Are you going to make me go back inside the tree?"

Leta takes a scrap of ribbon from her pocket. Ties her hair into a loose braid. Then she reaches toward him. Power flickers at her hands, wisps of grayish smoke. He pales and goes very still.

"I'm not going to *make* you do anything, Elan." Her fingers cast gently over his throat, then his wrist. Marking his pulse. More of the strange, bluish veins rise across her forearms as she examines him. "You're not dead anymore. What happens from now on is your choice."

There's a note of veiled anger in her voice. Turned inward, as though she is upset with herself. Her hands curl closed. Her magic dims. Elan glances at me. Then slowly, softly, he says, "I want to go home."

Leta nods. But all I feel from her, through the tether, is sorrow. She takes the cloth from Elan. My stomach clenches when I see the wound on his face. A deep, brutal cut from temple to jaw; it carves deeply across the corner of his eye. His lashes are matted with blood. His iris has turned crimson.

I drag in a breath. Resolved that those creatures in the woods will *never* harm my brother again. No matter what I have to do, I will protect him.

"I will make sure you go home," Leta tells Elan. "But I have to mend you first."

Arien gives her a wary look. "*You* can mend him?"

"I think so."

"What do you mean, *you think*? Shouldn't you be a little more certain?"

"I've not used my power to mend before, but I've had it done to me." She pushes back her sleeve and shows us her arm. The new scar she revealed when we first arrived in the woods. Now, I notice that it's healed black. Like the cut on my own hand, where she licked away my blood. "I can heal you, Elan. It—it will hurt, though."

Elan touches the cut on his cheek. He blinks. A trail of blackened blood oozes from his eye. "It already hurts."

"And there's one more thing." Her lashes dip. She stares down at her hands, fingers pressed against the scar on her palm. "I'll need you to trade with me."

I turn to her, appalled. "He's not going to *bargain* with you, Leta. How can you even ask that?"

"That's how it works. I don't make the rules."

Again, I catch a flicker of her well-deep sorrow from across the tether.

"I'll trade," Elan says quietly. "I just—I don't know what I can give you."

Leta settles herself closer to him. Her fingers stray to the end of her braid. She falls into a thoughtful silence. "I want a memory. I want your memory from when Moth brought you back."

He nods, shoulders drawn up in determination. "I can try."

Leta puts her hands on either side of Elan's face. The veins that lace her skin begin to darken. He shivers. "You're cold."

"Always." She cups her hands against her mouth. Breathes into them before touching him again. "Is that better?"

He grimaces. "Worse."

"At least she washed off the blood, first," Arien offers.

Elan laughs. "I guess that's an improvement, then."

Leta shakes her head at them both. She makes a show of rubbing her hands together to try to warm them before she continues.

Her eyes change. Not the pale gold from when she used her alchemy in the rituals. But a shimmering, moonlike silver. Shadows slither out from her hands. Her magic, as it wraps around Elan, is the color of night, streaked through with gold.

"Tell me," she says. "Tell me what you remember."

Haltingly, Elan begins to speak. "I was in the dark. Then she was there, the one you called Moth. But she wasn't alone. There were two others with her."

More shadows cloud the air. Elan tries to pull away, but Leta tightens her hold. "And then what did you see?"

"One of them had feathers. And eyes, so many eyes. She took out a knife and cut her wrist. One had antlers, and her face was all bone. She breathed out, and everything turned to frost. And I was—" He makes a sharp, hurt noise. "Please, I can't—"

Leta, teeth clenched, sends more of her magic over Elan. Her fingers flex, pressing hard against his skin. Her voice turns low and cold. "Keep going."

Elan bites back another cry. Scrunches his hands into the bedclothes until his knuckles go white. I pin my own hands between my knees. All I want to do is stop this, stop Leta. But I force myself to keep still. Watch her heal him. Watch her hurt him.

"They gave their breath and blood to the tree, and I was alive. Lady Moth, she caught me. I tried to get away, but I couldn't. I—"

The wounds on his face start to knit closed. Flesh drawn together by strands of magic. And as Leta finishes the spell, she starts to change. The air around her shivers. Her features blur. Between one blink and the next, she is no longer a girl but something entirely . . . *other*.

And then—I notice Leta's face. How her expression is almost a mirror image of Elan's, as he tries not to cry out in pain. She's terribly pale, and her breath comes out in sharp, fractured gasps.

It hurts Elan, this power. And it hurts her, too.

Finally, with a ragged sound, she releases my brother. The thick strands of her magic start to loosen. They drift apart, trailing into the air like smoke until they completely dissolve.

Elan slumps down onto the bed, curls up on his side. The new scar cuts blackly over his cheekbone. And his eyes are changed. The wounded one turned pure black, instead of golden brown. The same way Arien's eyes look when he uses alchemy.

I help him tuck the blanket tighter around himself. "You were very brave."

He glares at me. "I'm not going to say thank you. That *hurt*." He touches his cheek. Traces over the scars. His voice softens. "I guess we'll match."

I touch my own face. The marks on my brow, the edge of my mouth. "I guess we will."

A sudden bright shard of pain resonates through the tether. I look at Leta. She's so pale; the scant freckles on her cheeks standing out against her skin. Her arms are wrapped tightly around her waist. Like her stomach hurts. I reach for her, but she brushes past me. Moving toward the front door.

"Excuse me." Her voice wavers, like she's trying not to cry. "I'll be back in a moment."

The latch scrapes, and a flood of grayish light washes in from the forest. Then she closes the door, and we're back in firelit darkness. I get to my feet. Call over my shoulder to Arien and Elan as I cross the room. "Wait here."

They exchange a glance, and Arien snorts to Elan, "Where does he think we would go?"

Outside, the forest is watchful and still. Mist streaks low over the shadowed ground. Leta is a few paces away from the cottage, in a grove of ferns. Her head is bowed forward. Her hand pressed to her mouth.

I go to her, pull her into my arms. She sinks against me, and I stroke my hand over her hair. She's silent a long while, her face pressed to my shoulder as she fights back tears. She starts to move away, but I take hold of her hand. Reluctant to let her go.

In the faded forest light, she looks blurred and unreal. As frighteningly powerful as the creature she fought in the woods.

"The Lord Under and I—we were to rule this world. Together." She hesitates, then goes on. "He loved me."

I stroke my thumb against her palm. Her skin is so cold. I want to let the silence stay, filled by unsaid things. But though it hurts, I don't want her to have to lie, or hide from the truth of how she felt. Gently, I say, "You loved him, too."

She starts to shake her head. Then she turns her face from me, a flush of shame on her pale cheeks. "You must think me wretched, to care for someone so cruel. I don't care what he did to me. But he hurt you so much. He fed on your pain and your fear. And still, I loved him, even as I loved you." She starts to cry, the tears falling so fast that she can't hold them back. "He's been there ever since he held my hand through the Vair Woods. He's had my heart, always. You *both* do."

For a moment, I'm unable to speak or move. But I've always known. Their bond, their connection. I felt it in the Vair Woods. I felt it in my dreams. I am *part* of it now, and perhaps I always have been. I'm bound to him, too.

I put my hand on Leta's cheek, draw her back to whisper softly against her skin. "Leta. I—I understand. Your love isn't a thing I want to cage. Your heart is your own."

"I love him. And I love you." Sadness resonates from her, gray and bleak. "I made him a promise when I was saved from the Corruption. I know that it hurt you all, how I left. Giving myself up seemed like the only choice I had. But I never intended to stay in this world. All this time . . . whenever I felt you out there in the dark, all I wanted was to come home."

She moves toward me, steps into my arms. She holds on to me as though I'm about to disappear. I weave my fingers into her tangled hair. I start to tremble. Full of a fierce, unnamable tenderness.

I think of a midsummer night. An orchard. The scent of bonfire smoke. How I held her as she promised I would never lose her. I want, so badly, to believe that still. Even here, in the world of the dead.

I bend to her, graze my lips over hers. Almost expecting her to vanish beneath my touch. She sighs against my mouth. Her eyes sink closed. I feel the brush of her lashes on my cheek. I kiss a path from her jaw to the hollow of her throat. Her skin tastes of incense. Her hair smells of smoke. It makes me think of an altar.

I take her face between my hands. Lean down slowly, until my forehead rests against hers. "I love you, Violeta. What needs to be done with the other gods, to allow you to leave . . . we will help you. We'll find a way to make things right."

"No." She shakes her head, trying to pull away. "You don't understand. It's impossible."

"Tell me, Leta. What have you done?"

She gazes up at me, her eyes still silvered with remnants of the magic she cast. Ivy trails down from the branches above. Tangles around us, over us. We're framed in leaves. And, as I hold her in my arms, three words drift free from her bitten lips.

"He isn't dead."

Chapter Twenty-Three

VIOLETA

There was a time when all I knew were secrets. I hid. I lied. I kept the worst to myself, wanting to spare everyone from hurt. But now, as Rowan and I stand in the quiet darkness of the world Below, the truth like a spell in the air between us, a part of myself comes unlocked.

Rowan looks at me, the tether lit by his fear and confusion—and breathless *relief*. "Is that what you have been hiding from us, this whole time?"

Despite the ache of sadness in my chest, my mouth quirks into a wry smile. "What gave me away? The blood, or the magic, or the way I could be summoned at an altar?"

He arches a brow. "I can read all of your moods, Leta. But even without that, it wasn't exactly subtle that you had a secret."

My smile dims, and I let out a sigh that plumes into the

air. My gaze drifts toward the trees, where shadows hide the farther reaches of the woods. "I meant to destroy him, and completely claim his power. It's what he deserves, after all he's done. But in that final moment . . . I just couldn't."

Rowan takes my hand. His eyes are dark with apprehension. "The forest listens when you speak. You have a power meant for gods. I can't quite believe you are real. That you'll come back with us. That you're . . . mine."

There's a hesitant question in the space between us. I take his hand, pull him closer. I slide my fingers along his forearm to press against his wrist. The spell-thread shimmers between us, a pale glow in the dark. I let him feel the power that has bound us together between worlds, beyond death.

"I am real. And I will *always* be yours, Rowan Sylvanan. I have been, ever since you came to my village and told me I was the last person you ever wanted to meet."

He laughs at this, puts his arms around me. I close my eyes and let my head sink against his chest as he trails his fingers gently through my hair. I want to lose myself in this moment, our closeness. Make the whole world be still, for just a breath.

But then, a sound cuts through the trees. I turn sharply toward it; a harsh, skittering noise that comes from way out in the depths of the woods. Apprehension prickles across my skin, and a queasy sense of foreboding tightens my stomach.

Rowan looks nervously toward the dark. "Could Moth—or the others—get through the thorns?"

I start to shake my head, then waver. "None of them ever

did before. But I wasn't such a threat then." The knot in my stomach winds tighter, and a dizzy laugh escapes me. "I suppose when you try to unseat the god of death, you're bound to make some enemies."

Rowan gives me a scathing look. "I'm glad to see your wit hasn't suffered while you've been here."

I take a tentative step forward. Eyes narrowed at the space between the trees. Everything goes still, the branches frozen in unnatural silence. Then, swiftly, the wind rises again, tearing through the woods, whipping the trees back and forth. Rowan tightens his grasp on my hand, "Leta," he says, all warning, as he urges me back.

We turn and rush toward the cottage. The fierce wind pushes us forward, billowing our clothes, pulling my hair loose from its braid, and making the door slam behind us once we're inside.

I drag the latch across and lean my back against the wooden panels of the door, trying to catch my breath. Arien pushes himself up from the bed, where he was sitting beside Elan. "Leta, what's going on?"

"Tell them," Rowan says, "what you just told me."

I press my lips together, swallow past the tightness in my throat. "The Lord Under isn't dead."

The truth, given a second time, is still hard to voice. But once I've let the words free, I'm washed again by the same unsteady relief at not being so *alone* in this.

Arien tilts his head, puzzled. "You mean—"

He cuts off as the sound comes again from the woods, closer

now. It shudders against the walls and whines under the lintel with a guttural, drawn-out *howl*. An enormous crash makes the whole room shudder. A shower of bark and leaves falls loose from the ceiling. Then a sudden, otherworldly light flares outside, illuminating the cracks beneath the door and around the window before it falls back to darkness.

Cautiously, I edge closer to the window. Arien shoulders in beside me as I pull back the shutters. We peer outside, but it's pitch dark. All I can see is the reflection of my own face, blurred, in the glass.

Then, slowly, the light rises again. A horrified gasp catches in my throat. As the brightness spills between the trees, it reveals a forest that has entirely changed.

A forest that is . . . *ruined*.

The heartwood trees that border my cottage are destroyed. Their trunks torn open, deep wounds gouged into each one, sap bleeding onto the earth. Their branches are bent back, angled like broken limbs. It aches to look at them. Like the wounds have been carved through my own flesh.

"What—" I begin; then the strange light—which has dimmed—flares again. I turn my face away from the glass, eyes clenched shut against the overwhelming brightness. I blink and blink, and when my vision adjusts and I look back through the window, I realize there are *shapes* between the trees.

They're translucent as mist, but with a form that could almost be . . . human.

Rowan crosses the room and presses in, close, on my other

side. Clutching the edge of the shutter, I squint toward the ruined trees, trying to see more clearly.

"They look," Arien says, his voice slow with dread, "like the creatures from the failed ritual."

Rowan makes a strangled sound of agreement. Fear traces a path down my spine, a series of shudders. These creatures are made of mist, not mud. But they are eerily similar to the monsters that surged from the lake when our second attempt to mend the Corruption failed. The same elongated limbs. The same too-wide mouths that are all teeth.

Then something moves through the light, a figure more solid than the wraiths in the mist. Apprehension untangles from the depths of my stomach, spirals through the rest of my body.

Lady Moth walks out from between the trees, trailed by her sisters.

I slam the shutters closed and turn back to the room, pulse quickening. Rowan's hand slips from mine as he moves toward Elan. Through the tether, I see his despair and guilt, all the hurt he's carried since the night he watched his brother being dragged into the lake.

Now his expression is set with fierce determination. He puts his arm protectively around Elan and guides him to the back part of my cottage—as far from the window as possible.

I glance at Arien. "Go with them."

He shakes his head. He doesn't move.

"Arien. *Go*."

"No, Leta," he says. "We will fight them together."

His hand slips into mine, and a note of pleading shines in his magic-darkened eyes. Through all the time we tried to stop the Corruption, and through all my time in the world Below, I've fought and feared and given up pieces of myself. Tried to face the strength and ruthlessness of gods—to *match* that strength—alone.

Now, standing beside Arien, I feel as though we are back on the shore of the lake, the sigil carved beneath our feet, the ground open before us, the full moon overhead. And this feels like a chance to undo my mistakes from that last ritual—where I sacrificed myself and left him behind.

A chance to accept his help. For us to face the danger together.

I give him a single, terse nod. Then I reach toward the door and open the latch.

The air fills with a wretched *cry*—too snarled and hollowed to be human. A gust of icy wind pours into the room, extinguishing the fire.

Then the front wall of my cottage is ripped away.

A heartwood crashes through the roof with a hail of jagged splinters. The newly bared sky is lit up midday bright. I drop to one knee, slam my hand against the dirt. My fingers curl to claws, and the forest responds, a wall of thorns spiraling up from the floor.

It encircles us in a protective cage. Arien is right beside me, but—frantically—I realize that Rowan and Elan are gone.

The fallen heartwood has cut the space in halves, trapped us on one side, Rowan and Elan on the other.

I shove myself toward the tree, scraping at the wood. "Hold on!"

I unleash my power against the trunk, forcing it against the barrier with all my strength, desperate to make a way past, or *through*. But my magic washes uselessly over the wood, like a current of water diverting around a stone dropped into a stream.

Uprooted from the earth, the tree is severed from my connection. I bite back a growl, trying again as power sparks helplessly from my hands.

Another gust of wind spills through the room. With a sharp *wrench*, the side of the protective barrier I made, guarding Arien and me from the rest of the forest, tears loose. I falter back from the fallen tree, my magic scattering into a cloud of shadows.

Lady Moth strides forward, a handful of broken thorns clutched inside her bloodied fist. She throws them to the ground, scrubs her palm against her skirts.

She glowers at me, her eyes filled with murderous fury. "Violeta. I am here for what is rightfully *mine*."

I get to my feet, step out of the thorns. Arien is beside me. In the ruined woods surrounding my cottage, we face the sister gods.

Lady Moth, her wounded arm now healed to a gruesome scar.

Lady Owl, a bite-shaped cut at her wrist dripping blackened blood.

Lady Fawn, her breath rasping through the carved bone of her mask.

A terrible understanding comes over me, as I recall Elan's memories of his resurrection. *Breath and blood*. That was what they used. Pieces of life taken from a human girl who should not have been in the world of the dead.

They used my trades to resurrect Elan.

And—to create—

My eyes shift from tree to tree, my breath stilled in leaden terror. The mist-like creatures are not monsters at all, but *souls*, brought to life using the pieces of myself I gave to the gods in exchange for their help.

A fractured sound escapes me as I see what they have done. "I thought what happened in the Vair Woods was bad enough. But this—you've made monsters of the dead you swore to protect."

Lady Moth squares her shoulders unrepentantly. "You left us no choice, Violeta."

"No choice? For all you claim to care for this world, you've caused more hurt and ruin than the Lord Under ever did."

"Is that truly what you think?" Fawn says, voice sharp. She shifts closer, and beneath the depths of her bone mask, her gaze is all cold *hatred*. I can't believe I ever held her hand in the woods and thought we might find safety together.

She bares her fangs in a snarl. "How can this world be balanced while you remain here? While you refuse to step aside?"

"Is what you've done a better alternative?" I cry, gesturing toward the sister gods, the carnage they've caused.

Lady Owl lifts her chin toward the wounded trees. "It will heal. Once you are gone, it will heal. So, if you want it mended, then you know what needs to be done."

I take a single step forward, my feet heavy against the darkening ground. "I won't surrender this world to you. Not after what you did to the people in the Vair Woods. Not after the way you tried to hurt Elan. And especially not after *this*."

The three of them exchange a loaded glance. Moth holds up a hand, her claws gleaming in the ethereal light. "If you don't surrender willingly, Violeta, then we will remove you, by force."

She carves a swift line through the air between us. Another gust of ice-studded wind tears through the woods. I'm lost beneath a whirl of mist and cold. I see a blur of movement as she rushes forward, and there's just enough time for Arien and me to crouch low, braced for the fight to begin.

But she veers to the opposite side of the fallen tree. To where Rowan and Elan are trapped.

"No!" I turn sharply, close at her heels. Before I can catch her, Fawn is in front of me. Our eyes meet, and she glares at me with furious hatred.

"You can't save them," she says, teeth sharp as she bites out the words. "The only way to stop this is for you to *surrender*."

Arien rushes to my side, a fresh sigil marked on his wrist, the ink still wet, shadows wreathed around his outspread fingers. His magic spirals through the air and catches hold of Lady Fawn. The strands weave tightly around her ankles and wrists, stilling her before she can come any closer.

He darts a glance in my direction, tips his chin to the fallen tree. "Help them, Leta."

I push past Fawn as she struggles against Arien's shadows, drop to my knees beside the heartwood. My fingers dig into the earth. I close my eyes and I draw on my magic. I call to the forest.

There's a sibilant whisper, like a voice against my ear. The power in my veins gives a sharp *pull*, and a cascade of vines spirals up from beneath the tree. With a hideous, broken-bone crack, part of the fallen trunk finally tears loose, leaving behind a jagged edge of sap-streaked wood.

I see Elan, crouched in the ruin of stones that was once my kitchen hearth. Rowan stands before him, his knife in his hand, the blade drawn, and his sleeves pushed back. Beneath his skin, the darkened remnants of the magic that's been poisoning him writhe in wild, spreading lines.

He looks at me, and it's like the first night I saw him change, when he gave his blood to the cursed lakeshore. The scars at his wrists drip blackened water. His fingers curl, hooked like claws. Crimson stains the corners of his eyes, and his mouth opens in a snarl, bearing sharpened teeth.

Moth lets out a cold, cruel laugh. "Look at you. Monstrous *boy*. You'll not save your brother. He died then, and he'll die now."

"No," Rowan snaps. "He *won't*."

An icy rush of power slices through me as I call up vines and brambles from the earth, creating a barrier around Moth.

The thorns are interspersed with pieces of bone, pale shards of wood, serrated leaves as sharp as razors.

She falters, stopping just before she's impaled on the brutal spikes. Her fists clench. Trembling with unrestrained fury, she glances toward me. Then, with deliberation, she raises her hand. Crooks her fingers. The wraithlike souls billow around her. I watch, horrified, as her eyes gleam golden, her mouth opens, and, with a hollowed hiss, she *devours* them.

Their power fills her with a terrible brightness, gleaming from her skin like a silvered moon. The air around her shimmers. Her hand slashes out, the vines I grew dissolve, and she surges toward me, borne on a cloud of pale moths.

Their wings are tiny shards of glass. I cry out as they cut against my cheeks, my forearms. Everything turns dark as Arien throws my cloak over the both of us. He holds me close beneath the muffled dark, the moths beating furiously against the fabric.

Wretched, desperate, I take a breath and call out a shadow-shrouded command. "*Chmah*. Stop!"

The moths dissolve, evaporating into a cloud of harmless fog. I shove the cloak away, stride quickly to where Lady Moth has fallen to her knees. Smiling coldly up at me, she spreads her hands. "It's no good, Violeta. You have *my* name, but what of the others?"

Shivering, desperate, I watch Lady Owl drag the remaining souls toward her. Light gleams from her narrowed eyes, and her teeth snap together as she devours them. She drops to a crouch and shoves her hands against the earth.

Beneath her pressing palms, the ground begins to tremble. A crack opens, widening, and I falter back, catching hold of Arien as we struggle to keep our balance.

He pushes past me, rushes toward Rowan and Elan. His shadows weave together, forming a wall for them to shelter behind.

Lady Fawn, now freed from the snaring magic, charges after Arien. She rakes at his barrier with her claws, trying to force her way through. Arien pushes back, but he is no match for her. The shadows start to dissolve, faster than he can re-form them.

Desperately, I look from Fawn to Owl to Moth. I can *fight* them, but what I truly need is to make them *leave*.

"*Chmah,*" I call again. "I said *stop*. You will allow no harm to come to us. From anyone. Especially your sisters."

She bares her teeth at me, snarling, but she is powerless to resist. She turns on her sisters, caught by the force of my compulsion. She's fierce, strengthened by the power she's stolen from the souls. A cloud of wings envelops the three sisters, and a high-pitched, ear-splitting *scream* of anger fills the air.

In a blur of ice and mist and feathers, the sisters vanish.

We're left behind in a terrible silence. I clamber over the fallen tree, my boots crushing the magic-grown vines into the mud. Rowan catches me, his hands on my shoulders, his face all apprehension. "Are you hurt?"

"No." I look between him and Elan. They're both windswept

and mud stained, and Elan has fresh scratches on his scarred cheek. "Are *you* hurt?"

Rowan shakes his head. He tries to smile, but his eyes are solemn. "Arien kept us safe. I think your cottage and your garden caught the worst of it. And . . . the forest."

Slowly, I look around. My cottage has been leveled to a pile of thorn-wrapped wood. My garden is nothing but blackened, withered leaves, buried under the slowing fall of snow. And all around us, the mutilated trees stand like sentinels. Their trunks torn open, their voices lost, their souls . . . gone.

I swallow back a sharp, choked sob. Rowan pulls me close. I curl against him, so overcome by despair and relief that all I can do is cry. He holds me tightly, clutching at my waist, my hip, as though he doesn't ever want to let me go.

Arien drapes my cloak across my shoulders. I huddle beneath the soft weight of it, allow myself a final moment of stillness. Then I draw back and turn toward the wounded trees. "This *cannot* happen again. I need to stop them."

"We'll help you," Rowan says. The same determined promise he made before.

Arien nods agreement. "We'll find a way out of this, together."

I start to pace a restless arc, my hands scrunched into the folds of my cloak. "There's more to it—what I told you before."

Arien takes a step toward me. His fingers brush my arm, as though he wants to reassure himself that I am still here. "Leta, whatever it is, we are with you. You don't have to face this alone."

Silence draws out. When I speak again, my voice is soft as the snow still drifting around us. "I've told you how the Lord Under isn't dead. I used his name and made him my captive. I stole his power. But while he lives—I can't go home."

Arien's fingers clutch tighter into the sleeve of my cloak. He shakes his head, all words gone. Rowan, trembling with held back fear, draws me closer against him. "Leta—"

Before he can finish, Elan cries out. We all turn, watching in horror as he falls to his knees. His head bows forward, his hands scrape helplessly against the ground. I slip free of Rowan's arms, rush over and crouch in front of Elan. Put my fingers beneath his chin, tilting up his face so I can look at him more clearly.

"I—" He rasps, choked. "I can't—"

Horrified, I watch as the edges of him begin to blur. His features start to scatter, the way the gods do when their hold on a single form slips loose. His eyes are smears of darkness, his mouth a wordless grimace.

And behind him, the torn-open trees start to creak and groan with a hideous sound. Their branches stretch down eagerly. They catch at Elan, drag loose the blurring pieces of him like strands of mist caught up by a rising wind.

"*Elan!*" Rowan shouts, rushing forward. He grabs for his brother, clasping him tightly by the shoulders.

From the heartwoods, I feel an immeasurable, desperate *hunger*. The same fierce *need* that came from the Corruption when I stood beneath its heart. The same hunger that radiated from the shore of the lake, when it demanded a tithe from Rowan.

The trees are wounded, their souls torn away. And here is a boy—not dead, not anymore, but still close to that border—and they want him. They want Elan, to replace what was stolen.

I shove my hands into the earth, my veins alight with power. Patterns of frost trace over my skin, and my magic unfolds with an endless shiver. It *hurts*. It always hurts. The wrongness of using this stolen thing, the underlying wound of my carved-out memoires. But I push aside the pain. I close my eyes and reach to the woods. Call the forest to obey me.

"No." My voice is frost and midnight. Ashen as the burned-down pyres in the mourning fields. "Elan is not yours."

I feel the heartbeat of the forest beneath my palms. My own pulse slows to match it. One by one, the wounded trunks seal closed, leaving behind silver scars on their crimson wood.

As the forest quiets around me, I feel as if I could sink right down to the very depths of the world. Curl up between the roots of the trees and sleep forever as flowers grow between my ribs, nurtured by my heart's blood.

With effort, I sit back on my heels, the whole world spinning. I touch a hand to my nose—realize it is bleeding. Spots of darkness dance in front of my eyes. I blink them away.

Elan lets out a muffled cry as he slumps into Rowan's arms. I get back to my feet, pausing for a moment to lean against Arien as I fight another wave of dizziness. Rowan helps Elan to stand and I go over to them. Press a careful touch to Elan's wrist, my fingers marking his pulse. It beats faintly. His skin is almost translucent, a threat of the blur and fracture from before hidden just beneath the surface.

He looks at me, determined—even beneath the pallid fear that lines his features. "I want to go home, Violeta."

I'm filled by the same fierceness that spurs me whenever Arien is in danger. Elan belongs with us. Even if he was dead once, and part of the trees. I'll not send him back there, not if he doesn't want to go.

I take a long, wistful look at the remnants of what was— for the briefest moment—my home. Now there are only torn dresses and broken china, cracked stones and splintered wood. A forest of vengeful gods and ruined trees, a forest that wants to claim Elan. My power, alone, is not enough to hold it back forever.

I slide my fingers down to gently clasp his hand. "I promised to keep you safe," I tell him, "and I will."

As the mothlights flicker and the trees whisper around us, I lead my family out of the woods.

Chapter Twenty-Four

ROWAN

We walk quickly through the forest, lost in silence. Leta stays ahead of us, her gaze fixed on the crimson trees. Whenever the branches stir, she cuts them a warning look. One hand raised, a flash of magic across her palm. Even I can feel their coiled-back, restless hunger.

I'm overcome by dark foreboding, not all of it mine. It sings through the tether. From Leta to me. It's inescapable. The fear that all of this will *vanish*. That Leta will be lost beneath the darkness of her new power. That Elan will become a soul again, sealed back inside a tree.

All I can think of is the night on the shore when I watched him drown. The forest wants Elan. Wants to reclaim my brother. But I won't let it take him—no matter what.

Leta glances back at me. Her eyes are troubled, but she gives me a reassuring smile. "He will be safe, Rowan. I promise."

Arien makes a sound of fierce agreement. "We won't let you be hurt, Elan."

Elan is quiet, brows pulled into a deep frown. His newly mismatched eyes burn with fear and fury. I can feel how tense he is. Every part of him is focused on staying *here*.

"And what about you?" I ask Leta. "What will you do?"

She lets out a sharp sigh, tugs a hand through her hair. "I can't . . ." She trails off, swears beneath her breath. "Damn. *Damn*. It's all so *impossible*. I can't fight them. The sister gods won't settle for anything except power."

We move on, our silence heavier than before. I try to piece out the strangeness, the horror, of what we just saw. The ruthlessness of the sister gods, the terrible lengths they will go to as they try to gain control. And the Lord Under, held captive somewhere out in the forest. A death sentence pinned to him. His life the price for Leta's freedom.

There's no sound for a long time except the crunch of our feet over fallen leaves. Then Arien speaks. "Leta, what was that word you said, to make Lady Moth stop?" He tries to repeat it. That arcane command that came from her lips like a curse. But he can't shape the sound. "Was it a spell?"

"Her name," Leta says. "Her *true* name."

She stops so suddenly that I almost collide with her. At her feet, a cascade of vines unfurls. They lash the air, echoing her troubled mood. "I don't know the names of the others. But if I

312

could find them—" She shakes her head and sighs with frustration. "I need more *time*."

Arien puts his hand on her arm. Jaw set, eyes fierce, he regards her with determination. "Then stay." He looks between us. "We'll take Elan home. And when all this is done—you can follow."

Leta bites the corner of her mouth. A flush paints over her pale cheeks. Tears shimmer at the corners of her eyes. Then she puts her hand over Arien's. Pressing her lips together, she gives a resolute nod. "I promise—I *promise*—that I will follow you."

He doesn't waver. "I know you will."

She turns to me. Slips her hand into mine. Her fingers are very cold. Crescents of mud are embedded beneath her nails. But even like this—tired and worn—she's still a creature of silver and fire. With her skin veined by traces of magic, and the forest reaching to trail branches through her flame-bright hair, she looks so much like the icon that Arien painted for our altar. More spell than girl.

"I promise," she says again. And though her voice is only a whisper, her words feel sharp as a flare of magic.

All I wanted since I was brought to this strange world was to go home. For Leta to come back with me. The thought of leaving without her is unbearable.

I shift Elan to Arien, who slips his arm around my brother's shoulders. With Leta's hand in mine, I lead her away from them, along the path. We step into a sheltered grove.

She looks up at me. Ethereal and beautiful. I think again

of the poem. Those words, the only spell I could cast, with no magic of my own.

> *Fair as the moon,*
> *bright as the sun,*
> *majestic as the stars.*

I pull her closer. Bend to her. She exhales a frost-laced sigh. It whispers a caress against my mouth. "Tell me," I breathe, voice low. "Tell me I can take you home."

Her gaze falls to her wrist. Her fingers brush against the sigil. I feel the strength of the spell tying us together. A bond that will reach across the forest. Across the *worlds*.

Then she looks at me again. Her silver-hued eyes are all determination. "Rowan. You *are* my home."

She kisses me, and everything stills. The connection between us burns with an endless, golden fire. For the space of a heartbeat there is only her mouth against mine, the taste of blood and incense and candle smoke. A promise that can never be broken.

We draw apart. She laughs softly, tucking a wayward strand of hair away from my face. Her touch lingers against my cheek. Then, with a sigh, we turn back to the path and go on through the woods.

The trees rise taller around us. They're closer together now, in a way that makes everything shadowed. It starts to rain. We bow our heads against the persistent drip of water from the leaves. Leta pulls the hood of her cloak over her hair.

The path continues to slope down. The way is lined by

granite stones covered with lichen. In the trees on either side of us, more pale moths flicker inside hanging jars. We reach a flat space, paved with stones. On one side is the forest. Silent and shadowed.

On the other is a pale, enormous tree.

White as bone, it rises far above the woods. The trunk is shrouded by mist. But as we walk closer, the mist parts, and I can see the bark is carved. The pattern reminds me of alchemical sigils. But sharper, stranger.

There's an altar at the base of the tree. It's lined with unlit candles. The wooden shelf marred by melted wax. The frame where an icon should sit is empty, revealing a view of the open doorway that leads inside the tree. Beyond, is darkness.

I feel a *pull* from the center of my chest. I press my hand to my ribs. It's the same connection I felt in the Vair Woods. When Leta and the Lord Under and I all stood together.

I know what is inside that darkened space, behind the altar.

Leta glances at the tree. She pauses, one hand raised. Head tilted, as though she is listening to the darkness. I catch the shift of her moods. The verdant green of hidden secrets. The pale gray of despair. And strongest of all, fear.

"He's there, isn't he?"

She nods grimly. "The bone tree. It's the heart of the whole world Below. It's where he mended me. And where I—" She shakes her head, turns determinedly back to the path. But I take her hand before she can walk away.

The words she spoke after the fight with the gods echo through me. *While he lives—I can't go home.* I remember the way she looked at the altar when I summoned her. Stained with blood. Overcome by grief.

The Lord Under tore my life apart, piece by piece. But there's no delight in the thought of his destruction. And when I picture Leta going into that dark, alone, I feel so terribly *sad*.

"I could stay with you," I offer quietly. "When you . . ."

"No." More of her despair lights through the tether. "You need to stay with Elan. Keep him safe."

I cup my hand against her cheek. Her skin is streaked with sweat. I stroke her face, and she leans into my touch. Her eyes flutter closed. "You're frightened," I murmur.

"I'm fine."

"You're not."

She smiles faintly. "Usually, we're on the opposite sides of this argument. I sound like you. *I'm fine, I'm fine.*"

I press my forehead to hers. Brush my lips against her temple. She sighs against my cheek, her breath cold. Then she turns toward the opposite path. Leads us away from the strange, pale tree.

She walks slowly, head still tilted as she listens to the sounds of the forest. Her eyes narrow, searchingly, as she scans the trees. She holds one hand raised. Her fingers curled loosely in the empty air. It's as though she's following an invisible thread. I picture it—like the tether that binds us, but strung between her and the woods.

We go along the path. The bone tree vanishes completely behind us. Leta pauses, turns. She goes to the trees, traces her fingers against them. They shiver and curve back, revealing a shadowed space.

She examines it for a moment, then nods for us to follow her. We step into the darkness.

Beyond is a flight of stairs that leads into a hollowed space. The steps are worn. The stone furred with moss. Leta gazes down at them. "There are doorways in the world Below," she explains. "It's how the gods cross through to claim a soul. I can use this one to send you home."

Elan holds my arm for balance as we carefully descend the stairs. On our way down, Arien collects one of the lighted moth jars from a nearby branch. We reach the bottom step. He raises the light, and the silver glow reveals a bare circle of earth.

Leta takes off her boots. Sets them aside. Barefoot, she gathers up her skirts and walks out into the circle. She draws a ribbon from the pocket of her cloak. Ties half of her curls back. Her expression turns resolute.

She bends, starts to carve a sigil into the ground. The mark she inscribes is complex. Endless lines, linked together with angular flourishes. It's familiar, yet not. We all watch her in silence. Then, with slow realization, Arien says, "It looks like the sigil we used for our rituals. But it's in reverse."

Leta steps back and looks ruefully at the mark. "I have the Lord Under's power." She touches her wrist where the darkness lines her skin. "I know how to cross worlds to claim a soul. But I still have my own magic, too. I'm going to use alchemy on this doorway, to make a path home."

The rain starts to fall more heavily. Leta moves back from the mark, her hands outspread. The strange, clouded magic—shadows sparked with gold—spills out from her fingertips. The ground begins to tremble. The lines of the sigil fill with water. It collects at the heart of the spell. A deepening pool that rises and rises.

It becomes a lake. An ink-dark lake.

Arien looks down at the water with quiet awe. "Leta, this magic, it's—" He shakes his head, words lost. A flicker of fear crosses his expression. He steps closer to the outer lines of the sigil, not yet covered by water. He touches it, and shadows wisp around his fingertips.

Leta traces another mark at the edge of the spell. It begins to glow. A pale light that extends down into the depths of the lake. A path.

"Follow it into the water," Leta says. "You'll wake up at the surface, in the world Above."

Elan looks nervously at the spell. "Are you sure about this?"

Her mouth tilts into a wan smile. Trying to tease him, she says, "Don't you trust me?"

Arien makes a face at her. Then he turns to Elan. "We could go together."

Elan hesitates, considering the offer. Then he nods. Before they leave, Leta pulls Arien into an embrace. She holds him for a long time, her face buried against his neck. Then she steps back. She scrubs at her face with her sleeve. Fighting back tears. "Go ahead. I'll be so quick, you won't even have time to miss me."

He lets out a tired, sad laugh. "Be safe, Leta."

"You too, my love."

Elan reaches to Arien. Takes hold of his hand. They step into the water. Wade out until it reaches their knees. The light around them begins to darken. They move deeper. The water at their waists.

Even though I trust Leta, and her magic, I still can't escape the anxiety clawing at me. How similar this moment feels to when I watched Elan drown.

Leta puts her hand over mine. Offers me a reassuring glance. "Just think of how surprised everyone will be when Elan comes back."

"We're going to have to think of a way to explain this."

She smiles teasingly. "I'll tell everyone you can raise the dead."

Sighing, I shake my head at her. "You are completely unhelpful."

In the lake, the water closes over Arien and Elan. The surface turns still. They are gone.

I start to move forward, but Leta draws me back. "Wait. I have something I want to show you first."

I look at the unbroken surface of the lake. "Shouldn't I follow them?"

"It's all right. You have time for this."

We go back up the stairs. She guides me away from the path. We pass between close-crowded heartwoods. Then, we step out into a grove of trees.

The canopied sky of the forest is thinner here. The branches sparse. Some of the trees look smaller, newer. Some of the older, taller ones are black and dead.

At the center of the grove is a circle of stones. They're smoke stained. Like the place where we light bonfires in the village square.

Leta trails her fingers through the air. "This is where I came to mend the Corruption."

She looks up, and I look up. Above us, the misted sky has brightened. It must be close to morning, if this world even has mornings. There's no sign of what once was here. But I can picture it. Torn and ruined. Clawed and hungry. Picture Leta inside the stones as she faced that darkness.

All the weight of it—what she did, what she gave up—is layered between us. Slowly, I take her hand. Bend and kiss her folded knuckles. Then her palm, the scar across her heartline. "I love you, Violeta."

"And I love you." She smiles at me, and for the briefest moment she is only *Leta*. Not a creature of wild, brutal magic who will go to kill a god. But just a girl. Her hair tangled by the wind. Mud on the hem of her skirts.

"There's one more thing," she says quietly, "that I wanted you to see."

She leads me to the very edge of the grove. There are four trees, grown together in a half circle. Three of them have the same crimson bark as the rest of the forest. But the last . . . is different.

The trunk is torn by a deep, ragged cut that drips tears of sap. Like the trees near Leta's cottage, when the gods—the ones she called the sisters—came.

Slowly, I extend my hand. Touch the wounded trunk. Sap smears my skin. It's warm. But the tree beneath is cold and still.

"Elan," I manage, my voice gone unsteady.

Leta comes to stand beside me. "This is the heartwood that held his soul. The Lord Under showed it to me when I first came here to mend the Corruption."

"And these are . . ." I trail off, looking to the trees on either side of the one I've touched. I can't make myself say the words. *My mother. My father.*

"Your family." Her hand drifts beneath her sleeve. Her fingers cast over the scar on her arm. "The sister gods, they used my trades to free Elan. My breath and my blood. But what they did—I can't repeat it." She glances at the trees on either side of the one where Elan's soul slept. Her expression turns sorrowful. "Especially now. There's no way to resurrect anyone else. I'm sorry."

The note of apology in her voice sends an ache through me. "You have done enough. More than enough. You kept this world safe. You kept Elan safe." I put my hands on her shoulders. Stare down at her, levelly. "You don't need to be sorry for this."

Shakily, she touches the new sigils on my throat. I feel the spike of thorns. The wash of the lake. I shiver as power flickers from Leta's fingers. Shadows and mist. New moon dark. A frostbitten night.

"I can't bring back your family," she says, still solemn. "But I can mend you, Rowan. I didn't have time to do more than quiet it, before. Now I can take away this poison forever."

"With a trade."

Her lashes dip. She gives a slow nod. "Yes. With a trade."

"I watched you heal Elan. It hurts you, to use this power."

"It doesn't matter."

"It does." I catch her hand inside my own. Move her away, break the contact.

She pulls against my grasp, protesting. "Rowan—"

"I don't want to be mended. Let me be poisoned. Let me be a monster." I stare at her, full of certainty. It's not the first time I've spoken it aloud. But these words, at this moment, have a heaviness, a finality. "I don't want you to hurt yourself for me. Ever again."

She smiles, soft and sad. Then she guides me to touch the trees, where the souls of my parents are held. "Here. Close your eyes and listen."

I do as she says. Her magic twines around me. Beneath the sounds of the forest, I hear an unexpected noise. At first, it's just the wind. Stirring quietly through the leaves. Then it changes. And I hear . . . voices.

I can hear the voices of my mother and father.

I can *see* them. Images that come in flashes. A library filled with books. Winter roses in an overgrown garden. I see love and joy. I see grief. A sadness that's bleak and dark as the lake beneath a starless sky. It's all woven together. Sunlight and sorrow. Despair and tenderness.

My family is part of the forest now. They *are* the forest.

I start to cry. I try to fight against it at first, but I can't hold back the tears. Leta wraps her arms around me. I bury my face against her hair. She is crying, too. Quiet sobs that make her shoulders tremble.

We hold each other for a long time while the trees whisper all around us. Then I shift back. I touch her cheek, wipe away her tears. "What about your own family? Can you go to where they are, and see them like this?"

"No." She looks down at her arms, marked by scars and sigils. "All my power comes from the sacrifice of their memories. From my chance to be with them in death. I can't go back. All I can do is sever my connection to the Lord Under, and go home."

We walk out of the trees and make our way through the forest. As we go back down the stairs, I try to think of the life we'll have when all this is done. It's a sharp hurt. Grief and hope. Tied inextricably together.

We reach the lake. The surface is still, without even a single ripple. It reminds me, eerily, of when I gave myself to the Corruption. In tithes. In rituals. And then I think of the night when Leta stayed beside me. When she put her hands in the earth next to mine as I bled into the ground.

"Will you come with me," I ask her, "to the water?"

She smiles, her mouth trembling, eyes still damp with tears. "Yes. I will."

She takes off her cloak. Leaves it at the base of the stairs, beside her boots. She tightens the ribbon in her hair. Then slowly, we follow the path. Walk, together, into the water.

It catches hold of Leta's skirts, making them billow out. They spread behind her as we move deeper. A train of lace.

The edges of my vision begin to waver. I look back. The whole forest is a blur. Lost in shadows.

I'm beginning to dissolve. It's only Leta—her hand in mine, the tether between us—that keeps me from fracturing apart entirely.

The water is at my chest now. Leta stands on tiptoe, waves lapping at her shoulders. She pulls me closer. I can see her quickening pulse against the blue-veined hollow of her throat. Her hands are shaking.

I bend to her. She kisses me fiercely, desperately. Her teeth catch my lip. Her fingers dig sharp into my waist. Like she has claws. I swallow, tasting blood. The water rises higher. This is a tithe. A sacrifice.

A resurrection.

The tether between us burns and burns. She wraps her arms around me. Drags me beneath the surface. The water closes over our heads. The light goes dim. I let out a single, wretched breath that bubbles upward.

Then all is quiet.

Chapter Twenty-Five

VIOLETA

I drag myself from the water. My skin is ice. My heart is quiet. My hair is tangled with knots of lake grass.

I am in the world Below, and I am alone.

I put on my cloak, leave my feet bare. I pick up the moth-light Arien left behind. I walk away from the lake, slowly start to climb the stairs. It takes every piece of me not to falter.

I can't look back.

I think of Arien and Rowan and Elan on the shore in the world Above. Of Lakesedge Estate, vine wreathed and beautiful. My garden, lit by the russet glow of Harvestfall sunset. The library with its empty shelves, still waiting for me to unpack the books.

The kitchen where I can sit at the table with Clover, drink bitter tea and share stories, tease each other. I can almost imagine the lilt of her voice. *The girl and the monsters . . .*

I close my eyes against the tears that come. I want so badly to lose myself in this tender longing. But I still have so much left to face before I can ever go home.

When I reach the top of the stairs, the heartwoods begin to murmur. Branches bend to stroke my cheeks. I turn my face against the rasp of their leaves. The ground trembles under my bare feet. With a shiver, the water evaporates from my hair and my clothes. The silken fabric of my dress settles back around me with a rustle. And all around me, the forest starts to change.

The trees and stones reshape themselves, weaving together to form a narrow, walled space. The branches stretch above to form a cavernous ceiling. It reminds me of the parlor at Lakesedge. A place for secrets spoken in the night. A place for bargains to be made.

There's a single arched doorway at one end. At the other, limned in darkness, is a raised dais. Atop that—a throne.

It's carved of the same bleached wood as the bone tree. A curtain of vines spills down behind it, the tiny leaves like lace. There are candles set at intervals throughout the room. They flare alight as I move forward. The air is honey, filled with the scent of melting wax and decaying flowers.

I pull the ribbon free from my hair and let my curls fall loose around my shoulders. Slowly, I kneel. Press my hands against the ground. I close my eyes and call on every piece of the Lord Under's stolen magic that I've made my own. I taste dirt and ash, and feel the razed-bare *ache* of desolation inside my chest as I connect to the forest.

I think of snow and feathers, claws and bones. The ruthless

creatures who want power so desperately they will turn against the ones they were sworn to protect.

Tell me their names.

A high-pitched ringing fills my ears, closing out all other sounds. I think of the cries of the wounded trees. Elan, helpless in Lady Moth's arms. His eye turned bright with blood. I think of my family somewhere out in the woods. And though their memories are lost to me, my place at their side forsaken, the thought of their trees torn open, and their souls devoured, fills me with unshakable determination.

Tell me their names.

The knowledge is there. Close. So close. But no matter how hard I try to catch hold, it slips past me. Always out of reach.

I let out a breath and tilt my head back, open my eyes to stare out at the forest beyond the arched doorway. Something stirs between the heartwoods.

A shape appears, silhouetted against the trees. At my wrist, the spell ignites with a sharp, sudden flare. A thread unfurls, spiraling out into the distance. I press my hand to my ribs. My heart is wild.

At the other end of the thread—is Rowan.

My vision wavers, and I begin to cry, all the tears I've fought against now spilling free. "You came back."

"I never left." He smiles, hesitant and sad. "The lake started to claim me. But all I could feel was *you*. The spell that bound us. Leta, you gave your life to the Lord Under—and to this world—to protect me. I didn't want to leave you behind. I didn't want you to face this alone."

I get to my feet. Rowan comes toward me. As he moves closer, I can see what it has cost him, this return. Darkness spills over him, raised in lines, encircling his throat like a snare. The wounds at his wrists drip bloodstained water, and his eyes are threaded black, like ink has pooled within his irises.

I fall into his arms, the room a blur of leaves and candlelight. I'm crying so hard I can barely speak. "It isn't enough. All the power I have, and it still isn't enough to find their names."

He draws me close, and I curl against him. With a roughened whisper, he says, "Then let me help you. You need more strength, more magic, more darkness. Take it from me."

I pull back, shaking my head. "Rowan. *No.*" A sob catches in my throat as I think of him on his knees at the edge of the lake, head bowed forward as he gave his tithe to the Corrupted shore. "I'll not let it hurt you like that, not again."

His mouth tilts into a hard smile. "What was it that you said, after I turned into a monster, and you made that foolish bargain for the power to save me?"

"It wasn't foolish. You were going to *drown* me." I wipe my tears, scowl at him. Then, with a sigh, I relent. "I told you it was my choice."

"Well, this is *my* choice, Violeta. I want to help you. We will do this, together."

He holds out his hand, his palm upturned like an offering. Bruises of poison bloom from each of the sigils marking his skin. He is laced with shadows, the air shimmering dark around him. The boy and the monster, both now so intertwined they are one and the same.

I step toward him. Take his hand. Vines uncurl from the ground beneath my feet, spreading around us in tangles of juniper leaves. He bends to me. Mouth hovering above mine for a tremulous heartbeat. He kisses me, and I taste the poison in his mouth.

With my eyes closed, I dip my head in a solemn nod. "Together."

From the dark heart of my palms, wild roses burst free, clambering out to band my fingers. Their thorns are like claws. I drag one across Rowan's upturned palm, carving deep into his heartline. The blood that wells up is onyx dark, thick as tree sap. The thorns weave around us like a brutal handfasting, blood smeared between our pressed palms. The tether glows endlessly bright, turning the forest to gold.

Rowan drops to one knee, his gaze shuttering. I kneel beside him and shove our bound hands into the earth. I call to the darkness within him, feel it wash through his veins like a tide. It rises, fierce, then pours into *me*. Water fills my lungs and my mouth. I let out a choked breath, certain I'll drown beneath it.

Rowan lifts his unbound hand and shakily cups my cheek. "I'm here," he says, his voice like the waves. "I'm with you, Leta. Take the power you need."

His shoulders are squared, his head raised. This isn't the helpless surrender of those long-ago nights, when he fed himself to the Corruption piece by piece. This is a welcoming, a communion.

I close my eyes and feel the magic inside Rowan, a ruinous darkness grown from poison and my own tender alchemy. I feel

329

the magic of the Lord Under, who gave me a new life, built me a home from the woods, grew a garden with my sorrow. I catch hold of the power—all of it, all of it—and pull hard, as though it's a deep-rooted heartwood that I want to tear from the earth.

With an enormous *wrench* it all comes loose.

Magic fills me, overwhelming, devouring. I cry out as my bones shift, as my veins run cold. "Tell me," I call into the darkness. "Tell me the names of the other gods."

And the darkness answers. It speaks with words that are not words but sounds of sharpness and hunger. Snowdrifts and pale feathers. Words that weave stories of blood and ice and smoke. Of lives eternal, forged far beyond a time when I ever existed.

My eyes flutter open, and I stand up slowly. Blood drips from my fingers, still wrapped with thorns stippling the ground with crimson. Rowan stands beside me. I place my hand to his chest. I feel the stir of darkness beneath his skin, in his veins. Then he puts his hand over mine. A trail of black-petaled hellebores unfurls beneath our feet.

I gasp, drawing back to stare at him with incredulous wonder.

So many times, I've touched him and the Corruption both, but this—this is different. The wounds on his throat and wrists have clotted over, healed to the same blackened scars as the marks I left on Elan. He looks at me, and his eyes are clear. He takes a slow breath, sighs it out, and though I feel the catch and drag of poison in his lungs, it has become . . . softer.

The darkness is still *in* him, but the power has not ruined him. It's *part* of him. Settled against his bones, nestled beneath his heartbeat. It has stayed in the darkness of his eyes, the points of his teeth. Traces of *monster* that will always be part of him.

He touches the healed-over scars, searching for the words. "It's not a poison any longer, Leta."

Carefully, he takes something from the pocket of his cloak. A woven circlet of branches.

I stare at it, incredulous. "You kept my crown?"

"I found it in your cottage, after everything was ruined. I thought you might want it still."

He places the wreath on my hair—tender, reverent. I unwind the thorns from my fingers and put my hand against his cheek, feel the warmth of his skin beneath my cold, scarred palm. Then I turn and walk toward the dais.

Everything feels as careful and deliberate as the motions of a ritual. I climb the stairs. I sit on the throne. And then I call to the gods.

Moth. Fawn. Owl. The three who helped me, who hurt me. I call their names, softly at first, then louder, until they become the only sound in the whole of the woods. "*Chmah. Sova. Yelen.* Come to me."

Out beyond the archway, the forest stirs. A flutter of snow-flakes falls through the air. A pale moth circles the branches overhead. Shadows stretch across the ground, interwoven with strands of mist.

And they appear, the gods, walking toward me with reluc-tant, halting steps. We stare at each other across the laden silence. I'm pinned by their gazes, the steel-sharp fury in their eldritch eyes. Fawn glares at me, her mouth cut into a snarl. "What now, little *pet*? Why have you called us here?"

"I want to end this. All of this. The hurt and the destruction. The fights for power. We need to restore balance."

Moth lets out a harsh, bitter laugh. "You claim you want balance, yet you are the one who has brought ruin to this world."

I spread my hands. My fingers are dark with earth, my arms are bloodless pale, lined with the indigo veins of my magic. From the ceiling of the room, branches bend to frame my shoulders with their needled leaves. Outside, the voices of the souls rise to a melodic hum.

"We all own an equal share in this," I tell Moth. "But it ends now. Come to me. Kneel down."

They move forward. They kneel on the frost-covered earth, shoulder to shoulder.

Rowan has moved back to stand in a shadowed corner of the room. And now, as I command the gods, he looks at me the way he did when we were in the village at Summersend. When I stood beside the bonfire in my faerie-tale dress with a crown of flowers on my hair.

He looks at me like I am the most beautiful thing in the world.

Magic blooms at my palms, a garland of ashen flowers. I straighten my spine, feel the weight of power in my veins, the connection between girl and forest. I let Rowan watch me, see me, as I speak the names of the sister gods once again. As I speak the words that will keep everyone safe.

"*Chmah. Sova. Yelen.* You will return to your lands; you will remain behind your borders. You will not hurt anyone in the world Above or Below. You will protect the souls within your forests, leave them to sleep inside the trees. You will swear to what I ask."

There's a heartbeat, then silence; then in unison the sisters murmur, "We swear."

Lady Moth looks up. There's a spark in her eyes, more challenge than anger. "And will you, Violeta, swear the same?"

I hold her gaze steadily as I let my hands drop to my sides. She gets slowly to her feet, flanked by her sisters. And for all that I have the power to compel her, in this moment we face each other like equals. I bow my head to her. "I will."

Fawn and Owl nod to me with the barest, deferential motion. I watch as they begin to fade, as their features blur and soften until there's only the trees, the shadows.

Moth is the last to go. We stand before each other for a long time in an unmoving silence that stretches out, endless as the forest. I curl my fingers against my palms, tracing the crescent scar. She gives me a final look, and then, in a flurry of pale wings, she is gone.

I sink heavily back down onto the throne, hollowed by the immensity of what I've done. What still lies ahead. The Lord Under, held captive in the darkness, waiting for me to destroy him—unbind myself from his power, so I can end our bargain.

Rowan steps out from the shadows. As he moves toward me, more of the black-petaled hellebores bloom at my feet. The candles in the alcoves gutter out. By the time he reaches the dais, all the lights have dimmed except for two that burn on either side of the platform.

"I'm so afraid," I confess to him. "The Lord Under has been part of my life since he led me out of the Vair Woods. I have his magic. I have his name. All I ever wanted was to come home. But it still *hurts* so much, even with all he's done, to think that I'll—" My words catch on a sob. I take a deep breath, trying to will away the tears.

Rowan gazes up at me. "I understand, Leta."

I spread my hands, let out a helpless sigh. "I am so *changed*, Rowan. How can I ever come back, after this?"

"I'll not let you be lost," he says, with all the fierceness of a vow made at an altar. Then, his voice turns quiet. "I'd do anything—give anything—for you, Violeta. I would search for-ever to find you in the dark."

Then he kneels. He kneels at the bottom of the dais. He lowers his head. His dark hair falls forward and hides his face. He presses his hands to the ground like he's at observance. At the sight of him there, supplicant, goose bumps rise all over my skin.

An uncertain laugh escapes me. "You don't have to do that. You don't have to *bow* to me."

I nudge at him with my toes, still laughing. But then he catches hold of my foot, and his calloused fingers stroke the soft arch. I go quiet. It's as though we realize, both at once, this is the first time we've been truly alone.

Slowly, his hands slide farther up my legs. He pushes back my skirts until they are a froth of black lace around me. Then he waits, fingers tracing gently over the scars on my knees. I sink back against the throne, and my eyes flutter closed.

He bends. The warmth of his breath ghosts over my skin. I bite down on a gasp as he kisses my scars, one by one. I'm far away, above the trees, on the very edge of a precipice with all the forest before me. I look down and see souls and heartwoods and gods, and know that in another touch, another heartbeat, I'll be lost.

But I don't fall, not yet.

More flowers rise from the earth. They cover the trees, the throne, until all the world is rustling leaves and midnight petals. Rowan gets to his feet. He shifts closer, traces a fingertip against my cheek. "No matter how far you go, I'll always call you home."

I slide my hand down the line of his jaw. Tilt his face upward so I can look into his eyes. I love him so much that I can hardly dare to speak, to even whisper. A single word escapes me. *"Please."*

Rowan closes the last, transient space between us. He crushes his mouth against mine in a sharp, desperate kiss. Heat spirals through me. I make a tattered sound against his lips. Magic ignites through my veins, and the tether between us glows. I think of forever and gardens and sunlight. Of impossible things that are so far out of reach.

I close my eyes as he makes a languorous path all the way down to the soft curve of my hip, until he's on his knees again, his hands beneath my skirts. He threads his fingers into the ribbons that knot my undergarments closed. He pauses, his fingers caught in the loops, and casts a careful glance in my direction.

"Untie them," I rasp.

He pulls the ribbons loose in a single, silken whisper. Slides the crumpled fabric down my legs, over my feet. Then he lifts me back against the throne. His breath grazes over me, warm. I curl my toes and tangle my fingers in his hair as he kisses between my thighs.

He's learned my body so quickly, mapped the exact way to touch me and make me spiral apart into helpless shivers. My head falls back; my eyes find the branches above. My breath turns to urgent gasps, echoing through the frost-laden air. I start to come apart. Power lights my hands, and silvered sparks drift up to hang above us, like stars.

Rowan pulls me into his arms and holds me until I'm still. His hand slides to my waist, fingers fitting into the notches of my ribs. "Wait," I breathe. "Let me—"

I reach for my discarded cloak. Search the pockets for the ink pen I've carried with me from habit, though it's been so long since I've drawn a sigil on my skin. Carefully, I set the nib to my wrist and mark the spell that Clover taught me. I can still hear her voice, the teasing lilt as she explained how it would work. *You can use the tea, or you can use magic.*

Rowan watches as I write. "What are you doing?"

"It's a contraceptive spell."

A slow blush spreads across his face. "Is that what you want?" He strokes his fingers around the outside of the sigil, mindful of the still-fresh ink. "For me to take you to bed, in a way that would require this?"

"I mean, there's not really a *bed*." I start to laugh, and he scowls at me, which only makes me laugh harder. "Yes. That is exactly what I want."

He pauses, tentative, one hand raised between us. Then his fingers lace through my hair, the edge of his thumb strokes against my skin. I lean close. Breathe a wretched sigh against his mouth, then kiss him. Slow and soft.

He unties the sash of my dress. I wriggle my arms out of the sleeves, and the dress falls to the dais in a billow of cloth. He reaches behind me to unfasten all the tiny hooks on the back of my camisole, then he slips the straps down, one at a time.

I'm all undone, shivering at the feel of the forest air on my skin. I feel so strange and new and shy. I've never been like this in front of anyone before, completely unclothed. Carefully, I take the crown of branches from my hair and set it aside.

Everything blurs. Rowan takes hold of my hand, traces the tender inside of my wrist. The spell flickers alight, the thread spirals between us. He looks at me like I'm some gilt-painted creature inside an icon frame. "Leta. You're so beautiful."

I get to my feet and push him down onto the throne. A startled huff comes from his mouth as I climb onto his lap, my knees curved on either side of him. I bend forward, kissing him more roughly now, as his hands and mouth skim over me, touching me everywhere—breasts and belly and the curve of my waist—until my whole body feels like fire; even the soles of my feet are feverishly heated.

I don't feel shy now, not at all, even when he grabs hold of his shirt and wrenches it over his head in a single motion. Even when I feel how warm his bared skin is against my own. My heart starts to beat very fast. I'm immolated by endless, all-consuming *want*. But when he reaches for me, I catch his hands and hold him still.

"Don't rush." I look at him, veiled, through my lashes. "I don't want this to feel like the only moment we'll have."

Rowan nods, cheeks flushed. He starts to kiss me again. Slower now. I imagine that we're in his room with the window open and midsummer light pouring over us, the whole day— week, month, *lifetime*—ahead of us. I think of home.

I trail my fingers over him, going from scar to scar. Kiss each new sigil marking his throat and chest and wrists. Feel the shiver of poison beneath his skin, feel him gone taut with desire as my hand goes between us, unfastening.

I touch him, lost to this unguarded closeness, the way he's laid himself out before me, trusting, throat bared. How he presses his face into my shoulder and breathes out a harsh, hot sound against my neck when I tighten my grasp. His fingers dip between my thighs, and a coil of heat unwinds all through me.

We trade kisses and touches for a long time as pale light shimmers around us. A faint murmur comes from the trees, and mist curls gently through the branches. Everything is slow, slow, slow, like honey dripped from a spoon, like sap from the pale heart of a tree.

Everything is slow, but soon I start to feel like a fire kindled to bright flame from banked-up coals. I rock my hips against him, my breath coming out in stuttered gasps. I want him close and closer.

Rowan takes my face between his hands. He strokes my cheek, a tentative question in the gesture. "You're certain?"

I look at myself, my knees braced on either side of him, my whole body eagerly curled forward. I start to laugh. "If I'm certain of anything, it's *this*."

He laughs, too, and his gaze sparks in a way that sends a flutter of anticipation to my stomach. I kneel above him, and he takes hold of my waist. His fingers press into the small of my back as I lower myself down.

He gasps. I kiss the sound from his mouth, still laughing as we start to move together. I'm dizzy with how good it feels. Shards of pleasure spark between us, and I see the colors of his mood through the tether. We're so tightly bound right now—through love and through power—that I can't tell which part of the spell is his and which is mine.

I let him in, past the liminal borders of my body. I let him have all of me.

I think of the forest around us. We're nothing but leaf and air and the whisper of the wind. The world turns to rose-hued light as we both start to fall apart. The only sound is our helpless sighs, our formless words. Then stillness.

I close my eyes. Rowan strokes my hair. I tuck my head beneath his chin. He holds me for a long while, until the final candles on either side of us have almost burned down. I can hear the faint catch of the poison when he breathes. I can hear the steady beat of his heart.

Slowly, I get back to my feet. I start to collect the discarded pieces of my clothing and put them back on: the lace and ribbon undergarments, my silken dress. I pick up the crown, turn it distractedly between my hands. I set it back over my hair.

"Leta," Rowan begins, hesitant. "Do you remember the promise you made to us all when we went to the final ritual, to mend the Corruption?"

I bite my lip, tasting blood, as fresh tears fill my eyes. "Yes. I remember."

"You said we would all work together." He gets to his feet, his hand outstretched toward me. "Let me go with you, into the bone tree. Let me go with you, and we can see this through to the end."

Chapter Twenty-Six

VIOLETA

I walk out into the woods with Rowan at my side. The world Below is mist and moths and clouded light. Midnight-colored flowers, strands of delicate ferns. Candles burning in eldritch altars. I'm ready to go home, but there's a bittersweet ache at knowing I'll leave this all behind.

When I next return, it will be in death. At this moment, with my skin flushed from heat and kisses, with the Lord Under's power in my veins, death seems a faraway thing. Still, I can picture it. My soul inside a heartwood that grows alone, at the center of a barren grove. My voice a solitary whisper threading into empty air. My parents, and Arien, cleaved away from me forever.

Rowan traces his thumb across my palm. His expression is troubled, but he doesn't speak. There are no words left that can change the truth of this moment. For all my power, there is only one way this can end.

The bone tree rises in the distance, shrouded by fog that's gray as smoke. The light casts lilac through the branches above and on the ground, drifts of snow melt slowly back into the mud. A lingering trace of when Lady Moth passed through this part of the forest.

Magic burns across my skin, cold as a midwinter, as we follow the path out of the trees. We climb the slope, pause at the altar. The empty icon frames the still-open archway. I touch the candles, and they flare alight. Then, with Rowan holding my hand, I take seven slow steps into the darkness.

The carved walls of the tree shift around us. Vines and leaves and thorns unfolding as we move farther through the corridors. Finally, we reach the sepulcher. A heavy scent of rust and iron fills the air.

Rowan takes my face between his hands. He looks at me carefully, only the barest pieces of him visible in the dim light. His dark eyes, the angle of his jaw. The way the shadows still outline him, smudged beneath the sigils on his skin.

We breathe together. I feel the tether strung between us. The spell tying us from heart to heart, wrist to wrist. And then, slowly, another strand unfurls and stretches into the darkness.

Around my feet, a circle of ghost mushrooms blooms from the earth. Their glow lights the air with a pallid haze. At first there's nothing. Just the sepulcher, all shadows. Then a shiver, a rustle. A shape appears, like a fragment of quartz on the muddied bed of the lake.

The Lord Under, held captive inside the heart of the bone tree.

The tree has grown around him now, shards pierced through his chest, his wrists. There's a smear of dried blood across his mouth. Light filtering down from above paints silver on his hair and the sharp points of his antlered crown.

His eyes are closed. He is completely still, aside from the irregular motion of his chest as he takes a shuddering breath. A cloud of frost appears at his bloodied lips when he exhales. Rowan stares at him wordlessly. His fingers tighten against mine, and the tether turns dark with a conflict of emotions. Fear and wonder and despair.

The light shifts, and for a moment I see the Lord Under the way he must appear to Rowan. His inhuman features, a refraction of narrowed eyes and layered mouths. The slashes at his throat that shift in time with his breath. The brutal sharpness of his fanged teeth.

His lashes flutter; his eyes open slowly. He swallows down a mouthful of blood. He looks at me for an endless moment, his eyes filled with countless unnamable things.

Then his attention slides to Rowan.

"How strange that you have ended *here*, after you fought so hard to stay in the world Above." His voice comes with a tidal sound, liquid as melted ice. "And yet, you've reclaimed the brother I stole from you. You have done the impossible; finally spared him from death."

Rowan touches his throat, his fingers marking a distracted line over his scars, then across the sigils. I can sense his anger—at the Lord Under, at himself—when he says, "This should have ended so much differently."

The Lord Under shakes his head, the motion stilted by the snare of the bone tree. "There has only ever been one way this could end." He looks to me, clear-eyed even beneath the haze of his pain. "I felt it, you know, the magic you drew from the forest to subdue my sisters. It was . . . clever, my love."

We regard each other. The ghost-pale air is filled by the shimmer of my power, the light from the spell-thread that binds us all together. "I did what you taught me. Used my strength to keep the forest safe."

His gaze slants to the bloodied bone shards that cut through him. Clear evidence of how apt a pupil I've been. His mouth tilts into a wry smile, acquiescing. "I never doubted your strength. Though I admit, when I asked for your help to save my world, this was not quite what I anticipated."

My heart sinks, and I'm too sorrowful to be angry with him. "When I asked for your help, this wasn't what *I* anticipated, either."

His smile flickers, dims. "I gave you my power, my heart, my name. Was that not enough?"

"It—it was. And it wasn't."

"I offered you a world. And yet this is how you would answer me. You'd prefer destruction to staying at my side."

344

I raise my hand. Shadows unfurl, stretching across the sepulcher toward the Lord Under, in his prison of vines and branches. The bone tree shifts, shivers, beneath my magic. It starts to devour him—thorned vines tightening, more shards piercing through his chest. He makes a sharp, ruined sound. Blood blackens his mouth.

I feel as though I'm lost in the woods, where all the paths before me lead only to danger. Destroy him and be free. Spare him, and never return to the world Above. It doesn't matter that I am sorry, or that I love him. I can't leave while our bond exists. It's woven too deep, it can't ever be undone.

Flowers bloom at our feet, their petals a brilliant crimson. I can feel the spell-thread between us, strained, about to shatter.

"Leta, wait." Rowan takes hold of my arm, stilling me. He says my name like a plea, a warning. "You are not those brutal creatures in the woods."

My hands tremble, even as power gathers coldly at my palms. The truth is like a drawn blade. Tears sting my eyes, but I force them away, swallowing down a sob. "I have to do this, Rowan. What way is there out of death, but for death?"

Rowan looks between me and the Lord Under. His expression guarded, he slides his hand down my arm, circles my wrist. "If your bond can't be undone, then remake it. A new connection . . . between the three of us."

He presses gently against the sigil. I look at him: scarred and shadowed, a boy and a monster, pulled into the world of the dead by his love for me. As his thumb marks my pulse, I feel the heat and softness of the tether. I feel an older, sharper magic.

Strands of power that bind us—the three of us. Heart to heart to heart. A connection forged in promises and blood and power. "Rowan, do you truly want this?"

"Yes," he says quietly. "I do."

I look at the Lord Under. Truly *look*, as though there is a secret hidden beneath his features, one I have never been able to unveil. I see tenderness and despair, fury and hope. All of them and none of them.

I move closer. The space between us narrows until I am against him, thorns and leaves and bones between us. I think of moonless nights. Trees on an ashen field, the cold slither of shadows in my veins. I think of the Lady. How she spoke to me in that hallowed, light-limned place. Told me that my choice would impact the fate of lives, of worlds.

Told me to look into the heart of the creature I named.

I lean against the Lord Under, fit my cheek into the crescent of his shoulder. He reaches out, wrists still caught by the tree, and his fingers unsteadily stroke my hair.

Then Rowan's hand is at my waist. He curls behind me, bows his head. His lips brush the side of my throat, grazing a kiss against my pulse. I stand, held between him and the Lord Under. Threads of magic weave around us, until the air is lit gold and the three of us are encircled by the tether.

I close my eyes. I whisper a name that tastes of pine and ash and smoke. "*Rvth*."

A tremor shivers through the air, and the carved walls of the bone tree writhe and coil. Slowly, the vines loosen, and the shards that pierced through the Lord Under draw back, unfold.

He looks at me with surprise—unsettled and bared, the human emotion so strange on his features. We stand on level ground, facing each other. A girl and a god and both of us changed.

I start to cry, but I meet his gaze evenly. "I wanted to help you. I—I *wanted* you." He acknowledges this silently, and I go on, the heat of confession sending a flush across my cheeks. "I don't want to destroy you. I just want to go home."

"Truly home," he says quietly. "To the world Above."

"Yes." I bow my head, tears dripping over my cheeks. "I want you to honor the terms of the bargain I made in the ruined grove. I want what you promised before you twisted my words, before you tricked me. And in turn . . ." I glance at Rowan. His fingers tighten at my waist. He nods. "I offer the promise I made to you . . . but reforged."

The Lord Under rubs at his wrist where the wounds are already healing. Even the rends in his cloak, left from the piercing shards, have knit closed. He wipes a claw against the edge of his mouth, scraping away the blood.

Quietly, he starts to recite my promise. The words I spoke beneath in the ruined grove, the words I spoke with poison in my veins. "You will love me. You will worship me. You will never forget me, even after you've returned home."

"Yes," Rowan says, his voice turned solemn.

"Yes," I echo. "We will."

The Lord Under reaches for my hand, presses his stained claws against the scar on my palm. "For you to return to the world Above, all this will need to be undone. Your magic, your

347

power, our connection. Whatever you find after this moment, you will face it alone."

As though in response to his words, a drift of magic spirals up from my hand, the shadows traced by gold. It feels like danger, to do this. But all our bargains have come with the taste of fear. It's right that our final one should feel the same.

Slowly, I nod. "I'll give it all back. And in exchange . . . you'll give back what you claimed from me. My family—my memories of them, and our reunion when I return Below for the final time."

He tightens his hold on my hand, drawing me closer until I am once again in his arms. He strokes my hair back from my face, and his lips graze against my cheek. "Very well. I accept your bargain." He kisses me again. I feel the curve of his smile against my skin as he glances toward Rowan. "I accept—from *both* of you."

The air around us shimmers, and a cold drift of wind casts over me. I flex my hands open and closed, feel the dance of power in my veins. Feel it start to dissolve. My connection to this world is undone and remade, replaced by a whispered promise, a kiss in the dark, and a tether that is as delicate as spider silk.

This is the last time the Lord Under and I will be together as equals. This is the last time we will be together at all. But I don't want this to be the end. To turn my back on him and walk away.

"Please," I say, my voice soft. "Come with us to the shore."

He glances between us, and nods, once. "If that is what you wish."

Rowan takes my other hand, and we walk in a line out of the bone tree. When we step through the arch and back into the forest, the trunk knits closed, the scrolled bark changed to a solid surface. None of us speaks as we go the rest of the way through the woods.

At the top of the stairs that lead to the lake, a heartwood stretches its branches to me. Leaves trace gently across my cheek. I look at the ground and see one, final garland of flowers bloom in my footprints.

We go down the stairs, pause at the edge of the water. Our reflections stretch across the surface, three blurred shapes. I see the outline of my crown, branches curved above my tangled hair. Tenderly, I touch the woven stems. I take off the circlet and hold it in my shaking hands.

The Lord Under watches me for a moment; then he turns to Rowan and beckons him close. "It seems your life has become mine after all. In a sense. Tell me, are you sorry for that?"

"No," Rowan says, without hesitating. He unlaces his cuffs and pushes back his sleeves. He holds out his arms, showing the blackened scars, stark against his skin. The sigils, and the left behind traces of poison. "Because of you, I turned myself into a monster. Because I became that monster, I found Violeta. I'm not sorry for any of this."

The Lord Under makes a noise low in his chest. A laugh, a sigh, a sound filled with as much tenderness as an inhuman creature can manage. "I believe I will . . . miss you, Rowan Sylvanan. I look forward to your observance, though I suspect it won't be colored with quite the same fear."

He puts his hand on Rowan's cheek. Rowan goes very still, but he doesn't pull away—not even when the Lord Under touches the scar on his mouth, tracing his claw down the curve of it before breaking contact.

The Lord Under turns to me, and gestures to the silvered path leading into the lake. "The last of your magic will see you back. Then our bargain will be done."

This is the end of it. Of altars and shadows and whispers in the darkened woods. I hold out the wreath to him, the crown he gave me to wear as I ruled this world at his side. "Goodbye."

He takes the wreath. His hand goes to my cheek, his claws gentle as he follows the line of my jaw. He touches beneath my chin. I tilt my face up, and he bends to kiss me for the last time. "Goodbye, Violeta."

Rowan puts his arm around me. Together we follow the path until our feet are met by the shallow edge of the lake. As I step into the icy water, I feel a pull from the forest. One final *reach* from the trees—their branches bowed toward me, the threads of magic stranded through the air, still tied loosely to my body.

I force myself to go forward. I don't turn back, not until the water is so deep that it laps against my throat. Then I allow myself to look at the world Below.

The Lord Under watches from the shore, his cloak wrapped around him like a shroud of shadows. A faint hue of power lights between us, and I whisper his name. I watch as he starts to fade, until he's turned to silver and silence, lost in the trees.

I take another step, and the ground is gone. Rowan pulls me against his chest. I close my eyes, listen to the steady throb of his heart beneath my ear. He kisses me as the water washes over us. Held by him, I fall beneath the surface.

I swallow down the darkness, and let it take me away.

Chapter Twenty-Seven

VIOLETA

We rise up through waves and ice and shadows. In the distance, fractured light sparks and ripples. I stretch out my hand. My fingers touch water and water and water. The light grows brighter. Finally, we break through the surface. We're back in the world Above, sprawled out on the shore of the lake. Waves at our feet, sedge grass tangled around our wrists.

I collapse onto my side and dig my fingers into the mud, dragging in breath after desperate breath. The air smells of forest and woodsmoke and *home*.

Rowan reaches for me. He's trembling, stung tight with apprehension. I fall against him, knotting my hands in the sodden fabric of his shirt as I pull him close. He presses his face to the curve of my neck, lets out a ragged sigh of relief. "You're real."

"I am real," I repeat. "I am *yours*."

I kiss him, a kiss that is both a caress and a claim. Open mouthed and desperate; all sharp teeth and breathless sobs. We clutch at each other to the point of bruising. A tender, furious confirmation. He starts to cry, tears falling hot against his cheeks, and I taste them as he kisses me back.

Colors wash over me. His moods—hurt and relief and love. The spell-thread is still tied between us. We're still bound. It's softer now, faint, but *there*.

We draw apart. Get to our feet. There's a shout in the distance, and we turn to see Clover and Arien, rushing toward us. We meet them at the edge of the pale trees, beside a scatter of blankets and lanterns—they've been waiting for us.

Clover throws her arms around me. "It's you! It's really you!" She squeezes me tightly then draws back, taking me by the shoulders to look me over. Her mouth curves up into an uncertain smile. Gently, she touches my cheek. "I missed you, Violeta. So much."

All I can do is sink against her. "And I missed you."

She holds me for another moment; then steps aside as Arien comes to me. With a tentative hand, he untangles a leaf from my hair. "Leta—" he says, choked, starting to cry. "I knew you would come back. I *knew*."

The trust in his voice undoes me. I wrap my arms around him, bury my face into his chest. Feel the shudder and sigh of his sobs as we cling to each other.

It's so different from the last time I came back, when I reached the house only to be claimed by shadows. I am here. I am here. I am *here*.

Clover drapes a blanket around my shoulders. "Let's go home."

I nod, my eyes already blurred with more tears.

Rowan takes my hand, and we make our way into the pale trees. I turn back to look at the shore before it is eclipsed by the forest. It seems a lifetime since I was here at the last ritual. Now the earth is mended. The water is clear, stained only with the tannin of fallen leaves. We've given so much, worked so hard, to make this possible.

Though the sky is clouded, my eyes wince against the brightness from the veiled sun. Everything is both familiar and strange at the same time.

The trees thin to a graveled path, and the ground here is cut by a blackened mark, the earth scarred all the way from the jacaranda tree to the closed gate of my garden. When Rowan summoned me to the altar, I hadn't noticed this. Now, I realize, all the places he touched when he was overcome by the Corruption are still unhealed.

I turn to Arien and Clover, confused. "This didn't mend when you healed the shore?"

They shake their heads. We step across the scar, and a knot of worry starts to tighten in my chest. I can feel it calling to me, this lingering darkness, the same way the poison inside Rowan stirred beneath my touch. But I don't have the power to mend it anymore.

The house rises up, still the same—all faerie-tale loveliness, with ivy around the eaves and a curl of smoke drifting from the chimney. I press my hand to my mouth, overcome. I can see my bedroom window with the curtains drawn, a vase of dried flowers on the sill.

Inside, the kitchen is warm from the stove, the room washed amber from firelight and altar candles. Rowan and I stand at the hearth, water dripping from our clothes onto the floor around us. The hallway door opens, and Florence comes into the room with Elan close behind her.

He pushes forward, past Florence, and runs toward Rowan. They stand apart for a moment, held by a tremulous silence, then Rowan wraps his arms around Elan. His eyes close, tears slipping through his lashes as he stands with his cheek pressed hard against Elan's silvery hair.

"Well!" Florence exclaims, looking at all of us. Her gaze is flinty, stern, but her mouth wavers. "You've reached new heights of danger and foolishness. And—I am so *very* glad you're safe, and home."

Fresh tears fill my eyes as I step toward her. She touches my cheek, my lake-wet hair. Then, putting her arm around my shoulders, she guides me closer to the fire. I stretch out my hands, reaching for the warmth of the flames.

Rowan and Elan step apart. With a grimace, Rowan looks down at his mud-stained clothes. "I'm going to change," he tells me. "I'll find you some dry things, too."

He leaves the room, and I sit down on the hearth. Huddle, shivering, inside the blanket still wrapped around my shoulders. Elan kneels beside me. I feel strangely shy as we look at each other. He's neater now, with his silver hair tied back into a knot. But there's still a spark of the heartwoods about him, in

355

the way his darkened eye reflects the firelight, and the luminance of his fawn-gold skin.

"You're different," he says softly.

I press my fingers gently to where the scar and the sigil mark my wrist. "Only a little."

"You're not so scary now." A beat passes; his mouth tips into a smile. "Thank you for bringing me home."

I can't help but smile in return. "We're going to have to find a way to explain how you came back."

"Oh," he says, waving a hand and laughing as he glances at Clover and Arien. "We already figured that out. I'm Florence's wayward relation, sent here to keep out of trouble."

I look him over, contemplating this. With his silver hair and his scars and his mismatched eyes, he looks nothing like the round-cheeked boy from the portrait upstairs. He is taller, older, with a newfound sharpness in the lines of his face and the set of his mouth. So changed that only those who loved him most would recognize him.

Florence smiles, ruffles a hand through Elan's hair. "It's true enough, I suppose."

"It must have been some trouble, if Lakesedge Estate was the safer place," Arien snorts, teasing. "What did you *do*, Elan?"

Elan elbows him. "Is that any way to speak to a *guest*?"

They dissolve into laughter, shoving at each other. Clover steps around them as she goes to the stove, reaches for a cup on the shelves above the hearth. She pours out some tea, stirs in a generous spoonful of honey before she passes me the cup.

"Elan and Arien told us what happened—some of it, at

least," she says as she tugs a hand down the length of her braid. "How did you escape? Did you really have to *kill* the god of death?"

Florence, beside Clover, draws her fingers across her chest protectively.

"No," I tell them. "He isn't dead." I glance to Arien, take a careful sip of tea. It's hot, bitter beneath the honey. I'm not sure where to begin. "Rowan and I both made a new bargain with the Lord Under."

Arien stares at me, his mouth fallen open in shock. "After all that's happened, you're *still* bound to him? Both of you?"

"It isn't the same." I look down at my hands, curled around the teacup. There's still dark crescents of dirt from the world Below embedded under my nails. "I gave it up. All my power and magic, and my bond to the Lord Under. I gave it up so I could come back."

In the gold-hued quiet of the kitchen, I tell the bare, earnest truth. About the tricks and the promises. How I walked beside the lord of the dead and was—for a brief moment—more a god than a girl. How I learned and used the names of the sister gods. How Rowan and I made our final, enduring bargain with the Lord Under.

I don't share it all, though. There are some parts too fragile to speak aloud. Like the way I slipped into that strange, light-limned place and heard the Lady's voice. The raw tenderness in the Lord Under's eyes when he kissed me that first time. Or how I feel such grief that my terrible, wondrous magic has been replaced by hollow emptiness.

Rowan comes back into the room, dressed in new, neat clothes. His dark linen shirt looks freshly ironed, and he's cleaned the mud from his boots. The only sign of disarray is his still-damp hair, hanging in loose waves around his shoulders.

He passes me a clean dress, folded up tidily. "I tried to find the warmest one."

"Thank you," I say, taking it from him. I look toward the hallway, but I don't want to go upstairs to my room and be so far from everyone. Not yet.

With the dress in my arms, I go inside the stillroom, shut the door behind me. Beneath the garlands of drying flowers and herbs, I start to take off my clothes. My silken dress from the world Below is torn; the fabric stained with blood, the mothwings tattered.

But I set it aside carefully, draped over the end of Clover's workbench. Thinking how I can embroider the tears closed, the same way the Lord Under once mended my cloak.

From the kitchen, I can hear the companionable sound of voices, the scrape of the stove drafts as someone adds wood to the fire. I look at the new dress. It's the color of moss, with full skirts and a wide ribboned sash. There's a lace camisole and undergarments folded up alongside it, and a pair of ribboned socks.

I shiver my way into the new clothes. The dress has a pattern of vines stitched around the hem. I tie the sash, but when I reach behind me for the buttons, my fingers are so cold that I can't fasten them.

With a sigh, I slouch back against the edge of the worktable.

My gaze drifts toward the window, to the scar on the ground outside. I curl my fingers against my palms, feeling the aching emptiness where my power used to be.

There's a soft knock on the door. It opens slowly, then Rowan steps into the room. The air around us glitters with dust motes as he regards me in silence—my face turned to the window, the back of my dress still gaping open. "Do you need some help?"

I nod, my lips pressed together. I feel like I'm about to cry again.

He closes the door quietly and crosses the room. Gently, he lifts my hair aside and starts to fasten the buttons. As his fingers brush my nape, Rowan laughs to himself. "Do you remember the first time I did this for you?"

I smile, warmed a little by the memory. "Yes, I do."

"You have no idea how terribly I wanted to kiss you then."

My smile widens. "Oh, I might have had *some* idea."

He bends, and presses his lips to my neck. I shiver at the feel of his breath on my skin. A spark flickers across the tether, and then I feel how the other piece of the spell—once tied to the Lord Under—now stretches into empty darkness.

I blink back wayward tears; there seems to be an endless well of them, tinged with a confusion of emotions. I clench my hands to fists, stare outside at the wounded earth.

Rowan kisses my neck again. "You can miss him, Leta."

"I don't—" I shake my head, wanting to protest, but the words won't come. I turn to look at him, take his hands between my own. "I'm not sorry to be home. Not at all."

"You can miss him all the same." His voice goes quiet, gentle. "You don't have to hide it. If you hadn't loved him the way you did, then none of this would have been possible."

I nod, unable to trust myself to speak. Maybe the bittersweet ache will soften; maybe it won't. All I am certain of is that I don't regret what I did.

I chose it all—the bargains and the hurt and the sacrifice.

I chose to come home.

Rowan fastens the rest of my buttons. Then he says, "Tell me the rest of the story, Leta. The story from the wayside."

For a moment I'm confused. So used to the loss and the emptiness I find, whenever I reach for the stories I used to know. But the words rise unbidden, as though they have been placed against my tongue. "The maiden in the labyrinth?"

"I'm still waiting to hear how it ended."

I think of that long-ago night at the wayside cottage, when I lay beside Arien and told him the story, wishing I could weave safety for him with my words. I think of the shift of light, how I'd looked up to see Rowan watching me. Entranced.

I let out a shaky breath. "Beyond seven forests, beyond seven lakes, there was a monster who lived deep below the earth . . ."

The words of the story are familiar, now. Like I've never forgotten them. How the maiden finds her way through the tangled walls of the labyrinth, following an unfurled thread to trace her path back home.

And when I close my eyes, I can see my mother sitting beside the fire in our cottage. My father with Arien in his arms, and his gaze fixed on her as *she* tells the story. Listening, listening to her voice. His whole face lit up with tenderness.

"I remember them," I whisper. "I remember."

Rowan reaches into his pocket, brings out an object wrapped in a length of silken ribbon. A key—the key to my garden. I curl my fingers around it, the iron warming against my palm.

Then, resolved, I slip the ribbon over my head and walk back out into the kitchen. Clover and Arien are still beside the hearth. "I need your help," I tell them. "To mend the scar."

"Of course," Arien says. They both stand up. Arien pulls on his cloak, and Clover finds a pen and ink bottle in the still-room. They wait for me while I slip my feet into Clover's spare boots, left beside the kitchen door, and then we walk together out into the yard.

The grass is scattered with dandelions that have turned to silver moons. The seeds drift free as we pass. The gate to my garden is open, left unlocked. Inside, the altar where Rowan summoned me is still propped against a fallen branch.

It's so *strange* to see it there, this icon, capturing the moment when I was a magical, shadow-hued creature. I brush my fingers over the frame, over ridges of wax from the burned-down candles.

I look around the garden. The skeletal trees, the barren thorns, the place where the scar ends, beneath the altar. "I want to mend this," I say. "Together. Just like we did at the ritual."

Arien nods, his eyes turned solemn. We kneel at the altar, and Clover takes her pen, marks a sigil on her arm. Arien does the same, then he gives the pen to me.

I push back my sleeve and add a mark in the tender hollow of my forearm. The same spell I used to wake the garden, when Rowan first brought me here. The same spell I used, once, to grow a heartwood from a seed. As the ink flows over my skin, I wonder if this is the last time I'll feel like an alchemist.

We put our hands against the earth, side by side, our fingers touching. The new sigil glows warm on my wrist. The earth hums as I reach for the spark of my power.

It's soft and small, all candle smoke and tiny wings. So different from the endless strength I commanded in the world Below. Slowly, the strands of our magic start to weave together. This is all I have now. A gentle warmth, a single thread spun loosely through my fingers. But it will be enough.

And when I close my eyes and cast the spell . . . I see my father. His hands in the earth, seeds sprung to life beneath the touch of his power. Ink on his wrists, his eyes turned to gold as magic gleams up from his skin.

Instead of the ache and ruin I once felt in place of these memories, now there is only light and heat and *love*.

I sit back and look around. The trees are still autumn bare, brambles curved sharply beneath. But there are new flowers at the edges of the path. Crimson roses, black-petaled hellebores. We've mended the garden, and the wound left on the ground has been healed over. I smile, my throat gone tight, as I look at the spaces of still-bare earth, picturing where I will plant seeds when the weather turns warm again.

Clover puts her arm around my shoulders. "I'm so glad you're back, Leta."

I squeeze her hand, smile at Arien. "Home," I say quietly. "With all of you."

We stay together for a while, as clouds cover the sky and the light turns somber. A scent in the air promises rain, and there's a chill to the wind that makes all of us shiver. Arien and Clover go back to the house, but I linger behind, sitting on the fallen tree. The place where Rowan once kissed me as the poison devoured him.

A canopy of silvered ivy has grown above it now, and leaves rustle over me, stirred with a whisper that reminds me of the souls in the heartwoods.

I'm still there when Rowan comes to find me, carrying another cup of Clover's tea, balanced carefully so it doesn't spill. He passes me the cup, then takes off his cloak and places it over my shoulders. Sitting down beside me, he looks appreciatively at the mended garden.

"It seemed a nice way to spend the last of my magic," I say, holding out my hand to show him the faint glimmer over my fingertips. "This is all I have left now."

He takes my hand between his own. His fingers press my heartline, the way he did when he first drew out my power. A touch on my palm, a flare of light between us. "And it's perfect," he tells me. "You're perfect."

The darkness shifts briefly under his skin when he touches me. I trace my fingers over a bruise-like shadow, smudged beneath the sigil on his collarbone. "I'm sorry that I don't have enough magic to mend you."

Rowan shakes his head, mouth tilted into a rueful smile.

"I don't need to be mended. What I said to the Lord Under before we came home—it was the truth. I'm not sorry for what I've become, Leta. For all my mistakes, I can't regret how the darkness in my life was the reason I met you."

"I love you, Rowan."

"And I love you."

We sit together and share the tea, passing the cup back and forth. Rowan looks at the ivy woven around the fallen tree. He touches the curled edge of a leaf as he glances up at me, shy and curious. "Why did you kiss me that day when I came to you here, when I became a monster?"

"Maybe it was because you were a monster that I kissed you."

I laugh and he sighs, scowling, which only makes me laugh harder. He rakes a hand through his hair, tilts back his head to look at the sky, where a daylight moon is visible between the clouds—pale silver, and almost full.

"Leta," he says, still shy, "it will be the Autumndark bonfire soon. I wondered if you'd come with me and lead the observance chant. I wasn't going to go at all, but I decided that I want to be there, in the village. I want to be there with you."

At his words, I feel a slow warmth, thinking of Summersend, the rush of pride that filled me as I walked with him through the crowd toward the fire. Thinking of how it will be, to stay by his side at all the other bonfires, and festivals, and tithe days.

"Together then," I agree.

A flush spreads across his cheeks. He smiles—pleased and

unguarded, baring his crooked teeth. I pull him close and press my forehead to his, sighing happily. Then I kiss him.

He threads his fingers into my hair, stroking gentle circles against the nape of my neck. There's a softness in this, being with him beneath the rising dusk. The tender, unhurried way he kisses me back; the pale light of magic strung between us. I feel it woven around our hearts, trailing away into the distance where it fades into a quiet dark.

I think of shadows and mist, of caresses that are laced by frost. I think of sunlight and honey, the firelit kitchen, my room with the curtains drifting back and forth in the Harvest-fall breeze. And Rowan, Rowan—the boy, the monster, the boy—who followed me into the dark and brought me home.

I kiss him. I kiss him for a long time, surrounded by the silver leaves of the garden I mended with the last bright sparks of my remaining magic.

Chapter Twenty-Eight

ROWAN

In the crimson light of sunset, I prepare for the Autumndark bonfire. My shirt is embroidered, black on black, a pattern of thorns at the shoulders. My hair is held back in five-strand braids on either side of my face, woven tight at my temples then loosening to fall behind my shoulders. It's the same way my father wore his hair at every bonfire.

Elan comes into my room. His hair is braided back like mine, and dark lines are painted across his eyelids. He has a small brush, and a jar, held in one hand. "Want me to help with your ink?"

The Autumndark bonfire is a celebration of the end of harvest season, when we welcome the shorter days and longer nights. As well as the bonfire and the litany, we mark our features with black ink.

The last time I wore ink to the ceremony, our father had

painted it on for me. After that—after he died—it hadn't felt right. Instead, I went to the village in my gloves and my cloak. Tried very hard to stay hidden in the shadows.

But tonight, I want things to be different.

I turn to Elan as he offers the jar of thickened ink. "Yes, please."

He opens the jar. I feel his breath, tickling against my cheeks alongside the strokes of the brush. He marks a line across each of my eyelids. A curve that tapers to a point on either side of my nose. He paints another layer of ink on one side. Licks his thumb, wipes away a smudge.

When he's finished, he steps back. Examines his work. He considers me for a long time. His eyes narrowed. Then he starts to laugh. "You look exactly like Father."

I turn to the mirror. At first glance the reflection *is* our father. The same fawn-gold skin and dark, braided hair. But the more I look, the more I notice the differences. The way I have a line between my brows from frowning so much. How my eyes are solemn. Rather than lit by the easy friendliness he had.

"Somehow I don't think anyone will mistake me for him." I'm laughing, too. Though the sound catches in my chest. A softened ache.

When we leave my room and go down the stairs, the house is quiet and empty. Everyone else has already left for the village. To help prepare the fire. We collect our lanterns from where Florence left them beside the front door. I follow Elan outside.

We walk down the drive. Pass under the arched gateway.

The trees beyond are bare now. Branches crossing the faded, sunset sky.

The sun sinks lower as walk to the village. I feel so anxious. I've done this countless times. Stood before the village for every ritual. Tonight, though, my life isn't veiled by shadows. Elan is here, alive. Leta will be beside me.

We pass through a grove of olive trees. I sigh, and Elan glances curiously at me. "I can't believe you're nervous about leading the chant. You were in the world of the *dead*."

"Father always made this look so easy."

Elan pulls a hand contemplatively through his hair. The silver strands curl around his fingers. "Oh, he made *everything* look easy," he says wistfully, his eyes dark with sadness. "Remember the time my lantern tipped over by accident and set the bonfire alight? He just started the litany, pretended it was supposed to happen that way."

"By accident?" I raise a brow. "From what I recall, there wasn't much *accidental* about it."

Elan stretches his arms overhead, feigning innocence. "I don't know what you're talking about."

I look at him. Painted eyes, braided hair. The new shirt Clover made for him, because he's grown out of the clothes left from when he was fourteen. When he was last alive.

It's a strange thought. That he was *gone* and is now returned. And though in many ways he's the same as I remember— foolish and playful, making jokes with Arien—there's a new seriousness to him. Traces of the world Below. I see them in the way the light touches his skin. In the slow blink of his onyx eye.

The fields around the village are dark by the time we reach their outskirts. Braziers have been lit between the rows of the orchard groves. In the center of the village, the windows of the cottages are unshuttered. Their sills lined with candles. A crowd has gathered around the unlit fire. Everyone wears clothes decorated with careful embroidery: long dresses and loose-sleeved linen shirts. Their faces marked in varying designs of black ink.

I see Florence at a table, near the side of the square. Serving out spiced apple cider and squares of almas cake. Elan waves to her, and she smiles back. *Her wayward relation*. In the lantern light, they look so similar that it's an easy truth. The same silvery hair, the same golden skin.

Clover walks through the crowd toward us. Her hair is pinned into a coronet. Behind her glasses, her eyes are lined delicately. When she notices my appearance, she grins. "You dressed up!"

I scowl at her, embarrassed. "*Everyone* is dressed up."

"Of course, of course." She arranges her face into a serious expression. Elan snorts back a laugh. I roll my eyes at them both as we walk over to the altar.

Thea is by the icon. Her hair is in two long braids. Each tied with a silken ribbon that matches her dress. She wears a linen apron and holds a brush in her hand. She's almost finished covering the icon frame with a new coat of varnish.

Arien sits at the base of the altar, surrounded by his jars of paint. He glances up at me. Pushes his hair from his face, leaving a smudge across his cheek. Shyly, he looks at the icon. "I've just about finished."

The new paint shimmers with an otherworldly brilliance. The Lady's hands are a blaze of light, retouched in gold. Above her, the sky is filled with brightened leaves and flowers. "It's—" I laugh, shaking my head. "Arien, this is wonderful."

"You really like it?"

"I do."

He tugs at his sleeve, his smile widening as his cheeks start to flush. "Thank you. For letting me do this. And for—well, everything."

He starts to clear away the brushes and paint jars. Elan bends down to help him. "If we hurry," he says, looking side-long at Arien, "we can get some of Florence's cake before the litany."

Arien nods, his cheeks flushed even brighter. Together they pack the jars and brushes into Arien's satchel. While they're working, Keeper Harkness comes to the altar. He looks at the frame, his lantern held up. Proudly, Thea says, "Isn't it perfect?"

She shows him how she's smoothed the worn-down wood, and added extra varnish. There's a pleased light in his eyes as he listens to her. Even beneath his serious expression. "You've done good work, Calathea."

Thea wipes her hands on a cloth. She smiles at me, a teasing lilt in her voice. "It was very kind of you to ask for my help, Lord Sylvanan. It's been excellent practice."

"You're very . . . welcome, Thea."

Keeper Harkness turns to me. There's a pause; then he offers a small nod. "Lord Sylvanan. We're almost ready for you to begin."

"Thank you." I hesitate. Before I can lose my nerve, I go on quietly, "Rowan. I—You can call me Rowan."

He's silent for a moment. "Brin." Then his face softens. His mouth lifts, a slight smile. He smooths his hair. As though checking that none of his curls have escaped the impeccably tidy knot. "Your father and I, we never used our titles with each other, either."

He nods to me again, then turns and goes over toward the fire. Calling the crowd to gather. Clover takes a sparklight from her pocket. She passes it to me. "Good luck. You look very imposing, by the way."

She helps Thea take off her apron. They go into the square, joining the line around the unlit bonfire. I'm left alone in the darkness, beside the altar.

I take a deep breath. I can smell the cut greenery piled within the stones. I close my eyes. The scent of pine makes me think of another forest. Shadows and crimson trees.

There's a gentle pull from the spell at my wrist. The voices of the crowd soften. I look up as Leta walks out from between two of the cottages. There's a wreath of ivy on her hair. Her skirts are a trail of lace, her sleeves embroidered with constellations and crescent moons. Her face is unpainted except for her lips.

When our eyes meet, her darkened mouth curves up into a smile.

She walks across the square with her gaze fixed on mine. When she reaches me, I bend down and kiss her. Careful not to smudge the paint on her mouth. Her arms slide around my waist, and she leans against me. Just like with Elan, there's a solemnness to her. In the angle of her downcast lashes. The way her fingers curl against her palm, pressed to the scar. We're all of us marked by the world Below.

I touch her cheek, gently. "Are you ready?"

She nods. We step apart and walk into the crowd.

A murmur goes through the air as we move toward the fire. I catch scraps of words, of whispers. The same rumors that always follow me. Suddenly, my attempt to make tonight *different* feels so foolish. But Leta takes my hand. Her fingers mark the line on my palm. The scar left from the blood I gave to summon her.

"Together," she says, her words like a spell. "Remember?"

"Together," I echo.

I think of my father at the final bonfire he led. His voice resonant as he sang the litany. I think of myself in the world Below, my hands pressed to the soul trees. Seeing my family, in flashes of emotion and memory.

I'll never stand beside my father again as he chants for the crowd. I'll never be able to replace him. But I am here. And I can do this.

I take out my sparklight. Set it to my lantern. Then I pass it to Leta, who does the same. All through the crowd, lanterns illuminate the square, a wash of brightness.

With steady hands, I lift the candle from my lantern. Hold the flame beneath the piled branches at the base of the fire.

The wood catches alight. Smoke curls up with a pleasant, acrid scent.

Leta smiles at me, her mouth a dark heart. The faint thread between us—all that's left of the tether now—hums like a song. The new blaze of fire spirals upward, rises higher. Sparks scatter. The sky is turned silver by the Autumndark moon.

Then Leta starts to sing.

She's alone at first, her chanted words small against the night. Then others join, familiar voices; Arien and Florence and Clover. One by one, the song weaves through the crowd. The air is filled with the litany.

We make a slow path around the fire. The crowd follows. We circle the stones three times; then I start to walk away from the village. Everyone falls into line behind me. I lead them out of the square. Over to the fallow fields.

At the edge of the tilled ground, I kneel. Brin steps to the head of the line. Inclines his head to me. Then he leads the villagers onward. Everyone spreads out. The field is walled with lantern light.

I take off my gloves. Press my hands to the ground. Cut a mark into the soil with my poison-banded fingers, then scatter in a handful of crumbled leaves. I think of light, of life, of magic woven through the world.

Leta gets back to her feet. She gathers up her skirts. Goes out onto the field. She is just a girl with mud on her boots and a handmade crown of ivy on her hair. But for the barest moment, the scene blurs. And the shadows where she walks might be vines or flowers or thorns.

At the center of the field, she takes a handful of earth. Clutches it in her fist. She stands alone. A pale ghost against the darkness of the field. Tears glisten on her cheeks.

Then she looks up and smiles. She reaches toward me.

I walk to her. I take her hand. Around us, the voices soften. The crowd drifts away from the edges of the field. Back to the village, to continue the celebration. My part in the ritual is over.

I turn in the opposite direction. Take Leta into the quiet dark, out in the orchards beyond the field. We pause near one of the braziers, burning with a small, eager fire. Leta unlaces her boots. She climbs, barefoot, into one of the trees. She sits framed by the branches, her eyes turned toward the clouded sky.

"Thank you," I say. "For being with me for the chant."

She smiles down at me. "I'll be with you for all the chants. For everything." She takes the wreath from her hair, starts to unravel the leaves. Piece by piece, the ivy falls to the ground at my feet. Then she laughs. "The next bonfire is midwinter. That's your birthday. Maybe I'll surprise you and sing 'Many Years' instead of the litany."

"Don't you *dare*."

"You're absolutely no fun." Still laughing, Leta shakes her head. "I guess it's not such a surprise now that I've told you my plans."

There's a rustle from beyond the trees. Elan and Arien pick their way down the path toward us. Arien stretches his hands over the brazier. Light flickers over his fingers, smeared with paint rather than magic. He looks content, but beside him, Elan is solemn.

He notices me watching him. "I'm fine. It's just—I didn't

realize how strange it would feel to be here again. To see the fires, to hear the litany."

I put my hand on his shoulder. "Yes, I know."

"It's all I can think about sometimes," he admits. He glances toward Leta. "Those creatures—those gods. That whole *world*. It's a pity you can't just . . . magic the memories away."

He laughs, but there's a darkness in his eyes. Arien picks up a handful of dried leaves. Casts them into the brazier. They crackle and turn to smoke. He's thoughtful as he watches the smoke rise.

"I have an idea." He digs through his pockets. Finds a pencil and a folded scrap of paper. He goes over to sit beneath the tree. Smooths the paper out against his knees.

Elan watches him, one brow raised. "What are you doing?"

"I can't make you forget. But you can tell me. Whisper it."

He pats the ground beside him. Elan gives Arien a hesitant smile, then goes over and sits down. He cups his hand against Arien's ear. He starts to whisper.

Leta and I both watch as my brother whispers secrets and Arien fills the page with sketches. Some of the things he draws I recognize. A forest that is only shadow. A grove of wounded trees, sap oozing from their scarred trunks. A creature with cold eyes and a sharp, cruel smile.

When they're done, Arien gives the paper to Elan. He looks at it for a long time. Then he gets up and crosses to the brazier. Arien follows him. They stand side by side as Elan tears the paper, drops the pieces into the flames. Watches them burn. Ash, then smoke, then gone.

He wipes his eyes on his sleeve. Then he turns to Arien. Teasingly, he says, "Now I want a secret from you. It's only fair."

"Oh?" Arien laughs, startled. He hesitates for a moment. Then he whispers to Elan.

"My hair looks like *what*?" Elan touches his fingers to the silver strands, pleased. "Starlight?"

Arien folds his arms. "It's not really a secret if you blurt it out to everyone."

Elan laughs, not at all sorry. Two figures appear at the edge of the orchard—Clover and Thea, waving to us. "You go ahead," Leta tells Elan and Arien. "We'll walk home later."

Elan links his arm through Arien's as they go to join Clover and Thea. We watch them make their way out of the trees and across the field. Their voices fade. We're alone again.

I lean my head against Leta's knees. She trails her hand idly over my hair. "You did well, tonight at the fire."

"I'm never going to be like my father." It's the thought I've turned over all night. Ever since I looked in the mirror and saw his features echoed in my own.

"Maybe you won't. But does that matter?" She gestures to the fields and the village beyond. "You can tend to this, in your own way."

We stay together, watch the fire in the brazier as it dwindles to embers. When we go back to the village, the square is empty. I pick up two lanterns from the altar. Relight the candles with my sparklight. We walk home slowly, our lights like tiny stars beneath the night-draped trees that line the road.

When we reach the estate, the house is dark, except for a

single lamp in the front window. We go inside. Extinguish our lanterns. I look toward the parlor. We owe another observance, but neither of us moves to the closed door.

Leta watches the smoke dissipate from her candle. A wistful smile on her paint-dark mouth. I think again of her question about my father. The type of lord I want to be.

"There's no erasing what I am. What I've done. I'll never replace my father." I look down at my hands. My scarred palm, my fingers banded by poison. "I feel as though I'm trying to follow a path where he walked. But I can't follow him entirely. There are places where the ground has shifted. Where I'll have to find my own way."

"You might not be able to replace him," Leta agrees. There's quiet understanding in her voice. "But you don't have to follow that path."

I picture the future as it might unfold ahead of us. Harvests and bonfires and tithe days. I'll turn twenty on midwinter. Stand before the village as we circle the fire. Leta will sing the chant on the darkest night of the year.

"Even without the curse, my life will always feel like something I've stolen," I admit.

Leta takes my hands between her own. She bends to my wrists. Presses her lips against the scars. "All we've done to be here—crossed life, and death—that should leave a mark. But you've earned your place. Your life is not a stolen thing, Rowan Sylvanan."

I draw her into my arms. She curls against me. Then she winds her fingers through the laces on my shirt, untying them.

She moves slow, deliberately idle. She starts to kiss my neck as she works at the laces. When her teeth bite softly against my throat, a moan escapes me—louder than expected in the quiet hallway.

"Shh!" Leta hisses, laughing.

She pushes me back against the wall. Cages me with her arms. She tiptoes to kiss me again. I look down at her, remembering her sadness when she stood in the field at the end of the bonfire procession. "I know you're sorry for what you gave up."

She shakes her head. "I'm not . . ."

"The creature you were in the Vair Woods, when I summoned you to the altar, she's still a part of you. At the bonfire . . . you looked like magic."

"I still have some magic left," she teases. "Let me show you."

Her fingers trace over my wrist, over the sigil. The tether isn't the same as before. But when she kisses me and pushes her fingers into the spell, there's a spark of heat that makes me gasp.

I grab her waist and spin her around. We've traded places, I have her pinned with the wall at her back. I bend to kiss her again. Catch her breathless laugher against my mouth. I tighten my hold on her waist, push my knee between her thighs. She arches her back and rocks against me, her skirts rustling around us.

We stumble up the stairs. Across the landing, and into the hallway. By the time we reach my door, all I want is to pull her into my room and kiss her forever. Leta looks at me, her mouth curled up into a smile. "We should have gone in the other direction, to my room. There's much more space."

I knot my fingers through her hair. Pull until her head tilts back and bares her throat. "More space for what, exactly?" I trail my mouth down her neck, punctuating my words with more kisses. "You'll have to be very specific."

She pretends to consider my question. "How did you phrase it last time? Take me to bed? At least there's an actual bed this time." She laughs helplessly, the sound echoing through the house. "Or a chaise. I suppose that's close enough."

I put my hand over her mouth. "Shh. I was trying to be polite. What did you *want* me to say?"

She huffs out another laugh against my palm. Draws back, her face settled into seriousness. She lowers her eyes. Looking almost shy. "Take me to bed, Rowan. Please."

We go into my room. She pauses halfway to unlace her boots, drops them haphazardly on the floor. She pulls at my shirt; I bend my head and let her take it off. We fall together onto the bed, a tangle of breathless kisses.

She turns so I can unfasten the buttons on the back of her dress. Soon she's all bared, except for the key to the garden that is still on the ribbon around her neck. I thread my fingers through it and tug her closer. Bury my face in her tangled hair. Kiss her cheek, her neck, her shoulder.

She curls her leg around my waist as her hand delves between us. She pulls impatiently at my waistband. "Why do you always have so many buttons?" Her foot runs down my calf, and she pauses. Leans on one elbow to peer at me incredulously. "Are you still wearing your boots?"

"I'm getting to them, Leta."

She helps me undress, laughing. I lean over her. Golden heat glimmers through the tether as we sink onto the bed. She clutches my waist, urges me closer, gasping as I start to move against her. I kiss the sound from her lips. Kiss her until our breath is ragged. Until the remaining traces of her magic light across her hands.

I whisper her name, over and over. The way I did when I tried to call her out of the dark. She buries her face in my neck, starting to shatter apart. Her teeth find my throat, and I'm dragged right over the edge with her.

Once we've both spiraled into stillness, we curl together under the tumbled quilts. I stay awake long enough to watch her dream. The flutter of her lashes, the soft rhythm of her breath.

And I know, undoubtedly, that I am more hers than I ever was. Even more than the moment when I knelt before her in the world Below. The spell-thread between us is so pale now, almost invisible. But it doesn't matter.

We are bound by more than magic.

Chapter Twenty-Nine

VIOLETA

The hours before dawn know all my secrets.

I chase scraps of sleep through the last of the full-moon night, curled beside Rowan on his narrow bed. His arm is reassuringly heavy, draped over my waist. The room is warm, lit by flames that flicker softly in the fireplace. But when I dream, it's of a world filled with frost and whispers and secrets.

I'm in a skyless forest. I walk through the archway of the bone tree. Power burns through my veins. I call a name into the darkness, one that feels so familiar on my tongue, that leaves my mouth with a taste of blood and honey.

Rowan tightens his hold on my waist. His fingers tangle gently in my hair as he brushes it aside to kiss my throat. And beside his touch I feel another—cold and clawed and laced with shadows.

The name from my dream is gone as soon as my eyes blink open, slipped away into nothingness. The memory of the power lingers, but when I flex my hands, there are only the faint sparks of my magic.

I sit up and pull back the curtains. The glass is fogged with condensation. I clear a space and look outside. It's early, and beneath the clouds, the estate is all trees and dark. For a moment I'm disoriented—back in another world, encircled by heartwoods and the whispers of souls.

Rowan stirs, opening his eyes to regard me, silhouetted by the window. He traces his fingers down my arm until he finds the sigil. "Are you all right?"

"Yes. I dreamed, that's all."

"You're home, Leta." His thumb presses against the spell, and the tether hums faintly. "You're here. You're safe."

I take his hand and clasp it between my own, bending to brush a kiss over his knuckles. "I know."

"I thought we'd bring down the books from the attic today." His voice is soft, still edged with sleep. "Or maybe you can start your list of seeds. Clover has an almanac in her stillroom that has a list of what you can plant, and when."

"We don't have to do everything right now, you know," I laugh. "We have time."

"I like to hear you say that. *Time*."

I stroke my fingers over his cheek, following the line of scars from his brow to his jaw. "Truly, all I thought about today was eating Florence's leftover bonfire cakes for breakfast."

"I think Elan has already put a claim on those."

"Well, he can share."

Rowan looks up at me, his eyes darkly serious. I can tell that he's nervous, though he's trying not to let it show. "We owe our observance."

"Yes," I say. "We do."

He sits up and clasps my face between his hands. Still serious, he goes on, "I took my share of this bargain willingly, Leta. I don't want to hide from it, whatever lies between the three of us."

I look down at the crescent mark on my palm, thinking of how it felt in the heart of the bone tree, when Rowan stepped forward and put his arms around me while I was held by the Lord Under. How even in my dreams, the two of them are all tangled up together. I don't have words for it, the way they both have a claim on my heart.

I let my head bow, press my forehead against his. "Then come with me to the altar."

We get out of bed. I find my dress and my undergarments where I dropped them on the floor last night, shiver my way back into everything while I'm close to the fire. I'm still cold, even near the hearth, so I put on Rowan's cloak, too.

Rowan gets dressed in new clothes, taking a long time to smooth the creases from his shirt and neaten the laces at his collar. He puts on his boots and ties back his hair into a knot. Then together, we go out of the room.

I carry my boots, walking barefoot through the quiet halls. The sun has started to rise now, illuminating the house with the barest hints of early light. The library windows show a lilac sky when we pass the open door. I look at the empty shelves and imagine how they will be once all the books are unpacked.

I look at the table, scattered with notebooks where Arien and Clover have been working at sketches and lessons. I look at the portrait of Rowan's family and think of Elan—brought back, brought home. He's scarred and changed, with shadow-laced dreams. But he has a life ahead of him. A future.

And that is something I will have, as well.

The house is mine, and I'll wake it slowly. I have so much time to open the rooms, to chase away the dust, to bring back everything that was going to be locked up forever.

We walk down the stairs and go into the parlor, opening the door slowly so it doesn't make a sound. Inside, the curtains are still drawn, and the corners are dark. The icon is hidden by shadows.

It's the first time I've been in this room since the day I was poisoned, when Rowan carried me to the icon so I could call to the Lord Under. It makes my chest go tight to look at the place where I bled and begged, lived and died.

I move shakily toward the altar, gather up my skirts as I start to kneel. But it doesn't feel right, the thought of us with our heads bowed and our hands pressed to the floor over the faded stain of my blood. Rowan and I both made so many desperate choices here. I don't want this to be where we keep our final promise to the Lord Under.

I hesitate, and Rowan touches my shoulder. I turn to him. "I think we should go somewhere else."

He looks at me for a moment then nods, understanding. He

takes a candle and a sparklight from the altar shelf, and slips them into his pocket before he follows me out of the room.

Arien is in the kitchen, his sleeves rolled to his elbows as he kneads bread dough on the flour-dusted table. He blinks at us sleepily when we come through the door. His hair is a mess, and his eyes are shadowed with tiredness. "You're up early."

"So are you." I go over to him, wipe a smudge of flour from his cheek.

"It's my turn for chores."

I watch as he puts the dough in the cast-iron tin. He covers it with a cloth and sets it near the stove hearth to rise, the way Florence taught him. As he wets a cloth and wipes away the spilled flour from the table, I have an image of him in another kitchen. In a cottage where the air smelled of linseed oil, where candles burned ominously at the altar.

I remember the night of his magic gone wild. Of the flames and the fear, and how I knelt on shards of glass to protect him. Once, I thought the only way I could keep Arien safe was to put myself in danger. I never thought—never hoped—that he could have this. A home. A family. A place where his magic is seen as a gift, rather than something to be feared.

I ruffle my hand through his sleep-tangled curls. He leans his head against my shoulder and smiles at me. "What are you doing up, anyway?"

"We're . . ." I waver for a moment, not sure how to explain. Then, I square my shoulders. Take a breath. "We are going to the lake to make observance to the Lord Under."

Arien sighs and presses his head closer against me. Then he

starts to laugh. "If you're going outside, you might want your boots. There's frost on the ground."

I look down at my bare feet, and I start to laugh, too. Awkwardly, I drape the hem of Rowan's cloak over my arm and step into my boots. As I walk toward the door, one of the trailing laces catches under my heel, and I trip forward. Rowan grabs my arm before I can fall.

"You were really going all the way to the lake like this?" He shakes his head, then kneels down to tie up the laces for me.

I give him a lascivious grin. "Maybe I just wanted to have you at my feet again."

Arien snorts. He picks up the broom and starts to sweep the floor, giving us a pointed look. "I'm still here, you know."

Laughing, I hold out my hand to Rowan. He stands back up, and we go outside, into the garden. Our breath plumes in the cold air. The banks of fallen leaves are stippled with tiny crystals of ice, and one of the trees is strung with an enormous spiderweb, beads of dew dotted along each silken thread.

Through the open gateway, everything in my garden is covered with frost as delicate as lace—the brambles, the flowers, the branches of the fallen tree. I wander the path, thinking of all the seeds I will plant. How I'll wake the garden slowly, just like the house.

I want to keep Lakesedge a little tangled and a little wild, so there will always be part of the estate that remains as I saw it on the night I arrived. Wreathed in vines, full of secrets, like something from a fable. I love it so much; I don't want to tame it completely.

Most of the orchard is bare now, and the pomegranate is a skeletal bower. I pick strands of pale star jasmine as I walk, until I hold a cascade of flowers and leaves. Rowan cuts pieces from the brambles, careful to avoid the thorns.

We follow the path down the slope until it reaches the forest. Mist streaks through the pale trees, and the air smells damp. I hear the lake before it comes into view, the soft hiss and sigh of waves as the water laps back and forth. Our feet leave shallow prints in the earth as we cross the shore.

At the edge of the waves, I lower myself down slowly, feeling the cold press of wet sand against my knees. Rowan sits beside me. He places the altar candle onto the ground, encircled by the bramble vines.

The sun has started to rise, and streaks of lavender trace the sky above the lake. Rowan takes out the sparklight and clicks it against the candle, his hand cupped around the flame to protect it from the wind. I tear a handful of petals loose and scatter them over the water. The waves catch the flowers and start to claim them, drawing them farther and farther out, until there are shreds of leaves and pale star jasmine strewn across the surface.

I watch the petals sink. Watch the candle burn.

Rowan puts his hands over mine, and we press our palms against the ground. I start to chant the harvest litany. I picture my words sunk beneath the waves, alongside the flowers I offered. As though the song is swallowed up when it reaches the expanse of the lake.

Rowan rests his chin against my shoulder for a moment.

Then . . . he starts to chant, too. I turn to look at him, shocked. He blushes and smiles at me. His voice is quiet, uncertain. It's imperfect and lovely, and it feels like he's shared a secret to let me hear this, something that he's never revealed to anyone else.

Our voices weave together unsteadily at first, both of us slightly off-key and a beat too slow. Then we fall into rhythm. As we sing, I dig my fingers into the earth, and I listen, listen, listen to the dark.

I think of myself at the center of the forest, a crown of branches on my hair and flowers blooming at my feet. My eyes sink closed. At first, the shadows I see are only shadows. Then a murmur stirs through the air. A sound that might be the wind, might be the waves, might be my name.

I see feathers and snow and silver-winged moths. A swath of mist that takes on the form of a creature who is almost—but not quite—human. His features shift into eyes and teeth and slashes at his throat. His hand reaches toward me. I imagine the feel of it against my cheek. Cold and clawed, but gentle.

Rowan's fingers tighten against mine beneath the earth. The tether flickers with faint-hued colors, fear and awe. I glance down at his wrist, at the healed-over scars. Darkness shifts beneath his skin, but the wounds stay closed.

"You can see him, too," I say quietly. "Can't you?"

Rowan moves closer to me. His voice is a little unsteady, but he isn't afraid. "Yes. I can see him."

We chant the final lines of the litany and fall into silence. I take a deep, slow breath that tastes of mist and incense. Gradually, the shadows start to fade. I blink my eyes open to see lake and sky and pale clouds. The altar candle has burned out. A drift of smoke winds through the air.

Rowan reaches to me, tucks back a loose curl from my face with his dirt-streaked hand. The mud has left stains on his fingers like shadowed magic. He starts to kiss me—kissing away my tears. I hadn't realized I was crying.

For the first time since I came home, I feel warm—truly warm. Filled with love and gratitude for how we found each other among curses and shadows.

I think of the tangled garden, all thorns and vines and loveliness. The ivy-wreathed house with lace curtains over the windows and a library filled with books. Observance where the two of us will taste gentle echoes of the world Below. Picture it all unfolded before us. Magic and memory, power and love, family and safety.

I watch the last of the flower petals circle over the water. Slowly, they disappear beneath the surface. My palms are still pressed to the ground. I hear a final whisper—a voice, blurred as a fever dream but imprinted forever on my heart.

Then I draw back my hands from the earth, and all goes quiet.

Acknowledgments

When I set out on this path ten years ago with a short story about a girl, her brother, and a haunted estate, I never could have imagined it ending here. Two books—an entire series!— written and released into the world during an unprecedentedly chaotic time. I'm so grateful for everyone who has weathered this storm with me, and whose invaluable support, enthusiasm, and friendship have made this all possible.

To my agent, Jill Grinberg—thank you, endlessly, for being the most steadfast advocate for my work. Your enduring presence has kept me grounded through each step of this process. Thanks also to Sam Farkas, Denise Page, Sophia Seidner, and the entire team at JGLM—I feel so lucky to work with you all.

To my editor, Kat Brzozowski—I am so glad the fates brought us together. I truly appreciate all you've done; thank you for being so organized, answering my endless questions, and for your encouragement as I navigated revisions. It has been wonderful to celebrate the conclusion of my debut series with you. And to Tiff Liao—thank you for taking a chance on my weird goth book, and your notes on my early drafts of

Forestfall, which helped shape the beautifully haunted vibes of the world Below.

The Fierce Reads team—Morgan Rath and Katie Quinn, queens of publicity and marketing; Brian Luster, tireless copy-editor (sorry about all the echo words!); Rich Deas, art direction magician; Ann Marie Wong and everyone at Holt/MCPG, thank you for making the experience of publishing such a joyful one. And thank you to Tim O'Brien for the gorgeous US cover illustration.

My gratitude also to the team at Pan Macmillan Australia—Claire Craig, Brianne Collins, Tom Evans, and Candice Wyman. It's such a dream come true to see my books published in Australia, and I appreciate all your hard work so, so much. And to the team at Titan Books—Cat Camacho, Lydia Gittins, Michael Beale, Eleanor Thomas and Nat Mack—thank you for creating such a gorgeous edition for UK readers. Eleanor, I promise you can have first rights to the Lord Under.

Thank you so much to the authors and booksellers who provided generous early reviews—Rebecca Ross and Marissa Meyer, whose books have been such an inspiration to me; Cristina Maria Russell at Books & Books; Brittany Smith at B&N South Carolina; Kiersten Frost at Brookline Booksmith; and Kylie Ann Freeman at Indigo Books.

And thank you to everyone at Owlcrate who made so many of my author dreams come true with their special editions of my books.

To Jess Rubinkowski, Cyla Panin, Jessica Olson, Riss Neilson, Vanessa Len, and Kat Delacorte—your wonderful books have been such a delight and inspiration, and I'm so glad for your friendship in this whirlwind of writer life. And to Katrine Williamson, Cait Millard, and Mhari Tocher—thank you for the coffee dates and helping me to reconnect to the world outside of my work desk.

To my family—Mum, thank you for always filling my world with books and stories. Dad—I'm so glad I was able to capture the real-life magic you worked with plants in Leta's alchemy. Kim, thank you for encouraging me to embrace my artist soul. To Felix and Orson, the best part of becoming an author is being able to share it all with you.

To B., the Lisey to my Scott, the light to my dark, you see the truth of me and I love you so much. I can't express how much I appreciate all your patience when I was mired in deadlines, and for celebrating every milestone with me.

Finally, to the readers who discovered this story about a fierce, foolish girl and a troubled, monstrous boy, and who found a connection to the world inside these pages . . . Thank you for your kind words, your wonderfully creative photos and fan art and cosplays, and, most of all, thank you for reading.

These books—and all that dwells inside—are yours now. I am so glad to pass them gently into your hands.